# Palgrave Studies in C[illegible] Graphic Novels

Series Editor
Roger Sabin
University of the Arts London
London, UK

This series concerns Comics Studies—with a capital "c" and a capital "s." It feels good to write it that way. From emerging as a fringe interest within Literature and Media/Cultural Studies departments, to becoming a minor field, to maturing into the fastest growing field in the Humanities, to becoming a nascent *discipline*, the journey has been a hard but spectacular one. Those capital letters have been earned.

Palgrave Studies in Comics and Graphic Novels covers all aspects of the comic strip, comic book, and graphic novel, explored through clear and informative texts offering expansive coverage and theoretical sophistication. It is international in scope and provides a space in which scholars from all backgrounds can present new thinking about politics, history, aesthetics, production, distribution, and reception as well as the digital realm. Books appear in one of two forms: traditional monographs of 60,000 to 90,000 words and shorter works (Palgrave Pivots) of 20,000 to 50,000 words. All are rigorously peer-reviewed. Palgrave Pivots include new takes on theory, concise histories, and—not least—considered provocations. After all, Comics Studies may have come a long way, but it can't progress without a little prodding.

Series Editor Roger Sabin is Professor of Popular Culture at the University of the Arts London, UK. His books include *Adult Comics: An Introduction* and *Comics, Comix and Graphic Novels*, and he is part of the team that put together the Marie Duval Archive. He serves on the boards of key academic journals in the field, reviews graphic novels for international media, and consults on comics-related projects for the BBC, Channel 4, Tate Gallery, The British Museum and The British Library. The 'Sabin Award' is given annually at the International Graphic Novels and Comics Conference.

More information about this series at
http://www.palgrave.com/gp/series/14643

Erin La Cour • Simon Grennan
Rik Spanjers
Editors

# Key Terms in Comics Studies

*Editors*
Erin La Cour
Vrije Universiteit Amsterdam
Amsterdam, The Netherlands

Simon Grennan
University of Chester
Chester, UK

Rik Spanjers
University of Amsterdam
Amsterdam, The Netherlands

ISSN 2634-6370 ISSN 2634-6389 (electronic)
Palgrave Studies in Comics and Graphic Novels
ISBN 978-3-030-74973-6 ISBN 978-3-030-74974-3 (eBook)
https://doi.org/10.1007/978-3-030-74974-3



This Palgrave Macmillan imprint is published by the registered company Springer Nature Switzerland AG.
The registered company address is: Gewerbestrasse 11, 6330 Cham, Switzerland

# Contents

# Notes on Contributors

**Victoria Addis** teaches English at Derby Moor Academy. She is the author of numerous journal articles and the recipient of the ISAANZ Postgraduate Essay Prize, awarded by the Irish Studies Association of Australia and New Zealand.

**Maaheen Ahmed** is Associate Professor of Comparative Literature at Ghent University. She is the principal investigator for *Children in Comics*, a multi-researcher project funded by the European Research Council, which seeks to construct an intercultural history of comics through children.

**Eric Atkinson** is a PhD student at the University of California, Riverside, studying African American Literature with an emphasis on comics highlighting representations of the African American body. A former McNair Scholar and the 2008 winner of the S. Randolph Edmonds Young Scholar Competition, he is also a published author.

**Jan Baetens** is Professor of Cultural Studies at KU Leuven. He has published widely on word and image studies. Some recent publications are *Novelization. From Film to Novel* (2018), *The Film Photonovel: A Cultural History of Forgotten Adaptations* (2019), and *Rebuilding Story Worlds: The Obscure Cities by Schuiten and Peeters* (2020).

**Josip Batinić** is a PhD candidate in Digital Humanities at the University of Antwerp. His main area of interest is the adaptation and the assimilation of traditional media into the digital realm. He has been following developments in New Media, particularly those concerned with representing comics on the computer screen.

**Bart Beaty** is the author, editor, and translator of more than twenty books in the field of Comics Studies, including *Twelve-Cent Archie* (2015) and *Comics Versus Art* (2012). He is the general editor of the *Critical Survey of Graphic Novels* (2012, revised 2018–2019) and the lead researcher on the *What Were Comics?* project.

**Vasiliki Belia** is a PhD candidate in the Arts, Media, and Culture Programme at Maastricht University. She researches the role comics play in the contemporary cultural investment in the history of feminism. In the past she worked as researcher and lecturer in the Graduate Gender Programme at Utrecht University.

**Nicholas Burman** is a British writer with an MA in Comparative Cultural Analysis from the University of Amsterdam. He writes about comics, DIY culture, ambience, and the urban and has been published by *FRAME*, *Soapbox*, *The Comics Journal*, *The Quietus*, and *Simulacrum*.

**Giorgio Busi Rizzi** is a BOF post-doctoral fellow at Ghent University and a member of the ACME Comics Research Group. He holds a PhD in Literary and Cultural Studies with a joint supervision by the Universities of Bologna and Leuven, focusing on nostalgia in graphic novels.

**Freija Camps** is a lecturer in English Literature at the Vrije Universiteit Amsterdam. She holds a master's degree in Literary Studies from the Vrije Universiteit Amsterdam and a research master's degree in Gender and Ethnicity Studies from Utrecht University. Her research interests include the study of graphic medicine through an engagement with feminist theory and disability studies.

**Ayanni C. H. Cooper** is an English PhD candidate at the University of Florida, where she specialises in comics and animation studies. Her research interests include feminist critique, monster theory, science fiction, fantasy, magical girls, and robots (big or small).

**Rikke Platz Cortsen**, PhD, is Lecturer in Danish at The University of Texas, Austin, where she teaches Danish and Scandinavian culture, including a course on Northern European Comics. She has researched a wide variety of topics in Comics Studies and is focused on comics from the Nordic countries.

**Benoît Crucifix** is an ERC-funded post-doctoral researcher at Ghent University, working on children's drawings in European comics as part of the COMICS project. His dissertation inquired into comics memory in the contemporary graphic novel. He co-edited *Comics Memory: Archives and Styles* (2018) and *Abstraction and Comics* (2019).

**Geraint D'Arcy** is Lecturer in Media Practice at the University of East Anglia, Norwich. He is the author of *Mise en Scène, Acting, and Space in Comics* (2020) and *Critical Approaches to TV and Film Set Design* (2018).

**Paul Fisher Davies** has published in *Studies in Comics*, the *Journal of Graphic Novels and Comics*, and *The Comics Grid* amongst others, including academic work in comics form, encompassing sketchnoting, graphic articles, and cover illustration. His monograph *Comics as Communication: A Functional Approach* was published by Palgrave Macmillan in 2019.

**Rachel A. Davis** holds an MLitt in Comics and Graphic Novels from the University of Dundee, with a thesis entitled "What Came First: The Chicken's Instagram or the Egg's Twitter? Comics Authorship in the Internet Age" (2019). She is the Outreach Coordinator at Saving Jane, an NGO that uses comics to educate about human trafficking.

**Esther De Dauw** is a Comics Studies scholar focusing on superheroes, race, and gender. She is the author of *Hot Pants and Spandex Suits: Gender Representation in American Superhero Comic Books* (2021) and editor of *Toxic Masculinity: Mapping the Monstrous in Our Heroes* (2020).

**Enrique del Rey Cabero** is Lecturer in Hispanic Studies at the University of Exeter and Honorary Faculty Research Fellow at the University of Oxford, where he is the co-convener of the Oxford Comics Network at the Oxford Research Centre in the Humanities (TORCH).

**Zu Dominiak** is a cartoonist and a PhD researcher at the University of Dundee. Dominiak investigates the relationship between comics and museum and gallery institutions. Dominiak also creates science and public information comics and has an interest in formalist experimentation and making 3D comics.

**Glen Downey** is an award-winning educator, children's writer, comics reviewer, and consultant living in Oakville, Ontario. He earned a PhD in English from the University of Victoria in 1998, specialising in Victorian literature and Game Studies. His works have been published by Rubicon, Pearson, Scholastic, and Oxford Canada.

**Harriet E. H. Earle** is Lecturer in English at Sheffield Hallam University. She is the author of *Comics, Trauma, and the New Art of War* (2017) and *Comics: An Introduction* (2021). Her research interests include American comics and popular culture, protest narratives, and biopolitics.

**Monalesia Earle** is an independent researcher. Her book, *Writing Queer Women of Color: Representation and Misdirection in Contemporary Fiction and Graphic Narratives* (2019), received Honorable Mention for the Charles Hatfield Book Prize, and runner up for the John Leo and Dana Heller Award for Best Single Work in LGBTQ Studies.

**Elisabeth 'Lisa' El Refaie** is Reader in Visual Communication at Cardiff University. She is the author of two monographs on comics, *Autobiographical Comics: Life Writing in Pictures* (2012) and *Metaphor and Embodiment in Graphic Illness Narratives* (2019), and has also published widely on other forms of visual/multimodal communication.

**Charles Forceville** lectures and researches in media studies at the University of Amsterdam. He takes a cognitivist approach to visual and multimodal discourse, specifically metaphor, in genres including advertising, documentary, animation, comics, and cartoons. He recently published *Visual and Multimodal Communication: Applying the Relevance Principle* (2020).

**Hugo Frey** is Professor of Cultural and Visual History and Director of Arts and Humanities at the University of Chichester. He has written books on history, cinema, graphic novels, modern France, and Vietnamese folk theatre.

**Jean-Paul Gabilliet** teaches North American studies at the Université Bordeaux Montaigne, France. He specialises in the cultural history of comics in North America and Europe. His main books are *Of Comics and Men: A Cultural History of American Comic Books* (2010) and a biography, *R. Crumb* (2012).

**Madeline B. Gangnes** is Assistant Professor of Nineteenth-Century British Literature at the University of Scranton. She holds a PhD in English from the University of Florida and her MLitt in Comics Studies from the University of Dundee. She is assistant editor of *Studies in Comics* and editor of *Sequentials*.

**Steven Gerrard** is Reader in Film at Northern Film School, Leeds Beckett University. He is the author of *The Carry On Films* (2016) and *The Modern British Horror Film* (2017). He longs to be either Status Quo's rhythm guitarist or Doctor Who. He'll have a long wait.

**Mel Gibson** is Associate Professor of Childhood Studies at Northumbria University, specialising in teaching and research relating to comics, graphic novels, picture books, and fiction for children. Her most recent work focuses on girlhoods, agency, and contemporary comics.

**Benoît Glaude** is a researcher at Ghent University and a visiting lecturer at UC Louvain, Belgium. He has published several books about French-speaking comics, including *Aire libre, art libre?* (2011), *Jijé l'autre père de la BD franco-belge* (2019), his PhD on comics dialogues, *La Bande dialoguée* (2019), and a recently edited volume on novelisations in children's literature, *Les Novellisations pour la jeunesse* (2020).

**Daniel Merlin Goodbrey** is Principle Lecturer in Narrative and Interaction Design at the University of Hertfordshire. A prolific and innovative comic creator, Goodbrey has gained international recognition as a leading expert in the field of experimental digital comics. An archive of his work can be found at http://e-merl.com.

**Ian Lewis Gordon** teaches history at the National University of Singapore. His books include *Comic Strips and Consumer Culture* (1998), *The Superhero Symbol: Media, Culture, and Politics* (2019), *Ben Katchor: Conversations* (2018), *Superman: The Persistence of an American Icon* (2017), *The Comics of Charles Schultz* (2017), and *Kid Comic Strips* (2016).

**Simon Grennan** is Leading Research Fellow at the University of Chester. He is an awarded scholar of visual narrative, a graphic novelist, and co-producer of *The Marie Duval Archive*. Since 1990, he has been half of international artists team Grennan & Sperandio, producer of over forty comics and books.

**Thierry Groensteen** has curated the Comics Museum in Angoulême from 1993 to 2001 and was the chief editor of *Les Cahiers de la bande dessinée* and *Neuvième Art*. Groensteen teaches comics in Angoulême and is a publisher for Actes Sud. He has written more than thirty books and essays, including *The System of Comics* (1999), *Comics and Narration* (2011), and *An Expanding Art* (2015).

**Laurence Grove** (aka Billy) is Professor of French and Text/Image Studies and Director of the Stirling Maxwell Centre at the University of Glasgow. His research focuses on historical text/image forms and specifically *bande dessinée*. He co-edits *European Comic Art* and has authored twelve books, four exhibitions, and approximately sixty chapters.

**Ian Hague** teaches Contextual and Theoretical Studies at London College of Communication (UAL). His research interests include sensory and material culture. He is the author of *Comics and the Senses: A Multisensory Approach to Comics and Graphic Novels* (2014) and has co-edited collections on multiculturalism and violence in comics.

**Kathryn Hemmann** is the author of numerous essays on Japanese fiction, graphic novels, and video games. Hemmann's book *Manga Cultures and the Female Gaze* (2020) argues that an awareness of female creators can transform our understanding of media that is often assumed to take a male audience for granted.

**Olivia Hicks** holds a PhD degree from the University of Dundee. Her thesis was on the super-girl in British and American girls' comics and her research interests include queerness, fandom studies, genre theory, and whiteness studies. Her chapter on whiteness in *Cloak and Dagger* was recently published in *Unstable Masks* (2020), and her chapter on SuperCorp is included in the volume *Supersex* (2020).

**Ian Horton** is a Reader in Graphic Communication and a founder member of the Comics Research Hub (CoRH) at the University of the Arts London. He is associate editor of the *Journal of Graphic Novels and Comics* and his research is focused on comic books, graphic design, and illustration.

**David Huxley** is the editor of *The Journal of Graphic Novels and Comics*. He has written widely on comics and has also written and drawn for a range of British comics. His most recent publication is *Lone Heroes and the Myth of the American West in Comic Books* (2018).

**Laurike in 't Veld** is a lecturer at the Erasmus School of History, Culture and Communication and a research associate at the Centre for Historical Culture, Erasmus University Rotterdam. She is the author of *The Representation of Genocide in Graphic Novels: Considering the Role of Kitsch* (2019).

**Paul Jackson** is course leader for MA Graphic Branding and Identity at London College of Communication. He works as a commercial illustrator under the pseudonym Wesley Merritt and is undertaking a practice-based PhD at LCC exploring the notion and construction of an interface between drawing and worldbuilding.

**Ahmed Mauroof Jameel** is a writer and comics scholar based in the Maldives. His research interests span auteurism, artistic identity, the dynamics of collaboration, and creative process. Jameel's practice-based PhD focused on writer-artist collaboration in comics and utilised autoethnography to generate insight into the collaborative experience.

**Jasleen Kandhari** Awarded Sikh art historian, theorist and curator, Jasleen Kandhari is the Founding Director of The Association of Sikh Art & Cultural Heritage (ASACH), Indian textiles, art history lecturer at Oxford University, creator of the first Sikh superheroine comic, Super Singhani and curator of ASACH Sikh Comics exhibition at the Cartoon Museum, UK. Forthcoming monographs: Thames & Hudson Sikh Art & Architecture, Sikh Comics: A Critical Guide.

**Gene Kannenberg Jr** has written on topics from comics lettering to Peanuts parodies, and he has served as Chair of the International Comic Arts Festival. His cartooning work was included in the Minnesota Center for Book Arts' 2017 exhibit "Asemic Writing: Offline & In the Gallery," and in Abstraction et bande dessinée (2019). Follow his work on Instagram (@genekjr) and at comicsmachine.com.

**Ralf Kauranen,** DSocSci, is a sociologist and comics scholar based in the Department of Finnish Literature at the University of Turku. He is leading the project *Comics and Migration: Belonging, Narration, Activism,* funded by the Kone Foundation.

**Frederik Byrn Køhlert** is Lecturer in American Studies at the University of East Anglia, where he also directs the MA programme in Comics Studies. He is the author of *Serial Selves: Identity and Representation* *in Autobiographical Comics* (2019) and the editor of two companion book series on Gender, Sexuality, and Comics Studies.

**Katja Kontturi** holds a PhD in Contemporary Culture Studies. Her doctoral dissertation (2014) dealt with Don Rosa's Disney comics as postmodern fantasy. Kontturi's research interests include comics, speculative fiction, and geek culture. Kontturi is the second representative of Finland in the board of Nordic Network for Comics Research (NNCORE).

**David Kunzle** started his scholarly life with the PhD *The Comic Strip or Picture Story Before, with and After Hogarth (1450–1826)* and ended it with *Cham* and *Rebirth of the Comic Strip 1847–1870, a kaleidoscope* (2019 and 2021), with many other quite different topics in between, such as *Fashion and Fetishism* (2004), recently published in a Chinese language edition.

**Nicolas Labarre** is Assistant Lecturer in American Society and Culture at University Bordeaux Montaigne. He is the author of *Heavy Metal, l'autre Métal Hurlant* (2017), a transnational history of *Heavy Metal* magazine, and *Understanding Genres in Comics* (2020).

**Erin La Cour** is Assistant Professor of English Literature and Visual Culture at the Vrije Universiteit Amsterdam and co-founder and co-director of Amsterdam Comics. Her research focuses on the intermediality and mediality of comics in several socio-historical cultural milieux. Her latest project is a co-edited special issue of *Biography: An Interdisciplinary Quarterly* entitled "Graphic Medicine."

**Nicolle Lamerichs** is Senior Lecturer and team lead in Creative Business at HU University of Applied Sciences, Utrecht. She holds a PhD in Media Studies from Maastricht University (2014). In her book *Productive Fandom* (2018), she explores intermediality, affect, costuming, and creativity in fan cultures.

**Guy Lawley** is pursuing a PhD at Central Saint Martins on print technology in nineteenth-century comics, with supervisors Prof Roger Sabin and Dr Ian Horton. Conference papers include "Four Colours on Newsprint: The Printed Comic 1894–1986" and "Roy Lichtenstein vs. the Comic Book: Materiality, Process and Colour."

**Martin Lund** is Senior Lecturer in Religious Studies at Malmö University, Sweden. His main research interests are the intersections of identity, memory, religion, space and place, and activism with comics production. He is also interested in critically interrogating and developing the theory and method of interdisciplinary Comics Studies.

**Luis Miguel Lus Arana,** MDesS, PhD, is an architect and architecture scholar who has written extensively on the relationships between architecture and media, especially comic books. In the last decade he has taught theory and history of architecture. He is also architectural cartoonist Klaus (Klaustoon).

**Ilan Manouach** is a conceptual comics artist and a PhD researcher at Aalto University, Helsinki. He is mostly known for being the creator of *Shapereader*, an embodied system of communication designed for blind and partially sighted readers/makers of comics, and the director of the research programme Futures of Comics.

**Stuart Medley's** research focuses on pictorial communication. He makes comics and storyboards to plan services to reduce homelessness and unemployment. He has run comics workshops throughout Europe, China, and Australasia. Medley is a founder and Chair of the Perth Comic Arts Festival.

**Gert Meesters** is Associate Professor of Dutch Language and Culture at the University of Lille, where he does research on Dutch language comics in their international context. He has recently co-edited *Les métamorphoses de Spirou. Le dynamisme d'une série de bande dessinée* (2019) and (À Suivre) *Les archives d'une revue culte* (2018).

**Penelope Mendonça** has been an independent graphic facilitator and cartoonist for more than twenty-five years. Her graphics examining race, gender, class, disability rights, and health inequalities are widely published and translated. Her background in social care informs both her work on co-production and her PhD, which examined values-based cartooning.

**Jean-Matthieu Méon** holds a PhD in Political Science and is Senior Lecturer in Communication Studies at the Centre de Recherche sur les Médiations (University of Lorraine, France). He has published extensively on censorship, musical amateur practices, and comics. His work on comics explores, in particular, the institutional, professional, and artistic dimensions of their legitimation.

**Nina Mickwitz** teaches contextual and theoretical studies at London College of Communication. She is the author of *Documentary Comics* (2016) and a co-founder of the Comics Research Hub (CoRH) at the University of the Arts London. Her interests include the transnational mobilities of small press comics and peripheral comics cultures.

**John Miers** is Lecturer in Illustration at Kingston School of Art. His comics practice focuses on applying theories of visual metaphor and depiction to the production of autobiographical comics dealing with his experience of multiple sclerosis.

**Ann Miller** After working as a secondary teacher and textbook writer, Ann Miller lectured in French at the University of Leicester. She has written widely on (mainly French-language) comics and translated a number of theoretical works by comics theorists. She is a founding co-editor of the peer-reviewed journal *European Comic Art.*

**Pedro Moura** (Lisbon, 1973) holds a PhD in Comics and Trauma (Leuven and Lisbon). He writes regularly at his *Yellow Fast & Crumble* blog. Most of his waking life is comics-related; in his dreams, it gets worse. A published comics writer, now he co-owns a bookstore gallery in Lisbon.

**Bruce Mutard** is a comics maker and researcher, and a PhD candidate at Edith Cowan University. His graphic novels include *The Sacrifice* (2008), *The Silence* (2009), *A Mind of Love* (2011), *The Bunker* (2001), *Post Traumatic* (2017), and *Souffre Douleur* (2019). He produces Comics Studies as comics: *First Person Third*, *Vita Longa*, *Ars Breva*, and *Comics Law in Practice.*

**Joan Ormrod** is a senior lecturer at Manchester Metropolitan University and the editor of the *Journal of Graphic Novels and Comics.* Her research is interdisciplinary, crossing youth culture, comics, science fiction, and fantasy. Her latest publications are *Wonder Woman, the Female Body and Popular Culture* (2020) and articles on romance comics, fandoms, and promotional culture.

**Jasmine Palmer** is a recent graduate of the Literature in a Visual Culture MA Programme at Vrije Universiteit Amsterdam and is a junior research assistant for Dr Erin La Cour's Comenius Teaching Fellowship research project "Opening a Dialogue About Mental Health Through Comics and Creative Writing."

**Laura A. Pearson** is an assistant professor in the Department of English and Cultural Studies at Huron University (London, Canada). Some of her latest publications appear in *Magical Realism and Literature* (Cambridge Critical Concepts, 2020), *Representing Acts of Violence in Comics* (2020), and *Strong Bonds: Child-Animal Relationships in Comics* (UP of Liège, forthcoming).

**Nancy Pedri** is Professor of English at Memorial University of Newfoundland, Canada. Her major fields of research include Comics Studies, word and image studies, and photography in literature. She is the author of *A Concise Dictionary of Comics* (2022) and co-author of *Experiencing Visual Storyworlds: Focalization in Comics* (2022).

**Marco Pellitteri** (1974), a mass media sociologist, is an associate professor in the School of Humanities and Social Sciences, Xi'an JiaoTong-Liverpool University (China). He is the author, among others, of the books *Sense of Comics* (1998), *The Dragon and the Dazzle* (2010), and *Mazinga Nostalgia* (1999, 4th ed. 2018).

**Daniel Peretti** is Assistant Professor of Folklore at Memorial University of Newfoundland. He writes about myth, comic books, legends, and festivals, and material culture. His book, *Superman in Myth and Folklore* (2017), combines all these topics.

**David Pinho Barros** teaches animation and Comics Studies at the School of Arts of the Catholic University of Portugal. He holds a PhD in Literary, Cultural, and Interartistic Studies from the University of Porto and the KU Leuven with a thesis on clear line comics and cinema.

**Anna Poletti** is Associate Professor of English Language and Culture at Utrecht University, and co-editor of *Biography: An Interdisciplinary Quarterly*. Her most recent book is *Stories of the Self: Life Writing After the Book* (2020).

**Barbara Postema** is a senior lecturer at Massey University New Zealand. Her monograph *Narrative Structure in Comics* (2013) was released in a Brazilian translation in 2018. She has contributed to the likes of *Image [&] Narrative*, the *Journal of Graphic Novels and Comics*, *The Cambridge History of the Graphic Novel*, and *Abstraction and Comics*.

**Camilla Prytz** holds an MA in English Literature in a Visual Culture from Vrije Universiteit Amsterdam in 2020. She is one of the two authors behind "Comprehending Colour: An Approach to Reading and Understanding Colour in Comics" published in *Digressions*.

**JoAnn Purcell,** PhD, is faculty and coordinator of Illustration at Seneca College. Her doctoral research in Critical Disability Studies at York University used her background as an artist and registered nurse to create comics alongside disability. She also holds an MA in Art History from York University and a BScN from the University of Toronto, and is a graduate of the Ontario College of Art.

**Dona Pursall** As a PhD researcher of the European project "Children in Comics," Dona Pursall explores childhood and identity through the development of British "funnies," particularly in relation to times of socio-political unrest and change. Her thesis wrangles with the ways in which humorous comics can be studied, child readership and comics representations.

**Julie Rak** holds the Henry Marshall Tory Chair in the Department of English and Film Studies at the University of Alberta, Canada. She is the author of the forthcoming *False Summit: Gender in Mountaineering Nonfiction* (2021) and many other books, collections, and articles about nonfiction, popular culture, and print culture.

**Chris Reyns-Chikuma** is Professor of French and Cultural Studies at the University of Alberta, Canada. He teaches and researches French bande dessinée, comics, and manga. He published many articles on the three traditions. His most recent one is "#spirou4rights: a critical perspective on promoting human rights through comics" in *MCF*.

**Kees Ribbens** is endowed Professor of Popular Historical Culture and War at Erasmus University Rotterdam and senior researcher at NIOD Institute for War, Holocaust and Genocide Studies in Amsterdam. He is a member of the editorial board of *European Comic Art* and has published widely on war in comics.

**Josh R. Rose** is Faculty of Art History and Art Appreciation at Brookhaven College in Texas. A scholar of Surrealism, he has recently begun focusing on the intersection of comics and art history. Additionally, he curated the 2016 exhibition "Heroes in the Making: The Art of Comics Production."

**Christopher Rowe** holds a PhD in Screen and Cultural Studies from the University of Melbourne. He has published articles on science fiction cinema, digital literature, and comics and is the author of the book *Michael Haneke: The Intermedial Void* (2016).

**Brian Ruh** is an independent scholar and holds a PhD in Communication and Culture from Indiana University. He is the author of *Stray Dog of Anime: The Films of Mamoru Oshii* (2004).

**Houman Sadri** is Associate Professor of English at the University of South-Eastern Norway, specialising in popular culture, comics, and myth- and folklore-based narratives. He is the co-editor of *Broken Mirrors: Representations of Apocalypses and Dystopias in Popular Culture* (2019) and reviews editor at *MAI: Feminism and Visual Culture.*

**Joe Sutliff Sanders** is university lecturer at the University of Cambridge and a member of the Centre for Research in Children's Literature at Cambridge. He is the author or editor of six books, the newest of which is an analysis of *Batman: The Animated Series.*

**Andrea Schlosser** is a graduate student of American studies at Ruhr University Bochum in Germany. Her academic areas of expertise include Comics Studies, queer studies, and Holocaust studies. Schlosser is the recipient of a full scholarship for her graduate studies by the Rosa Luxemburg Foundation in Germany.

**Greice Schneider** is a professor in the Department of Communications of Universidade Federal de Sergipe (Brazil) and is the author of *What Happens When Nothing Happens: Boredom and Everyday Life in Contemporary Comics* (2017). Her publications have appeared in *Studies in Comics*, *European Comic Art*, and *Scandinavian Journal of Comic Art.*

**Doug Singsen** is Associate Professor of Art History at the University of Wisconsin-Parkside. His book *The Invisible Costume: Whiteness and the Construction of Race in American Comics and Graphic Novels*, co-written with Josef Benson, is forthcoming.

**Rik Spanjers** is Lecturer in Media Studies at the University of Amsterdam. He obtained a PhD in 2019 with a research project on World War II representation in comics. He has published in *Image [&] Narrative*, co-wrote an exhibition on Japanese popular culture for the Tropenmuseum, and reviews comics for several outlets. He is also co-founder and co-director of Amsterdam Comics.

**Roel van den Oever** is Assistant Professor of English Literature at Vrije Universiteit Amsterdam. He is the author of the book *Mama's Boy: Momism and Homophobia in Postwar American Culture* (2012).

**Jos van Waterschoot** (1965) is curator of comics and book history at the Heritage Collections (Allard Pierson) of the University of Amsterdam. He writes comics reviews for various comics magazines as well as comics scenarios.

**Essi Varis,** PhD, has researched comics, literature, and narrative theory since 2013. Her doctoral dissertation, which she defended in the University of Jyväskylä, Finland, in 2019, suggests a new cognitive theory for understanding multimodal fictional characters. She is investigating speculative thought and imagination at the University of Helsinki.

**E. Dawson Varughese's** research explores visual arts and literary responses to post-millennial "New India." She publishes on Indian genre fiction in English, Indian graphic narratives, domestic Indian book cover design, and public wall art. Her most recent book is *Visuality and Identity in Post-millennial Indian Graphic Narratives* (2017).

**Lukas R. A. Wilde** is research associate at Tübingen University's Department for Media Studies. His PhD monograph received the Roland-Faelske-Award 2018 for the best dissertation in Comics and Animation Studies. His main areas of interest include pictorial semiotics, media theory, Japanese popular culture, web comics, and animation.

**Peter Wilkins** designs programmes for at-risk and refugee youth for the Training Group at Douglas College in Vancouver, Canada. He holds a PhD in English from The University of California, Irvine, and is an editor of *The Comics Grid: Journal of Comics Scholarship* and co-founder of *Graphixia: A Conversation About Comics.*

**Benjamin Woo** is Associate Professor of Communication and Media Studies and director of the Research on Comics, Con Events, and Transmedia Lab at Carleton University in Ottawa, Canada. He is the author of *Getting a Life: The Social Worlds of Geek Culture* (2018).

**Daniel Worden** is an associate professor in the Department of English and the School of Individualised Study at the Rochester Institute of

Technology. He is the author of *Neoliberal Nonfictions: The Documentary Aesthetic from Joan Didion to Jay-Z* (2020) and the editor of *The Comics of Joe Sacco: Journalism in a Visual World* (2015).

**Lydia Wysocki** is an educational researcher at Newcastle University, using sociocultural theory to explore how what people read influences how they understand the social world. She founded and leads Applied Comics Etc., working with subject specialists and comics artist-writers to make comics that communicate specific information.

**Nicholas Yanes,** PhD, examines entertainment as an academic and consultant. His dissertation explored the business history of EC Comics/*Mad Magazine*. His first book, *Iconic Obama* (2012), analysed Obama's media impact. His second book, *Hannibal for Dinner* (2021), examines NBC's *Hannibal.* He's written for *Casual Connect*, *GameSauce*, *Sequart*, MGM's *Stargate Command*, and *ScifiPulse.*

# Introduction: Key Terms in Comics Studies

*Erin La Cour, Simon Grennan, and Rik Spanjers*

Over the last 25 years, the field of Comics Studies has become firmly established in Anglophone academia. The number of comics-specific book series, journals, and conferences has steadily increased, and the field continues to gain ground in universities through comics courses and degree programmes at the bachelors and masters levels. While this bodes well for the future of the field, comics scholars as of yet do not have a set disciplinary home. Instead, they are housed in a wide range of departments including, but not limited to, media studies, literature, communication, history, and art and design.

This breadth of disciplinary expertise has benefitted Comics Studies in terms of flexibility, adaptability, and permeability. It has created a field with a particularly broad lexicon of terms, derived from a wide range of academic traditions. While positive on the one hand, on the other, the heterogeneity of approaches and terms used does not always reflect or advance the current condition of the field. Because knowledge transfer from one discipline to another remains uneven and often accessible only by osmosis, specialisations and particular methodologies have arisen that stand in direct contrast to and often disengaged from others.

---

The original version of this chapter was revised. A correction to this chapter can be found at https://doi.org/10.1007/978-3-030-74974-3_2



E. La Cour et al. (eds.), *Key Terms in Comics Studies*, Palgrave Studies in Comics and Graphic Novels,
https://doi.org/10.1007/978-3-030-74974-3_1

*Key Terms in Comics Studies* seeks to open the dialogue on comics scholarship across these diverse fields and approaches so as to engender access to and an analysis of comics-specific theorisations, histories, and methodologies. We decided to call this book *Key Terms in Comics Studies* in our preliminary talks about it during the second international Amsterdam Comics Conference in 2018 in order to underscore precisely what the entry on comics in this book outlines: that in English the word "comics" has expanded to describe the medium, and thereby encompasses multiple genres, styles, origins, practices, and histories.

Focused on Anglophone Comics Studies, this book compiles terms and critical concepts in current use, including those from other languages that have been adopted by and are currently applied in English.

We discussed and discussed again the conditions that any possible term must meet to be included in the book. *Key Terms in Comics Studies* includes terms and critical concepts that are used in specific ways in current Anglophone Comics Studies. Each entry is syncretic rather than exhaustive, balancing overview, accuracy, and brevity. Seeking to provide an outline of meanings and uses, the entries are 250 words or fewer, placed in alphabetical order, and substantiated with examples and references. Entries are explicitly cross-referenced to each other via the use of capitalisation on the first occasion when they appear in another entry. References to primary sources are included in the text, rather than reference lists.

Like each term, the glossary also does not claim to be exhaustive. Instead, we envision *Key Terms in Comics Studies* as a start in mapping a continually changing taxonomy and highlighting contemporary points of overlap and discord across disciplines that beg further development.

Besides being a collection of terms, this book has also become a collection of scholars—a fortunate side effect of our search for contributors. When sending out invitations to contribute, we were guided by the specialisations implied by particular key terms and cognisant of the wide range of points of view and types of experience that make the field so vibrant and diverse. Together, the nearly 100 international experts who we invited to co-create this book show a developed tacit knowledge of the different approaches that are current in the field, as well as the concepts that are deployed in it.

Part of the joy of making *Key Terms in Comics Studies* has been the rekindling of old friendships, making new contacts, and discovering new insights. We would like to thank all of our contributors for their expertise, creativity, and collaboration.

## Abstract Comics

Abstract comics are EXPERIMENTAL COMICS that adopt the CONSTRAINT of not using REPRESENTATIONALLY figurative IMAGES or CONVENTIONALLY NARRATIVE SEQUENCES. Instead, a sense of READING momentum is engendered by shifts in direction, texture, or tone of the ART across sequences of PANELS, creating sequential dynamism (Molotiu 2012). Robert Crumb and Saul Steinberg experimented with abstract imagery and non-narrative comics during the twentieth century (Molotiu 2016: 120), but as a GENRE, abstract comics really found their stride in the twenty-first century. Andrei Molotiu published an anthology of abstract comics by numerous practitioners in 2009, which he introduced with a manifesto of sorts. Aarnoud Rommens et al. followed this up in 2019 with a volume combining creative work and scholarly articles. Thierry Groensteen differentiates between abstract and infranarrative comics, arguing that while both show iconic solidarity, abstract comics use sequences of only abstract images, whereas infranarrative comics use figurative or representational images in sequences that do not produce any straightforward narrative (2011: 9–19). Some practitioners of abstract and infranarrative comics include Derek A. Badman, Olivier Deprez, Gene Kannenberg, Renée French, Eric Labé, Mark Laliberte, Andrei Molotiu, Carlos Santos, Fiona Smyth, and Yuichi Yokoyama.

Barbara Postema

### *References*

Groensteen, T. (2011) *Comics and Narration*. Translated from French by A. Miller, 2013. Jackson: University Press of Mississippi.

Molotiu, A. (2016) "Art Comics" in Bramlett, F., Cook, R., and Meskin, A. (eds.) *The Routledge Companion to Comics*. Abingdon: Routledge, pp. 119–127.

Molotiu, A. (2012) "Abstract Form: Sequential Dynamism and Iconostasis in Abstract Comics and in Steve Ditko's *Amazing Spider-Man*" in Smith, M. J. and Duncan, R. (eds.) *Critical Approaches to Comics: Theories and Methods*. Abingdon: Routledge, pp. 84–100.

Molotiu, A. (2009) *Abstract Comics*. Seattle: Fantagraphics.

Rommens, A., Crucifix, B., Dozo, B., Dejasse, E., and Turnes, P. (eds.) (2019) *Abstraction and Comics/Bande dessinée et abstraction*. Liège: La Cinquième *Couche*/Presses Universitaires de Liège.

## Abstraction

Discourse on comics abstraction has largely focused on the FORMAL qualities of comics, that is, abstraction in terms of the IMAGE, PANEL, or PAGE LAYOUT (which raise questions about REPRESENTATION and MIMESIS) and of SEQUENCE (including considerations of NARRATIVE). As Aarnoud Rommens points out, this focus insists on clear definitions of what comics *are*, especially in relation to LITERATURE and ART, which problematically "effects a reification of comics: rather than descriptive, definitions become prescriptive in the production of artefacts in accordance with the 'law' of the medium whose inner workings (the 'structure of comics') it supposedly 'objectively' describes" (2019: 26–27). Current research into comics abstraction has moved away from such pitfalls and towards a consideration of what comics *do*—that is, how they engage with social and political DISCOURSE, especially in terms of perceived disciplinary boundaries and hierarchies. In thinking of abstraction as a "stepping aside, a movement away from the mainstream, suggesting the possibilities for art to maneuver within self-organized, withdrawn initiatives in the field of cultural production" (Lind 2013: n.p.) comics abstraction can be afforded a plurality of avenues to explore that can engender a rethinking of the engagement and/or disengagement of comics with its MATERIALITY, INTERMEDIALITY, TRANSMEDIALITY, SELF-REFLEXIVITY, and MEDIUM-specificity (Baetens 2011; Beaty 2012; La Cour 2019)—as well as of the parameters for abstraction more broadly.

Erin La Cour

### *References*

Baetens, J. (2011) "Abstraction in Comics," *SubStance* 40(1), pp. 94–113.

Beaty, B. (2012) *Comics versus Art*. Toronto: University of Toronto Press.

La Cour, E. (2019) "Social Abstraction: Toward Exhibiting Comics as Comics" in Rommens, A., Crucifix, B., Dozo, B., Dejasse, E., and Turnes, P. (eds.) *Abstraction and Comics/Bande dessinée et abstraction*, Volume 1. Liège: La Cinquième *Couche*/Presses Universitaires de Liège, pp. 401–417.

Lind, M. (2013) "Interview: On Abstract Possible," *Abstract Possible*, 2 April 2013, n.p. Available at: http://abstractpossible.org/2011/04/05/on-abstract-possible-2/ [Accessed 1 August 2020].

Rommens, A. (2019) "Introduction" in Rommens, A., Crucifix, B., Dozo, B., Dejasse, E., and Turnes, P. (eds.) *Abstraction and Comics/Bande dessinée et abstraction*, Volume 1. Liège: La Cinquième *Couche*/Presses Universitaires de Liège, pp. 25–61.

## Actively Multisensory Comics

Although all comics are multisensory, some are more active than others in their engagement with the SENSES other than sight, which is CONVENTIONALLY understood as the dominant or only sense involved in the READING of comics. In so doing, actively multisensory comics emphasise the range of MATERIAL resources that are available to CREATORS in conveying meaning. Examples include Sally Anne Hickman's *Edible Comics* (2013), Dominique Grange and Tardi's *1968–2008…N'Effacez Pas Nos Traces!* (2008, packaged with an audio CD), Art Spiegelman's *In the Shadow of No Towers* (2004, a large, hard cardboard book), and Fumi Yoshinaga's *Antique Bakery* (1999–2002, a manga series that featured scratch and sniff covers). Some titles include such features as a novelty, while others make use of comics' materiality to make more serious points or to integrate a varied experience into their narratives. Active engagement with multisensory materiality can also open comics up to new AUDIENCES, as can be seen in the way that audiocomics such as Marvel's *Daredevil* #1 Audio Edition (2011) or tactile comics like Philipp Meyer's *Life* (2013) enable blind and visually impaired readers to engage with the MEDIUM (Lord 2016). Scholarship on comics and the senses is relatively limited (Hague 2014), but related concepts such as materiality have grown in importance in COMICS STUDIES since the mid-2010s.

Ian Hague

### *References*

Hague, I. (2014) *Comics and the Senses: A Multisensory Approach to Comics and Graphic Novels*. Abingdon: Routledge.

Lord, L. (2016) *Comics: The (Not Only) Visual Medium*. MSc. Massachusetts Institute of Technology. Available at: http://hdl.handle.net/1721.1/106761 [Accessed 30 April 2020].

## Activism

Activism is a collective group's championing of a political, social, economic, or environmental cause. Those who participate in activism, activists, are considered a social IDENTITY group (Horowitz 2017: 1). The group is defined by their shared cause and policy stemming from a belief that society can be bettered with their desired change. The comics MEDIUM has HISTORICALLY been used for communicating activist causes. Examples of this include Benton Resnick, Alfred Hassler, and Sy Barry's *Martin Luther King and the Montgomery Story*, originally published by The Fellowship of Reconciliation, and Jaime Cortez's *Sexile/Sexilo*, published by the Institute for Gay Men's Health in partnership with Gay Men's Health Crisis and AIDS Project Los Angeles. These comics advocate for civil rights for Black Americans and QUEER people's health and well being, respectively. REPRESENTATION is key when analysing activist comics. Since comics are "produced by individuals or groups of individuals who bring to their works their own preexisting ideas," comics scholars must contextualise how an activist movement or cause is represented in a text to discern between DOCUMENTARY and PROPAGANDIST discursive elements (Duncan et al. 2015: 344).

Rachel A. Davis

## *References*

Duncan, R., Smith, M. J., and Levitz, P. (2015) *The Power of Comics: History, Form, and Culture.* 2nd edition. London: Bloomsbury Academic.

Horowitz, J. (2017) "Who Is This 'We' You Speak of? Grounding Activist Identity in Social Psychology," *Socius* 3(1–17), pp. 1–17.

## Adaptation

Adaptation is the process of reproducing a work of ART or aspects of a work of art, from one REGISTER in another register, or versions of aspects of a work of art in the same register (Hutcheon 2006: 8). While adaptation is often thought of as STORY adaptation, according to Jan Baetens, it "is less a relationship between two objects than a cultural practice that explores new relationships between all aspects of the literary and artistic institution, such as artist, originality and style" (2018). Adaptation shares functional characteristics with TRANSLATION and with TRANSMEDIA productions in which the affordances of each register allow or disallow register-specific aspects of storytelling (Barnstone 1993). Both the process and the products of adaptation focus upon comparative stylistic analysis within registers, such as Karasik and Mazzucchelli, *City of*

*Glass* (1994), in which different drawing styles indicate the traits of different characters and between different registers, such as Grennan, *Dispossession: A Novel of Few Words (2015*), in which the LITERARY voice of Victorian novelist Anthony Trollope is replaced by a specific drawing style.

Simon Grennan

## *References*

Baetens, J. (2018) "Adaptation: A Writerly Strategy?" in Mitaine, B., Roche, D., and Schmitt-Pitiot, I. *Comics and Adaptation*. Jackson: University Press of Mississippi, pp. 31–46.

Barnstone, W. (1993) *The Poetics of Translation*. New Haven: Yale University Press.

Hutcheon, L. (2006) *A Theory of Adaptation*. Abingdon: Routledge.

Lynch, D. (2016) "Between the network and the narrative: Transmedia storytelling as a philosophical lens for creative writers," *New Writing* 13(2), pp.161–172.

## Advertising

In the early twentieth century, SUNDAY FUNNIES in America were a staple of newspaper publishing and by the 1930s increasingly contained advertising for products such as Jell-O, Lux, and Rinso. Selling advertising space for COMIC STRIPS in the Sunday funnies generated in the region $1,000,000 per annum for newspapers in 1933 ("The Funny Papers" 1933: 98–101). Advertising was also central to COMIC BOOK PUBLISHING throughout much of the twentieth century. Charles Atlas' bodybuilding courses were early examples of such advertisements in the FORM of comic strips. Advertisements for Hostess Twinkies bars (featuring SUPERHEROES from both Marvel and DC) appeared in many titles released by these publishers in the 1970s. The American comic book has its origins, at least in terms of format, in premiums, or free giveaway comics. In the early 1930s Harry I. Wildenberg and M. C. Gaines of the Eastern Colour Printing Company experimented with the PRINTING process to create half-tabloid sized giveaways for customers of companies such as Canada Dry, Gulf Oil, and Wheatena (Goulart 1991: 18–20). Strictly speaking these were not advertising but are best considered as promotional or public relations comics (Horton 2017); Sol Davidson has suggested all these types can be termed impact comics (Davidson 2005: 340–342).

Ian Horton

## *References*

Davidson, S. M. (2005) "The Funnies' Neglected Branch: Special Purpose Comics," *International Journal of Comic Art* 7(2), pp. 340–57.

Goulart, R. (1991) *Over 50 Years of American Comic Books*. Lincolnwood: Publications International, Ltd.

Horton, I. (2017) "Comic Books, Science (Fiction) and Public Relations" in Collister, S. and Roberts-Bowman, S. (eds.) *Visual & Spatial Public Relations: Strategic Communication Beyond Text*. Abingdon: Routledge, pp. 29–52.

"The Funny Papers," *Fortune*, April 1933.

## Aesthetics

Aesthetics is a field of philosophy that covers a wide range of topics surrounding not only ART, but all forms of aesthetic subjective experience. Strictly speaking, the term was coined by Alexander Gottlieb Baumgarten in the eighteenth century to refer "to cognition by means of the senses" (Baumgarten 1750; Goldman 2005: 255), establishing a turning point in philosophy. Depending on the moment in time, the discipline may accommodate distinct problems such as aesthetic categories (beauty and the sublime, for instance) (Plato c. 428/42–348/347 BC, Burke 1757); questions of taste and aesthetic judgement (Hume 1777; Kant 1790); art as creation and construction (Hegel 1818–1829; Halliwell 1986); the nature of aesthetic experience (Dewey 2005); the ontology of works of art (Currie 1988; Goodman 1968; Wollheim 1980); the debate between POPULAR CULTURE and art (Carroll 1998; Eco 1994; Shusterman 1991); or the nature of perception (Gombrich 1960), among others. Discussions on comics and aesthetics include philosophical approaches to what makes comics an art FORM (Meskin 2007, 2012; Harvey 1979; Carrier 2000; Baetens 2011); the debate on comics' cultural legitimation (Eco 1994; Groensteen 2000, 2006); and the relationship between comics and the ART WORLD (Beaty 2007, 2012; Frey and Baetens 2019).

Greice Schneider

## *References*

Baetens, J. (2011) "Historicising achronism: Some notes on the idea of art without history in David Carrier's *The Aesthetics of Comics*," *Image [&] Narrative* 12(4) pp. 130.

Baumgarten, A. (1750) *Aesthetica*. Reprint 1961. Hildesheim: Georg Olms Verlag.

Beaty, B. (2007) *Unpopular Culture: Transforming the European Comic Book in the 1990s*. Toronto: University of Toronto Press.

Beaty, B. (2012) *Comics versus Art*. Toronto: University of Toronto Press.

Burke, E. (1757) *A Philosophical Enquiry into the Origin of our Ideas of the Sublime and Beautiful*. Reprint 1968. Boulton, J. T. (ed.) Notre Dame: University of Notre Dame Press.

Carrier, D. (2000) *The Aesthetics of Comics*. University Park: The Pennsylvania State University Press.

Carroll, N. (1998) *A Philosophy of Mass Art*. Oxford: Oxford University Press.

Currie, G. (1988) *An Ontology of Art*. London: Macmillan.

Dewey, J. (1934) *Art as Experience*. Reprint 2005. London: Penguin.

Eco, U. (1964) *Apocalypse Postponed*. Reprint 1994. Bloomington: Indiana University Press.

Frey, H. and Baetens, J. (2019) "Comics Culture and Roy Lichtenstein Revisited: Analysing a Forgotten 'Feedback Loop,'" *Art History* 42(1) pp.126–152.

Goldman, A. (2005) "The Aesthetic" in Gaut, B. N. and Lopes, D. (eds.) *The Routledge Companion to Aesthetics*. 2nd edition. Abingdon: Routledge, pp.255–266.

Gombrich, E. H. (1960) *Art and Illusion: A Study in the Psychology of Pictorial Representation*. Princeton: Princeton University Press.

Goodman, N. (1968) *Languages of Art: An Approach to a Theory of Symbols*. Indianapolis: Bobbs-Merrill.

Groensteen, T. (2000) "Why are comics still in search of cultural legitimization" in Magnussen, A. and Christiansen, H.-C. (eds.) *Comics and Culture: Analytical and Theoretical Approaches to Comics*. Copenhagen: Museum Tusculanum Press, pp. 29–42.

Groensteen, T. (2006) *Un objet culturel non identifié*. Angoulême: Éditions de l'an 2.

Halliwell, S. (1986) *Aristotle's Poetics*. London: Duckworth.

Harvey, R. C. (1979) "The aesthetics of the comic strip," *Journal of Popular Culture* 12(4), 640–652.
Harvey, R. C. (1996) *The Art of the Comic Book: An Aesthetic History.* Jackson: University Press of Mississippi.
Hegel, G. W. F. (1818–1829) *Aesthetics: Lectures on Fine Art.* Translated from German by T. M. Knox, 1975. Oxford: Oxford University Press.
Hume, D. (1777) *Essays Moral, Political and Literary.* Reprint 1985. Miller, E. F. (ed.) Indianapolis: Liberty Classics.
Kant, I. (1790) *Critique of Judgment.* Translated from German by J. H. Bernard. Reprint 1931. London: Macmillan and Co.mpany.
Meskin, A. and Cook R. T. (2012) *The Art of Comics: A Philosophical Approach.* Hoboken: Wiley-Blackwell.
Meskin, A. (2007) "Defining Comics?" *The Journal of Aesthetics and Art Criticism* 65(4), pp. 369–379.
Plato (c. 428/42–348/347 BC) *Complete Works.* Translated from Greek by J. M. Cooper and D. S. Hutchinson et al., 1997. Cooper, J. M. and Hutchinson, D. S. (eds.) Indianapolis: Hackett.
Shusterman, R. (1991) "Form and Funk: The Aesthetic Challenge of Popular Art," *British Journal of Aesthetics* 31(3), pp. 203–213.
Wollheim, R. (1968) *Art and Its Objects.* Reprint 1980. Cambridge: Cambridge University Press.

## Affect

Affect theory refers to "an approach to history, politics, culture, and all other aspects of embodied life that emphasizes the role of nonlinguistic forces" (Schaefer 2019: 1). There is no single theory of affect, but a number of distinct notions across disciplines can be condensed into two main views: the first, rooted in psychology and neurosciences, considers affect as "a primary innate biological motivating mechanism" (Tomkins 1982). It aims to organise a system of universal elemental affects. In this context, the term is sometimes used interchangeably with emotions, moods, and feelings. A second main approach, more associated with the humanities, understands affect as an "intensive force" (Ott 2017) that should not be confused with a broader notion of feeling, but rather with a more abstract concept, outside consciousness. Disseminated by Gilles Deleuze and Félix Guattari (1980), affect here comprehends the non-conscious experience of intensity and the body's capacity to act and to be affected (Massumi 2002). More recent works in CULTURAL THEORY and MEDIA studies have tried to reconcile both views, focusing on a HYBRID approach (Ngai 2005; Ahmed 2010; Grossberg 2013). In COMICS STUDIES, the notion of affect appears in a broad range of contexts (Worden 2006; Hague 2014; Reiser 2014).

Greice Schneider

## *References*


Ahmed, S. (2010) "Happy Objects" in Gregg, M. and Seigworth, G. J. (eds.) *The Affect Theory Reader*. Durham: Duke University Press, pp. 29–50.

Deleuze, G. and Guattari, F. (1980) *A Thousand Plateaus: Capitalism and Schizophrenia*. Translated from French by B. Massumi, 2004. New York: Continuum.

Grossberg, L. (1992) *We gotta get out of this place: Popular conservatism and postmodern culture*. Abingdon: Routledge.

Hague, I. (2014) *Comics and the Senses: A Multisensory Approach to Comics and Graphic Novels*. Abingdon: Routledge.

Massumi, B. (2002) *Parables for the Virtual: Movement, Affect, Sensation*. Durham: Duke University Press.

Ngai, S. (2005). *Ugly Feelings*. Cambridge: Harvard University Press.

Ott, B. L. (2017) "Affect in Critical Studies" in *Oxford Research Encyclopedia of Communication*. Available at: https://oxfordre.com/communication/view/10.1093/acrefore/9780190228613.001.0001/acrefore-9780190228613-e-56?print [Accessed 9 July 2020].

Reiser, J. (2014) "'Thinking in cartoons': Reclaiming Spiegelman's *In the Shadow of No Towers*," *Journal of Graphic Novels and Comics* 5(1), pp. 3–14.

Schaefer, D. O. (2019) *The Evolution of Affect Theory: The Humanities, the Sciences, and the Study of Power*. Cambridge: Cambridge University Press.

Tomkins, S. S. (1982) "Affect theory" in Ekman, P., Friesen, W. V., and Ellsworth, P. (eds.) *Emotion in the human face*. Cambridge: Cambridge University Press, pp. 353–395.

Worden, D. (2006) "The Shameful Art: McSweeney's Quarterly Concern, Comics, and the Politics of Affect," *MFS Modern Fiction Studies* 52(4), pp. 891–917.

## Album

In the eighteenth century, “album” (“white tablet” in Latin) was the standard English and French term to refer to notebooks designed for inserting pictures or DRAWINGS, and for publications containing mostly IMAGES (Lesage 2013). It was the word used by Rodolphe Töpffer, the “Father of the Comic Strip,” to name the books in which he had his first picture STORIES published in the 1830s. In French-speaking European countries, “album” became the “natural” appellation of hardbound books containing picture stories or a majority of pictures (Filliot 2012). When the comics MEDIUM turned into a POPULAR CULTURAL phenomenon, by becoming a staple of ILLUSTRATED children’s magazines in the early twentieth century, comics albums became quasi-luxury COMMODITIES for a few decades, most often purchased as birthday or holiday gifts. From the 1930s to the early 1960s, Franco-Belgian comics magazine publishers regarded albums as a secondary niche MARKET. By 1966, the runaway success of René Goscinny and Albert Uderzo’s *Astérix* prompted a progressive economic and cultural change: in twenty years the album succeeded the magazine as the dominant format of European comics PUBLISHING. By the early 1980s, it inspired the US comics industry to market GRAPHIC NOVELS next to periodical FLOPPIES (Gabilliet 2005).

Jean-Paul Gabilliet

### *References*

Filliot, C. (2012) “Les premiers albums de bande dessinée au XIXe siècle: Quelle identité éditoriale, quel usage culturel et social?” in Alary, V. and Chabrol-Gagne, N. *L’Album: le parti pris des images*. Clermont-Ferrand: Presses Universitaires Blaise-Pascal, n.p.

Gabilliet, J.-P. (2005) “Du comic book au graphic novel: L’européanisation de la bande dessinée américaine,” *Image [&] Narrative* 6(2), n.p. Available at: http://www.imageandnarrative.be/inarchive/tulseluper/gabilliet.htm [Accessed 15 August 2020].

Lesage, S. (2013) “Album” in Groensteen, T. (ed.) *Dictionnaire esthétique et thématique de la bande dessinée, Neuvième art 2.0*. Available at: http://neuviemeart.citebd.org/spip.php?article536 [Accessed 30 July 2020].

## Allegory

An allegory is a device by which a text contains a second, partially obscured, meaning or message in which characters, settings, and events act as analogues to external, often real-world situations, places, and figures. Gary Johnson points to shared attributes between allegory and "synecdoche, metonymy, simile and metaphor" (2012: 4), noting that, in the case of the latter, the lines between the two concepts are often blurred or obscured (ibid.: 6–7). Examples of allegorical NARRATIVES include FABLES, MYTHS, scripture, and FOLKLORE-based texts in which the AUDIENCE'S familiarity with the original narrative allows for an easier understanding of the deeper truths or ideas to be transmitted. Northrop Frye maintains that allegory is structurally intrinsic to all narrative texts (1990: 54), in as much as criticism and interpretation of a text must lead to its transformation into "a parable or illustrative fable" (ibid.: 53). This corresponds to the idea that allegory is simultaneously a "mode of reading and a strategy for writing" (Mailloux 2010: 254). In SUPERHERO comics, the X-Men have often been interpreted as an allegory for the negative experiences of minorities and other marginalised societal groups.

Houman Sadri

### *References*

Frye, N. (1957) *Anatomy of Criticism*. Reprint 1990. Princeton: Princeton University Press.

Johnson, G. (2012) *The Vitality of Allegory*. Columbus: The Ohio State University Press.

Mailloux, S. (2010) "Hermeneutics, Deconstruction, Allegory" in Copland, R. and Struck, P. T. (eds.) *The Cambridge Companion to Allegory*. Cambridge: Cambridge University Press, pp. 254–265.

## Allusion

To allude is to make an intentional but casual reference to another work. It is useful to think of allusions as "micro-texts" embedded in the structure of a larger NARRATIVE (Leitch 2007: 121)—they are INTERTEXTUAL, though the REFERENT might come from any aspect of life. Allusions have been defined in many ways, including "phraseological adaptation," in reference to purely verbal ART (Machacek 2007: 523). A typology might categorise them by intention: for example, SATIRICAL, such as a team of accountants yelling "Accountants Assemble!" when mobilising for action (Walton 2006: 200); or HERMENEUTIC, such as Alison Bechdel's reference to the Daedalus MYTH to characterise her father in *Fun Home: A Family Tragicomic* (2007) (ibid.: 12). The dividing line between allusion and other types of intertextuality (embedded NARRATION, PASTICHE, echo, PARODY) is difficult to draw. Characteristic of allusion is the hope that a part of the AUDIENCE will understand the reference, which allows for the allusion to remain below the radar of other segments of the audience.

Daniel Peretti

## *References*

Leitch, T. (2007) *Film Adaptation and Its Discontents: From* Gone with the Wind *to* The Passion of the Christ. Baltimore: The Johns Hopkins University Press.

Machacek, G. (2007) "Allusion," *PMLA* 122(2), pp. 522–536.

Walton, R. (2006) *Ragmop: A Brief History of Crime.* Toronto: Planet Lucy Press.

## Alterity

Alterity is the state of otherness. Western metaphysics initially understood the relation between self and other as binary. Immanuel Kant's conception of the will to act characterised the self as independent of the other (1998: 543). But in order to live a free life, we have to recognise that the other also has a form of AUTONOMY. Emmanuel Levinas focuses on alterity as entirely separate from the self, and so we are in relation to the other, with obligations to others (1991: 53–81). Subsequent debate about alterity concerns incorporation. Edmund Husserl argued that the other presents itself or gives itself to the cogito through experience (2001: 73). Martin Heidegger argued that the other has being in its own right and consciousness involves proximity to or being "between" others (1996: 124). Alterity later becomes an explanation for women's and minority subjugation: Simone de Beauvoir identified alterity as the ontological status of women

(2009: 26), Gayatri Chakravorty Spivak asked whether the subaltern other can be represented fully in normative systems (1988: 87, 104), and Jacques Derrida asked whether there was even a self/other relation at all, because "every other is wholly other" (1995: 84). Hélène Cixous identified alterity as the space where binary, phallocentric logic can be escaped (1976: 893). Alterity initially was confined to descriptions of human relations, but Karen Barad's POSTHUMANIST and David Abram's ECOLOGICAL approaches see alterity as an important principle for all existence (Barad 2007: 26, Abram 2010: 181).

Julie Rak

## *References*

Abram, D. (2010) *Becoming Animal: An Earthly Cosmology.* New York: Pantheon Books.

Barad, K. (2007) *Meeting the University Halfway.* Durham: Duke University Press.

de Beauvoir, S. (1949) *The Second Sex.* Translated from French by C. Borde and S. Malovany-Chevallier, 2001. New York: Vintage.

Cixous, H. (1976) "The Laugh of the Medusa," *Signs* 1(4), pp. 875–893.

Derrida, J. (1992) *The Gift of Death.* Translated from French by D. Wills, 1995. Chicago: University of Chicago Press.

Kant, I. (1781) *Critique of Pure Reason.* Translated from German by P. Guyer and A. W. Wood, 1998. Cambridge: Cambridge University Press.

Husserl, E. (1900) *Logical Investigations.* Translated from German by Findlay, J. N., 2001. Abingdon: Routledge.

Heidegger, M. (1927) *Being and Time.* Translated from German by J. Stambaugh. Reprint 1996. Albany: SUNY Press.

Levinas, E. (1961) *Totality and Infinity: An essay on exteriority.* Translated from French by A. Lingis, 1991. Berlin: Springer.

Spivak, G. C. (1988) "Can the Subaltern Speak?" in Nelson, C. and Grossberg, L. (eds.) *Marxism and the Interpretation of Culture.* Basingstoke: Macmillan Education, pp. 271–313.

## Alternative Comics

Comics produced outside the mainstream PUBLISHING industry are dubbed alternative comics. Broadly, this term refers to several qualities: THEME, STYLE, AUDIENCE, PRODUCTION, and distribution. UNDERGROUND COMIX provided a template with their adult SUBJECTS and auteur approach (Estren 1974: 20). Hatfield distinguishes between “independent” comics (including GROUNDLEVEL COMICS) and alternative comics: while both are produced beyond the purview of large publishers, the former presents mainstream subjects, while the latter “more often denotes satirical, political, and autobiographical elements inherited from underground comix” (Hatfield 2005: 26). Regardless of tone, alternative comics proliferated from the 1980s onward with the rise of the DIRECT MARKET and more grassroots production methods, such as ZINES; some even transcended to mainstream acceptance, like Mirage Studios’ *Teenage Mutant Ninja Turtles* (1984–2015). Simultaneously, major publishers experimented with “alternative” FORMATS (see DC’s Vertigo imprint) and mainstream publishers today regularly release titles that would have been described as alternative comics decades before. DIGITAL creation and distribution, more diverse themes and CREATORS, and the rise of platforms like Webtoons further complicate the need for this distinction.

Josh R. Rose

### *References*

Estren, M. J. (1974) *A History of Underground Comics.* San Francisco: Straight Arrow Books.

Hatfield, C. (2005) *Alternative Comics: An Emerging Literature.* Jackson: University Press of Mississippi.

## Amar Chitra Katha

Often translated from Hindi as “immortal picture stories,” the Indian Amar Chitra Katha series of comics was started in 1967 by Anant Pai. Amar Chitra Katha comics centre on heroes who “fought on behalf of Hindus or those under the protective net of Hindu rulers” (Chandra 2008: 2). Amar Chitra Katha’s MARKET has been chiefly urban, middle

CLASS, and English-speaking, and targets 8–18-year-olds in a bid "to teach them what it means to be Indian" (McLain 2009: 12). However, Amar Chitra Katha has always enjoyed a broader READERSHIP, proving to be "a medium that has helped Indians living in postcolonial India and throughout the world define what it means to be Indian" (ibid.: 3). Typically, Amar Chitra Katha comics are 32 pages long. NARRATIVE TEXT, visual IMAGES, and SPEECH BALLOONS are employed, inspired by American comics that were in circulation in India during the 1950s and 1960s (e.g. *Phantom* and *Mandrake*). Amar Chitra Katha hallmarks include Indian heroes (usually those from the epics, e.g. *Ramayana* and the *Mahabharata*), patriotism (medieval kings, colonial freedom fighters, and brave hearts), as well as animal FABLES (such as *Panchatantra*).

E. Dawson Varughese

## *References*

Chandra, N. (2008) *The Classic Popular: Amar Chitra Katha, 1967–2007.* New Delhi: Yoda Press.

McLain, K. (2009) *India's Immortal Comic Books: Gods, Kings and Other Heroes.* Bloomington: Indiana University Press.

## Angle

Angle is a COMPOSITIONAL choice concerning the FRAMING of the subject, which determines the spatial PERSPECTIVE through which the READER will apprehend the visually represented elements. It is one of the terms amply employed in COMICS STUDIES whose origin can be directly traced back to FILM studies. Its cinematic ancestry is most easily detected in vocabular conjugations such as the one denounced by Bart Beaty when he writes, "'Camera angle,' for example, is routinely used to describe compositional framing in comics even though no camera is employed in the construction of the image" (2011: 108). One of the most adopted variations on this expression, which is less cinematic and more general, is "angle of view" (Cohn 2011), or "angle of vision," which Ann Miller uses abundantly in her theoretical work. Miller highlights the importance of this factor in all compositional strategies in comics, but explains that it is only likely to be noticed by the reader "if it is high or low" (2007: 94). Non-standard angles are usually used as resources of hyperbole, as Thierry Groensteen exemplifies when studying a PANEL from *Corentin*. He writes, "This image is framed in a slight low angle shot to render the assailant's stature even more menacing" (2007: 120).

David Pinho Barros

## *References*

Beaty, B. (2011) "In Focus: Comics Studies Fifty Years After Film Studies—Introduction," *Cinema Journal* 50(3), pp. 106–110.

Cohn, N. (2011) "A different kind of cultural frame: An analysis of panels in American comics and Japanese manga," *Image [&] Narrative* 12(1), pp. 120–134.

Groensteen, T. (1999) *The System of Comics*. Translated from French by B. Beaty and N. Nguyen, 2007. Jackson: University Press of Mississippi.

Miller, A. (2007) *Reading Bande dessinée: Critical Approaches to French-language Comic Strip*. Bristol: Intellect.

## Animation

Animation commonly refers to a kind of moving IMAGE with a specific visual AESTHETIC that is easy to tell apart from that of live-action FILM. Its essential difference from film consists in it not having its constitutive FRAMES recorded from a live-action source; instead, it is created and arranged manually. At least, this was the case in its early analogue stages, when each "'frame' of animation was given visual form by reference to a physically existing image of some sort" (Stabile 2013: 111). In recent times, Omar O. L. Martinez has identified animation as "distinct type of moving image with solely illusory movement" (2015: 42), an all-encompassing definition with an elaborate set of criteria that applies to both analogue and digital, frame-by-frame and automatic, intentional, and accidental examples of animation. By the 1980s, animation moved its focus from primarily manipulating physical images to manipulating digital data. Computer generated imagery and similar digital tools and techniques allowed animators to transfer the laborious task of creating in-between frames to programmable algorithms. Such computer-assisted digital animation is used so often in contemporary moving image culture that "it is possible to come to a conclusion that 'animation' as a separate medium in fact hardly exists any more" (2006: 35).

Josip Batinić

### *References*

Stabile, C. A. and Harrison, M. (eds.) (2003) *Prime time animation: Television animation and American culture*. Abingdon: Routledge.

Martinez, O. O. L. (2015) "Criteria for defining animation: A revision of the definition of animation in the advent of digital moving images," *Animation* 10(1), pp. 42–57.

Manovich, L. (2006) "Image future," *Animation* 1(1), pp. 25–44.

## Annual

The ANNUAL is an aspect of the COMIC BOOK industry that has been poorly documented from a historical standpoint. One of the earliest American annuals is 1949's *Archie Annual*; there is no definitive first annual documented (Gill et al. 1949). With that said, comic books coming out monthly meant that only twelve issues would be produced a year. However, annuals were a way to give a series a thirteenth issue. These issues often contained more pages and frequently contained various reprints or shorter stories. As the comic book industry evolved, annuals shifted from being standalone issues to parts of ongoing story arcs. Further, annuals were sometimes self-contained crossover events. For example, *Bloodlines* was a crossover event that was only told in annual issues made by DC Comics in 1993 (Raspier et al. 1993).

Nicholas Yanes

### *References*

Gill, R., Schwartz, S., Montana, B. and Shorten, H. (1949) *Archie Annual.* New York: Archie Comic Publications Incorporated.

Raspier, D., Velluto, S., Gemdjian, A. and Chaifez, S. (1993) *Bloodlines.* Burbank CA: DC Comics.

Van As, T. (2020) "What Are Comic Book Annuals?" *How To Love Comics.* n.p. Available at: https://www.howtolovecomics.com/2020/08/19/what-are-comic-book-annuals/ [Accessed 3 November 2020].

## Anti-Hero

An anti-hero is a protagonist who lacks one or more of the traditional positive attributes of a HERO. Often morally ambivalent, such characters can tend to perform heroic tasks for selfish or venal reasons, or be seen to commit excessively violent or criminal acts in order to serve their perception of the greater good (including an ambivalence about the collateral damage their actions may cause). The vigilante nature of traditional SUPERHERO characters can serve to blur the lines between heroes, anti-heroes, and VILLAINS—Chris Gavaler notes that in terms of extralegality there is, after all, little difference "whether the hero kills, castrates or leaves criminals tied to lampposts" (2015: 166)—but the willingness to take a life is often the benchmark of such characters (in simple terms, The Punisher kills while Batman, as a rule, does not).

Houman Sadri

### *References*

Gavaler, C. (2015). *On the Origins of Superheroes.* Iowa City: University of Iowa Press.

## Applied Comics

Applied comics are comics with a specific job to do. They communicate information to a target AUDIENCE, a goal that shapes choices made throughout the comics-making process and differs from a general category of non-fiction comics. Applied comics are typically made as a COLLABORATION between subject specialist(s) and comics CREATOR(S), though one person might take on both roles. In addition to the usual drafting and editorial work, a coproduction approach can involve the intended end users in making decisions about the comic, particularly when navigating ETHICAL considerations and sensitive information. Any ART and NARRATIVE STYLES might be chosen to connect the content with its target audience, and this is likely to be a crucial discussion for a project team. Planning for the distribution of an applied comic to its target READERSHIP can make SELF-PUBLISHING more appropriate than commercial PUBLISHING, particularly when applied comics are free at the point of use. Though some comics-FORM public information campaigns might require large-scale distribution with logistical challenges, other comics might be distributed to a small network or made as part of a closed group (particularly in EDUCATION or healthcare settings) with associated confidentiality issues. Related fields include infographics, data VISUALISATION, GRAPHIC FACILITATION. Subfields include GRAPHIC MEDICINE, science comics, and comics used as a method within academic research.

Lydia Wysocki

## *References*

Czerwiec, M. K., Williams, I., Squier, S. M., Green, M. J., Myers, K. R., and Smith, S. T. (2015) *Graphic Medicine Manifesto*. University Park: The Pennsylvania State University Press.

Graham, R. (2011) *Government Issue: Comics for the People, 1940s–2000s*. New York: Abrams Comic Arts.

Wysocki, L. (2018) "Farting Jellyfish and Synergistic Opportunities: The Story and Evaluation of Newcastle Science Comic," *The Comics Grid: Journal of Comics Scholarship*, 8(1), pp.6–14.

Wysocki, L. and Leat, D. (2019) "Collaborative Comic as Boundary Object: The Creation, Reading, and Uses of Freedom City Comics/ Cómic colaborativo como Objeto de Frontera: la creación, lectura y usos de Freedom City Comics," *Tebeosfera* 3(10), n.p. Available at: https://revista.tebeosfera.com/documentos/comic_colaborativo_como_objeto_frontera_la_creacion_lectura_y_usos_de_freedom_city_comics.html [Accessed 14 August 2020].

## Archetype

An archetype is a primary model of a CHARACTER, IMAGE, motif, or symbol. The psychologist Carl Jung developed the notion of psychological archetypes in the early twentieth century. For Jung, archetypes are images or forms that arise out of man's collective unconsciousness. Cultural archetypes, which pre-exist culturally instead of psychologically, occur in various storytelling formats and are imbued with meaning and connotations prior to their inclusion. The archetype pre-exists the text and adds meaning to the text. Archetypes may reveal universal roles within societies or may be created out of the MYTHOLOGICAL or religious framework on which a society is based. It can be difficult to differentiate between archetypes and the STEREOTYPES with which they are infused. Some criticisms of the concept suggest the use of culturetypes instead (Meyer 2003). Culturetypes represent roles, images, or objects made meaningful within a specific social or cultural context as opposed to archetypes, whose claim to universality cannot be supported. Examples of archetypes include, but are not limited to, the hero, the mask, or the quest for a sacred object. An oft-cited discussion on comics and archetypes is Umberto Eco's influential "The Myth of Superman" (1972).

Esther De Dauw

## *References*

Eco, U. (1972) "The Myth of Superman," *Diacritics* 2(1), pp. 14–22.

Meyer, M. D. E. (2003) "Utilizing mythic criticism in contemporary narrative culture: Examining the 'present-absence' of shadow archetypes in *Spider-Man*," *Communication Quarterly* 51(4), pp. 518–529.

Osborn, M. (1990) "In defense of broad mythic criticism: A reply to Rowland," *Communication Studies* 41, pp. 121–127.

## Architecture

PAGE architecture is a term common to both comics and graphic design, used to describe aspects of the DESIGN, PAGE LAYOUT, and visual COMPOSITION of a page's contents. Elements of comics such as PANELS, GUTTERS, and CAPTION BOXES are sometimes described as being parts of the architecture that provide a page with its underlying structure. Within the visual NARRATIVES of comics, the DEPICTION of architecture is often an important element in establishing a STORY'S locale. The urban setting of many comics narratives has meant that depictions of architecture have "long been a prominent fixture of the comics page" (Labio 2015: 312). Will Eisner includes the study of architecture in the "range of diverse disciplines" that should form part of a comics ARTIST'S EDUCATION (2008: 159). Architecture also plays an important role in "gallery comics," a type of HYBRID comics "made specifically for exhibition" (Gravett 2013: 131). Gallery comics operate as "architecturally mediated" ART installations that are experienced via the READER'S navigation of "a real world, three dimensional environment" (Goodbrey 2016: 16).

Daniel Merlin Goodbrey

## *References*

Goodbrey, D. M. (2016) "Images in Space: The Challenges of Architectural Spatiality in Comics" in Ebrahim, S. and Peppas, M. (eds.) *Framescapes: Graphic Narrative Intertexts.* Oxford: Inter-Disciplinary Press, pp. 15–29.

Gravett, P. (2013) *Comics Art.* London: Tate Publishing.

Eisner, W. (1985) *Comics and Sequential Art: Principles and Practices from the Legendary Cartoonist.* Reprint 2008. New York: W. W. Norton & Company.

Labio, C. (2015) "The Architecture of Comics," *Critical Inquiry* (41)2, pp. 312–343.

## Archive

In broad terms an archive is a collection of documents and the facility in which they are stored. More than a simple accumulation of records, as Jacques Derrida attests, the archive carries with it its historical connotation of "arkhé," which "names at once the *commencement* and the *commandement*"—meaning that even the most benignly intended archives fall prey to consignation and authorisation (1995: 1). Moreover, he argues, any archival project, through its act of collection necessarily excludes certain information, thereby working "*a priori* against itself" (ibid.: 12). Discussions of archival theory have been explored primarily in COMICS STUDIES through the CLOSE READING of comics that likewise discuss archival theory, especially as it pertains to the complications of WRITING into HISTORY the lives of peoples and cultures that have been excluded from view in local, state, and national archives as well as in the LITERARY CANON, due to factors including GENDER, RACE, CLASS, ETHNICITY, and (DIS)ABILITY (see Cvetkovich 2008; Rohy 2010; La Cour 2013 and 2021; Ahmed and Crucifix 2018). Other approaches to the archive include considerations of the history, SERIALITY, and MATERIALITY of comics as SELF-REFLEXIVE archival projects (see Crucifix 2017).

Erin La Cour

## *References*

Ahmed, M. and Crucifix, B. (eds.) (2018) *Comics Memory: Archives and Styles.* London: Palgrave Macmillan.
Crucifix, B. (2018) "From loose to boxed fragments and back again: Seriality and archive in Chris Ware's *Building Stories,*" *Journal of Graphic Novels and Comics* 9(1), pp. 3–22.
Cvetkovich, A. (2008) "Drawing the Archive in Alison Bechdel's *Fun Home,*" *WSQ: Women's Studies Quarterly* 36(1–2), pp.111–128.
Derrida, J. (1995) *Archive Fever: A Freudian Impression.* Translated from French by E. Prenowitz, 1996. Chicago: University of Chicago Press.
La Cour, E. (2021) "Alison Bechdel: *Dykes to Watch Out For*" Domsch, S., Hassler-Forest, D., and Vanderbeke, D. (eds.) *Handbook on Comics and Graphic Narratives.* Berlin: De Gruyter, pp. 527–541.
La Cour, E. (2013) *The "Graphic Novel": Discourses on the Archive.* PhD. University of Amsterdam.
Rohy, V. (2010). "In the Queer Archive: *Fun Home,*" *GLQ: A Journal of Lesbian and Gay Studies* 16(3), pp. 340–361.

## Art

Comics have been critiqued as art, NARRATIVE or SEQUENTIAL art, anti-art, minor art, degraded art, invisible art, and non-art. The fissure is one of construction and intention, between CREATOR, AUDIENCE, and industry; as Anastasia Salter contentiously notes: "high art demands an artist, and an original, while comics produce collaborations, and indistinguishable copies" (2016: 355). CANONISATION causes separation on grounds of terminology, such as comics versus GRAPHIC NOVELS. Andrei Molotiu's term "art comics" challenges the subservience of the sequential to the visual, of ILLUSTRATION to narrative storytelling (2016: 119). Legitimacy debates focus on comic art exhibitions or publications and their position as diametrically opposed to commercial or POPULAR CULTURAL forms (Beaty 2012: 212). Considering comics within a distinct ART WORLD, allowing for critique which moves beyond FORM, embraces their HYBRID nature and appreciates their commercial, subversive, or so-called unsophisticated qualities (Beaty 2012: 44–46). Rodolphe Töpffer's theory of "doodles" aligned awkwardness and expression with naïve and "anti-academic" traditions of art, appreciating individuality and robustness over AESTHETIC unity (Smolderen 2014: 27–31). The comics-as-art DISCOURSE remains problematised within wider high- versus low-brow subjectivity, as ironically noted by Art Spiegelman when he claimed: "I've been designated not as a comic book artist because I did something that got a Pulitzer Prize" (qtd. in Beaty 2012: 101).

Dona Pursall

## *References*

Beaty, B. (2012) *Comics versus Art*. Toronto: University of Toronto Press.

Molotiu, A. (2016) "Art Comics" in Bramlett, F., Cook, R., and Meskin, A. (eds.) *The Routledge Companion to Comics*. Abingdon: Routledge, pp. 119–127.

Salter, A. (2016) "Comics and Art" in Bramlett, F. Cook, R., and Meskin, A. (eds.) *The Routledge Companion to Comics*. Abingdon: Routledge, pp. 348–357.

Smolderen, T. (2000) *The Origins of Comics: From William Hogarth to Winsor McCay*. Translated from French by B. Beaty and N. Nguyen, 2014. Jackson: University Press of Mississippi.

## Art World

According to Howard Becker, the art world is the network of interactions between fine ARTISTS, critics, ART galleries, MUSEUMS, art magazines, and the "art market" (1982: 34–39). Comics emerged in the late nineteenth century's CULTURAL INDUSTRY outside of the art world and initially enjoyed very limited proximity to it—regardless of Pablo Picasso's enthusiasm for turn of the century SUNDAY FUNNIES and Bauhaus co-founder Lyonel Feininger's 1906–1907 *art-nouveau* feature "The Kin-der-Kids." Comics' penetration into the fine artists' visual vocabulary began only in the 1940s with Kurt Schwitters and continued with the rise of POP ART, particularly in Roy Lichtenstein's works (Varnedoe and Gopnik 1990: 153–229). Since the late twentieth century, comics have become frequent objects and subjects of contemporary ART (Wagstaff 1987; Rosenberg and Sterckx 2009). In parallel to the fine artists' appropriation of the MEDIUM, two significant trends have emerged since the 1980s: the gradual multiplication of EXHIBITS of original comic artwork in fine art galleries and museums and a growing MARKET of original comics art that high-profile galleries and auction houses have increasingly publicised and taken over since the turn of the twenty-first century (Beaty 2012).

Jean-Paul Gabilliet

## *References*

Beaty, B. (2012) *Comics versus Art*. Toronto: University of Toronto Press.

Becker, H. S. (1982) *Art Worlds*. Berkeley: University of California Press.

Rosenberg, D. and Sterckx, P. (2009) *Vraoum! Trésors de la bande dessinée et art contemporain*. Paris: Maison Rouge/Editions Fage.

Varnedoe, K. and Gopnik, A. (1990) *High & Low: Modern Art and Popular Culture*. New York: The Museum of Modern Art.

Wagstaff, S. (1987) *Comic Iconoclasm*. London: Institute of Contemporary Art.

## ARTHROLOGY

Arthrology is the term used by Thierry Groensteen for the articulation of independent and interdependent FORMAL items constituting the comics PAGE. With the term SPATIO-TOPIA, Groensteen discusses the organisation of the elements out of which comics consist in SPACE (Groensteen 2007: 21). Arthrology describes the ways in which these elements are articulated, or drawn together. It is divided into two sub-classes. First, restricted or restrained arthrology, which governs the linear relations between elements on the comics page and is concerned with how meaning is created by the articulation of elements that are formally adjacent to one another (ibid.: 103). Second, general arthrology is the network of elements that surpasses the spatio-TEMPORAL SEQUENCE of NARRATIVE. BRAIDING, the most prominent example of general arthrology, creates relations between panels or other elements in comics that are removed from each other spatially (ibid.: 146).

Rik Spanjers

## *References*

Groensteen, T. (1999) *The System of Comics.* Translated from French by B. Beaty and N. Nguyen, 2007. Jackson: University Press of Mississippi.

## Artist

Comics are either made by a single artist (often called a "complete" AUTHOR or CREATOR, in charge of both SCRIPT and artwork) or by a team of artists (often working following a strict division of LABOUR in an industrial studio setting: editing, scriptwriting, artwork, LETTERING, COLOURISATION). The distinction between these two systems, which includes a large set of intermediary positions (DRAWINGS can be made by more than one person; conversely a whole team can COLLABORATIVELY assume various functions, successive instalments or versions of the same work can be done by different artists), is neither chronological or geographical nor GENRE-related. There is, however, a strong relationship with the artistic and CULTURAL-INDUSTRIAL context in which comics are made. In analogy with auteur theory in FILM, which claims that a single agent, generally the director, is in control of all aspects of a collaborative work, the increased cultural legitimacy of comics has transformed artists into authors and authors into auteurs, a situation that is often at odds with the legal regulations of the PUBLISHING industry which does not always offer individual authorship as well as ownership to its "employees," as exemplarily shown by the first Donald Duck cartoons, made by Carl Barks but signed by Walt Disney.

Jan Baetens

## *References*

Ahmed, M. (2017) "Comics and authorship: An introduction," *Authorship* 6(2). Available at: https://www.authorship.ugent.be/article/view/7702 [Accessed 3 August 2020].

Friedlander, K. (2018) "The Editor, the Author Function, and the Social Function: A Methodological Survey," *Journal of Graphic Novels and Comics* 9(2), pp. 157–172.

Peeters, B. (2003) *Lire la bande dessinée*. Paris: Flammarion.

## Assemblage

Assemblages are non-hierarchical, organic multiplicities connected through various processes and can be stabilised or destabilised through new connections in larger or smaller assemblages through the different connections between components. From the French "agencement," assemblage was coined as a term by Gilles Deleuze and Félix Guattari and was later clarified and developed by Manuel DeLanda with an emphasis on how assemblages are "wholes characterised by relations of exteriority" (2006: 10). This means assemblages are defined by the way they attach and re-attach to other parts and reconfigure their assemblage. In comics assemblage can denote the FORMAL assemblage of elements within a comic (Cortsen 2012), the similarity between urban environments and comics (Dittmer 2014), the POST/HUMAN body as it relates to SUPERHEROES within the assemblage of the corporate world of comics and interrelated with READER assemblages and critical assemblages (Jefferey 2016), or to describe how PANELS are put together by the comics reader (Cohn 2013). Assemblage describes amorphous and diverse collections of objects, elements, and DISCOURSE that are in a process of disconnecting and re-connecting with other assemblages. As such, assemblage can be scaled for comics analysis to examine assemblages within the panel to the larger scale of comics interrelated with a global multimedial world.

Rikke Platz Cortsen

### *References*

Cohn, N. (2013) "Navigating comics: An empirical and theoretical approach to strategies of reading comic page layouts," *Frontiers in Psychology*, n.p, Available at: https://www.frontiersin.org/articles/10.3389/fpsyg.2013.00186/full [Accessed 10 July 2020].

Cortsen, R. P. (2012) *Comics as Assemblage: How Spatio-temporality in Comics is Constructed*. PhD. University of Copenhagen.

DeLanda, M. (2006) *A New Philosophy of Society: Assemblage Theory and Social Complexity*. New York: Continuum.

Deleuze, G. and Guattari, F. (1980) *A Thousand Plateaus*. Translated from French by B. Massumi, 2004. New York: Continuum.

Dittmer, J. (2014) "Narrating urban assemblages–Chris Ware and Building Stories," *Social & Cultural Geography* 15(5), pp. 477–503.
Jefferey, S. (2016) *The Posthuman Body in Superhero Comics–Human, Superhuman, Transhuman, Post/Human.* London: Palgrave Macmillan.

## Audience

As Ien Ang (1991) observes, an audience is an abstract construct, produced by techniques of measurement and distinct from individual MEDIA consumers. In comics, as in other PRINT media, audiences are estimated from sales and circulation figures, though these data are rarely available complete and unabridged. Even at their best, they only indicate how many copies a given COMIC BOOK has sold, not how many people they reach nor what those READERS think, feel, or do in the moment of RECEPTION. Audiences are never neutral: they are always constructed for a particular purpose and inevitably shaped by prior assumptions. For instance, recent backlashes against the presence of women in comics' subcultural spaces (Scott 2013; Cicci 2018) and more diverse REPRESENTATIONS in SUPERHERO comics (Fu 2015; Hunt 2019) rely on naturalised claims about who "counts" in the comics audience. These claims are only possible because sales data that do not measure library or institutional sales and MARKET research surveys conducted in COMIC SHOPS construct an audience of comic book FANS (Woo 2018, 2020), side-lining other readers and their experiences of READING (Cedeira Serantes 2019: 19).

Benjamin Woo

### *References*

Ang, I. (1991) *Desperately Seeking the Audience.* Abingdon: Routledge.
Cedeira Serantes, L. (2019) *Young People, Comics, and Reading: Exploring a Complex Reading Experience.* Cambridge: Cambridge University Press.
Cicci, M. (2018) "The Invasion of Loki's Army? Comic Culture's Increasing Awareness of Female Fans" in Click, M. A. and Scott, S. (eds.) *The Routledge Companion to Media Fandom.* Abingdon: Routledge, pp. 193–201.

Fu, A. S. (2015) "Fear of a Black Spider-Man: Racebending and the Colour-Line in Superhero (Re)Casting," *Journal of Graphic Novels and Comics* 6(3), pp. 269–283.

Hunt, W. (2019) "Negotiating New Racism: 'It's Not Racist or Sexist. It's Just the Way It Is,'" *Media, Culture & Society* 41(1), pp. 86–103.

Scott, S. (2013) "Fangirls in Refrigerators: The Politics of (In)Visibility in Comic Book Culture," *Transformative Works and Cultures* 13, n.p. Available at: http://journal.transformativeworks.org/index.php/twc/article/view/460 [Accessed 1 August 2020].

Woo, B. (2018) "Is There a Comic Book Industry?" *Media Industries Journal* 5(1), pp. 27–46.

Woo, B. (2020) "Readers, Audiences, and Fans" in Hatfield, C. and Beaty, B. (eds.) *Comics Studies: A Guidebook.* New Brunswick: Rutgers University Press, pp. 113–125.

## Author

In COMICS STUDIES, the terms ARTIST, CREATOR, and WRITER are often used interchangeably, although each emphasises a different aspect of the creative process. While typically artist highlights DRAWING, writer SCRIPTING, and creator both, whether individually or in a team, the term author connotes an often singular and legal ownership of the entire finished product. In his influential article "The Death of the Author" (1967), Roland Barthes explores the limitations of traditional conceptions of authorial ownership in the study of LITERATURE, particularly as it pertains to the interpretation of a work. He contends that authorship presents a tyrannical foreclosure of meaning that can only be broken by the birth of the READER. In response to Barthes' propositions, Michel Foucault reminds us that the author's name "can group together a number of texts and thus differentiate them from others" (1969: 123), calling to mind the problematic exclusionary practices of valorisation of certain individuals and works in the CANON. He argues therefore for a consideration not just of interpretation but also of DISCOURSE, writing that "unlike a proper name, which moves from the interior of a discourse to the real person outside who produced it, the name of the author remains at the contours of texts (…). It points to the existence of certain groups of discourse and refers to the status of this discourse within a society and a culture" (ibid.: 123). Owing to the historical relationships between comics, team production, and mass production, authorship remains a contested idea in Comics Studies, and the term has increasingly been relegated as an anachronism or avoided altogether.

Erin La Cour

## *References*

Barthes, R. (1967) "The Death of the Author" in Heath, S. (ed.) *Image, Music, Text.* Translated from French by S. Heath, 1977. London: Fontana, pp. 142–148.

Foucault, M. (1969) "What is an Author?" in Bouchard, D. F. (ed.) *Language, Counter-Memory, Practice: Selected Essays and Interviews.* Translated from French by D. F. Bouchard and S. Simon, 1977. Ithaca: Cornell University Press, pp. 113–138.

## AUTOBIOGRAPHY

Autobiography tells a chronological narrative of a person's life from their birth to the moment of WRITING. As a LITERARY GENRE, it emerged during the eighteenth century (Rak 2004). Autobiography is commonly understood as involving a pact between the READER and the AUTHOR that is sealed by the NARRATOR, protagonist, and author having the same name (Lejeune 1975; Miller 2007), a feature adapted in autobiographical comics in the form of the autobiographical avatar (Whitlock 2006). This fidelity grounds the reader's expectation "that an author takes to narrate his life directly (her life, or a part of it, an aspect of it) in a spirit of truth" (Lejeune qtd. in Miller 2007: 538). Every autobiography must negotiate the tension between the reader's expectation that the author is SELF-REFLEXIVE regarding the limitations of MEMORY and self-knowledge, and the author's own self-questioning (Miller 2007). These genre characteristics are shared by MEMOIR and other types of LIFE WRITING, which together are key cultural sites where questions of IDENTITY, experience, and meaning are explored.

Anna Poletti

## *References*

Lejeune, P. (1975) "The Autobiographical Pact" in Eakin, P. J. (ed.) *On Autobiography*, 1989. Translated from French by K. Leary. Minneapolis: University of Minnesota Press, pp. 3–30.

Miller, N. K. (2007) "The Entangled Self: Genre Bondage in the Age of Memoir," *PMLA* 132(2), pp. 537–548.

Rak, J. (2004) "Are Memoirs Autobiography? A Consideration of Genre and Public Identity," *Genre* 37(3–4), pp. 483–504.

Whitlock, G. (2006) "Autographics: The Seeing "I" of the Comics," *MFS Modern Fiction Studies* 52(4), pp. 965–979.

## Autographics

The term autographics was coined in 2006 by Gillian Whitlock, who argues that the "subject positions that narrators negotiate in and through comics" (966) is different from a LITERARY AUTOBIOGRAPHY specifically because of the visual presentation of the self. The often re-quoted question by Hillary Chute (2010), "What does it mean for an author to literally reappear—in the form of a legible, drawn body on the page—at the site of her inscriptional effacement?," is especially pertinent to autographics, as various theories from LIFE WRITING suggest that the SUBJECT position for embodied lives lived outside the normative social structure can make space for subjugated knowledge; autographics bring forward first-person accounts of lives in MATERIAL FORM and refuse to be silenced. Autographics can be traced back to at least the early 1970s, a decade in which the rise of the independent, personal, and often transgressive COMIX and ZINE movements reacted against the CENSORSHIP of the COMICS CODE (Gardner 2008).

JoAnn Purcell

## *References*

Chute, H. (2008) "The Texture of Retracing in Marjane Satrapi's *Persepolis*," *Women's Studies Quarterly* 36(1–2), pp. 92–110.

Gardner, J. (2008) "Autography's Biography, 1972–2007," *Biography* 31(1), pp. 1–26.
Whitlock, G. (2006) "Autographics: The Seeing 'I' of the Comics," *MFS Modern Fiction Studies* 52(4), pp. 965–979.

## Autonomy

Autonomy is the freedom to govern oneself. The form governance takes is a matter of some debate in philosophy: political autonomy, for instance, refers to the right of a group to govern itself, while personal autonomy refers to an individual's ability to make decisions and be held morally accountable for them (Dworkin 1988: 34–47). An individual has autonomy when freedom, the ability to choose and reason are all possible for an agent to exercise. Plato and Aristotle both identified autonomy with rationality and saw rationality as essential to the human soul and community harmony (Plato 2008: 436 b6–C1; Aristotle 1999: 10–11). Immanuel Kant connected autonomy to moral choice and the location of morality in an individual, rather than in the state or religious authority (Kant 1996: 17). Later iterations of autonomy understand decision-making and accountability as hallmarks of individualism and authenticity. This is the essence of personal autonomy, when individuals decide for themselves what is right (Dworkin 2015: 11–14). Subsequent work on autonomy connects it to liberalism and the ideas of individual freedom, agency, and social responsibility, accompanied by debates about the role of justice in determining whether actions are truly free (Rawls 1971), the possibility of autonomy for women within patriarchy (Christman 1995: 17–39), or the pull of social obligations in a liberal framework that, despite itself, sometimes reframes autonomy as relational (Kymlicka 1989).

Julie Rak

## *References*

Aristotle (c. 340 BC) *Nicomachean Ethics*. Translated from Greek by W. D. Ross, 1999. Kitchener: Batoche Books.

Christman, J. (1995) "Feminism and Autonomy" in Bushell, D. (ed.) *"Nagging" Questions: Feminist Ethics in Everyday Life*. Savage: Rowman & Littlefield, pp. 17–39.

Dworkin, G. (1988) *The Theory and Practice of Autonomy*. Cambridge: Cambridge University Press.

Dworkin, G. (2015) "The Nature of Autonomy," *Nordic Journal of Studies in Educational Policy* 2, pp. 7–14.

Kant, I. (1784) "An answer to the question: What is Enlightenment?" in Gregor, M. (ed.) *Practical Philosophy*. Translated from German by M. Gregor, 1996. Cambridge: Cambridge University Press, pp. 11–22.

Kymlicka, W. (1989) *Liberalism, Community, and Culture*. Oxford: Oxford University Press.

Plato (c. 428/42–348/347 BC) *Great Dialogues of Plato*. Translated from Greek by W. H. D. Rouse, 2008. New York: Signet Editions.

Rawls, J. (1971) *A Theory of Justice*. Cambridge: Harvard University Press.

## Avant-Garde

Avant-garde ("vanguard" in French) became the most common noun and adjective in French and English in the nineteenth century to qualify "radical" ruptures with dominant "academic" forms by means of FORMAL innovations in the ARTS (Keller 1991). Avant-garde comics are defined in contrast with "mainstream" PRODUCTION. From the mid-nineteenth century to the 1960s, the cultural confinement of the MEDIUM to the domains of ILLUSTRATED books, children's books, newspapers, and MASS PRODUCED periodicals did not allow the emergence of any space of radical creative innovation, with the exception of G. Herriman's "Krazy

Kat"—an atypical, anti-commercial artefact in the field of NEWSPAPER STRIPS (Heer and Worcester 2004: 22–34). In Western Europe and America, the comics' most significant avant-garde phase took place in the context of the 1960s socio-cultural effervescence, with the rise of "UNDERGROUND" creators using the counter-cultural press and small-press comic magazines to express resistance to the post-World War II conservatism and consumerism (Gabilliet 2018). By the mid-1970s, the underground's decline ushered in ALTERNATIVE COMICS, a catchall category including all types of non-mainstream production regardless of their adherence to any agenda of revolutionary innovation (Beaty 2006; Hatfield 2005; Mazur and Danner 2014).

Jean-Paul Gabilliet

## *References*

Beaty, B. (2007) *Unpopular Culture: Transforming the European Comic Book in the 1990s.* Toronto: University of Toronto Press.

Gabilliet, J.-P. (2018) "Underground Comix and the Invention of Autobiography, History and Reportage" in Baetens, J., Frey, H., and Tabachnick, S. *The Cambridge History of the Graphic Novel.* Cambridge: Cambridge University Press, pp. 155–170.

Hatfield, C. (2005) *Alternative Comics: An Emerging Literature.* Jackson: University Press of Mississippi.

Heer, J. and Worcester, K. (2004) *Arguing Comics: Literary Masters on a Popular Medium.* Jackson: University Press of Mississippi.

Keller, J.-P. (1991) *La nostalgie des avant-gardes.* Geneva: Editions Zoé/ La Tour d'Aigues: Editions de l'Aube.

Mazur, D. and Danner, A. (2014) *Comics: A Global History, 1968 to the Present.* London: Thames and Hudson.

## Bande Dessinée

Literally meaning "drawn strip," bande dessinée is the French equivalent to comics. One definition is that bande dessinée is a "French-language mixture of images and written text that together form a narrative" (Grove 2010: 16). French language is key, as a reminder that bande dessinée is not uniquely French, but also encapsulates worldwide cultures, including those of Belgium (e.g. Hergé, but equally the tradition of *Spirou*), Switzerland (e.g. Rodolphe Töpffer, Cosey, Zep), Québec (e.g. Julie Doucet, and Michel Rabagliati), and Africa (e.g. Marguerite Abouet). In France, bande dessinée has the epithet of NINTH ART, implying a high-culture status traditionally surpassing that of Anglophone equivalents. The reasons for bande dessinée's importance and specificity remain conjectural (Grove 2014; Miller 2007; Screech 2005), but the following might be considered: the development of ILLUSTRATED journals in France in the nineteenth century; the use of bande dessinée journals post-war for wide-spread PROPAGANDA (e.g. *Vaillant* (communist) and *Coeurs Vaillants* (Catholic)); critical engagement with the SEMIOTICS of the bande dessinée from the 1960s onwards (e.g. the work of Thierry Groensteen; Groensteen 1999); the existence of both mainstream and counter-cultures (epitomised from 1959 by the journal *Pilote*); and active state sponsorship (e.g. for the NATIONAL centre in Angoulême).

Laurence Grove

### *References*

Groensteen, T. (1999) *The System of Comics.* Translated from French by B. Beaty and N. Nguyen, 2007. Jackson: University Press of Mississippi.

Grove, L. (2010) *Comics in French: The European Bande Dessinée in Context.* New York: Berghahn Books.

Grove L. (2014) "Bande dessinée: État present," *French Studies* 68(1), pp. 78–87.

Miller, A. (2007) *Reading Bande dessinée: Critical Approaches to French-language Comic Strip.* Bristol: Intellect.

Screech, M. (2005) *Masters of the Ninth Art: Bandes dessinées and Franco-Belgian Identity.* Liverpool: Liverpool University Press.

## Biography

Biography is a form of LIFE WRITING in which "scholars of other people's lives document and interpret those lives from a point of view external to the subject" (Smith and Watson 2010: 5). Written by comics ARTISTS, professional and amateur historians, journalists, and novelists, biography can have a range of intentions—from establishing a "definitive" account of the life of a famous person, to writing the lives of everyday people into the historical record. The aim of the biographer is to identify and interpret whatever factual information is available on the SUBJECT and organise this creatively into a NARRATIVE that "add[s] up to some overall idea of the subject, so that their biography, for the moment, will give the truest answer to the question: What was she, or he, like?" (Lee 2009: 124). To achieve this, they must sift the pile of facts that might be available and offer READERS "the creative fact; the fertile fact; the fact that suggests and engenders" (Woolf 1942: 197). For this reason biography can be thought of as a "love-match" between "Invention" and "Truth" (Holmes 15). Yet this match is always partly shaped by the context of the biographer themself: "A biography is always involved with the social and cultural politics of its time and place, so its assumptions change about what is major or minor, permitted or shocking, mainstream of alternative" (Lee 2009: 126).

Anna Poletti

### *References*

Lee, H. (2009) *Biography: A Very Short Introduction*. New York: Oxford University Press.

Smith, S. and Watson, J. (2010) *Reading Autobiography: A Guide for Interpreting Life Narratives*. 2nd edition. Minneapolis: University of Minnesota Press.

Woolf, V. (1939) "The Art of Biography" in *The Death of the Moth and Other Essays*, 1942. San Diego: Harcourt Brace, pp. 187–197.

## Black and White

The shift from black and white to COLOUR comics is often explained in technical and commercial terms: since colour was (and still is) more difficult as well as more expensive to PRINT than black and white, it is considered a key marketing tool, hence the use of colour in the SUNDAY FUNNIES as opposed to the daily instalments of the same comics. If the former cannot be denied, the latter is however problematic, since many comics ARTISTS strongly resisted the use of colour. Some of them had started in black and white and considered the strength and singularity of their STYLE would be jeopardised by colour (this was the initial position of Hergé). Others simply lacked the technical and financial means to work in colour (as happened with the Xeroxed works in the 1960s UNDERGROUND COMIX). Still others prove reluctant to colour for strategic reasons (sticking to a DIY approach of the culturally upgraded GRAPHIC NOVEL in order to challenge the industrial streamlining of full colour SUPERHERO comics). However, uneventful as well as artistically challenging uses of black and white can be found in all periods, GENRES, and contexts.

Jan Baetens

### *References*

Baetens, J. (2011) "From Black & White to Color and Back," *College Literature* 38(3), pp. 111–128.

Groensteen, T. (1993) *Couleur directe/Direct Colour.* Thurn: Kunst der Comics.

Smolderen, T. (2000) *The Origins of Comics: From William Hogarth to Winsor McCay.* Translated from French by B. Beaty and N. Nguyen, 2014. Jackson: University Press of Mississippi.

## Boredom

Boredom is defined as a subjective state of mind related to loss of meaning and an "experience without qualities" that emerges with a modern idea of TEMPORALITY and the COMMODIFICATION of attention (Goodstein 2005). The various DISCOURSES on boredom usually refer to a cluster of feelings associated with the loss of meaning itself: some identify a serious and more glamorous form of boredom, closer to the melancholic ennui (Kuhn 1976; Svendsen 2005), while others consider it a trivial, casual, and temporary experience (Spacks 1995; Ngai 2005). This dialectical and ambiguous relationship also affects a shifting in the dynamics of attention and distraction (Crary 2001), and work and leisure (Klapp 1986). Boredom is considered both as a plague and as a source of creativity (Raposa 1999), as it destroys and enhances experience (Benjamin 1992) and shortens and elongates time (Heidegger 1995). The subject has become a relevant topic in COMICS STUDIES, especially after the 1990s, with the emergence of ALTERNATIVE and AUTOBIOGRAPHICAL comics (Hatfield 2005). Boredom and everyday life appear as a reaction to eventful plots and extraordinary STORYWORLDS. It manifests not only as a topic, but also as a deliberate AESTHETIC category (Schneider 2016).

Greice Schneider

## *References*


Benjamin, W. (1955) *Illuminations.* Translated from German by H. Zohn, 1992. Arendt, H. (ed.) London: Fontana.

Crary, J. (2001) *Suspensions of Perception: Attention, Spectacle and Modern Culture.* Cambridge: The Massachusetts Institute of Technology Press.

Goodstein, E. S. (2005) *Experience without Qualities: Boredom and Modernity.* Stanford: Stanford University Press.

Hatfield, C. (2005) *Alternative Comics: An Emerging Literature.* Jackson: University Press of Mississippi.

Heidegger, M. (1927) *Being and Time.* Translated from German by J. Stambaugh. Reprint 1996. Albany: SUNY Press.

Klapp, O. (1986) *Overload and Boredom: Essays on the Quality of Life in the Information Society.* Westport: Greenwood.

Kuhn, R. C. (1976) *The Demon of Noontide: Ennui in Western Literature.* Princeton: Princeton University Press.

Ngai, S. (2005) *Ugly Feelings.* Cambridge: Harvard University Press.

Raposa, M. L. (1999) *Boredom and the Religious Imagination.* Charlottesville: University Press of Virginia.

Spacks, P. (1995) *Boredom: The Literary History of a State of Mind.* Chicago: University of Chicago Press.

Svendsen, L. F. H. (2005) *A Philosophy of Boredom*. London: Reaktion Books 2005.
Schneider, G. (2016) *What Happens When Nothing Happens: Boredom and everyday life in contemporary comics*. Leuven: Leuven University Press.

## Braiding

Within a comics SEQUENCE, each PANEL is articulated with the previous and the following one, entering into TEMPORAL and logical relationships. But certain IMAGES can also DIALOGUE *in absentia*, establishing links between distant PAGES. As Jan Baetens and Pascal Lefèvre noticed, "a comic requires a reading that discerns, behind linear relations, aspects or fragments of panels that may form a network with aspects or fragments of other panels" (1993: 72). I use the term braiding ("tressage") to denote the operation that manages the type of relationship that is not restricted to BREAKDOWN (1999: 173–186). We can take just one famous example, the smiley badge in *Watchmen*, by Alan Moore and Dave Gibbons (1986–1987). It appears both in the very first and the very last panels of the work, and it forms a network with a large number of other circular motifs. The badges, and more generally the circle, are patterns that structure the NARRATIVE and have vast symbolic implications. Braiding is never essential for the construction and the understanding of the STORY—at least at a first level of meaning, which is satisfactory in itself. But, when detected, it always leads to an enrichment, a deepening of the meaning.

Thierry Groensteen

## *References*

Baetens, J. and Lefèvre, P. (1993) *Pour une lecture moderne de la bande dessinée*. Amsterdam-Bruxelles: Sherpa-CBBD.
Groensteen, T. (1999) *The System of Comics*. Translated from French by B. Beaty and N. Nguyen, 2007. Jackson: University Press of Mississippi.
Groensteen, T. (2015) *The Expanding Art of Comics. Ten Modern Masterpieces*. Translated from French by A. Miller, 2017. Jackson: University Press of Mississippi.

## Breakdown

A COMIC is a collection of non-moving IMAGES. It is divided into PAGES, tiers and PANELS, nested elements that are physical, perceptual, and SEMANTICAL units. In a comic, the action is articulated in "packets." As Barbara Postema puts it: "The frames and gutters function to separate and connect the images at the same time" (2013: 56). That is what is referred to as the operation of breakdown ("découpage"): choosing what is going to be REPRESENTED and distributing the action over a given number of panels. Breakdown is usually the job of the SCRIPTWRITER, but sometimes the ARTIST takes responsibility for it. Breakdown divides up the flow of NARRATIVE information: it determines the MODE of enunciation (ICONIC or LINGUISTIC) and it distils the information along a TEMPORAL axis. Breakdown has its "figures of speech": question and answer, ANGLE *versus* reverse angle, narrow shot *versus* wide shot, objective vision *versus* subjective vision, and so on. And it is primarily concerned with RHYTHM. In the work of novice AUTHORS, NARRATION may seem flawed, because the segmentation of the action is either excessively brutal or lacking in pace. MANGAS have a different rhythm: they are more descriptive and more analytical than Occidental comics.

Thierry Groensteen

### *References*

Postema, B. (2013) *Narrative Structure in Comics. Making Sense of Fragments.* Rochester: Rochester Institute of Technology Press.

Groensteen, T. (1999) *The System of Comics.* Translated from French by B. Beaty and N. Nguyen, 2007. Jackson: University Press of Mississippi.

## Canon

In COMICS STUDIES, the term canon is used in two related but significantly different manners. Within comics FANDOM, canon refers to the STORIES within a fictional STORYWORLD that are deemed to be officially part of an ongoing NARRATIVE. Within comics scholarship, canon refers to tendencies to position certain works as the most important in the field. In the realm of SUPERHERO stories, which often encompass literally thousands of works, canon is "the official or popularly recognised history of a factional universe" (Fu 2015). DC Comics, for instance, regularly marked some tales as "imaginary stories" to suggest that they existed outside the canon of character continuity. Kuskin notes that many creators of superhero stories are themselves canonisers when they work to build on stories by their predecessors (Kuskin 2008). In the scholarly community, the canon refers to certain works like Spiegelman's *Maus* (1986 and 1991) that are highly taught, widely published on, and frequently cited. Benjamin Woo and Bart Beaty (2016) have argued that canons presuppose implicit notions of value and distort the ability of scholars to fully come to terms with relations between works by narrowing avenues of investigation. In the scholarly tradition, the canon is those works that are implicitly held to be important.

Bart Beaty

### *References*

Beaty, B. and Woo, B. (2016) *The Greatest Comic Book of All Time: Symbolic Capital and the Field of American Comic Books.* London: Palgrave Macmillan.

Fu, A. S. (2015) "Fear of a Black Spider-Man: Racebending and the Colour-Line in Superhero (Re)Casting," *Journal of Graphic Novels and Comics* 6(3), pp. 269–283.

Kuskin, W. (2008) "Batman in the Trash: Canon Construction and Bibliography," *English Language Notes* 46(2), pp. 58–69.

## Caption Box

Sometimes called "narrative box," the caption box is the rectangle containing a TEXT that gives information from the NARRATOR to complement the text in the SPEECH BALLOONS coming from the characters.

It is usually put in one of the corners of the FRAME. The caption box can usually be found at the top left of the frame for two reasons: first, because Western cultures read from left top to right and down and, second, because this position is the least obstructive to the DRAWING, as there is often less relevant visual information in this part of the frame (e.g. the sky). Used more profusely at the beginning of comics, like arrows, caption boxes are usually sparser as the comic progresses because the CREATORS and READERS become accustomed to the comics' VISUAL LANGUAGE (Witek 2009). Caption boxes usually contain brief information about place, and/or time, but they could also provide the narrator's comments about elements in the STORY (e.g. characters and mood). For readability, they at times also use a COLOUR clearly different from those used in the PANEL and a similar lettering throughout the work for consistency. However, ARTISTS have played with the caption box in various ways to create surprise effects, AESTHETIC contrast, ironic counterpoint, or to convey more information through the colour (e.g. the use of blue for Dr Manhattan's caption boxes in *Watchmen* (1986–1987)) or the lettering (e.g. *Astérix and the Goths* (1961–1962)).

Chris Reyns-Chikuma

## *References*

Groensteen, T. (2010) "The Monstrator, the Recitant and the Shadow of the Narrator," *European Comics Art* 3(1), pp. 1–21.

McCloud, S. (1993) *Understanding Comics: The Invisible Art*. New York: Harper Perennial.

Witek, J. (2009) "The Arrow and the Grid" in Heer, J. and Worcester, K. (eds.) *A Comics Studies Reader*. Jackson: The University Press of Mississippi, pp. 149–156.

## CARICATURE

The word caricature originates from the Italian "caricare," meaning to load, or to charge (Wright 1865: 415). Caricatures are portraits that exaggerate the features of those who are depicted to achieve COMEDY and/or critique. The rise of caricature is often connected to Romanticism, during which the already existing FORM of caricature became, through newly available PRINT TECHNOLOGIES and the works of ARTISTS such as William Hogarth, Honoré Daumier, and George Cruikshank, a prominent artform as well as a form of social and political critique (see Rose 2016; Haywood 2013). A substantial portion of the early twentieth-century theorisation of caricature was undertaken in the Warburg Institute against the background of the rise of fascism in Germany by E. H. Gombrich and Ernst Kris. These scholars saw a history of caricature that was not just comedic exaggeration, but rather a manipulation of the external features to fit the internal truths of character as well as a way of conducting anti-PROPAGANDA (Rose 2016: 9–11). The terms CARTOON and caricature are often used interchangeably. For specialists, however, cartoons are associated with SCHEMATISATION, while caricature emphasises exaggeration. That being said, the HISTORIES of both terms, cartoon with Rodolphe Töpffer and caricature with Hogarth and others, are inextricably entangled with the history of comics (Smolderen 2014).

Rik Spanjers

## *References*

Haywood, I. (2013) *Romanticism and Caricature*. Cambridge: Cambridge University Press.

Rose, L. (2016) *Psychology, Art, and Antifascism: Ernst Kris, E. H. Gombrich, and the Politics of Caricature*. New Haven: Yale University Press.

Smolderen, T. (2000) *The Origins of Comics: From William Hogarth to Winsor McCay*. Translated from French by B. Beaty and N. Nguyen, 2014. Jackson: University Press of Mississippi.

Wright, T. (1865) *Caricature & Grotesque in Literature and Art*. London: Virtue Brothers & Co.

## Cartoon

In ART historical terms, the cartoon was a full-scale DRAWING used to plan out and transfer a DESIGN to a surface for an oil painting or other large visual artworks during the Renaissance; cartoons represented a preliminary step in a longer process. Today, the cartoon style is characterised by the simplification of shapes in drawing, often for HUMOROUS effect. In his 1854 *Essai de physiognomonie*, Rodolphe Töpffer extolls the many virtues of "simple line drawing" (cartooning) as a means of REPRESENTATION in picture-STORIES (Töpffer 1965: 6–10). The single-PANEL cartoon in the nineteenth century usually consisted of a drawing with a TYPESET caption, often an exchange of dialogue, and possibly SPEECH BALLOONS or labels describing a visual METAPHOR, a technique still common among some contemporary editorial cartoonists. As American newspaper cartoonists began subdividing their cartoons into multiple scenes or panels, usually in a horizontal or vertical arrangement, this PAGE LAYOUT, along with the humorous nature of the drawings, led to them being christened COMIC STRIPS (the British equivalent, "strip cartoon," focuses more on the FORM than the humour expressed within it). Scott McCloud differentiates between comics and single-panel cartoons, with the latter lacking his key concept of juxtaposition (1993: 20–21). However, contemporary single-panel cartoons, such as those appearing in the *New Yorker*, often rely on the juxtaposition of IMAGE and caption, the one re-interpreting the other for COMEDIC effect.

Gene Kannenberg Jr

## *References*

McCloud, S. (1993) *Understanding Comics: The Invisible Art*. New York: Harper Perennial.

Töpffer, R. (1845) *Enter: The Comics*. Translated from French by E. Wiese (ed.), 1965. Lincoln: University of Nebraska Press.

## Cartoonist

The identities of visual ARTISTS, their materials, and the circumstances in which they work have often been bundled together with the things they produce (Joseph 2019: 19 and 12). According to this idea, "It is taken for granted that a 'main' creator loads a work with meaning"—that is, intends a product to have specific significance—and produces what Barthes calls a "final signified," or unitary statement in the form of the work (Jameel 2016: 176, Barthes 1977: 147). The circumstances under which a CARTOONIST works overwhelmingly contradict this idea. These circumstances involve team production and collaboration as part of a distributed business. Team production involves groups producing work that is not individually attributable to them (Blair 2003: 399). Collaboration requires the mutual mediation of intention (Brienza and Johnston 2016: 2). A distributed business requires teams and individuals to undertake different work with common aims that are not achievable by them alone (Agarwal and Rudolph 2008: n.p.). Brienza and Johnston call the distributed business of comics "comics work" (2016: 2). Woo further notes that these relationships are still often replaced by an "occupational imaginary," in the form of a named cartoonist. This is a fictional idea of the cartoonist as the single, motivating creator—in fact, an avatar of all the collaborators—even if they are also a real person working as part of a team (2016: 190).

Simon Grennan

## *References*

Agarwal, S. and Rudolph, S. (2008) "Semantic description of distributed business processes." Stanford: AAAI Spring Symposium. Unpublished paper. Available at: https://www.researchgate.net/publication/221250734_Semantic_Description_of_Distributed_Business_Processes [Accessed 11 January 2021].

Barthes, R. (1961–1973) *Image, Music, Text.* Translated from French by S. Heath (ed.), 1977. London: Fontana.

Blair, M. (2004) "Locking in Capital: What Corporate Law Achieved for Business Organisers in the Nineteenth Century," *51 UCLA Law Review 2003–4*, pp. 387–455.

Brienza, C., and Johnston, P. (2016) "Introduction" in Brienza, C. and Johnston, P. (eds.) *Cultures of Comics Work.* London: Palgrave Macmillan, pp. 1–17.

Ahmed, J. (2016) "Negotiating Artistic Identity in Comics Collaboration" in Brienza, C, and Johnston, P. (eds.) *Cultures of Comics Work.* London: Palgrave Macmillan, pp. 175–188.

Joseph, M. (2019) *Victorian Literary Businesses: the management and practices of the British publishing industry.* London: Palgrave Macmillan.

Woo, B. (2016) "To the Studio! *Comic Book Artists: The Next Generation* and the Occupational Imaginary of Comics Work" in Brienza, C. and Johnston, P. (eds.) *Cultures of Comics Work.* London: Palgrave Macmillan, pp. 189–202.

## Celebrity

The notion of what constitutes celebrity has undergone dramatic evolutions due to internet connectivity, social MEDIA, and various innovative multimedia platforms. According to Peter Ward, "we consume media, we consume people, and these people (...) are transformed into celebrities as they participate in processes of production, representation and consumption" (2019: 1). Participants in the global comics community—like ILLUSTRATORS, WRITERS, COSPLAYERS, and live-action actors—are consistently MEDIATED, both through their work (PRODUCTION) and in their reciprocal INTERACTION with FANS (REPRESENTATION). Social media may seem the most obvious point of connection to the comic-celebrity, but CONVENTIONS, conferences, and meet-and-greets also function as places where "Fandom is literally transformed into an open market—a place where celebrity guests become commodities for the consumption of devout fans" (Duchesne 2010: 22). Moreover, blurring the boundaries of reality, comic characters can be celebrities in their own right, in that both the illustrated and live-action figures "we encounter through our consumption of media form a resource to process our own sense of who we are (...) and our place in the world" (Ward 2019: 5).

Ayanni C. H. Cooper

### *References*

Duchesne, S. (2010) "Stardom/Fandom: Celebrity and Fan Tribute Performance," *Canadian Theatre Review* 141, pp. 21–27.

Deshaye, J. (2014) "The Metaphor of Celebrity, Three Superheroes, and One Persona or Another," *The Journal of Popular Culture* 47(3), pp. 571–590.

Redmond, S. (2019) *Celebrity*. Abingdon: Routledge.

Ward, P. (2020) *Celebrity Worship*. Abingdon: Routledge.

## Censorship

Censorship is the practice of suppressing or banning MATERIAL such as books, FILMS, or news reports, based on its content or perceived RECEPTION within society. Typically, this is because the material is considered obscene, politically objectionable, or a threat to NATIONAL security. The word comes from the Latin "censere," meaning "to appraise or judge" (OED 2020: n.p.). Censorship typically happens at government level, but can be enforced at any level of society by government agencies or private companies. There are many rationales for censorship, dependent on the censoring agent. The most visible type is likely moral censorship, the removal of material deemed obscene. During the 1960 UK obscenity trial for *Lady Chatterley's Lover*, E. M. Forster wrote that the "law tells me that obscenity may deprave and corrupt, but as far as I know, it offers no definition of depravity or corruption" (Rolph 1990: 55). Political and religious censorship allows for control to be maintained by the filtering of information to the public and is among the most common types internationally. Sweden officially abolished censorship in 1766, though there are restrictions on child pornography and hate speech. The 1954 COMICS CODE is an example of censorship aimed specifically at comics.

Harriet E. H. Earle

## *References*

Oxford English Dictionary (2020) "Censorship" in *Oxford English Dictionary*. Oxford: Oxford University Press.

Rolph, C. H. (ed.) (1990) *The Trial of Lady Chatterley*. London: Penguin Books.

## Chaperoned Reading

The chaperoning theory emerged as a response to a problem found at the intersection of COMICS STUDIES and children's LITERATURE studies. I (2013) offer the theory as a way of solving the difficulty of separating comics from PICTURE BOOKS, two iconotexts with abundant FORMAL similarities. The theory begins by noting Roland Barthes' argument that IMAGES have infinite meanings that are narrowed by any TEXT that accompanies them (1985). Comics and picture books routinely use images accompanied by words, but, I note, the READER in charge of TRANSLATING those words is dramatically different between the two. Picture books anticipate a dual READERSHIP—a proficient reader speaking the words aloud to a listening reader who observes the images—and thus I conjecture that picture books SCRIPT a situation in which one reader, usually older, has an opportunity to shape the words that direct the meaning of the images, thus allowing power over the meaning of the images. Comics, however, anticipate a solitary reader who reads the words and chaperones their meaning as they narrow the meaning of the images. I argue that this difference helps to explain the HISTORICAL, ideological, and formal differences between two otherwise very similar forms. I have since expanded the theory with Charles Hatfield (2017).

Joe Sutliff Sanders

## *References*

Barthes, R. (1982) *The Responsibility of Forms: Critical Essays on Music, Art, and Representation*. Translated from French by R. Howard, 1985. Berkeley: University of California Press.

Hatfield, C. and Sanders, J. S. (2017) "Bonding Time or Solo Flight? Picture Books, Comics, and the Independent Reader," *Children's Literature Association Quarterly* 42(4), pp. 459–486.

Sanders, J. S. (2013) "Chaperoning Words: Meaning-Making in Comics and Picture Books," *Children's Literature* 41, pp. 57–90.

## Childishness

Referring to childlike qualities, childishness has negative connotations. Based on assumptions and dismissive of children's behaviour, all things childish are deemed inappropriate for adults. Childishness therefore evokes non-normative and even deviant behaviour. Comics have long been relegated to the realm of childishness: made for, while also harming, children on the one hand, and too childish to merit adult attention on the other. Correspondingly, the move for comics legitimation has often insisted on how "comics have grown up" (Pizzino 2016: 21–45). The childishness associated with comics should perhaps not be dismissed completely and calls for a re-evaluation of the elements of comics connoted as childish. This holds for the CARTOONISH STYLE of many comics that, like CARICATURE and other so-called primitive, non-REALISTIC styles, have been looked down upon (Camden 2018), even though they are laden with centuries of DRAWING HISTORY (Smolderen 2014). Childishness is also present in the indulgence of comics in the playful and illogical (Bukatman 2012; Smolderen 2014) and in their deployment of

REPETITION and slapstick (Ahmed 2019). In light of these different childish connections with comics—in style, NARRATION, or HUMOUR, among other possibilities—the figure of the child has recently been proposed as embodying comics (Chaney 2017).

Maaheen Ahmed

## *References*

Ahmed, M. (2019) "Children in Comics: Between Education and Entertainment, Conformity and Agency" in Aldama, F. L. (ed.) *Oxford Handbook for Comic Book Studies.* Oxford: Oxford University Press, 1–19.

Bukatman, S. (2012) *The Poetics of Slumberland: Animating Spirits and the Animated Spirit.* Berkeley: University of California Press.

Chaney, M. (2017) *Reading Lessons in Seeing: Mirrors, Masks and Mazes in the Autobiographical Graphic Novel.* Jackson: University Press of Mississippi.

Camden, V. (2018) "'Cartoonish Lumps': The Surface Appeal of Alison Bechdel's *Are You My Mother?*" *Journal of Graphic Novels and Comics* 9(1), pp. 93–111.

Pizzino, C. (2016) *Arresting Development: Comics at the Boundaries of Literature.* Austin: University of Texas Press.

Smolderen, T. (2000) *The Origins of Comics: From William Hogarth to Winsor McCay.* Translated from French by B. Beaty and N. Nguyen, 2014. Jackson: University Press of Mississippi.

## Children's Comics

Although, as Hatfield has noted, there is a persistent belief "that comics [themselves] are somehow rooted in childhood" (2004), children's comics generally refer to visual NARRATIVES written specifically for young people, whether for EDUCATIONAL purposes or the trade MARKET. Such comics are categorised in this way for different reasons, including their subject matter, complexity, and reading level. A point of contention in defining children's comics is the extent to which they should be seen as separate and distinct from children's PICTURE BOOKS. As Meskin (2007) has noted, it is challenging to make such a distinction. For instance, the argument that children's comics are distinct because their ILLUSTRATIONS are necessary to understand the narrative does not always hold, nor is it specifically the case that picture books can always be understood in the absence of their illustrations (2007). Nonetheless, children's comics are generally understood to have features that distinguish them as comics (PANELS, GUTTERS, encapsulation, CLOSURE, THOUGHT BUBBLES and SPEECH BALLOONS, and narrative CAPTION BOXES), but intended for pre-adolescents. "Graphic readers," whether for the trade market or the classroom, are a subset of children's comics for very young readers. They are organised by subject or theme and then levelled to ensure a developmental approach to READING, often relying on the kind of panel organisation "in which words and pictures send essentially the same message" (1994). There are, however, notable examples of wordless children's comics in which a narrative, intended for young readers, is told entirely through SEQUENTIAL IMAGES.

Glen Downey

## *References*

Hatfield, C. (2004) "Introduction: Comics and Childhood," *ImageTxT* 3(3), n.p.

McCloud, S. (1994) *Understanding Comics (The invisible Art)*. New York: HarperCollins.

Meskin, A. (2007) "Defining Comics?" *Journal of Aesthetics and Art Criticism*, 65(4), pp. 369–379.

## Class

That comics are READING MATERIAL for the lower classes is an assumption made in almost every country from the nineteenth century on. This typically locates both READERS and MEDIUM as in deficit, although it may also be celebratory, as when Will Allred argued that American comics were "created by the working class for the working class" (2012: 261). Class can be significant with regard to specific characters or titles. For instance, Kevin Michael Scott said of *Daredevil* (1964–) that "no other comic (…) placed its hero so squarely in the realm of the poor and working classes" against "the corrupting bargain made between government, crime, and wealth (…) to profit from [them]" (DiPaolo 2018:169 and 171). In another example, Andrew Alan Smith discusses how Ben Grimm continues to perform a working-class identity despite accruing wealth and EDUCATION, suggesting class is a "sticky" factor in self-definition (DiPaolo 2018). Another link involves comics created to generate social aspiration amongst working-class readers. An example was the British girls' comic *Girl* (Hulton Press 1951–1964), which offered COMIC STRIPS about "acceptable" activities for middle-class girls, including ballet; "respectable" careers, such as nursing; and school STORIES focused on fee-paying schools, not those available free to all (Gibson 2015).

Mel Gibson

## *References*

Allred, W. (2012) "The Working Class in American Comics" in Brooker, K. (ed.) *Blue-Collar Pop Culture: From NASCAR to Jersey Shore,* Volume 2. Oxford: Praeger, pp. 261–274.

DiPaolo, M. (ed.) (2018) *Working-Class Comic Book Heroes: Class Conflict and Populist Politics in Comics.* Jackson: University Press of Mississippi.

Gibson, M. (2015) *Remembered Reading: Memory, Comics and Post-War Constructions of British Girlhood.* Leuven: University of Leuven Press.

## Clear Line

Coined as "klare lijn" in 1977 by Dutch COMIC BOOK ARTIST Joost Swarte, clear line ("ligne claire") was created to define the STYLE pioneered by Hergé and developed together with his assistants Bob de Moor, E. P. Jacobs, and Jacques Martin, among others (Brok et al. 1977; Rivière 1976). Swarte's definition encompassed all aspects of Hergé's style, understanding it as clarity of thought that extended to the NARRATIVE, the PAGE LAYOUT, or the construction of the STORY. Generally speaking, it is used to define a synthetic graphic style characterised by its economy, with no unnecessary detailing; the use of precise, smooth, and continuous lines with little thickness variation; and a clear division of areas in the DRAWINGS, filled in with flat COLOURS. Perhaps the most distinctive of the styles that characterised the Brussels School (École de Bruxelles) of Belgian comics, the term was later extended to younger generations of AUTHORS whose style shared the philosophy of Hergé's work, such as Joost Swarte, Ever Meulen, and Henk Kuijpers, in the Netherlands; Yves Chaland, Ted Benoit, Serge Clerc, and Floc'h, in France; Vittorio Giardino, in Italy; and Max and Daniel Torres in Spain, among others (Lecigne 1983; Pomier 2005).

Luis Miguel Lus Arana

## *References*

Rivière, F. (1976) *L'école d'Hergé*. Grenoble: Jacques Glénat.

Brok, H., Pommerel, E. and Swarte, J. (1977) *De klare lijn*. Rotterdam: Rotterdamse Kunststichting.

Lecigne, B. (1983) *Les Héritiers d'Hergé*. Bruxelles: Magic Strip.

Pomier, F. (2005) *Comment lire la bande dessinée?* Paris: Klincksieck.

## Close Reading

The concept of close reading comes from LITERARY studies, where it refers to a formalist reading method promoted by New Criticism, which still widely taught (Brummett 2019) and discussed (Rabaté 2020) in modern literary studies, which consists of a scrupulous word-for-word analysis of a short text (poem, short story, passage from a novel, etc.). The close reading of a COMIC is an empirical analysis of the relationships between all the SIGNS—not just the words—visible on the surface of the PAGE, at the level of a comics page (Eco 1976), a daily COMIC STRIP (Karasik and Newgarden 2017), or even a single IMAGE (Fresnault-Deruelle 2014), including an evaluation of its impact on the interpretation of the entire work. A potential risk in close reading is to fall into formalist essentialism by over-generalising and decontextualising the analysis of such a limited excerpt. As Jan Baetens and Hugo Frey recommend, "it is crucial to underline the importance of close-reading of individual works that have to be seized also in the dynamics of the reading process" (2017: 201).

Benoît Glaude

## *References*

Baetens, J. and Frey, H. (2017) "'Layouting' for the Plot: Charles Burns and the Clear Line Revisited," *Journal of Graphic Novels and Comics* 8(2), pp. 193–202.

Brummett, B. (2019) *Techniques of Close Reading*. 2nd edition. London: SAGE.

Eco, U. (1965) "A Reading of Steve Canyon." Reprint 1976. *20th Century Studies* 15–16, pp. 19–33.

Fresnault-Deruelle, P. (2009) "Image Readings" in Miller, A. and Beaty, B. (eds.) *The French Comics Theory Reader*. Translated from French by A. Miller and B. Beaty. Reprint 2014. Leuven: Leuven University Press, pp. 231–236.

Karasik, P. and Newgarden, M. (2017) *How to Read Nancy: The Elements of Comics in Three Easy Panels*. Seattle: Fantagraphics.

Rabaté, J.-M. (2020) "When Did Close Reading Acquire a Bad Name?" in James, D. (ed.) *Modernism and Close Reading*. Oxford: Oxford University Press, pp. 113–130.

## Close-Up

Close-up refers to a particular way of presenting a DRAWING, in which a specific element of the IMAGE is foregrounded in a PANEL so as to take up the visual field of most of the enclosing FRAME (although it is possible to have a close-up without a frame). While used across the visual ARTS, the close-up is most familiar from FILM, where it is one of the three standard framings that also include medium shots and long shots, both of which are techniques also used in comics. According to Ivan Brunetti, "a close-up focuses on and emphasizes something important to the narrative (e.g. a facial expression)" (2011: 51), but the technique has received very little critical attention in COMICS STUDIES, where it is commonly assumed to play the same NARRATIVE role as in film, with its rhetorical meaning readily understood by READERS versed in VISUAL LANGUAGE. As such, the close-up uses "a sliver of information to refer to the whole" (Cohn 2012: 106) and can be understood as a narrative technique comparable to FOCALISATION, PERSPECTIVE, pacing, and RHYTHM. In addition, the use and prevalence of the close-up may vary depending on the GENRE, FORM, and NATIONAL context of a comic.

Frederik Byrn Køhlert

## *References*

Brunetti, I. (2011) *Cartooning: Philosophy and Practice*. New Haven: Yale University Press.

Cohn, N. (2012) "Comics, Linguistics, and Visual Language: The Past and Future of a Field" in Bramlett, F. (ed.) *Linguistics and the Study of Comics*. London: Palgrave Macmillan, 92–118.

## Closure

One of the laws of Gestalt psychology, closure describes our habit of constructing wholes from parts. Closure was first popularised in COMICS STUDIES by Scott McCloud (1993). Playing a central role in McCloud's endorsement of comics as a SEQUENTIAL ART (based on Will Eisner's comics theories), closure emphasises the importance of the SPACE between PANELS in NARRATIVES, which engenders "a kind of magic only comics can create" (ibid.: 93). Other theorists have since nuanced McCloud's claim (Mikkonen 2017: 38–40) and pointed out connections with existing LITERARY and NARRATOLOGICAL concepts. Hannah Miodrag draws parallels between closure and Wolfgang Iser's theorisation of filling gaps as an essential part of the READING process (2013). For Miodrag, comics function as a web rather than a sequence and the gap-filling takes place on all levels within, between, and beyond comics panels and PAGES. Considering comics as "an art of tensions," Charles Hatfield highlights "the interplay of different codes of signification" in between panels (2005: 44). Building on propositions to reconsider closure by turning to theories of visual narrative processing (Kukkonen 2013; Cohn 2013: 68–69), Chris Gavaler and Leigh Ann Beavers argue for understanding closure "as a subset of inference" (2018: 3). Jan Baetens and Hugo Frey warn against overemphasising and generalising the role of the space between panels (2014: 121–122).

Maaheen Ahmed

## *References*

Baetens, J. and Frey, H. (2014) *The Graphic Novel: An Introduction.* Cambridge: Cambridge University Press.

Cohn, N. (2013) *The Visual Language of Comics: Introduction to the Structure and Cognition of Sequential Images.* London: Bloomsbury Academic.

Gavaler, C. and Beavers, L. A. (2018) "Clarifying Closure," *Journal of Graphic Novels and Comics* 11(2.1), pp. 182–211.

Hatfield, C. (2005) *Alternative Comics: An Emerging Literature.* Jackson: University Press of Mississippi.

Iser, W. (1972) "The Reading Process: A Phenomenological Approach," *New Literary History* 3(2), pp. 279–299.

Kukkonen, K. (2013) *Contemporary Comics Storytelling.* Lincoln: University of Nebraska Press.

McCloud, S. (1993) *Understanding Comics: The Invisible Art.* New York: Harper Perennial.

Mikkonen, K. (2017) *Narratology of Comic Art.* Abingdon: Routledge.

Miodrag, H. (2013) *Comics and Language: Reimagining Critical Discourse on the Form.* Jackson: University Press of Mississippi.

## Collaboration

Collaboration is a common arrangement when more than one person is involved in a creation. The etymology of the term is co-labour, to work together. The common understanding of a comics collaboration is operationalised and negotiated between a comics ARTIST and the WRITER, with both usually being named on the cover. However, the creation of a PUBLISHED comic often requires the additional knowledge and labour of editors, INKERS, COLOURISTS, DESIGNERS, PRINTERS, and others. Roland Barthes asserts that "a text is made up of multiple writings, drawn from several cultures and entering into mutual relations of dialogue, parody, contestation" (1977: 148), and in doing so disputes the intractable MYTHOLOGY of the singular individual genius. With this, the definition of collaboration might necessarily expand to include all who contribute substantially to the work. Of specific note in GRAPHIC MEDICINE and COMICS JOURNALISM, a cogent argument can be made that the person(s) whose STORY is being recreated is also a significant contributor. Re-operationalising collaborations to name all contributors is a form of resistance to hegemonic cultural systems. As a FORM for picturing embodiments and the stories lived in them, comics can be powerful creations of mutual exchange.

JoAnn Purcell

## *References*

Barthes, R. (1967) "The Death of the Author" in Heath, S. (ed.) *Image Music Text.* Translated from French by S. Heath, 1977. London: Fontana, pp. 142–148.

Tolich, M. (2010) "A critique of current practice: Ten foundational guidelines for autoethnographers," *Qualitative Health Research* 20(12), pp. 1599–1610.

## Collectors

Already in the early twentieth century, the first collectors saved the comics sections of Sunday newspapers and later clipped their favourite NEWSPAPER STRIPS. With the growth of the comics magazine industry the first FANZINES that enjoyed confidential distribution as far back as the 1930s were instrumental in the progressive construction of collectors' networks. The latter were structured around the exchange of information about their common hobby as well as the mutual sale and purchase of comics. By the 1960s collectors were among the key actors of the emerging comics FANDOM movements kindled by the NOSTALGIA of individuals born between the 1920s and 1940s in America and Europe for GOLDEN AGE comics (Gabilliet 2016; Schelly 1999). It is essential to distinguish comics READERS from comics collectors; although collectors are sometimes heavy readers, their primary practices give pride of place to the accumulation, either targeted or combined, of various comics-related artefacts—magazines, books, toys, and published or unpublished original ART, as well as the PRODUCTIONS of certain AUTHORS or PUBLISHERS (Rhoades 2008). Simultaneously, many of them play key roles in the dissemination of non-academic scholarship about the MEDIUM (Pustz 1999: 110–147).

Jean-Paul Gabilliet

### *References*

Gabilliet, J.-P. (2016) "'Âge d'or de la bd' et 'Golden Age of Comics': Comparaison des notions fondatrices de la bédéphilie dans l'aire franco-belge et aux États-Unis (1961–2015)," *Le Temps des medias, Revue d'histoire* 27, pp. 139–152.

Pustz, M. (1999) *Comic Book Culture: Fanboys and True Believers.* Jackson: University Press of Mississippi.

Rhoades, S. (2008) *A Complete History of American Comic Books.* New York: Peter Lang.

Schelly, B. (1999) *The Golden Age of Comic Fandom.* Revised edition. Seattle: Hamster Press.

## COLOUR

Colour has always been present in comics, from the crudely coloured Epinal PRINTS to more sophisticated mid-nineteenth-century works using black-plus-one colour techniques and, somewhat later, the full-colour Sunday instalments of US NEWSPAPER comics. Colour was vital for cultural and commercial reasons. It was an eyecatcher meant to seduce, while only important CREATORS were given the possibility to use colour; although in certain cases they were forced to do so by their patrons in order to keep up with the increasing colourisation of all print culture. At the same time, colour was also a huge problem, for it often relied upon a harmful division of LABOUR. Until the 1980s, DRAWING and colouring remained separate operations, generally executed by different agents (the ARTIST first made the drawing and only after that someone else, generally underpaid women, added colour). Moreover, printers did not always follow very closely the instructions, with frequent mismatches between AUTHORIAL intentions and actual print. Today, most artists work in "direct colour," merging drawing and colouring, while better and cheaper printing techniques have lifted most of the MATERIAL, financial, and artistic obstacles to colour. But in AVANT-GARDE and EXPERIMENTAL works, BLACK AND WHITE continues to be the default option.

Jan Baetens

## *References*

Baetens, J. (2011) "From Black & White to Color and Back," *College Literature* 38(3), pp. 111–128.

Groensteen, T. (1993) *Couleur directe/Direct Colour*. Thurn: Kunst der Comics.

Smolderen, T. (2000) *The Origins of Comics: From William Hogarth to Winsor McCay*. Translated from French by B. Beaty and N. Nguyen, 2014. Jackson: University Press of Mississippi.

## Colourist

Comics colourists, adding COLOUR to BLACK AND WHITE artwork, potentially enhance its AESTHETIC/decorative qualities, NARRATIVE clarity, and emotional ambience, with the colourist's position as ARTIST (Uhlig 2016: 54–55), dedicated craftsperson, or worker on an industrial PRODUCTION line (Priego 2010: 198–203) influencing actual outcomes. Additionally, shifts in the colourist's role have related to four phases of production/PRINTING TECHNOLOGY. Since the 1990s, full-colour IMAGES increasingly are created DIGITALLY (Gibbons and Pilcher 2017: 136–146), often for onscreen consumption. Most printed comics still require one printing plate each for cyan (blue), magenta (red), yellow, and black—CMYK (Bann 2006: 36–37). Originally, for mechanical colour separation, colourists did not make finished colour artwork, but only sketched colour guides (Cassel 2012: 24, 122). Colour separators then created by hand three images—using Ben Day dots and their successors—for CMY plates. The black line artwork was printed over these. Flat, unmodulated "four-colour" images resulted, with a limited range of tints (Hackleman 1924: 231–235). The "blue-line method" maintained the black line plate, but colourists now painted colour images for printing under it, separated into CMY components photographically (and later by electronic scanning) (Lawley 2018). Full process colour ("couleur directe") separated all four CMYK plates directly from full-colour artwork, abandoning the discrete black line ART. Many artists now executed their own colours (Groensteen 1993). Digital production, replicating this process with computers, includes a separate colourist role partly for commercial expediency.

Guy Lawley

### *References*

Bann, D. (2006) *The All New Print Production Handbook*. Hove: RotoVision.

Cassel, D. (2012) *Marie Severin: The Mirthful Mistress of Comics*. Raleigh: TwoMorrows.

Gibbons, D. and Pilcher, T. (2017) *How Comics Work*. Hove: RotoVision.

Groensteen, T. (1993) *Couleur directe/Direct Colour*. Thurn: Kunst der Comics.

Hackleman, C. (1924) *Commercial Engraving and Printing*. Indianapolis: Commercial Engraving Publishing Company.

Lawley, G. (2018) "Black and white and blue all over" in Hathaway-Price, D. (ed.) *Fanscene 1*. Wallasey: David Hathaway-Price, pp. 98–105.

Priego, E. (2010) *The Comic Book in the Age of Digital Reproduction*. PhD. University College London. Available at: http://dx.doi.org/10.6084/m9.figshare.754575 [Accessed 28 April 2020].

Uhlig, B. (2016) "Hidden Art: Artistic References in Mattotti's 'Docteur Jekyll & Mister Hyde,'" *Image [&] Narrative* 17(4), pp. 43–56.

## Comedy

The very term COMIC implies that comedy is a central feature of the MEDIUM and in America in the early twentieth century the NEWSPAPER STRIPS were known as the (SUNDAY) FUNNIES ("The Funny Papers" 1933). According to Roger Sabin, "The great age for comedy comics was c. 1935–65. (…) selling in numbers that were never matched before or since—in other words, millions rather than thousands" (1996: 27). Sabin goes on to suggest that this success was due to changes in the FORM such as simplified artwork, removal of captions, and brighter COLOURS, that made more fluid joke telling possible (1996: 27–29). Joseph Witek also argues that there are key formal features, for example, spatial simplification and the use of emanata, underpinning what he calls the CARTOON MODE of comics which are closely linked to anthropomorphic characters in children's comics (2012: 27–30, 34–42). Yet despite their commercial success, in COMICS STUDIES "Notably less attention has been awarded to comics that are funny—whether daft, deadpan or exponents of slapstick gags" (Mickwitz et al. 2020: 10). This is in part because such comics are associated with children and as the medium (and Comics Studies) sought legitimacy adult THEMES have been deemed more worthy of attention.

Ian Horton

## *References*

"The Funny Papers," (1933) *Fortune*, April 1933.

Mickwitz, N., Hague, I., and Horton, I. (2020) "Introduction" in Mickwitz, N., Hague, I., and Horton, I. (eds.) *Representing Acts of Violence in Comics.* Abingdon: Routledge, pp. 1–16.

Sabin, R. (1996) *Comics, Comix and Graphic Novels: A History of Comic Art.* London: Phaidon Press.

Witek, J. (2012) "Comics Modes: Caricature and Illustration in the Crumb Family's Dirty Laundry" in Smith, M. J. and Duncan, R. (eds.) *Critical Approaches to Comics: Theories and Methods.* Abingdon: Routledge, pp. 27–42.

## Comic Book

The modern American comic book is a 36–page saddle-stapled magazine (32 interior pages plus covers), typically 6-3/4" × 10-1/8". The format can be traced back to the 1930s, when previously published NEWSPAPER STRIPS first began to be collected in booklets. PRINTED on newspaper presses, the pages were folded into quartos, yielding magazines approximately 7-1/2" × 10-3/8". Early publishers quickly standardised the comic book's length at 64 pages, eventually reducing page counts to 52 and then 36 pages including ADVERTISING, primarily to keep the 10-cent price point that had been established in the 1930s. Beginning with issues dated February 1961, Dell Comics raised their prices to 15 cents, followed soon by DC and then other companies increasing to 12 cents per issue (Wells 2012: 49–50); prices have steadily increased to this day. Further cost-cutting measures included gradually reducing the number of STORY pages to 17 and increasing paid advertising pages, although the contemporary commercial comic book usually includes approximately 22 story pages. As periodicals, comic books as a rule do not stay in print like non-SERIALS do. Exceptions have included Gilberton Publishing's *Classics Illustrated* series (1941–1962) and many of the UNDERGROUND COMIX of the 1960s and 1970s, which went through multiple printings, often with increased pricing.

Gene Kannenberg Jr

## *References*

Wells, J. (2012) *American Comic Book Chronicles: 1960–1964.* Raleigh: TwoMorrows.

## Comic Strip

As Ian Gordon notes, "there is no distinct aesthetic that isolates the comic strip" (2020: 13), but it is a short FORM comics work most commonly appearing in daily NEWSPAPERS. Daily comic strips tend to range from a single PANEL to as many as four panels, while Sunday comic strips tend to stretch to as much as a full page. Comic strips are known for their brevity and their frequency. Many have been published daily for multiple decades. While it has distinct traditions in several NATIONAL comics fields, the comic strip is most closely tied to the tradition of daily newspaper publishing in the US beginning in the 1890s. The most popular comic strips at the turn of the twentieth century featured recurrent characters (like Rudolph Dirks' *Katzenjammer Kids* (1897–1913)), but by the 1910s ongoing SERIALISED NARRATIVES had been identified as an excellent way to develop READER loyalty. The 1920s and 1930s inaugurated a celebrated era of adventure strips (Chester Gould's *Dick Tracy* (1931–1977); Harold Gray's *Little Orphan Annie* (1924–1968)). While certain strips targeted an adult READERSHIP through the inclusion of topical material (Walt Kelly's *Pogo* (1948–1975), Garry Trudeau's *Doonesbury* (1970–2014)) or innovative AESTHETICS (George Herriman's *Krazy Kat* (1913–1944)), the comic strip has been profoundly all-ages and often addresses an AUDIENCE of children as much as it does adults (Charles Schulz's *Peanuts* (1952–2000); Bill Watterson's *Calvin and Hobbes* (1985–1995)).

Bart Beaty

## *References*

Gordon, I. (2020) "Comic Strips" in Hatfield, C. and Beaty, B. (eds.) *Comics Studies: A Guidebook.* New Brunswick: Rutgers University Press, 13–24.

## Comics

The term comics is derived from "comic" and was first used to refer to early American NEWSPAPER STRIPS. Since that time, comics has become the most widely used word describing the MEDIUM. Seeing as how the term was originally used in relation to American comics, it still connotes, and, to a certain extent, privileges the American tradition. Another flaw of the term is that it implies that the medium of comics is closely connected to comedy, which is not wholly accurate (Gardner 2012: ix). Near synonyms of comics, as well as attempts to circumvent negatively perceived connotations of the term—such as GRAPHIC NOVEL, graphic narrative, and COMIX—have been more and less successful. None of them, however, have been able to displace comics. The word comics, then, also has its advantages. Among them are its seniority and its relative inclusiveness towards the vast range of different traditions and FORMS associated with the medium.

Rik Spanjers

### *References*

Gardner, J. (2012) *Projections: Comics and the History of Twenty-First-Century Storytelling*. Palo Alto: Stanford University Press.

## Comics Ages (Golden Age, Silver Age, Bronze Age)

Whether defined by dynasties or decades (Smith 1998), periodisation is a common feature of historical narratives. It divides the flow of time into discrete units that are explicitly or implicitly different from one another in some meaningful way. In COMICS STUDIES, the most influential periodisation has been the Ages of Comics scheme, which divides the HISTORY of comics into a Golden Age, Silver Age, Bronze Age, and so on. It directly recalls the Ages of Man defined by Hesiod in *Works and Days* (c. 700 BC), while faintly echoing the archaeologist's divisions of Stone Age, Bronze Age, and Iron Age. The Ages of Comics first appeared in the nostalgia-oriented FANDOM of the 1960s (Gavaler 2018: 7, 9) and was later integrated into industrial discourse as part of publishers' "memory management" (Méon 2018: 195). Fans and scholars have proposed new labels to correct the system or extend it to the present (Lewis

2003; Resha 2020). However, the Ages of Comics are conceptually incoherent, really only describe American SUPERHERO COMIC BOOKS, overemphasise CHARACTER debuts, and tend to totalise or essentialise (Woo 2008). Recent scholarship has offered some alternatives. Gabilliet (2010) absorbs the Ages scheme within a broader history that attends to rises and falls in sales, the emergence and decline of PUBLISHERS, and generations of CREATORS, while Kidman's (2019) periodisations focus on the comic-book industry's relations with other media industries through licensing agreements.

Benjamin Woo

## *References*

Gavaler, C. (2018) *Superhero Comics.* London: Bloomsbury Academic.

Kidman, S. (2019) *Comic Books Incorporated: How the Business of Comics Became the Business of Hollywood.* Oakland: University of California Press.

Lewis, A.D. (2003) "One for the Ages: Barbara Gordon and the (Il-) Logic of Comic Book Age-Dating," *International Journal of Comic Art* 5(2), pp. 296–311.

Méon, J.-M. (2018) "Sons and Grandsons of Origins: Narrative Memory in Marvel Superhero Comics" in Ahmed, M. and Crucifix, B. (eds.) *Comics Memory: Archives and Styles.* London: Palgrave Macmillan, pp. 189–209.

Resha, A. (2020) "The Blue Age of Comics," *Inks: The Journal of the Comics Studies Society* 4(1), pp. 66–81.

Smith, J.S. (1998) "The Strange History of the Decade: Modernity, Nostalgia, and the Perils of Periodization," *Journal of Social History* 32(2), pp. 263–285.

Woo, B. (2008) "An Age-Old Problem: Problematics of Comic Book Historiography," *International Journal of Comic Art* 10(1), pp. 268–279.

## Comics Code

The Comics Code was created in 1954, as a regulation tool created in response to a US Senate investigation into comics. The code was controlled by the Comic Magazine Association of America (CMAA) and was in effect until 2011. The criticism of comics that led to the code's creation came in three phases: criticism of their effect on children's READING; of the books' failure to uphold social morals; and, finally, of the behavioural effects, "which desensitised children to violence and promoted juvenile delinquency" (Nyberg 2017: 25). In the early 1950s, psychiatrist Fredric Wertham suggested that COMIC BOOKS caused juvenile delinquency, despite scant evidence. Wertham's claims, backed by many supporters, led to the 1953 United States Senate Subcommittee on Juvenile Delinquency, which decided to allow self-regulation within the industry. In 1954, he published *Seduction of the Innocent.* PUBLISHERS policed their own output, and newsstands were only allowed to stock comics that bore the CCA ("Comics Code Approved") stamp. The 1960s' rise of UNDERGROUND comics circumvented the CMAA by distributing via HEAD SHOPS, allowing underground ARTISTS to achieve success without the CCA stamp. By 2011, few publishers were still following its guidelines, and the CMAA had little power over publication and distribution.

Harriet E. H. Earle

## *References*

Nyberg, A. K. (2017) "The Comics Code" in Bramlett, F., Cook, R., and Meskin, A. (eds.) *The Routledge Companion to Comics.* Abingdon: Routledge, 25–33.

Wertham, F. (1954) *Seduction of the Innocent: The Influence of Comic Books on Today's Youth.* New York: Rinehart.

## Comics Journalism

The term comics journalism (also referred to as "graphic journalism" or "graphic reporting/reportage") was first used in the mid-1990s by Maltese American CARTOONIST Joe Sacco to describe his nonfiction comics about current events (Williams 2005). Since then, this GENRE has become an increasingly popular way to bear WITNESS to a range of socio-political events and circumstances, with a focus on the experiences of ordinary, subaltern people in crisis situations (Hodapp 2015). Works under this banner employ a variety of approaches, FORMATS, and

STYLES; in addition to words and DRAWINGS, some also include PHOTOGRAPHS and other DOCUMENTARY source MATERIALS. Comics journalism is praised for its ability to tell intimate STORIES that invite READER engagement and empathy through the use of multiple viewpoints, the mixing of REALISTIC and symbolic elements, and the tensions between distinct SEMIOTIC MODES (Schack 2014). Most graphic journalists include themselves as a character, thus emphasising the interpretative nature of all journalistic processes and challenging established notions of professional objectivity and authenticity (Nyberg 2012; Weber and Rall 2017). The genre also raises important questions about how to respect the VOICE, dignity, and safety of vulnerable SUBJECTS (Orbán 2015), and how such a time-consuming form of reportage can maintain newsworthiness.

Elisabeth 'Lisa' El Refaie

## *References*

Hodapp, J. (2015) "The postcolonial Joe Sacco," *Journal of Graphic Novels and Comics* 6(4), pp. 319–330.

Nyberg, A. K. (2012) "Comics Journalism: Drawing on Words to Picture the Past in *Safe Area Goražde*" in Smith, M. J. and Duncan, R. (eds.) *Critical Approaches to Comics: Theories and Methods.* Abingdon: Routledge, pp. 116–128.

Orbán, K. (2015) "Mediating distant violence: Reports on non-photographic reporting in *The Fixer* and *The Photographer*," *Journal of Graphic Novels and Comics* 6(2), pp. 122–137.

Schack, T. (2014) "'A failure of language': Achieving layers of meaning in graphic journalism," *Journalism* 15(1), pp. 109–127.

Weber, W. and Rall, H.-M. (2017) "Authenticity in comics journalism: Visual strategies for reporting facts," *Journal of Graphic Novels and Comics* 8(4), pp. 376–397.

Williams, K. (2005) "The case for comics journalism," *Columbia Journalism Review* 43(6), pp. 51–55.

## Comics Shop

In North America, COMIC BOOKS were traditionally carried by magazine retailers, in newsstands and convenience stores. The first speciality shops appeared in the mid-1960s, generally in neighbourhoods frequented by teenagers, young adults, hippies, and college students. In the 1970s, the emergence of the DIRECT MARKET of non-returnable, heavily discounted comics purchased directly from PUBLISHERS multiplied the number of shops and fuelled the growth of a clientele of FANS/COLLECTORS whose patterns of demand fragilised the retailers' MARKET following speculative bubbles in the mid-1980s and early 1990s (Gabilliet 2010: 138–158). Comics shops are central to the fan subculture. Alongside comics, many of them carry a wide array of related MERCHANDISE (posters, clothes, toys, trading cards, etc.) that epitomises the extension of the comics hobby well beyond the purchase of READING MATERIAL. The shops are also privileged spots for informal meeting and exchange—to the point of sometimes appearing forbidding to non-fan customers (Pustz 1999). In Europe, where the rise of comics shops in the 1970s coincided with the growth of the ALBUM market (on which general bookstores also cashed in), speciality stores are frequently perceived as alternate types of bookstores rather than specifically subcultural venues.

Jean-Paul Gabilliet

### *References*

Gabilliet, J.-P. (2005) *Of Comics and Men: A Cultural History of American Comic Books.* Translated from French by B. Beaty and N. Nguyen, 2010. Jackson: University Press of Mississippi.

Pustz, M. (1999), *Comic Book Culture: Fanboys and True Believers.* Jackson: University Press of Mississippi.

## Comics Studies

Near the end of the 1980s, the perception of comics in Anglophone MEDIA shifted with the rise of the GRAPHIC NOVEL (Sabin 2010: 87). This newfound respectability helped establish Comics Studies (Sabin 2019), a field of inquiry that certainly already was present in different

NATIONAL contexts both within and outside of academia, albeit often only because of the specific interest of individual researchers. One peculiarity of Comics Studies is that while since the 2000s a sizeable number of journals, conferences, and PhDs written on comics have come into being, much of this research takes place within wider disciplinary contexts (La Cour and Spanjers 2016: 1). Comics scholars often work in LITERATURE, ART HISTORY, CULTURAL STUDIES, and media studies departments. Thus, while Comics Studies is certainly a field of inquiry, it can be said to lack disciplinary mass in the FORM of Comics Studies programmes in universities, even though there are now a handful of such programmes in existence. More recently, comics scholars have started re-examining the biases that the history of the discipline as well as its emplacement in various university systems have instilled in Comics Studies. Among these critiques are: general discussions of the state of Comics Studies (Chute and Jagoda 2014; Aldama 2018; Singer 2019); discussions of the graphic novel as a concept that privileges a certain type of comics over others (La Cour 2013; Beaty and Woo 2016; Spanjers 2019); and discussions of the racial and gender biases of Comics Studies (Chute 2010; Whaley 2015; Earle 2019; Whitted 2019).

Rik Spanjers

## *References*

Aldama, F. L. (2018) *Comics Studies Here and Now*. Abingdon: Routledge.

Beaty, B. and Woo, B. (2016) *The Greatest Comic Book of All Time: Symbolic Capital and the Field of American Comic Books*. London: Palgrave Macmillan.

Earle, M. (2019) *Writing Queer Women of Color: Representation and Misdirection in Contemporary Fiction and Graphic Narratives*. Jefferson: McFarland.

La Cour, E. (2013) *The "Graphic Novel": Discourses on the Archive*. PhD. University of Amsterdam.

La Cour, E. and Spanjers, R. (2016) "Integration, Appropriation, Rebellion: Comics' Sociability in the Milieux of Art and Literature," *Image [&] Narrative* 17(4), pp. 1–4.

Sabin, R. (2019) *Comics in the Academy, Three Questions*. Available at https://www.youtube.com/watch?v=G7LIDcyIhbw [Accessed 3 August 2020].
Sabin, R. (1993) *Adult Comics: An Introduction*. Abingdon: Routledge.
Singer, M. (2019) *Breaking the Frames: Populism and Prestige in Comics Studies*. Austin: University of Texas Press.
Spanjers, R. (2019) *Comics Realism and the Maus Event: Comics and the Dynamics of World War II Remembrance*. PhD. University of Amsterdam.
Whaley, D. E. (2015) *Black Women in Sequence: Re-Inking Comics, Graphic Novels, and Anime*. Seattle: University of Washington Press.
Whitted, Q. (2019) *EC Comics: Race, Shock, and Social Protest*. New Brunswick: Rutgers University Press.

## Comix

Comix refers primarily to the UNDERGROUND comics of the 1960s and 1970s. Underground comix were sold through HEAD SHOPS rather than newsstands and featured explicit SEXUAL content, frequent depictions of drug use, scathing SATIRE of mainstream society, psychedelic-inspired AESTHETICS, and absurdist HUMOUR (Danky and Kitchen 2009; Rosenkranz 2002; Skinn 2004). The term became closely identified with the underground movement and was used as part of the title of many underground comics, such as *Zap Comix* and *Wimmen's Comix* (Robbins et al. 2016). The term has sporadically been used in other ways before and after the heyday of underground comix. Its most notable earlier use was in Charles Schulz's *Peanuts* COMIC STRIP, where it appeared in the titles of various COMIC BOOKS read by Charlie Brown and other characters. Art Spiegelman, who participated in the underground movement of the 1960s and 1970s, later used the alternate spelling of "commix" to describe the mixture of words and IMAGES in the comics MEDIUM (1988).

Doug Singsen

### *References*

Danky, J. and Kitchen, D. (2009) *Underground Classics: The Transformation of Comics into Comix*. New York: Abrams.
Robbins, T., et al. (2016) *The Complete Wimmen's Comix*. Seattle: Fantagraphics.

Rosenkranz, P. (2002) *Rebel Visions: The Underground Comix Revolution, 1963–1975*. Seattle: Fantagraphics.

Skinn, D. (2004) *Comix: The Underground Revolution*. New York: Thunder's Mouth.

Spiegelman, A. (1988) "Commix: An Idiosyncratic Historical and Aesthetic Overview," *Print* 42(6), pp. 61–73, 195–196.

## Commodity

A commodity is a consumer good characterised by its interchangeable character (regardless of its origin) and its economic value exclusive of any social, moral, or AESTHETIC value. Raw MATERIALS or cash crops are commodity goods because they are initially undifferentiated—unlike works of ART that, at least in our contemporary culture, are primarily defined in terms of uniqueness. "Commodification" occurs when MARKET values replace social values, substituting standardisation for singularity (Bourdieu 1985). Any cultural product, from MASS PRODUCED popular MUSIC or LITERATURE to AVANT-GARDE art, pertains to interactions between cultural consumption and economic specificity (e.g. a classical opera marketed as an inexpensive CD). Until the 1960s, comics in Western countries would enjoy a commodity status in cultural hierarchies because they were overwhelmingly perceived as disposable, escapist, lowbrow material churned out in assembly-line fashion by mass PUBLISHING industries (newspapers and popular periodicals) for a supposedly undiscriminating market of young and/or uneducated readers (Gabilliet 2010: 244–249). However, the once dominant perception of the MEDIUM as commodity has evolved considerably in the last few decades thanks to the rise of the GRAPHIC NOVEL, which has drawn comics closer to the aesthetic value judgement systems attached to literature (Beaty and Woo 2016).

Jean-Paul Gabilliet

### *References*

Beaty, B. and Woo, B. (2016) *The Greatest Comic Book of All Time: Symbolic Capital and the Field of American Comic Books*. London: Palgrave Macmillan.

Bourdieu, P. (1985) "The Market of Symbolic Goods," *Poetics* 14(1–2), pp. 13–44.
Gabilliet, J.-P. (2005) *Of Comics and Men: A Cultural History of American Comic Books*. Translated from French by B. Beaty and N. Nguyen, 2010. Jackson: University Press of Mississippi.

## Composition

Composition in comics refers to the judicious arrangement of the visual elements within a singular PANEL. This includes choices of placement of VANISHING POINT, of FRAMING, such as the distribution of elements along horizontal-vertical and left-right axes or the distance-ANGLE relations to represented objects, choices of LINE-work, COLOUR, dark-light contrast ratio, not to mention STYLISTIC options. Composition may also entail decisions upon the use of emanata, verbal matter (SPEECH BALLOONS, CAPTION BOXES, ONOMATOPOEIAS, and other TEXTS), visual METAPHORS, and other expressive tools at the disposal of the AUTHOR. These choices turn the panel into a "medium of control" (Eisner 1985: 40) allowing for the STORY to flow visually and NARRATIVELY, while "techniques operate quietly in the background" (McCloud 2006: 18). This can act either in a CONVENTIONAL, expected fashion, reinforcing its legibility, or in a jarring, surprising way, looking for remarkable effects. The linear arrangement of panels in narrative relationships pertains to TRANSITIONS and SEQUENCE. When referring to the composition of the panels within a whole PAGE, spread or beyond that, one properly refers to PAGE LAYOUT, but sometimes these terms are used interchangeably.

Pedro Moura

### *References*

Eisner, W. (1985) *Comics and Sequential Art*. Tamarac: Poorhouse Press.
McCloud, S. (2006) *Making Comics. Storytelling Secrets of Comics, Manga and Graphic Novels*. New York: Harper.

## Constraint

Constraint is the practice of applying a "globally active device whose nature is neither grammatical nor discursive" to the PRODUCTION of a work (Baetens 2003: n.p.). Jan Baetens distinguishes between "constraint" and "rule," as "either the grammatical structure of a given language or the discursive norms imposed by genres and/or contexts," and "device," "a stylistic means of underlining local textual phenomena" (ibid.). Further, Thierry Groensteen distinguishes between "constraints which can be considered generative (they produce new works) and constraints which can be considered transformational (they modify existing works)" (Groensteen 1997: 17, qtd. in Baetens 2003: n.p.). Constraint was developed by the Oulipu group ("Ouvroir de littérature potentielle" 1960 (Roubaud 2005)) and adopted in the comics REGISTER by Oubapo ("Ouvroir de bande dessinée potentielle" 1992), exemplified by Queneau's *Exercises in Style* (1981) and (although not a member of Oubapo) Madden's *99 Ways to Tell a Story: Exercises in Style* (2005), in which a single STORY is told or shown in different STYLES. The adoption of constraints often explicitly involves a critical assessment of the conditions under which spontaneously produced works emerge (Grennan 2015).

Simon Grennan

### *References*

Baetens, J. (2003) "Comic strips and constrained writing," *Image [&] Narrative* 7, n.p. Available at: http://www.imageandnarrative.be/inarchive/graphicnovel/janbaetens_constrained.htm [Accessed 11 May 2020].

Grennan, S. (2015) *Dispossession: A novel of few words.* London: Jonathan Cape.

Groensteen, T. (1997) "Un premier bouquet de contraintes" in Oubapo (eds.) *Oupus* 1. Paris: L'Association, pp. 13–59.

Queneau, R. (1981) *Exercises in Style.* London: Calder.

Madden, M. (2005) *99 Ways to Tell a Story: Exercises in Style.* New York: Chamberlain Bros.

Roubaud, J. (2005) "The Oulipo and Combinatorial Art" in Mathews, H. and Brotchie, A. (eds.) *Oulipo Compendium.* London: Atlas, pp. 37–44.

## Convention (Public Fan Gathering)

The first public gatherings geared towards comics FANS appeared in the mid-1960s. In the USA, where the main annual event is San Diego Comic-Con (Bolling and Smith 2014), comic conventions, the first of which took place in 1964, have replicated the pattern established by SCIENCE FICTION conventions since the 1930s, with venues accommodating both dealers booths offering back issues, MERCHANDISE, original ART, and areas dedicated to panels about comics-THEMED topics (Gabilliet 2010: 265–267). In Europe, it was the tradition of art events, such as salons or festivals, that shaped the earliest comics-themed gatherings. The first one, the "International Salon of Comics" held in Bordighera, Italy, in 1965, was organised by academics, EDUCATORS, and various public intellectuals. The International Salon of Comics comprised a series of lectures and panels as well as exhibits of comic art, with only a small area for PUBLISHERS booths. As of 1966, the annual event moved to Lucca where it became Europe's main comics salon until its French replica, created in Angoulême in 1974, took over Lucca's leadership by the early 1980s. Although American-type comic-cons and European-type festivals nowadays share many features, the former are concerned primarily with profitability while the latter emphasise cultural agendas (Lesage 2013).

Jean-Paul Gabilliet

### *References*

Bolling, B. and Smith, M. J. (eds.) (2014) *It Happens at Comic-Con: Ethnographic Essays on a Pop Culture Phenomenon*. Jefferson: McFarland.

Gabilliet, J.-P. (2005) *Of Comics and Men: A Cultural History of American Comic Books*. Translated from French by B. Beaty and N. Nguyen, 2010. Jackson: University Press of Mississippi.

Lesage, S. (2013) "Angoulême, 'la ville qui vit en ses images'? Politisation de la culture et institutionnalisation du festival" in Fléchet, A. and Goetschel, P. (eds.) *Une histoire des festivals XXe–XXIe siècle*. Paris: Editions de la Sorbonne, pp. 252–264.

## Conventions

Conventions of comics are those forms of meaning-making that have been deployed repeatedly, by one or more CREATORS, over time, such that they become recognised, unmarked choices among a community of READERS and ARTISTS. These may include norms of FORMAT, (PAGE) LAYOUT, approaches to REPRESENTING certain participants and processes in comics form, and accepted METAPHORS or conceptualisations that come to underpin comics PRODUCTION and RECEPTION. There has been little serious formalisation of such conventions. Wally Wood's "22 Panels that Always Work" (Wood and Crouch 1980) has become a popular example of the sharing of conventions amongst colleagues; Mort Walker's *The Lexicon of Comicana* (2000) playfully proposes a number of conventions with technical terms coined, few of which have caught on, with the notable exception of emanata. Part of the work of comics theory, such as that by Thierry Groensteen (2009, 2013) and Scott McCloud (1993), is to elucidate comics conventions and how they work. Conventions may be described at several levels: the conventions of a system as a whole, developing by phylogenesis; conventions acquired and deployed by a creator, ontogenesis; and conventions established within a text, logogenesis (Davies 2020). Hannah Miodrag (2013) notes this latter as a "*langue* of the text."

Paul F. Davies

### *References*

Davies, P. F. (2020) "Comics and Heteroglossia" In Giddens T. (ed.) *Critical Directions in Comics Studies.* Jackson: University Press of Mississippi, pp. 158–178.

Groensteen, T. (1999) *The System of Comics.* Translated from French by B. Beaty and N. Nguyen, 2007. Jackson: University Press of Mississippi.

Groensteen, T. (2011) *Comics and Narration.* Translated from French by A. Miller, 2013. Jackson: University Press of Mississippi.

McCloud, S. (1993) *Understanding Comics: The Invisible Art.* New York: Harper Perennial.

Miodrag, H. (2013) *Comics and Language: Reimagining Critical Discourse on the Form.* Jackson: University Press of Mississippi.

Walker, M. (1980) *The Lexicon of Comicana.* Reprint 2000. Lincoln: iUniverse.

Wood, W. and Crouch, B. (1980) *The Wallace Wood Sketchbook.* Bridgeport: Bill Crouch.

## Convergence

The term "media convergence" refers to various dynamics that are rarely systematically interrelated. Starting from the observation that most MEDIA content and media TECHNOLOGIES are digital nowadays, as technologies are merging into multi-functional devices (Meikle and Young 2012), heterogeneous forms of media and INTERMEDIALITY cannot be differentiated ontologically anymore, with recourse to their material properties. This concern can be traced to the exchanges between PRINTED and DIGITAL COMICS (Kashtan 2018). A cultural perspective, often attributed to Henry Jenkins (2006), further investigates how practice-based and institutional aspects of media and media "dispositifs" (including CONVENTIONALISED habits or "protocols") are also converging, such as earlier distinctions between mass and interpersonal communication (Jensen 2010), or between producer and recipients (Bruns 2008). Especially relevant for COMIC BOOKS is their integration into larger TRANSMEDIA franchises (Yockey 2017). As a business strategy, this is also called transmedia STORYTELLING. Woo has pointed out, for instance, that the American comic book industry "does not produce 'comic books' but intellectual property that circulates across multiple media, ranging from film, television, and video GAMES to licensed MERCHANDISE and even Broadway theater" (2018: 39).

Lukas R. A. Wilde

### *References*

Bruns, A. (2018) *Blogs, Wikipedia, Second Life, and Beyond: From Production to Produsage*. New York: Peter Lang.

Jenkins, H. (2006) *Convergence Culture. Where Old and New Media Collide*. New York: New York University Press.

Jensen, K. (2010) *Media Convergence: The Three Degrees of Network, Mass, and Interpersonal Communication*. Abingdon: Routledge.

Kashtan, A. (2018) *Between Pen and Pixel. Comics, Materiality and the Book of the Future*. Columbus: The Ohio State University Press.

Meikle, G. and Young, S. (2012) *Media Convergence: Networked Digital Media in Everyday Life*. London: Palgrave Macmillan.

Woo, B. (2018) "Is There a Comic Book Industry?" *Media Industries Journal* 5(1), pp. 27–46.

Yockey, M. (ed.) (2018) *Make Ours Marvel. Media Convergence and a Comics Universe*. Austin: University of Texas Press.

## Cosplay

Cosplay is a form of dress-up in which FANS represent existing fictional characters, usually in self-made outfits. Fans cosplay their favourite characters at a CONVENTION, such as San Diego Comic-Con. The term "cosplaying" was coined in the 1980s by the GAME designer Takahashi Nobuyuki when he observed fan costuming at an American convention (Bruno 2002). Cosplay is a material, embodied expression, based on existing STORYWORLDS, and a form of INTERMEDIALITY (Lamerichs 2018). The process of creating costumes can be understood as a critical making process (Crawford and Hancock 2019) in which fans often learn from each other (Okabe 2012). The eventual cosplay performance is a form of imaginative play and re-enactment, through which fans form social communities and ties (Mountfort et al. 2018; Winge and Eicher 2018). It allows fans to experiment with their IDENTITY, body, and GENDER (e.g. cross-play). In this sense, fans construct their identity actively, for instance in terms of gender (Lamerichs 2011), SEXUALITY (Gn 2019), or age (Skentelbery 2019). The cosplay community, however, is a lived culture like any other and is not necessarily inclusive or welcoming. Analysing the context and values of a specific cosplay community or performance is therefore essential.

Nicolle Lamerichs

### *References*

Bruno, M. (2002) "Cosplay: The Illegitimate Child of SF Masquerades, and Costuming a World Apart: Cosplay in America and Japan." *Glitz and Glitter Newsletter, Millennium Costume Guild,* October 2002.

Crawford, G. and Hancock, D. (2019) *Cosplay and the Art of Play: Exploring Sub-Culture through Art.* Berlin: Springer.

Gn, J. (2019) "Queer Simulation: The Practice, Performance and Pleasure of Cosplay," *Continuum: Journal of Media & Cultural Studies* 25, pp. 583–593.

Lamerichs, N. (2011) "Stranger than fiction: Fan identity in cosplaying," *Transformative Works and Cultures* 7, n.p. Available at: https://journal.transformativeworks.org/index.php/twc/article/view/246/230 [Accessed 5 August 2020].

Lamerichs, N. (2018) *Productive Fandom: Intermediality and Affective Reception in Fan Cultures.* Amsterdam: Amsterdam University Press.

Mountfort, P., Peirson-Smith, A., and Geczy, A. (2018) *Planet Cosplay: Costume Play, Identity and Global Fandom.* Bristol: Intellect.

Okabe, D. (2012) "Cosplay, Learning, and Cultural Practice" in Ito, M., Okabe, D., and Tsuji, I. (eds.) *Fandom Unbound: Otaku Culture in a Connected World.* New Haven: Yale University Press.

Skentelbery, D. (2019) "I Feel Twenty Years Younger. Age-Bending Cosplay," *FNORD.* Available at: https://readfnord.wordpress.com/2019/07/02/i-feel-twenty-years-younger-age-bending-cosplay/ [Accessed 5 August 2020].

Winge, T. M. and Eicher, J. B. (2018) *Costuming Cosplay: Dressing the Imagination.* London: Bloomsbury Academic.

## Creator

Used as a synonym for ARTIST, AUTHOR, or WRITER, the term creator has become increasingly popular in COMICS STUDIES in the twenty-first century. Creator is often preferred because it does not overemphasise either the visual (artist) or the verbal (author or writer) aspects of comics creation. As such, the term creator is used most often in relation to comics made by one person (Round 2010: 20). There are exceptions to this rule. Comics can be made by multiple creators, but in those cases the different roles of the creators are more often made explicit through job titles such as writer, artist, LETTERER, COLOURIST, and so on. In the case of comics that are created by a team, the term creator can also refer to the one who is seen as responsible for the work as a whole in the sociocultural setting of the work in question. A comics creator in this sense might be likened to a FILM director or, in case of SERIAL PUBLISHING, a showrunner (Blakey 2017). The term maker has been used in comics scholarship in a similar fashion as creator, but with slightly different connotations.

Rik Spanjers

## *References*

Blakey, E. (2017) "Showrunner as Auteur: Bridging the Culture/ Economy Binary in Digital Hollywood," *Open Cultural Studies* 1(1), pp. 321–332.

Round, J. (2010) "'Is this a book?' DC Vertigo and the Redefinition of Comics in the 1990s" in Williams, P. and Lyons, J. (eds.) *The Rise of the American Comics Artist: Creators and Contexts.* Jackson: University Press of Mississippi, pp. 14–30.

## Critical Race Theory

Critical Race Theory originated as an academic movement when, in 1982, scholars of colour studying at Harvard Law School became, according to lawyer and founding Critical Race Theorist Kimberlé Williams Crenshaw, "frustrated by the currency of arguments that cast doubt on the viability of race as a unit of analysis or the utility of race consciousness in deconstructing hierarchy" (2011: 1264). Those frustrations matured across multiple academic disciplines to become a critical lens to examine the dynamic relationship between RACE and power within a society. This theory posits that race is socially constructed (as opposed to biologically determined) and that race functions alongside other social identities like GENDER, CLASS, and SEXUALITY to reinforce systems of power that oppress certain racial groups to the advantage of others (Ruiz De Castilla and Reyes Garcia 2014: 173). Mass MEDIA is one such system. Political scientist Stephen M. Caliendo observes that "all information that we encounter is framed," and comics can interpret harmful racial ideologies through its distinct VISUAL LANGUAGE as objective information or truths for a large, unassuming READERSHIP (2011: 76). As such, Critical Race Theory advocates for an end to oppressive racial ideology and practices through critical evaluation and INTERSECTIONAL DISCOURSE.

Rachel A. Davis

## *References*

Caliendo, S. M. (2011) "Race, Media, and Popular Culture" in Caliendo, S. M. and McIlwain, C. D. (eds.) *The Routledge Companion to Race and Ethnicity*. Abingdon: Routledge, pp. 73–81.

Ruiz De Castilla, C. and Reyes Garcia, Z. E. (2014) "From sexual siren to race traitor: Condoleezza Rice in political cartoons" in Howard, S. C. and Jackson, II, R. L. (eds.) *Black Comics: Politics of Race and Representation*. London: Bloomsbury Academic, pp. 169–187.

Williams Crenshaw, K. (2011) "Twenty Years of Critical Race Theory," *Connecticut Law Review* 43(5), pp. 1253–1352.

## Cultural Theory

Cultural theory informs approaches to the study of culture, offering "a series of overlapping, sometimes consistent, sometimes contradictory and antagonistic, contiguous (if not always common) discussions" across different academic disciplines and schools of thought (Oswell 2010: xl). Since the emergence of Cultural Studies, a broad set of cultural theory approaches relies on the assumption that culture "is not so much a set of *things*—novels and paintings or TV programmes and comics—as a process, a set of *practices*" (Hall 1997: 2). Subsequently, these "things" do not hold static meaning, but "[i]t is by our use of things, and what we say, think and feel about them—how we represent them—that we *give them a meaning*" (Hall 1997: 3). This concern with cultural REPRESENTATION as "signifying practice" is central to analytical approaches that investigate how cultural texts relate to the DISCOURSES they emerge from and constitute. In so doing, cultural theory informs various (cross-)disciplinary approaches that seek to analyse the ideological function of cultural texts to affirm, resist, or subvert dominant ideologies, for example, hierarchies of GENDER, RACE, CLASS, ETHNICITY, and DIS(ABILITY). Important to the study of comics and ideology, for example, have been issues of representation, power, and subjectivity (Barker 1989; Cortsen et al. 2015; Hague 2017).

Freija Camps

## *References*

Barker, M. (1989) *Comics: Ideology, Power, and the Critics*. Manchester: Manchester University Press.

Cortsen, R. P., La Cour, E., and Magnussen, A. (eds.) (2015) *Comics and Power: Representing and Questioning Culture, Subjects and Communities.* Cambridge: Cambridge Scholars.

Hague, I. (2017) "Comics and Cultural Studies" in Bramlett, F., Cook, R., and Meskin, A. (eds.) *The Routledge Companion to Comics.* Abingdon: Routledge, pp. 424–432.

Hall, S. (1997) *Representation: Cultural Representations and Signifying Practices.* London: SAGE.

Oswell, D. (2010) "Editor's Introduction: Cultural Theory—Genealogies, Orientations and Territories" in Oswell, D. (ed.) *Cultural Theory: Volume 1, Legacies and Innovations.* London: SAGE, pp. xxi–xlviii.

## Culture Industry

Theodor Adorno and Max Horkheimer's term culture industry referred to the PRODUCTION of anything "removed from the naked necessity of life" (Adorno 1991: 109). As part of the Frankfurt School Adorno and Horkheimer critiqued the prevalence of the culture industry's outputs as inauthentic entertainment that functioned as instruments of social control, as opposed to authentic mass culture made by people for their true self-expression and enjoyment. The social and political context of the Frankfurt School's work shaped their view that even when AUDIENCES professed to enjoy those products, it was never out of true freedom but only ever "euphoria in unhappiness" (Marcuse 1964: 7) as permitted within capitalism. Though scholars have moved on from this justifiable pessimism it can still be useful to differentiate between comics as authentic self-expression, as normative social control, and/or as elite forms of ART. At any scale of production, as IMAGETEXTS created by humans, all comics are cultural products that are shaped by the social, economic, and political contexts in which they are made. Scholars of comics must be critical in asking whose voices are REPRESENTED or marginalised, and whose way of life is presented as normal, desirable, or abhorrent.

Lydia Wysocki

### *References*

Adorno, T. (1947) *The Culture Industry: Selected Essays on Mass Culture.* Reprint 1991. Bernstein, J. M. (ed.) Abingdon: Routledge.

Marcuse, H. (1964) *One-Dimensional Man: Studies in the Ideology of Advanced Industrial Society.* Abingdon: Routledge.

## Dénouement

Dénouement (from French "to untie") refers to the point in a plot where the knots of the NARRATIVE are untied and the last conflicts following the climax are resolved. Paradoxically, this untying of the plot-knots can be thought of as tying together the narrative plot strands into a thread that ends the STORY. Since Aristotle's *Poetics*, this unravelling, after the central pivotal point in the story, has been considered the part of any narrative that has the potential for catharsis or impacting the AUDIENCE emotionally with the conclusion of events (Butcher 1902). In comics, this conclusion to the complications of a narrative can happen in the telling or the showing of the story or in a combination of both. Because comics allows for visual-only content, the denouement of a narrative can be expressed in a single or several PANELS without TEXT or can take place through performative acts supported by STYLISTIC or FORMAL qualities, such as PAGE LAYOUT or COLOUR and style changes. The SERIALISED nature of COMIC BOOKS often breaks the narrative off before the climax and leaves the reader waiting on a cliff-hanger for the next issue where the climax and denouement will occur.

Rikke Platz Cortsen

### *References*

Butcher, S. H. (1902) *The Poetics of Aristotle*. London: Macmillan and Company.

## Depiction

Depiction is a unique type of visual REPRESENTATION defined by both seeing the MATERIALS that constitute the depiction, whilst also VISUALISING the object of the depiction. The experience of this phenomenon differs from both vision and visualisation (or visual imagining), in that it always involves an experience of simultaneously seeing a graphiotactic array, the surface on which it is inscribed, and the situation of vision, plus visualising the absent object of the depiction (Wollheim 1980: 11–14 and 205–226, Wollheim 1987: 21 and 46, Thomas 1999: 227). Robert Hopkins notes that the phenomenology of depiction "differs from that of other types of experience (…) due both to the thought of an absent object and to the awareness of the marked surface" (1998: 16). Hence, the experience of depiction has both a definitive structure (which distinguishes it from the structure of other types of visual representation) and a unique phenomenology, in that the essential dual experience of vision (seeing MARKS) and visualisation ("seeing-in" the object of depiction) is unlike any other experience of visual representation.

Simon Grennan

## *References*

Thomas, N. (1999) "Are theories of imagery theories of imagination? An active perception approach to conscious mental content," *Cognitive Science* 23, pp. 207–245.

Hopkins, R. (1998) *Picture, Image and Experience: A Philosophical Enquiry.* Cambridge: Cambridge University Press.

Wollheim, R. (1968) *Art and Its Objects.* Reprint 1980. Cambridge: Cambridge University Press.

Wollheim, R. (1987) *Painting as an Art.* Princeton: Princeton University Press.

## Design

Comics are rarely studied as design objects or in relation to the principles and processes of graphic design and PRODUCTION methods of PRINTING (exceptions include Farmer 2006; Gray 2017; Murray 2013; and Rogers 2006). The importance of design in production, before computers, has been noted by Ernesto Priego: "everything was put together as a coherent textual whole by a graphic and editorial designing team" (2014). Comics are a sub-category of magazine PUBLISHING and many of the roles, such as the art director, are identical. At Timely Comics (later Marvel Comics), editor Stan Lee fulfilled the function of art director before Sol Brodsky joined as production manager additionally producing graphics such as the mastheads for *The Fantastic Four* (1961–) and *The Avengers* (1963–) (Zimmerman 1985: 15–18). Similarly, Jan Shepard and Kevin O'Neill worked as art directors on many titles for the publisher IPC including *2000 AD* (1977–), producing mastheads for STORIES such as Judge Dredd as well as LAYOUTS (Bishop 2007: 21–22 and 40–41).

This process was revolutionised in the 1980s by the Apple Macintosh computer, with whole COMIC BOOKS such as *Shatter* (1985–1988) (Case and Athanas: 1986) being produced using this new TECHNOLOGY. By the end of the 1990s all design was digitally achieved.

Ian Horton

## *References*

Bishop, D. (2007) *Thrill-power Overload: 30 years of 2000 AD.* Oxford: Rebellion.

Case, J. and Athanas, C. (1986) *Shatter.* Chicago: First Comics.

Farmer, C. (2006) "Comic Book Color and the Digital Revolution," *International Journal of Comic Art* 8(2), pp. 330–346.

Gray, M. (2017) *Alan Moore, Out from the Underground: Cartooning, Performance, and Dissent.* London: Palgrave Macmillan.

Murray, P. R. (2013) "Behind the Panel: Examining Invisible Labour in the Comics Publishing Industry," *Publishing Research Quarterly* 29(4), pp. 336–343.

Rogers, M. C. (2006) "Understanding Production: The Stylistic Impact of Artisan and Industrial Methods," *International Journal of Comic Art* 8(1), pp. 509–517.

Priego, E. (2014) "Comic Books: Art Made in the Assembly Line," *Graphixia* 153, n.p. Available at: http://www.graphixia.ca/2014/02/comic-books-art-made-in-the-assembly-line/ [Accessed 5 August 2020].

Zimmerman, D. J. (1985) "Sol Brodsky Remembered," *Marvel Age* 1(22), pp. 12–25.

## DÉTOURNEMENT

Détournement is the SITUATIONIST practice of altering found objects in order to undermine their normal ideological meaning and replace it with a revolutionary social critique. The term derives from the French word "*détourner*," which means to divert or turn around (Zacarias 2020). Comics were one of the Situationists' preferred targets for détournement, along with ADVERTISEMENTS and Hollywood FILMS (Marcus 1989: 178–79).

Doug Singsen

## *References*

Marcus, G. (1989) *Lipstick Traces: A Secret History of the Twentieth Century*. Cambridge: Harvard University Press.

Zacarias, G. (2020) "Détournement in Language and the Visual Arts" in Zacarias, G. and Hemmens, A. (eds.) *The Situationist International: A Critical Handbook*. London: Pluto, pp. 214–235.

## Dialogic

As conceptualised by Mikhail Bakhtin, a cultural work is said to be dialogic if it exists in a state of overt dialogue with other works or with a broader cultural environment. When used in conjunction with its counter-concept, "monologic"—designating works which fail to acknowledge their own contexts, the HISTORY and GENRES in which they partake—dialogic typically carries positive connotations. Dialogism, the quality of being dialogic, differs from INTERTEXTUALITY both in the sense that dialogic texts invite future interactions in addition to engaging with previous texts and in the notion that dialogic works also interact with a range of social practices. The latter meaning implies that "dialogic" can be used to describe analytical frameworks for COMICS STUDIES that seek to locate the READING of comics within broader contexts and practices, from a pragmatic, AESTHETIC, or political standpoint (Hudson 2010; Pinti 2019). The MULTIMODALITY of comics, which connects them to the other Bakhtinian concept of POLYPHONY, means that this dialogic approach can also be applied at the level of the individual comics, to describe the interplay between the various SEMIOTIC systems at work in the MEDIUM, and between the various CREATORS involved (Christiansen 200: 118).

Nicolas Labarre

### *References*

Christiansen, H.-C. (2000) "Comics and Film: A Narrative Perspective" In Magnussen, A. and Christiansen, H.-C. (eds.) *Comics and Culture: Analytical and Theoretical Approaches to Comics*. Copenhagen: Museum Tusculanum Press, pp. 107–122.

Hudson, R. (2010) "The Derelict Fairground: A Bakhtinian Analysis of the Graphic Novel Medium," *CEA Critic* 72(3), pp. 35–49.

Pinti, D. (2019) "Bakhtinian dialogics. Comics Dialogics: Seeing voices in *The Vision*" in Smith, M., Brown, M., and Duncan, R. (eds.) *More Critical Approaches to Comics: Theories and Methods*. Abingdon: Routledge.

## Diegesis

Diegesis is now frequently used as a neologism for the STORYWORLD. Pascal Lefèvre describes diegesis in the comics REGISTER as "the fictive space in which the characters live and act (…) versus the extradiegetic space" of the world encompassing the story (2009: 157). This is a typical contemporary use. However, Plato defines diegesis as a MODE of REPRESENTATION that includes both NARRATOR and story, so that the act of telling itself is a prerequisite of the definition, relative to what is told, as nothing can be told that is not NARRATED (Plato 2008: 3.392c–398b). On the other hand, he describes MIMESIS as a mode where representations are made through simulation rather than telling and take place entirely in the present without a narrator. Because Plato's distinction arises from his theorisation of the difference between the registers of poetry and painting, Gérard Genette's exploration of the significant transformations that diegesis and mimesis have undergone since Plato, in terms of meaning and usage in different languages, is important in mapping the historical overview of the shifts in this DISCOURSE as it pertains to registers (Genette 1988: 18, 43, and 45).

Simon Grennan

### *References*

Genette, G. (1979) *Narrative Discourse Revisited*. Translated from French by J. E. Lewin, 1988. Ithaca: Cornell University Press.

Lefèvre, P. (2009) "The Construction of Space in Comics" in Heer, J. and Worcester, K. (eds.) *A Comics Studies Reader*. Jackson: University Press of Mississippi, pp. 157–162.

Plato (c. 375 BC) *Republic*. Translated from Greek by R. Waterfield, 2008. Oxford: Oxford University Press.

## Digital Comics

The term digital comics encompasses a broad spectrum of comics whose PRODUCTION and distribution involves the use of digital TECHNOLOGIES. Although a PRINT comic can be digitised and viewed on electronic devices, scholars generally agree that such comics would need to be "a 'new expression' of the original work, rather than the 'same expression' in a new (…) format" in order to be properly termed digital (Aggleton 2018: 5). Indeed, digital comics use digital tools and methods (hyperlinks, Scott McCloud's concept of the "infinite canvas" (2000), audio/video, interactive HTTP elements, etc.) in order to experiment with new ways of representing the defining features of the MEDIUM of comics: SPEECH BALLOONS, PANELS, GUTTERS, and so on, the predetermined TEMPORAL elements that compromise READERS' control over pacing (Goodbrey 2013; Daniels n.d.). In their use of digital technologies, digital comics inevitably blend with other digital MEDIA—notably ANIMATION and video GAMES—resulting in HYBRID FORMS that are difficult to reduce to a single medium. For this reason, digital comics, and especially those that employ SOUND and moving IMAGES, are often argued to "contradict comics' conception of space as representation of time—the 'conceptual fundament of the medium'" (Bukatman 2011: 134).

Josip Batinić

### *References*

Aggleton, J. (2018) "Defining digital comics: A British Library perspective," *Journal of Graphic Novels and Comics* 10(4), pp. 1–17.

Bukatman, S. (2011) "Online Comics and the Reframing of the Moving Image" in D. Harries (ed.) *The New Media Book*. London: BFI Publishing, pp. 133–143.

Daniels, E. C. (n.d.) "The Digital Comics Manifesto." *Screendiver*. Available at: http://screendiver.com/digital-comics-manifesto [Accessed 15 September 2019].

Goodbrey, D. (2013) "Digital Comics—New Tools and Tropes," *Studies in Comics* (4)1, pp. 185–198.

McCloud, S. (2000) *Reinventing Comics: How Imagination and Technology are Revolutionizing an Art Form*. New York: Paradox Press.

## Direct Market

Comics distribution changed dramatically in the 1970s and 1980s, resulting in the direct MARKET. Unlike traditional newsstand distribution where unsold products could be returned, this approach focused on specialty shops pre-ordering discounted titles that could not be returned—essentially a subscription model (Hatfield 2005: 22). This decreased the financial risks for PUBLISHERS during a period of industry instability. The direct market likely originated with secondary distribution to HEAD SHOPS developed for UNDERGROUND COMIX, although Gary Groth argued that the direct market was "the belated result of the pop-culture craze surrounding Marvel Comics from the late '60s and early '70s" (1983). Regardless, the direct market resulted in explosive specialty retail growth: by 1990 some 400 comic stores opened in the UK and 4000 in the US (Sabin 1996: 157). While it effectively siloed exposure and AUDIENCE, it propelled the rise of ALTERNATIVE COMICS and the industry economic bubble of the 1990s.

Josh R. Rose

## *References*

Groth, G. (1983) "What the Direct Sales Market Has Wrought, Part Two: The Comics Renaissance," *The Comics Journal* 85, pp. 8–11.

Hatfield, C. (2005) *Alternative Comics: An Emerging Literature*. Jackson: University Press of Mississippi.

Sabin, R. (1996) *Comics, Comix and Graphic Novels: A History of Comic Art*. London: Phaidon Press.

## Disability Comics

Disability comics is a GENRE under the larger umbrella of PATHOGRAPHICS, a term credited to Anne Hunsaker Hawkins in 1998 by Susan Merrill Squier (2015), and further defined as "narrative[s] of illness." It is important to note here that disability does not equate to ILLNESS, but there are INTERSECTIONS in embodied experiences. The history of this genre is embedded in LITERATURE and the medical humanities. The NARRATIVES are written as AUTOGRAPHICS, or by a family member, a caregiver, or medical personnel, and provide a source of knowledge of the experience of living *with* or *beside* disability. The growth of disability narratives is often collected under GRAPHIC MEDICINE, which provides an organising support network. The umbrella of medicine and the common story arc of treatment and recovery are counter to current disability studies DISCOURSE (Kolářová 2014) for disability is as much a part of life as ability and wellness, and the heroic narrative of "overcoming" undermines those who live with it. Kateřina Kolářová (2014) expands on Lauren Berlant's (2006) work in this area and prescribes making room for negativity and failure as generative conditions to be included in the collective cultural rhetoric. Jay Dolmage and Dale Jacobs (2016) wrote about the unique ability of comics to visually depict *crip time* defined as a different experience of time by those living with or caring for someone with a disability and in comics PANELS can be portrayed through the extension or shortening of TIME or through the lack of progress or resolution.

JoAnn Purcell

## *References*

Berlant, L. (2006) "Cruel Optimism," *differences: A Journal of Feminist Cultural Studies* 17(3), pp. 20–36.

Dolmage, J. and Jacobs, D. (2016) "Mutable Articulations: Disability Rhetorics and the Comics Medium" in Foss, C., Gray, J., and Whalen, Z. (eds.) *Disability in Comic Books and Graphic Narratives.* London: Palgrave Macmillan, pp. 14–28.

Kolářová, K. (2014) "The Inarticulate Post-Socialist Crip: On the Cruel Optimism of Neoliberal Transformations in the Czech Republic," *The Journal of Literary and Cultural Disability Studies* 8(3), pp. 263–280.

Squier, S. (2015) "The Uses of Graphic Medicine for Engaged Scholarship" in Czerwiec, M. K., Williams, I., Squier, S., Green, M., Myers, K., and Smith, S. (eds.) *Graphic Medicine Manifesto.* University Park: The Pennsylvania State University Press, pp. 41–66.

## Disability Studies

Disability studies is an area of interdisciplinary scholarly inquiry that gathers its methods and critical theory from sociology, health, anthropology, FEMINISM, QUEER and RACE studies, and the visual and performative ARTS (Gleeson 1999 and Snyder et al. 2002). Disability can be difficult to delineate, but is most often defined as physical, developmental, cognitive, and/or psychosocial impairments that can create challenges in the activities of daily living. Disability is also created by attitudinal biases, social conditions, and physical environments that restrict some bodies' full participation in society. Disability occurs at the juncture of expectation and function in the body and in the lived physical and psychosocial space. The VISUALISATION of the embodiment of disability in comics can make this FORM a vital source and method of scholarly inquiry. A foundational concept in disability studies is the mantra "nothing about us without us" ("Nothing About Us Without Us" 2004), as speaking for another can silence and re-inflict marginalisation and create a hierarchical difference.

JoAnn Purcell

## *References*

Gleeson, B. (1999) *Geographies of Disability.* Abingdon: Routledge.

Snyder, S. L., Brueggemann, B., Garland-Thomson, R. (2002) *Disability Studies: Enabling the Humanities.* New York: Modern Language Association Publishing.

"'Nothing About Us Without Us': Recognizing the Rights of People with Disabilities." (2004) *UN Chronicle Online Edition* XLI (4). Available at: https://web.archive.org/web/20070614173650/http://www.un.org/Pubs/chronicle/2004/issue4/0404p10.html [Accessed 17 August 2020].

## Discourse

In LINGUISTICS, discourse refers to any utterance longer than a sentence, and by extension to individual acts of communication, whether written or spoken. Following the work of POSTSTRUCTURALISTS, discourse also refers to a coherent system of utterances produced by an institution or a social body (Foucault 1969: 135–40). In the context of comics, examples such as "North American Comics Discourse" (Fischer 2010) or "industry discourse" refer to a range of significant utterances within specific spheres, construed in both cases as forming a coherent set of communicative acts, inscribed in a specific HISTORICAL and cultural context. In NARRATOLOGY, "narrative discourse" is commonly contrasted with the plot of the STORY, in a way which parallels the distinction between *SYUZHET* and *FABULA* for Russian formalists, describing the story as it is told by contrast with its underlying structure (Genette 1979: 26–27). This use builds on the notion that MODES of discourse or discourse modes (both translations of "mode du discours") can be organised to form a taxonomy of specific relationships between FORM and content, and are akin to other taxonomical categories, such as GENRES.

Nicolas Labarre

## *References*

Fischer, C. (2010) "Worlds within Worlds: Audiences, Jargon, and North American Comics Discourse," *Transatlantica: Revue d'études américaines/American Studies Journal*, n.p. Available at: http://journals.openedition.org/transatlantica/4919 [Accessed 8 May 2020].

Foucault, M. (1969) *Archaeology of Knowledge and the Discourse on Language*. Translated from French by A. M. Sheridan Smith, 1972. New York: Pantheon Books.

Genette, G. (1979) *Narrative Discourse: An Essay in Method*. Translated from French by J. E. Lewin, 1980. Ithaca: Cornell University Press.

## Distant Reading

Distant reading is the opposite of CLOSE READING. It uses processes of ABSTRACTION—including but not limited to quantification—to "[reframe] the scale of literary inquiry" (Underwood 2017: n.p.), analysing whole LITERARY fields or corpora rather than focusing on individual texts. Given how many COMIC BOOKS there are and how few of them constitute "plausible texts," comics seem well suited to this approach (Beaty and Woo 2016: 5–6). A distant reading may use methodological frameworks such as content analysis (Spiggle 1986; Peterson and Gerstein 2005; Cocca 2014) and corpus LINGUISTICS (Dunst et al. 2017; Cohn et al. 2019; Bateman et al. 2019). Insofar as they pose empirical questions about cultural texts, analyses of industry data, reviews and citations, READERS and AUDIENCES, and PARATEXTS such as advertisements or LETTER COLUMNS may also constitute a kind of distant reading. Given the MULTIMODAL nature of comic ART, scholars have been hampered by the need to code/annotate manually. However, experiments with crowdsourced annotations (Tufis and Ganascia 2018) and automated coding of visual elements (Douglass et al. 2011; Dunst and Hartel 2018) show promise.

Benjamin Woo

## *References*

Bateman, J. A., Veloso, F. O. D., and Lau, Y. L. (2019) "On the Track of Visual Style: A Diachronic Study of Page Composition in Comics and Its Functional Motivation," *Visual Communication*. Available at: https://doi.org/10.1177/1470357219839101 [Accessed 5 August 2020].

Beaty, B. and Woo, B. (2016) *The Greatest Comic Book of All Time: Symbolic Capital and the Field of American Comic Books*. London: Palgrave Macmillan.

Cohn, N., Axnér, J., Diercks, M., Yeh, R. and Pederson, K. (2019) "The Cultural Pages of Comics: Cross-Cultural Variation in Page Layouts," *Journal of Graphic Novels and Comics* 10(1), pp. 67–86.

Cocca, C. (2014) "The 'Broke Back Test': A Quantitative and Qualitative Analysis of Portrayals of Women in Mainstream Superhero Comics, 1993–2013," *Journal of Graphic Novels and Comics* 5(4), pp. 411–428.

Douglass, J., Huber, W. and Manovich, L. (2011) "Understanding Scanlation: How to Read One Million Fan-Translated Manga Pages," *Image [&] Narrative* 12(1), pp. 190–227.

Dunst, A. and Hartel, R. (2018) "The Quantitative Analysis of Comics: Towards a Visual Stylometry of Graphic Narrative" in Dunst, A., Laubrock, J., and Wildfeuer, J. (eds.) *Empirical Comics Research: Digital, Multimodal, and Cognitive Methods*. Abingdon: Routledge, pp. 43–61.

Dunst, A., Hartel, R., and Laubrock, J. (2017) "The Graphic Narrative Corpus (GNC): Design, Annotation, and Analysis for the Digital Humanities," *14th IAPR International Conference on Document Analysis and Recognition*, pp. 15–20. Available at: https://www.computer.org/csdl/proceedings-article/icdar/2017/3586d015/12OmNzZmZjy [Accessed 5 July 2020].

Peterson, B. E. and Gerstein, E. D. (2005) "Fighting and Flying: Archival Analysis of Threat, Authoritarianism, and the North American Comic Book," *Political Psychology* 26(6), pp. 887–904.

Spiggle, S. (1986) "Measuring Social Values: A Content Analysis of Sunday Comics and Underground Comix," *Journal of Consumer Research* 13(1), pp. 100–113.

Tufis, M. and Ganascia, J.-G. (2018) "Crowdsourcing Comics Annotations" in Dunst, A., Laubrock, J., and Wildfeuer, J. (eds.) *Empirical Comics Research: Digital, Multimodal, and Cognitive Methods*. Abingdon: Routledge, pp. 85–103.

Underwood, T. (2017) "A Genealogy of Distant Reading," *Digital Humanities Quarterly* 11(2), n.p. Available at: http://www.digitalhumanities.org/dhq/vol/11/2/000317/000317.html [Accessed 15 July 2020].

## Documentary

Documentary extends the claim that its REPRESENTATIONS refer to actual and HISTORICAL events and persons, thus distinguishing it from a fictional REGISTER that might include environments and characterisation with real-world counterpoints. In COMICS STUDIES the term documentary has emerged in response to the notable expansion in comics work that uses WITNESSING as methodology and presents "encounter" as a prominent feature. However, documentary can also describe the process of using ARCHIVAL sources to retrospectively construct a NARRATIVE. Documentary comics have been situated in relation to a range of historical precursors, including but not limited to illustrated JOURNALISM. Jeff Adams' 2008 account privileges the agenda of social change characterising nineteenth-century social REALISM. Hillary Chute (2016) constructs a GENEALOGY of DRAWING as a tool of documentary witnessing that includes Goya's *The Disasters of War* (1810–1820). Other approaches have drawn on theories of audio-visual documentary (Lefèvre 2011; Mickwitz 2016). The umbrella term documentary captures concerns shared by comics journalism, BIOGRAPHY, AUTOBIOGRAPHY, and comics performing advocacy: narrative construction and notions of authenticity, credibility and claims to truth, questions of intent, AFFECT and the ETHICS of representation.

Nina Mickwitz

### *References*

Adams, J. (2008) *Documentary Graphic Novels and Social Realism.* New York: Peter Lang.

Chute, H. (2016) *Disaster Drawn: Visual Witness, Comics, and Documentary Form.* Cambridge: Harvard University Press.

Lefèvre, P. (2011) "The various modes of documentary comics" in Grunewald, D. (ed.) *Der doumentarische Comic—Reportage und Biographie.* Berlin: Bachmann Verlag, pp. 50–60.

Mickwitz, N. (2016) *Documentary Comics: Graphic Truth-telling in a Skeptical Age.* London: Palgrave Macmillan.

## Double Face-Out

Coined by Rosalind Krauss in 1999, double face-out is a MISE-EN-SCÈNE that is associated with the comics REGISTER and the PHOTONOVEL, in which the visually REPRESENTED exchange between two characters conflates the time in which each character acts and reacts to the other. Hence, "both characters appear together, the instigator somewhat in the background looking at the reactor who tends to fill the foreground, but, back turned to the other, is also facing forward out of the frame. (…) [The] double face-out presents us with the mannerism of a dialogue in which one of the two participants is not looking at the other" (Krauss 1999: 300).

Simon Grennan

### *References*

Krauss, R. (1999) "Reinventing the Medium," *Critical Inquiry* 25(2), pp. 289–305.

## Drawing

Drawing encompasses a wide range of types of activity (as a verb), object (as a noun), TECHNOLOGY, and environment. It is a group of types of visual REPRESENTATION. Drawing always devolves to MARK making, although the etymologies of the word in different languages indicate a wide variety of ideas (including a shared root of the English word "drag" as distinct from the meaning "to arrange" in French). Central to theorisations of drawing are relationships between actions of the body and the mark, described as TRACE and INDEX (Grennan 2017: 15) and autography (Rosand 2002: 61, Gardner 2011: 64). The concept of the representation of a unique subject by the drawn mark gives rise to methods of STYLISTIC analysis, focusing on types of formal resemblance between marks and on the MATERIAL and social ecology of their PRODUCTION (Lawrence 2008; Munsterberg 2009: 21–27). Of similar significance are theorisations of drawing systems in which the topological location of the mark is guided by strict visual correspondence to the relative functions and items of an independent system, such as WRITING and SPATIAL PROJECTION SYSTEMS, theorisations of the phenomenon of DEPICTION and of the significance of the COLOUR of the mark (Poirier 1987: 57).

Simon Grennan

## *References*


Gardner, J. (2011) "Storylines," *SubStance* 40(1), pp. 53–69.

Grennan, S. (2017) *A Theory of Narrative Drawing*. London: Palgrave Macmillan.

Lawrence, P. (2008) "The Morelli Method and the Conjectural Paradigm as Narrative Semiotic," *Watermark* 2, pp. 103–116.

Munsterberg, M. (2009) *Writing About Art*. Scotts Valley: CreateSpace.

Poirier, M. (1987) "The 'disegno-colore' controversy reconsidered," *Explorations in Renaissance Culture* 13, pp. 52.

Rosand, D. (2002) *Drawing Acts: Studies in graphic expression and representation*. Cambridge: Cambridge University Press.

## Ecocriticism

Ecocriticism refers to a set of CULTURAL THEORIES and INTERDISCIPLINARY work that shares "a commitment to environmentality" (Buell 2005: 11). While the term emerged in academic DISCOURSE in the 1970s, the concern with the REPRESENTATION of the natural environment can be traced to earlier works in cultural theory (ibid.: 13). According to Cheryll Glotfelty, these writings in ecocriticism share "the fundamental premise that human culture is connected to the physical world, affecting it and affected by it" (1996: xix). In turn, various contributions to ecocriticism also question the seeming opposition between nature and human culture that characterises "anthropocentric dominance over the earth" (Zapf 2016: 82). Environmental critiques of this divide emphasise the need to rethink the relation between nature and culture in order to challenge the "commonsensical assumption that the world exists as a background for the human subject" (Alaimo 2016: 1). Rather, as proposed by Donna Haraway, the human is not separate from nor central to ecology, but is always entangled in a "becoming-with" worldly matter, as "human beings are with and of the earth, and the biotic and abiotic powers of this earth are the main story" (2016: 55). While still a nascent area of research in COMICS STUDIES, current scholarship has reconsidered the use of the FUNNY ANIMAL and the theory of ASSEMBLAGE in light of the environment (Bealer 2014).

Freija Camps

### *References*

Alaimo, S. (2016) *Exposed: Environmental Politics and Pleasures in Posthuman Times*. Minneapolis: University of Minnesota Press.

Bealer, A. H. (2014) *Graphic Environments: Performing Ecocriticism at the Confluence of Image and Text*. PhD. University of Utah. Available at: https://collections.lib.utah.edu/details?id=196484 [Accessed 5 July 2020].

Buell, L. (2005) *The Future of Environmental Criticism: Environmental Crisis and Literary Imagination*. Oxford: Blackwell.

Glotfelty, C. (1996) "Introduction: Literary Studies in an Age of Environmental Crisis" in Glotfelty, C. and Fromm, H. (eds.) *The Ecocriticism Reader*. Athens: University of Georgia Press, pp. xv–xxxvii.

Haraway, D. J. (2016) *Staying with the Trouble: Making Kin in the Chthulucene*. Durham: Duke University Press.
Zapf, H. (2016) *Literature as Cultural Ecology: Sustainable Texts*. London: Bloomsbury Academic.

## Education

Education is a broad-based term in COMICS STUDIES that can be applied in several contexts. The term "comics in education" refers to the use of educational or trade comics in a classroom setting, and the broader discussion of their efficacy in PEDAGOGICAL practice. Comics have long been recognised for their ability to motivate students (Yang 2003). Their rise as a tool for literacy development has led to an ongoing discussion of their full potential, not just to simplify complex material for students, but to show how they themselves "can articulate ideas and meaning through the use of the visual" (Sousanis 2019: 37). "Educational comics" can either refer to comics developed by educational PUBLISHERS for the classroom or to comics published for educational or training purposes, such as those used for medical or military training (which are termed APPLIED COMICS), with the idea that "an abundant amount of research support[s] the contention that presenting visuals and text together positively affects student learning" (Muzumdar 2016: 1). When published by an education press, comics are often levelled, curricularly aligned, and designed to meet standards and expectations for use with young readers to which trade publications are not bound. Such standards vary depending on the educational MARKETS for which the works are developed. A "comics educator" is loosely defined as a teacher who is intentional about including comics or graphic novels in their pedagogical practice.

Glen Downey

### *References*

Muzumdar, J. (2016) "An Overview of Comic Books as an Educational Tool and Their Implications for Pharmacy," *Innovations in Pharmacy* 7(4), pp. 1–10.
Sousanis, N. (2019) "Articulating Ideas and Meaning through the Use of Comics," *Learning Landscapes* 12, pp. 33–38.
Yang, G. (2003) "Strengths of Comics in Education," *Comics in Education*, n.p. Available at: https://www.humblecomics.com/comicsedu/strengths.html [Accessed 13 April 2020].

## Etching

Etching is a PRINTING technique for the detailed REPRODUCTION of IMAGES used from the sixteenth century onwards but gaining prominence in the seventeenth century. The basic principle involves the ARTIST cutting the image on the metal plate by working through an acid-resistant wax-based additional ground, with the subsequent application of acid leaving only the incisions. These grooves are then filled with ink, which is transferred to paper via pressure from a printing press (MacLean 2012). The process parallels engraving, whereby the artist works directly onto the metal using a burin or sharp precision cutter. The reproduction of images through the TECHNOLOGY of etching also followed on from manuscript ILLUMINATIONS and then woodcut ILLUSTRATIONS (a carving made directly into a block of wood that was then inked) before being largely superseded by LITHOGRAPHY. Illustrations of this type were key to early printed proto-comics (Kunzle 1973), or picture NARRATIVES. Examples include individual illustrations and CARICATURES, but also the TEXT/image culture of the emblem book (Grove 2005), certain "*images d'Épinal*," and discrete series of etched images that together tell a STORY, such as Jacques Callot's *Les Grandes Misères de la guerre* (1633).

Laurence Grove

### *References*

Grove, L. (2005) *Text/Image Mosaics in French Culture: Emblems and Comic Strips.* Aldershot: Ashgate/Routledge.

Kunzle, D. (1973) *History of the Comic Strip, Volume 1: The Early Comic Strip 1450–1825.* Berkeley: University of California Press.

MacLean, R. (2012) "Book Illustration: Engraving and Etching." *University of Glasgow Library Blog.* Available at: https://universityofglasgowlibrary.wordpress.com/2012/08/28/book-illustration-engraving-and-etching/ [Accessed 3 August 2020].

## Ethics

Ethics, also known as moral philosophy, governs right or wrong behaviour based on agreed-upon principles in specific contexts. Ethics has a foundational but fluid place in the comics industry. The MEDIUM lends itself to unfettered self-expression and as such often falls outside of local ethics or federal or international laws. HISTORICALLY, the voluntary COMICS

CODE of the 1950s outlined rules for (North American) COMIC BOOK PUBLISHERS in reaction to a public outcry that comics were ruining children's minds (Nyberg 1998). Society outgrew the Code and it was dismantled in 2011. Ethics also needs to be considered when telling the STORIES of others, as consent from the SUBJECT(S) can be complicated by their vulnerability, their cognition, or by a power imbalance. Ethics can also extend to the READER as well. Arthur Frank (1995) explores the ethics of witness and testimony specifically in terms of illness. He defines testimony not only as one of seeing, but also of being with illness. Comics can bridge the gap between CREATOR and reader, not only by combining IMAGES and TEXT, but also by mixing in the reader's perspective as a participant.

JoAnn Purcell

## *References*

Frank, A. W. (1995) *The Wounded Storyteller: Body, Illness, and Ethics.* Chicago: The University of Chicago Press.

Nyberg, A. K. (1998) *Seal of Approval: The Origins and History of the Comics Code.* Jackson: University Press of Mississippi.

## Ethnicity

Max Weber provided a succinct definition for "ethnic groups" in 1922 as "human groups (other than kinship groups) who cherish a belief in the common origins of such a kind that it provides a basis for the creation of 'community'" (1978: 364). From this, the understanding of ethnicity as a type of social IDENTITY arose. Often confused as synonymous with RACE, ethnicity differs as members of an ethnic group are defined by their shared "origin," which can be cultural, racial, geographical, HISTORICAL, and/or LINGUISTIC. Mass MEDIA like comics are a vessel for ethnographic ideology with the potential to STEREOTYPE nuanced ethnic cultures into exotic "others" (Ibrahim 2011: 12). Comics scholars must take this potentiality into account when examining texts about ethnic groups. INTERSECTIONALITY provides one critical framework for contextualising ethnicity by understanding its nuances and societal expressions through its relationship to other social identities like GENDER, CLASS, SEXUALITY, and NATIONALITY. An increasing body of scholarship is exploring how texts and the comics FORM itself can be used as EDUCATIONAL tools and facilitate DISCOURSE between different ethnic groups (Norton 2003; Juneau and Sucharov 2010; Chantal 2013).

Rachel A. Davis

## *References*

Chantal, C. M. (2013) “Panels for Peace: Contributions of Israeli and Palestinian Comics to Peace-Building,” *Quest: Issues in Contemporary Jewish History* 5, pp. 205–231.

Ibrahim, V. (2011) ”Ethnicity” in Caliendo, S. M. and McIlwain, C. D. (eds.) *The Routledge Companion to Race and Ethnicity*. Abingdon: Routledge, pp. 12–20.

Juneau, T. and Sucharov, M. (2010) “Narratives in Pencil: Using Graphic Novels to Teach Israeli-Palestinian Relations,” *International Studies Perspectives* 11(2), pp. 172–183.

Norton, B. (2003) “The motivating power of comic books: Insights from Archie comic readers,” *The Reading Teacher* 57(2), pp. 140–147.

Weber, M. (1922) “Race Relations” in Runciman, W. G. (ed.) *Max Weber: Selections in Translation*. Translated from German by E. Matthews, 1978. Cambridge: Cambridge University Press, pp. 359–369.

## Exegesis

Exegesis is originally a term used in the context of the Bible, referring to the close analysis and subsequent interpretation of a text. It is now common for it to be used more broadly, being applied to the READING of HISTORICAL, philosophical, or LITERARY documents. Exegesis can follow a number of approaches, exploring for example the relevance of the background of the AUTHOR, the social and chronological context, LINGUISTIC expression, or psychology-based connotations. In the case of comics, the HYBRID nature of the FORM adds an extra dimension to any exegesis, as this is likely to include not just TEXT, but also IMAGE, and the interaction of the two. Examples of landmark studies in the exegesis of comics include: Barthélemy Amengual's CLOSE READING of José Cabrero Arnal's *Pif le Chien* (1955), as one of the first book-length studies to offer a close reading of a comic; Fredric Wertham's controversial interpretation of the negative psychological effect of comics upon children (1954); Umberto Eco's analysis of the duality of Superman (1972), placing the character in a popular literary and social context; Thierry Groensteen's SEMIOTIC analysis of the workings of comics (1999); and Trina Robbins's presentation of comics from a FEMINIST standpoint (1999).

Laurence Grove

## *References*

Amengual, B. (1955) *Le Petit Monde de Pif le chien: Essai sur un 'comic' français.* Algiers: Travail et Culture d'Algérie.

Eco, U. (1972) "The Myth of Superman," *Diacritics* 2(1), pp. 14–22.

Groensteen, T. (1999) *The System of Comics.* Translated from French by B. Beaty and N. Nguyen, 2007. Jackson: University Press of Mississippi.

Robbins, T. (1999) *From Girls to Grrrlz: A History of Female Comics from Teens to Zines.* San Francisco: Chronicle Books.

Wertham, F. (1954) *Seduction of the Innocent: The Influence of Comic Books on Today's Youth.* New York: Rinehart.

## Experimental Comics

Experimental comics find new ways to create expression, and in the process test the CONVENTIONS and boundaries of comics. The experimentation can be applied in the visual STYLE, FORMAL elements, NARRATION, or MATERIAL and format. Creators, such as the French experimental comics collective Oubapo ("Ouvroir de bande dessinée potentielle"), which was inspired by the example set by the OuLiPo movement (Oubapo 1997), often set themselves deliberate CONSTRAINTS (Madden 2005), such as restricting the number or shape of PANELS; limiting the TEXT they include; or ensuring that a comic will be legible when READ in different directions. A further constraint is only using a single IMAGE, repeated in every panel, with only the text changing, or no images at all. Experimental comics can be challenging to read. However, degrees of experimentation differ, and some mainstream comics successes can also be seen as highly experimental; see, for example, Alan Moore and J. H. Williams III's *Promethea #2* (2005) for non-linear narration and the disintegration of PAGE LAYOUTS; Richard McGuire's *Here* (2014) for consistent use of a single SPACE and POINT OF VIEW; and Chris Ware's *Building Stories* (2012) and Jason Shiga's *Meanwhile* (2010) for making READERS ASSEMBLE a narrative themselves.

Barbara Postema

## *References*

Madden, M. (2005) *99 Ways to Tell a Story: Exercises in Style.* New York: Chamberlain Bros.

Oubapo (1997) *OuPus 1.* Paris: L'Association.

## Fable

The term fable is often applied to any traditional or widely known STORY; such is the case with Thomas Bullfinch's *The Age of Fable* (1867), which retells MYTHS and LEGENDS. More technically it refers to a story whose primary function is to impart a moral lesson to its AUDIENCE, a lesson that is often made explicit in the conclusion; this is the case with the famous collection by Aesop (c. 620–564 BC). These stories can be transmitted in any MEDIUM, including oral tradition and COMIC BOOKS, and are usually very short (Hansen 2002: 41). Fables were ILLUSTRATED in an approximation of the comic format as early as 1905 (Kuo 2013). They often combine simple plots with one-dimensional characters—commonly depicted as ANIMALS—to foreground the relationships and thus provide little room for alternative interpretations. In comic books, fables are perhaps most prominent in the series *Fables*, written by Bill Willingham (2002–2015). Willingham's work shows the broad range of tale types encompassed by the term; the characters of the series are taken mostly from LITERARY fairy tales and oral tradition.

Daniel Peretti

### *References*

Hansen, W. (2002) *Ariadne's Thread: A Guide to International Tales Found in Classical Literature*. Ithaca: Cornell University Press.

Kuo, S. (2013) "The Art of Making Animals Laugh: Benjamin Rabier's Comic-Illustration of *Les Fables de La Fontaine*," *Newphilologus* 97, pp. 21–33.

## Fabula

A fabula is a STORY in its widest sense. For Russian formalists, the fabula was the "aggregate of mutually related events reported in the work" (Tomashevsky 2012: 49). These did not have to form causal or chronological sense and could extend beyond the boundaries of the work's representative field. The fabula was considered secondary or as "raw material" (Selden et al. 1997: 35) forming a backdrop to the emotional events of the SYUZHET. Due to the later revisions of Gerard Genette (1980) and FILM NARRATOLOGISTS such as David Bordwell (1985: 49–57), contemporary usage affords the fabula higher regard and wider scope: it is "external to any actual work" (Gaudreault and Marion 2004: 61) and exists within our mind collected through the action of the syuzhet, or is known prior to its realisation. Fabula is derived from the Latin for "a telling." Hence, a story is sometimes considered to have the capacity to root various "tellings" across different media (Gaudreault and Marion 2004: 67, Flores-Silva and Cartwright 2019: 391). This expanded definition is particularly important in comics because it gives us a sense of narrative coherence despite the discrepancies and manipulations of TIME, which are particular to the comics form (Cook 2017 17–26, Pratt 2009).

Geraint D'Arcy

## *References*


Bordwell, D. (1985) *Narrative in the Fiction Film.* Madison: University of Wisconsin Press.

Cook, R. T. (2017) "Narrative, Time Travel and Richard McGuire's *Here*" in Ursini, F., Mahmutovic, A., and F. Bramlett (eds.) *Visions of the Future in Comics: International Perspectives.* Jefferson: McFarland, pp. 12–30.

Flores-Silva, D. and Cartwright, K. (2019) "Fabula," *New Literary History* 50(3), pp. 387–391.

Gaudreault, A. and Marion, P. (2004) "Transécriture and Narrative Mediatics: The Stakes of Intermediality" in Stam, R. and Raengo, A. (eds.) *A Companion to Literature and Film.* Oxford: Blackwell, pp. 58–70.

Genette, G. (1979) *Narrative Discourse: An Essay in Method.* Translated from French by J. E. Lewin, 1980. Ithaca: Cornell University Press.

Pratt, J. H. (2009) "Narrative in Comics," *Journal of Aesthetics and Art Criticism* 67(1), pp. 107–117.

Selden, R., Widdowson, P., and Brooker, P. (1997) *A Reader's Guide to Contemporary Literary Theory.* London: Prentice Hall.

Tomashevsky, B. (2012) "Thematics" in Lemon, L. T., Reis, M. J., and Morson, G. S. (eds.) *Russian Formalist Criticism: Four Essays.* Lincoln: University of Nebraska Press, pp. 46–64.

## Fairy Tales

Commonly defined as children's STORIES about magical beings, fairy tales, related to FOLKLORE and MYTH, have travelled across cultures over time. Regarding ADAPTATIONS created for children, Chris Duffy's (2013) anthology comic is representative. Fairy tales may also engage adult READERS with their consideration of issues of SEXUALITY and morality, as exemplified by Bill Willingham's *Fables* (2002–2015), which incorporates characters from a number of fairy tales. Marina Warner (2014) is a key theorist in relation to how these tales reflect changing social concerns, behaviours, and contexts through retelling. Warner (1995) also analyses who tells the tales and how, considering FILM alongside traditional oral storytelling. This is not the only approach to these tales, however. Bruno Bettelheim (1976), for instance, analysed them in terms of Freudian PSYCHOANALYSIS and was concerned with how they might help children understand problems such as separation anxiety and sibling rivalries. This work is seen as problematic but still represents an important way of thinking about fairy tales and, in particular, children's responses to them. Another key approach is to look at the origins of these tales, as exemplified by Jack Zipes (2013) who did so via engagement with cognitive science and evolutionary theory, amongst other fields.

Mel Gibson

### *References*

Bettelheim, B. (1976) *The Uses of Enchantment: The Meaning and Importance of Fairy Tales*. London: Thames and Hudson.

Warner, M. (1995) *From the Beast to the Blonde: On Fairy Tales and Their Tellers*. New York: Vintage.

Warner, M. (2014) *Once Upon a Time: A Short History of the Fairy Tale*. Oxford: Oxford University Press.

Zipes, J. (2013) *The Irresistible Fairy Tale: The Cultural and Social History of a Genre*. Princeton: Princeton University Press.

## Fanboy/Fangirl

Fanboy/fangirl describes an extreme fan who exhibits "excessive interest and inappropriate emotional attachment" to a particular character, ARTIST, WRITER, GENRE, or PUBLISHER of COMIC BOOKS (McCracken 2010). Harry McCracken (2010) suggests that the term arose from the conflict between comics fans and SUPERHERO fans. Fanboy can be a derogatory term that implies they are cultural dupes in their unquestioning obsession and CHILDISHNESS. Alternatively, it has been adopted as a badge of honour by some fans. In an early study, that did not account for the internet, Matthew Pustz (1999) analysed the ways the term as a concept was perceived and used within FANDOM. The fluid uses of it are explored by Simon Locke (2012) who revisits earlier studies of fanboys to argue that their own use of the term challenges "the downgrading of their cultural activity" and enables them to articulate authenticity (835). The use of fanboy ignores the activities of fangirls. Male academics are accused of favouring fanboy and industrial practices and excluding the significance of fangirls in the HISTORY of and practices of fandom and fan production (Scott 2011). The rise in ADAPTATIONS of superhero comics in TRANSMEDIA universes led to increasing cultural influence of this subworld in comic book fandom.

Joan Ormrod

### *References*

Locke, S. (2012) "'Fanboy' as a revolutionary category," *Participations* 9(2), pp. 835–854.

McCracken, H. (2010) "Fanboy! The Strange True Story of the Tech World's Favorite Put-Down." *Technologizer: A Smarter Take on Tech*, 17 May 2010. Available at: https://www.technologizer.com/2010/05/17/fanboy/ [Accessed 23 April 2020].

Pustz, M. (1999) *Comic Book Culture: Fanboys and True Believers.* Jackson: University Press of Mississippi.

Scott, S. (2011) *Revenge of the Fanboy: Convergence Culture and the Politics of Incorporation.* PhD. University of Southern California. Available at: http://digitallibrary.usc.edu/cdm/ref/collection/p15799coll127/id/439159 [Accessed 15 July 2020].

## Fandom

Fandom refers to the cultural domain of AUDIENCES that actively group around existing fiction, including television, FILM, and comics. Popular imagery surrounding FANS tends to depict the fan as deviant, tragic, or violent (Bailey 2005). These negative depictions were argued against by the first scholars of fandom, who explored its creative and social elements, and its subversion of POPULAR CULTURE (Jenkins 1992; Bacon-Smith 1992; and Grossberg 1992). The RECEPTION of fans adds to existing STORYWORLDS and can be seen as productive, AFFECTIVE, and critical (Lamerichs 2018 and Hills 2002). Particularly in comics fandom, fans widely engage in MATERIAL and visual fan practices, such as COSPLAY and COLLECTING (Woo 2018). Through active consumption, READERS become producers, and some even create their own independent comics, thereby adding new voices to the established industry. From a socio-political PERSPECTIVE, comic producers profit from this free LABOUR of fans (Stanfill 2019). The cultures of fans are not only positive. Gate-keeping is common, as well as instances of sexism (Scott 2019) and RACISM (Pande 2018). Fandom is an umbrella term that captures many cultures, communities, platforms, and practices (Click and Scott 2017 and Booth 2018). To study fans means to look at these local instances and expressions.

Nicolle Lamerichs

### *References*

Bacon-Smith, C. (1992) *Enterprising Women: Television Fandom and the Creation of Popular Myth.* University Park: The University of Pennsylvania Press.

Bailey, S. (2005) *Media Audiences and Identity: Self-construction in the Fan Experience.* London: Palgrave Macmillan.

Booth, P. (ed.) (2018) *A Companion to Media Fandom and Fan Studies.* Hoboken: Wiley-Blackwell.

Click, M. A. and Scott, S. (eds.) (2017) *The Routledge Companion to Media Fandom.* Abingdon: Routledge.

Grossberg, L. (1992) "Is there a Fan in the House? The Affective Sensibility of Fandom" in Lewis, L. (ed.) *The Adoring Audience: Fan Culture and Popular Media.* Abingdon: Routledge, pp. 50–67.

Hills, M. (2002) *Fan cultures.* Abingdon: Routledge.
Jenkins, H. (1992) *Textual Poachers: Television Fans and Participatory Culture.* Abingdon: Routledge.
Lamerichs, N. (2018) *Productive Fandom: Intermediality and Affective Reception in Fan Cultures.* Amsterdam: Amsterdam University Press.
Pande, R. (2018) *Squee from the Margins: Fandom and Race.* Iowa City: University of Iowa Press.
Scott, S. (2019) *Fake Geek Girls: Fandom, Gender, and the Convergence Culture Industry.* New York: New York University Press.
Stanfill, M. (2019) *Exploiting Fandom: How the Media Industry Seeks to Manipulate Fans.* Iowa City: University of Iowa Press.

## Fantasy

Fantasy is both a sub-GENRE of speculative fiction and a strategy of NARRATION or WORLD-building that presents obvious, often magical or supernatural divergences from common knowledge concerning the real world (Hume 1984). There are no absolute rules for distinguishing fantasy from other speculative genres, such as SCIENCE FICTION, HORROR, or fairytales. Rather, fantasy is usually recognised as fantasy by genre-typical anti-REALIST features, such as the introduction of secondary worlds, substitution of creative impossibilities for scientific possibilities, and a sense of wonder or estrangement evoked in the protagonist and/or the READER (Attebery 1992: 11–14, 106–107, Mendlesohn 2008; Tolkien 1983). As the word "imagination" suggests, fantasy and visual expression are closely intertwined, and (series of) DRAWINGS remain the easiest way of sharing imagery that only exists in one's mind (Tolkien 1983). Indeed, many foundational comics from Winsor McCay's *Little Nemo in Slumberland* (1905–1927) to Osamu Tezuka's main works (1982–1989) are classifiable as fantasy. Moreover, as comics rarely strive for photorealism, STYLISTIC choices in visual expression can make even comics based on real life appear fantastical, for example, Art Spiegelman's *Maus* (1980–1991) (Todorov 1973; Varis 2019, 88–89).

Essi Varis

## *References*

Attebery, B. (1992) *Strategies of Fantasy.* Bloomington: Indiana University Press.

Hume, K. (1984) *Fantasy and Mimesis. Responses to Reality in Western Literature.* Abingdon: Routledge.

Mendlesohn, F. (2008) *Rhetorics of Fantasy.* Middletown: Wesleyan University Press.

Todorov, T. (1970) *The Fantastic: A Structural Approach to a Literary Genre.* Translated from French by R. Howard, 1973. Ithaca: Cornell University Press.

Tolkien, J. R. R. (1983) "On Fairy-Stories" in Tolkien, C. (ed.) *The Monsters and the Critics and Other Essays.* London: George Allen and Unwin, pp. 109–161.

Varis, E. (2019) "Alien Overtures. Speculating About Nonhuman Experiences with Comic Book Characters" in Karkulehto, S., Koistinen, A.-K., and Varis, E. (eds.) *Reconfiguring Human, Nonhuman and Posthuman in Literature and Culture.* Abingdon: Routledge, pp. 79–107.

## Fanzine

Fanzines, like ZINES of all types, are SELF-PUBLISHED magazines created by and for special interest groups. The earliest fanzines emerged out of SCIENCE FICTION FANDOM in America in the 1930s and included both science fiction and comics as topics (Schelly 2010: 3, Sabin 1993: 63, 174–175, Triggs 2010: 17). English language fanzines dedicated to comics first appeared in the 1950s, but the 1960s and 1970s saw a boom with the launch of many titles such as *Alter Ego* (1961–), *Comic Media News* (1973–1980), *The Comic Reader* (1961–1984), *Ka-Pow* (1967–1968), and *Xero* (1960–1963) (Goulart 1991: 313–317, Sabin 1993: 63–64, 174–175, Schelly 2010: 3–12). These contained articles about comics, CREATOR interviews, INDICES of COLLECTIBLE comics, and COMIC STRIPS, ILLUSTRATIONS, and short stories by FANS themselves, many of whom went on to work in the COMIC BOOK profession (Sabin 1993: 63–64, Schelly 2010: 6–7). In Europe fanzines such as *Giff Wiff* (1962–1967) and *Phenix* (1966–1977) in France and *¡Bang! Fanzine* *de los tebeos* (1968–1977) in Spain were launched in the 1960s with the expressed aim of raising the status of comics (Grove 2013: 230–240, Valencia-García 2018: 17–18). Fanzines were the wellspring of JOURNALISM and criticism about comics with some such as *Alter Ego* and *The Comics Journal* (1977–) making the transition to regular magazines in terms of PRODUCTION values and distribution (Sabin 1993: 85, Schelly 2010: 126–30).

Ian Horton

## *References*

Goulart, R. (1991) *Over 50 Years of American Comic Books*. Lincolnwood: Publications International, Ltd.

Grove, L. (2010) *Comics in French: The European Bande Dessinée in Context*. New York: Berghahn Books.

Sabin, R. (1993) *Adult Comics: An Introduction*. Abingdon: Routledge.

Triggs, T. (2010) *Fanzines: The DIY Revolution*. London: Thames and Hudson.

Schelly, B. (2010) *Founders of Comics Fandom*. Jefferson: McFarland.

Valencia-García, L. D. (2018) "Tintin in the *Movida madrilène*: Gender and Sexuality in the Punk Comic Book Zine Scene," *European Comic Art* 11(2), pp. 12–33.

## Feminism

Several waves of feminism have intersected with comics, sometimes represented and debated within titles, sometimes co-opted by feminism. Regarding the latter, second-wave feminism adopted Wonder Woman as an icon when Gloria Steinem put her on the cover of the first issue of feminist flagship *Ms* in 1972 (Ormrod 2018: 545). In comics, the second wave appeared in mainstream titles such as Gerry Conway and John Buscema's *Ms Marvel* (1977–1979), where the very title showed an engagement with feminism, albeit in a rather constrained way (Gibson 2015). Later comics, especially by women creators engaged with AUTOBIOGRAPHY, tend to explore issues in a way that is in line with the notion of plural feminisms, rather than a singular variant dominated by Western middle-CLASS white women. INTERSECTIONALITY (Collins and Bilge 2016) can be seen across a number of comic GENRES, both fiction and non-fiction. Sana Amanat, Gwendolyn Willow Wilson, and Adrian Alphona's *Ms Marvel* (2014–) is also significant in relation to REPRESENTATIONS of intersectional feminism via the adoption of the title by Kamala Khan, a young Pakistani-American Muslim. Her admiration for the previous Ms Marvel, Carol Danvers, now Captain Marvel, is explored in the comic (Wilson et al. 2016), but is also interrogated, and the characters can be seen as representing differing generational approaches to feminisms (Gibson 2018).

Mel Gibson

## *References*

Amanat, S. and Wilson, G. W. et al. (2014) *Ms Marvel.* New York: Marvel Comics.

Collins, P. H. and Bilge, S. (2016) *Intersectionality.* Cambridge: Polity Press.

Conway, G. and Bushema, J. et al. (1977–1979) *Ms Marvel.* New York: Marvel Comics.

Gibson, M. (2015) "Who does she think she is? Female comic-book characters, second-wave feminism, and feminist film theory" in Gibson, M., Huxley, D., and Ormrod, J. (eds.) (2015) *Superheroes and Identities* Abingdon: Routledge, pp. 135–146.

Gibson, M. (2018) "'Yeah. I think there still is hope.' Ms Marvel: Youth, Ethnicity, Faith, Feminism and Fandom" in Goodrum, M., Prescott, T., and Smith, P. (eds.) *Gender and the Superhero Narrative* Abingdon: Routledge, pp. 23–44.

Ormrod, J. (2018) "Wonder Woman 1987–1990: The Goddess, the Iron Maiden and the Sacralisation of Consumerism," *Journal of Graphic Novels and Comics* 9(6), pp. 540–544.

Wilson, G. W., Alphona, A., Andolpho, M., and Miyazawa, T. (2016) *Ms. Marvel Volume 6: Civil War II.* New York: Marvel Worldwide, Inc.

## Fic

Fic is an abbreviation of "fanfic" or "FAN fic," which in turn is an abbreviation of "fan fiction." The term initially was coined in 1944 and meant "fiction about fans," but was later used to describe fiction WRITTEN by fans that take place within popular fictional WORLDS, which remains the current meaning (Hellekson and Busse 2014: 5–6). Fic is a type of LITERARY fiction based on MEDIA such as FILMS, books, COMICS, GAMES, but also real people, such as musicians or sports players (Waysdorf 2015: n.p.). Fics often offer alternative STORIES to the ones they are based on. They sometimes feature fan-created or self-inserted characters, such as "Mary Sue" type (Chander 2007: 598). They sometimes combine separate pieces of media. They are usually unauthorised and not written for profit, but for enjoyment. They are primarily shared on the internet (Fathallah 2017: 9).

Zu Dominiak

## *References*

Fathallah, J. (2017) *Fanfiction and the author: How fanfic changes popular cultural texts.* Amsterdam: Amsterdam University Press.

Hellekson, K. and Busse, K. (2014) *The Fan Fiction Studies Reader.* Iowa City: University of Iowa Press.

Chander, S. (2007) 'Everyone's a Superhero: A Cultural Theory of "Mary Sue" Fan Fiction as Fair Use', *California Law Review*, 95, pp. 597–626.

Waysdorf A. (2015) "The creation of football slash fan fiction," *Transformative Works and Cultures* 19, n.p. Available at: https://journal.transformativeworks.org/index.php/twc/article/view/588 [Accessed 9 July 2020].

## Film

Comics theorists have been wary of adopting hand-me-down frameworks of analysis from film studies. However, certain approaches that were first applied to film have proved productive in relation to comics, if only to emphasise differences. SEMIOTICS, the search for specific signifying practices, which had helped film scholars to account for the constructed nature of the cinematic illusion, was valuable in enabling comics scholars to identify the codes and operations at work in comics (Groensteen 2011). PSYCHOANALYTIC film criticism set out to uncover repressed scenarios in mainstream cinema (Metz 1982), and although the forms of imaginary identification offered by the filmic apparatus seem inapplicable to comics, Benoît Peeters and others have shown how METAPHOR and metonymy, key resources of comics, give access to the unconscious of the comics text through condensation, REPETITION, and displacement (Peeters 1984; Tisseron 1987). The theorisation of filmic NARRATION offered a model for considering the INTERACTION of verbal and visual narrating instances, subsumed within an overall narrational process (Gaudreault 1988; Groensteen 2011). Finally, Gilles Deleuze's taxonomy of IMAGES, including those imbued with AFFECT and MEMORY, supports his argument that cinema is itself a mode of thought, an insight that offers much to comics research (1986).

Ann Miller

## *References*


Deleuze, G. (1983) *Cinema I. The Movement-Image*. Translated from French by H. Tomlinson and B. Habberjam, 1986. Minneapolis: University of Minnesota Press.

Gaudreault, A. (1988) *Du littéraire au filmique: Système du récit*. Paris: Méridiens Klincksieck.

Groensteen, T. (1999) *The System of Comics*. Translated from French by B. Beaty and N. Nguyen, 2007. Jackson: University Press of Mississippi.

Groensteen, T. (2011) *Comics and Narration*. Translated from French by A. Miller, 2013. Jackson: University Press of Mississippi.

Metz, C. (1977) *Psychoanalysis and Cinema: The Imaginary Signifier*. Translated from French by C. Britton, A. Williams, B. Brewster, and A. Guzzetti, 1982. London: Macmillan.

Peeters, B. (1984) *Les Bijoux ravis: Une lecture moderne de Tintin*. Brussels: Magic Strip.

Tisseron, S. (1987) *Psychanalyse de la bande dessinée*. Paris: PUF.


## Floppy

As popular nomenclature, floppy refers to the traditional saddle-stitched pamphlet COMIC BOOK that emerged in 1920s North America. Though it describes the MATERIALITY of an array of objects like BANDE

DESSINÉE ALBUMS, ZINES, and "one-shot" comics, the term typically references MASS PRODUCED, SERIALISED, American comic book issues, roughly twenty-five pages long. Christy Uidhir links individual floppies with seriality as a format of publication related to NARRATIVE experience (2016). Floppy seems to have gained traction just as trade paperbacks and GRAPHIC NOVELS proliferated, suggesting a needed shorthand to describe this printed form, despite earlier attempts like Michael Barrier and Martin Williams' "comic-book comic" (1982). It further coincided with broader cultural acceptance of comics through bookstores and libraries. Thus, Carol Tilley has urged library collections to engage with the floppy equally as with bound comic volumes (Tilley and Bahnmaier 2018: 62).

Josh R. Rose

## *References*

Barrier, M. and Williams, M. (eds.) (1981) *A Smithsonian Book of Comic-Book Comics.* Washington: Smithsonian Institution Press.

Tilley, C. L. and Bahnmaier, S. (2018) "The Secret Life of Comics: Socializing and Seriality," *The Serials Librarian* 74, pp. 54–64.

Uidhir, C. M. (2016) "Comics and Seriality" in Bramlett, F., Cook, R., and Meskin, A. (eds.) *The Routledge Companion to Comics.* Abingdon: Routledge, pp. 264–272.

## FOCALISATION

First coined by narrative theorist Gérard Genette in 1972, focalisation complements terms such as NARRATIVE, omniscience, VOICE, PERSPECTIVE, and POINT OF VIEW, for example, as it means to distinguish that "narration refers to the voice that speaks [whereas] focalisation refers to the perspective from which the narrative is recounted" (Kukkonen 2013: 45). Further, based on the three distinct types—internally focused, externally focused, and omniscient narrator—focalisation is a rhetorical move that makes the distinction of narrative agency coming to terms with questions of authenticity and fictionality. For comics, as the visual perspective of the IMAGE and narrative voice do not always match, the depiction is meant to elicit a particular understanding. In other words, the STYLE of the LINES, the use of COLOUR, ANGLE of GAZE, and vagueness work to present "subjective ideas and opinions about those events" that reflect the entangled relationship between the ARTIST, their perspective, the TEXT, the AUDIENCE, and interpretation, or what Roland Barthes (1977: 17–18, 43) termed a connotative layer (Fischer and Hatfield 2011: 70). Largely charged as graphic focalisation, it means to MEDIATE the emotional and cognitive SENSE of perspective from the literal, ocular sense.

Eric Atkinson

## *References*

Barthes, R. (1961–1973) *Image, Music, Text.* Translated from French by S. Heath (ed.), 1977. London: Fontana.

Fischer, C. and Hatfield, C. (2011) "Teeth, Sticks, and Bricks: Calligraphy, Graphic Focalisation, and Narrative Braiding in Eddie Campbell's *Alec*," *Substance* 40(1), pp. 70–93.

Genette, G. (1979) *Narrative Discourse: An Essay in Method.* Translated from French by J. E. Lewin, 1980. Ithaca: Cornell University Press.

Kukkonen, K. (2013) *Studying Comics and Graphic Novels.* Hoboken: John Wiley & Sons.

## Folklore

Folklore refers to traditional culture, including verbal ART, handmade objects, customs, beliefs, and MUSIC—with recent folklore definitions also including digital traditions. It is also the name of the academic discipline that studies folklore (sometimes called folkloristics). Once thought of as survivals of archaic modes of civilisation, folklore is now conceptualised as an everyday activity in which all people engage. Generally, folklorists focus on UNMEDIATED performances such as storytelling and dance, and MATERIAL culture in the form of handmade objects. This would exclude many comics because of their standardised MASS PRODUCTION. Nonetheless, folklorists began studying comics in 1950 (Brewster 1950). Popular DISCOURSE often considers comics to be a type of modern folklore (Peretti 2016). Comics CREATORS employ folklore in the form of ADAPTATION (de Vos 2013) or ALLUSION. A COMIC BOOK can also portray the performance of folklore, such as a character telling a folktale or joke. Furthermore, comics can appropriate and rework folklore, inserting new characters into old STORIES or vice versa: comic book creators "borrow themes and ideas current in traditional and contemporary folklore" (Banks and Wein 1998: n.p.). Finally, FANS of comics often employ the content of comics in the making of their own folklore, such as costumes and tattoos.

Daniel Peretti

## *References*


Banks, A. and Wein, E. (1998) "Folklore and the Comic Book: The Traditional Meets the Popular," *New Directions in Folklore* 2, n.p. Available at: https://scholarworks.iu.edu/journals/index.php/ndif/article/view/19861/25933 [Accessed 2 August 2020].

Brewster, P. (1950) "Folklore Invades the Comic Strips," *Southern Folklore Quarterly* 14, pp. 97–102.

de Vos, G. (2013) "Folklore, Mythology, and the Comic Book Format: A Contemporary Tradition" in Beaty, B. and Weiner, S. (eds.) *Critical Survey of Graphic Novels: History, Theme, and Technique.* Amenia: Salem Press, 100–103.

Dundes, A. (1980) "Who Are the Folk?" in *Interpreting Folklore.* Bloomington: Indiana University Press, pp. 1–19.

Peretti, D. (2016) "Comics as Folklore" in *The Folkloresque: Reframing Folklore in a Popular Culture World.* Logan: Utah State University Press, pp. 104–120.


## Form

Comics as a form emerged in the eighteenth century when Rodolphe Töpffer "employed cartooning and panel borders, and feature[d] the first independent combination of words and pictures seen in Europe" (McCloud 1993: 17). COMIC STRIPS were born in the 1890s with Richard Felton Outcault's *Hogan's Alley* in the US and were circulated as "Sunday supplements" in NEWSPAPERS (Chute 2017: 8). The 1930s brought forth the stand-alone COMIC BOOK, consisting of 32 pages and characterised as a "collection of comic-strip stories [which was] made up of one sustained story, often an installment in series" (Chute 2008:

453). Due to MASS REPRODUCTION, early comics were regarded as "semiliterate" (McCloud 1993: 3) and were PRINTED on "cheap paper meant for fishwrap" (Chute 2017: 11). Although first associated with youth culture, comic books could also be darker and bleaker like Winsor McCay's *Little Nemo in Slumberland* (1905), catering to a more mature READERSHIP. In the 1970s the GRAPHIC NOVEL appeared. Though Richard Kyle coined the term in 1964, it was POPULARISED by Will Eisner who tried to sell his work to mainstream PUBLISHING houses in 1978. Hillary Chute claims that the format of the graphic novel differs from its predecessors by its "expressive, long-form narrative[s]" (ibid.: 19), thereby not considering the plethora of works labelled "graphic novels" simply for marketing purposes (Sabin 1993). More recently, WEBCOMICS have emerged, which "encompass all genres, from traditional gag cartoons to sophisticated online graphic novels and experiments digital art" (Eisner 2008: 151) and can be published and updated without "the months-long lead times of print publishing" (ibid.).

Andrea Schlosser

## *References*

Chute, H. (2017) *Why Comics? From Underground to Everywhere.* New York: Harper Perennial.

Chute, H. (2008) "Comics as Literature? Reading Graphic Narrative," *PMLA* 123(2), pp. 452–465.

Eisner, W. (1985) *Comics and Sequential Art: Principles and Practices from the Legendary Cartoonist.* Reprint 2008. New York: W. W. Norton & Company.

McCloud, S. (1993) *Understanding Comics: The Invisible Art.* New York: Harper Perennial.

Sabin, R. (1993) *Adult Comics: An Introduction.* Abingdon: Routledge.

## FRAGMENTATION

Comics are, in part, "an art of fragments, of scattering, of distribution" (Groensteen 2009: 22), where fragmentation unfolds both in SPACE and in TIME. This dimension is core to FORMAL and NARRATOLOGICAL approaches to comics that emphasise comics

READING as a process of "making sense of fragments" (Postema 2013). Fragmentation is described in terms of gaps, with a strong emphasis on the GUTTER, and is connected to the processes linking these fragments together, such as SEQUENCE, CLOSURE, and ARTHROLOGY. Besides identifying the linkage between fragments that READERS infer, scholars have suggested that fragmentation situates openness at the core of the meaning-making process (Ahmed 2016). The CULTURAL-HISTORICAL strand in COMICS STUDIES ties this fragmentation to specific publication contexts. The emergence of the COMIC STRIP appears as an engagement with the "fragments of modernity" (Gardner 2012: 7), resulting from urban development, experiments with MOTION and vision, and the rise of the NEWSPAPER STRIPS and later SYNDICATION. SERIALISATION relies on a fragmentation that can take many forms: endless REPETITION and variation, open-ended NARRATIVE continuity, and a strictly planned coherence aimed at book publication. This publication over time organises fragmentation according to commercial and MATERIAL CONSTRAINTS that yield different cultural practices (Lesage 2019).

Benoît Crucifix

## *References*

Ahmed, M. (2016) *Openness of Comics: Generating Meaning within Flexible Structures.* Jackson: University Press of Mississippi.

Gardner, J. (2012) *Projections: Comics and the History of Twenty-First Century Storytelling.* Stanford: Stanford University Press.

Groensteen, T. (1999) *The System of Comics.* Translated from French by B. Beaty and N. Nguyen, 2007. Jackson: University Press of Mississippi.

Lesage, S. (2019) *L'Effet livre: Métamorphoses de la bande dessinée.* Tours: Presses universitaires François-Rabelais.

Postema, B. (2013) *Narrative Structure in Comics: Making Sense of Fragments.* Rochester: Rochester Institute of Technology Press.

## Frame

The frame is the often-black LINE that encloses some comics PANELS, while others do not have one. By metonymy, the term is often used as a synonym for panel. Similarly, a FILM frame refers to the IMAGE projected on the screen or to a still image of the PHOTOGRAPHIC film, both of which appear to be surrounded by a rectangular black frame (Kemp 1996: 11–12, Peretz 2017: 87–88). The notion of picture frame comes from ART history, where its study (Schapiro 1969; Phelan 2006) deals with the MATERIAL object—that is the ornamental and protective border edging the picture—as well as with pictorial framing and the AESTHETIC and DIEGETIC boundaries of the image. From a functional point of view (Groensteen 2007: 39–57), a comics frame outlines the image by affecting the framing (Schmid 2021) of its content and by delimiting an off-frame, or even by determining its general meaning via an expressive frame. On the other hand, it visually shapes a GRID on the PAGE—or the "hyperframe," as coined by Thierry Groensteen (2007: 30)—which affects the whole READING process. NARRATOLOGY has also appropriated the concept of frame (Berlatsky 2009: 171–173) to study the embedding of NARRATIVE levels.

Benoît Glaude

## *References*

Berlatsky, E. (2009) "Lost in the Gutter: Within and Between Frames in Narrative and Narrative Theory," *Narrative* 17(2), pp. 162–187.

Groensteen, T. (1999) *The System of Comics*. Translated from French by B. Beaty and N. Nguyen, 2007. Jackson: University Press of Mississippi.

Kemp, W. (1996) "The Narrativity of the Frame" in Duro, P. (ed.) *The Rhetoric of the Frame: Essays on the Boundaries of the Artwork*. Cambridge: Cambridge University Press, pp. 11–23.

Peretz, E. (2017) *The Off-Screen: An Investigation of the Cinematic Frame*. Stanford: Stanford University Press.

Phelan, R. (2006) "The Picture Frame in Question: American Art 1945–2000" in Wolf, W. and Bernhart, W. (eds.) *Framing Borders in Literature and Other Media*. Amsterdam: Rodopi, pp. 159–175.

Schapiro, M. (1969) "On Some Problems in the Semiotics of Visual Art: Field and Vehicle in Image Signs," *Semiotica* 1(3), pp. 223–242.

Schmid, J. (2021) *Frames and Framing in Documentary Comics*. London: Palgrave Macmillan.

## FUMETTI

Fumetti is an Italian word for comics. The term is also used in the singular form (the "fumetto" or a "fumetto") to designate the ART FORM or a specific work. An archaic meaning of "fumetto" refers to a sauce for cooking, but in the 1940s the Italian public started to designate comics "storie a fumetti" ("stories with little smoke clouds"), as the SPEECH BALLOONS were named "fumetti" ("fumo" meaning "smoke"). Thus, the current use of "fumetti" is based on a synecdoche: one element of the LANGUAGE indicates the whole art form. The use of the word in English is incorrect: "fumetti" does not refer to picture STORIES based on PHOTOGRAPHS or still FRAMES from movies; the correct names for such forms are "fotoromanzo" and "cineromanzo," that is, "PHOTONOVEL" and "cinenovel" (historical examples are the magazines *Grand Hotel* (1946) and *Bolero Film* (1947)). Both forms are Italian inventions. "Fumetti" started to appear in the late nineteenth century: early pioneers were Casimiro Teja, Antonio Rubino, Attilio Mussino, and Sergio Tofano. Among the most popular characters are *Tex* (1948), *Diabolik* (1962), and *Dylan Dog* (1986). Among the most celebrated ARTISTS of all time are Gianni De Luca, Grazia Nidasio, Guido Crepax, Andrea Pazienza, Tanino Liberatore, Vittorio Giardino, and Gipi.

Marco Pellitteri

### *References*


Barbieri, D. (1990) *Valvoforme e valvocolori*. Milan: Idea Books.

Becattini, A., Boschi, L., Gori, L., and Sani, A. (2012) *I Disney italiani*. Battipaglia: NPE.

Bono, G. and Stefanelli, M. (eds.) (2012) *Fumetto! 150 anni di storie italiane*. Milan: Rizzoli.

Boschi, L. (2007) *Irripetibili: Le grandi stagioni del fumetto italiano*. Rome: Coniglio.

Carabba, C. (1973) *Il fascismo a fumetti*. Florence: Guaraldi.

Faeti, A. (2013) *La storia dei miei fumetti: L'immaginario visivo italiano fra Tarzan, Pecos Bill e Valentina*. Roma: Donzelli.

Fasiolo, F. (2012) *Italia da fumetto: Il graphic journalism e la narrativa disegnata che raccontano la realtà italiana di ieri e di oggi*. Latina: Tunué.
Gadducci, F. (2006) *Notes on the Early Decades of Italian Comic Strips*. Pisa: Felici.
Gadducci, F., Gori, L., and Lama, L. (2011) *Eccetto Topolino: Lo scontro culturale tra il fascismo e il fumetto*. Battipaglia: NPE.
Genovese, R. (2009) *L'avventurosa storia del fumetto italiano: Quarant'anni di fumetti nelle voci dei protagonisti*. Rome: Castelvecchi.
Tosti, A. (2016) *Graphic Novel: Storia e teoria del romanzo a fumetti e del rapporto fra parola e immagine*. Latina: Tunué.

## Funny Animal

Rooted in cultures of CARICATURE and MEMORY, the funny animal—or "not-so-funny animals" since at least Robert Crumb's *The Goose and the Gander Were Talking One Night* (1988) and the canonisation of Art Spiegelman's *Maus* (1980–1991) (Witek 1989: 111)—is a graphic GENRE "encrusted with connotations" (Hatfield 2005: 4). Because the funny animal contributes to multiple genres, it also constitutes a MODE. Global examples and extensive funny animal GENEALOGIES abound. Jared Gardner has written on the HISTORICAL relationships between the American and European funny animal (2014); Brian Cremins on the SELF-REFLEXIVE and global-ranging funny animal (2016); Daniel Yezbick on the funny animal as "one of the comics industry's most familiar and malleable traditions" (2012); and Joshua T. Anderson on funny animals and "Re-Animalating Native Realities" (2019). Decouple funny from animal in the context of the (Western) liberal humanist tradition built on beast FABLES and manufactured binaries, and it becomes clear how TROPES of "Othering" and creaturely SCHEMATICS avail this mode to exploit the asymmetrical DISCOURSES of humanity and animality (i.e. based on CLASS, GENDER, RACE, SEX, species, etc.). Jimmy Swinnerton's early twentieth-century misogynistic, tiger-headed *Mr. Jack* (1903–1935) is often considered the seminal American funny animal. A contemporary, twenty-first-century example is Nina Bunjevac's catwoman Zorka of *Heartless* (2012), in which the funny animal self-reflexively undermines and reaffirms status-quo conformity in terms of cis and heteropatriarchal white supremacist traditions embedded in the myth of the "North American Dream."

Laura A. Pearson

## *References*


Anderson, J. T. (2019) "Re-Animalating Native Realities: The Funny Animals and Indigenous First Beings of Native Realities Press," *Inks* 3(1), pp. 249–272.

Cremins, B. (2016) "Funny Animals" in Bramlett, F., Cook, R., and Meskin, A. (eds.) *The Routledge Companion to Comics.* Abingdon: Routledge, pp. 146–153.

Gardner, J. (2014) "Invasion of the Funny Animals." *Public Books,* 15 November 2014. Available at: http://www.publicbooks.org/invasion-of-the-funny-animals/ [Accessed 19 August 2020].

Hatfield, C. (2005) *Alternative Comics: An Emerging Literature.* Jackson: University Press of Mississippi.

Pearson, L. (2014) "Alternative Paradoxes in *Heartless*: Reading (Un-) Love in Nina Bunjevac's 'Bitter Tears of Zorka Petrovic.'" *Comics Forum,* 27 May 2014. Available at: https://comicsforum.org/2014/05/27/alternative-paradoxes-in-heartless-reading-un-love-in-nina-bunjevacs-bitter-tears-of-zorka-petrovic-by-laura-a-pearson/ [Accessed 19 August 2020].

Witek, J. (1989) *Comic Books as History: The Narrative Art of Jack Jackson, Art Spiegelman and Harvey Pekar.* Jackson: University Press of Mississippi.

Yezbick, D. (2012) "Funny Animals: Whimsy and Worry in the World of Animal Narratives" in Beaty, B. and Weiner, S. (eds.) *Critical Survey of Graphic Novels: History, Theme, and Technique.* Amenia: Salem Press, 211–215.

## Gag

In show business a gag is a joke, trick, or STORY that makes people laugh, with "gag" referring to the gagging that the AUDIENCE experiences when the funny part is revealed. In comics, the gag appears in various forms and has been a staple of the MEDIUM since its inception. A gag CARTOON is a one-PANEL cartoon that offers an immediate laugh. "[T]he haiku of cartooning" (Harvey 2009: 35), it has developed into a GENRE of its own, becoming a key feature of established HUMOUR magazines and securing its prominence as an essential variety of visual humour (Inge 1984). A gag COMIC STRIP is a SERIALISED strip with several panels, in which the first panels build up to the last panel, which contains the pay-off. The popularity of both gag cartoons and strips demands that the ARTIST provides a gag-a-day (Waugh 1947), which in some series changes into a more sustained NARRATIVE going beyond the mere guffaw (The Comics Journal 1997). The art of making a good gag requires timing and a good understanding of what the READER will find amusing, as well as an in-depth knowledge of how SPATIALITY, LINE, and RHYTHM work (Karasik and Newgarden 2017). Recently, many blog- and WEBCOMICS employ the use of gags in strips and one-panel cartoons.

Rikke Platz Cortsen

### *References*


The Comics Journal (1997) "'Dear Sparky…'": Comics Artists from Across the Medium on the Legendary Cartoonist and Creator of *Peanuts*," *The Comics Journal* 200, pp. 49–68.

Harvey, R. C. (2009) "How Comics Came to Be: Through the Juncture of Word and Image from Magazine Gag Cartoons to Newspaper Strips, Tools for Critical Appreciation Plus Rare Seldom Witnessed Historical Facts" in Heer, J. and Worcester, K. (eds.) *A Comics Studies Reader*. Jackson: University Press of Mississippi, pp. 25–45.

Inge, M. T. (1984) "'The New Yorker' Cartoon and Modern Graphic Humor Author(s)," *Studies in American Humor* New Series 2, 3(1), pp. 61–73.

Karasik, P. and Newgarden, M. (2017) *How to Read Nancy: The Elements of Comics in Three Easy Panels* Seattle: Fantagraphics Books.

Waugh, C. (1947) *The Comics*. London: Macmillan.

## Game

Jesper Juul describes a game as "a rule-based system with a variable and quantifiable outcome, where different outcomes are assigned different values, the player exerts effort in order to influence the outcome, the player feels emotionally attached to the outcome, and the consequences of the activity are negotiable" (2005: 36). The popularity of games as a pastime, particularly in the forms of sports and video games, has often seen them become the subject of comic NARRATIVES, ADAPTATIONS, and/or TRANSMEDIA tie-ins. Comic series and characters have similarly formed the basis for many adaptations into video-, card-, and board-game formats. Video games and the video game industry were of particular influence to the development of the early WEBCOMICS scene, being widely recognised at the time as forming the most popular GENRE of webcomics (Campbell 2006: 49). DIGITAL COMICS SEQUENCES are at times used within video games to progress the narrative of the game. Some video games such as *Framed* (Boggs 2014) and *A Duck Has an Adventure* (Goodbrey 2012) attempt a more direct HYBRIDISATION between the qualities of comics and games. These hybrids have been described as "game comics" and can be considered as a type of hypercomic that makes "specific use of the key characteristics of comics in the mechanics of their gameplay" (Goodbrey 2015: 8).

Daniel Merlin Goodbrey

### *References*

Campbell, T. (2006) *A History of Webcomics.* San Antonio: Antarctic Press.

Goodbrey, D. (2015) "Game comics: An analysis of an emergent hybrid form," *Journal of Graphic Novels and Comics,* (6)1, pp. 3–14.

Juul, J. (2005) *Half-real.* Cambridge: The Massachusetts Institute of Technology Press.

## Gaze

The gaze is powerful. In constructing both the object and the subject of knowledge, it plays an important role in mechanisms of repression (Foucault 1963; Butler 1993). The male gaze, for instance, affects the constant objectification of women in CULTURAL PRODUCTION

(Mulvey 1975). However, as bel hooks' discussion of the oppositional gaze suggests, the gaze can also be a means of countering repression. Several comics scholars have examined the critique and subversion of the male gaze by contemporary female comics artists (Chute 2010; Oksman 2016; Køhlert 2019). This also holds for MANGA, especially manga aimed at female readers or made by female artists (Meyer 2013; Hemmann 2020). Further, comics scholarship has broached the distracted gaze of the crowd (Balzer 2010), the vampire's gaze (Round), and the relationship between gaze and subjectivity in comics (Packard 2017). In considering the detached gaze in Adrian Tomine's comics, Greice Schneider shows how REPRESENTATIONS of characters' gazes "guides our expectations and makes different elements interact, transforming the images into potential scenes" (Schneider 2012: 74). The gaze is therefore closely connected to PERSPECTIVE, "a key aspect of transmission and mediacy in narratives" (Mikkonen 2017: 151). In comics, however, it is often very difficult to determine through whose eyes we see at a given moment.

Maaheen Ahmed

## *References*


Balzer, J. (2010) "'Hully Gee, I'm a Hieroglyphe'—Mobilising the Gaze and the Invention of Comics in New York City, 1895" in Ahrens, J. and Meteling, A. (eds.) *Comics and the City: Urban Space in Print, Picture and Sequence*. New York: Continuum, pp. 19–31.

Butler, J. (1993) *Bodies That Matter: On the Discursive Limits of Sex*. Reprint 2011. Abingdon: Routledge.

Chute, H. L. (2010) *Graphic Women: Life Narrative and Contemporary Comics*. New York: Columbia University Press.

Foucault, M. (1963) *The Birth of the Clinic: An Archeology of Medical Perception*. Translated from French by A. Sheridan. Reprint 2004. Abingdon: Routledge.

Hemmann, K. (2020) *Manga Cultures and the Female Gaze*. London: Palgrave Macmillan.

hooks, b. (1992) *Black Looks: Race and Representation* Boston: South End Press.

Køhlert, F. B. (2019) *Serial Selves: Identity and Representation in Autobiographical Comics*. New Brunswick: Rutgers University Press.

Meyer, U. (2013) "Drawing from the body—The self, the gaze and the other in Boys' Love manga," *Journal of Graphic Novels and Comics* 4(1), pp. 64–81.
Mikkonen, K. (2017) *Narratology of Comic Art*. Abingdon: Routledge
Oksman, T. (2016) *"How Come Boys Get to Keep Their Noses?" Women and Jewish American Identity in Contemporary Graphic Memoirs*. New York: Columbia University Press.
Packard, S. (2017) "The Drawn-Out Gaze of the Cartoon: A Psychosemiotic Look at Subjectivity in Comic Book Storytelling" in Reinerth, M. S. and Thon, J.-N. (eds.) *Subjectivity across Media: Interdisciplinary and Transmedial Perspectives*. Abingdon: Routledge, pp. 111–124.
Mulvey, L. (1975) "Visual Pleasure and Narrative Cinema," *Screen* 16(3), pp. 6–18.
Round, J. (2014) *Gothic in Comics and Graphic Novels: A Critical Approach*. Jefferson: McFarland.
Schneider, G. (2012) "Lost Gazes, Detached Minds: Strategies of Disengagement in the Work of Adrian Tomine," *Scandinavian Journal of Comic Art* 1(2), pp. 58–81.

## Gekiga

Usually translated as "dramatic pictures," "gekiga" differs from other MANGA terms like SHŌNEN and SHŌJO in that it does not purport to REPRESENT an intended AUDIENCE for its STORIES but rather differentiates itself by its content (Schodt 1983). Said to be coined by artist Yoshihiru Tatsumi in the late 1950s, "gekiga" differentiate themselves from other types of manga by their THEMES (serious, adult stories often of loss and alienation) and ARTISTIC STYLES (grounded and REALISTIC, with fewer stylised expressions). At the outset, "gekiga" had a strong working-CLASS element to it, telling stories of hardscrabble lives on the fringes of society in the postwar years (Rosenbaum 2012: 269–271). Although the rebellious students of the 1960s picked up some proletarian principles from "gekiga," the FORM was changing and adapting to Japan's increasing affluence (Ōtsuka 2015). Similar to the way that the more mainstream shōnen manga was becoming professionalised and more acceptable to the culture at large in the late 1960s and early 1970s, so too did "gekiga" change, becoming focused more on entertainment and less on the social critiques that had initiated the form.

Brian Ruh

## *References*

Ōtsuka, E. (2015) "Otaku Culture as 'Conversion Literature'" in Galbraith, P. W., Kam, T. H., and Kamm, B. (eds.) *Debating Otaku in Contemporary Japan: Historical Perspectives and New Horizons.* London: Bloomsbury Academic, pp. xiii–xxix.

Rosenbaum, R. (2012) "The Gekiga Tradition: Towards a Graphic Rendition of History" in Iadonisi, R. (ed.) *Graphic History: Essays on Graphic Novels And/As History.* Cambridge: Cambridge Scholars Publishing, pp. 260–284.

Schodt, F. L. (1983) *Dreamland Japan: Writings on modern manga.* Berkeley: Stone Bridge Press.

Suzuki, S. (2013) "Tatsumi Yoshihiro's Gekiga and the Global Sixties: Aspiring for an Alternative" in Berndt, J. and Kümerling-Meibauer, B. (eds.) *Manga's Cultural Crossroads.* Abingdon: Routledge, pp. 48–62.

## Gender

Different strands of gender theory and FEMINIST criticism have sought to define the way gender is REPRESENTED in heteronormative and patriarchal culture, while also questioning the DISCOURSES that constitute the notions of "men" and "women." For example, PSYCHOANALYTIC feminist theory approaches these matters from the perspective of "sexual difference" to explain female subjectivity and corporeality (Irigaray 1993: 5). In turn, feminist POSTSTRUCTURALIST Judith Butler questions this essentialist notion of "woman" beyond its strategic and political uses, and proposes to understand gender not as natural but as performatively constructed: "gender is always a doing, though not a doing by a subject who might be said to preexist the deed" (2006: 34). Drawing on Michel Foucault's *The History of Sexuality* (1990), Butler establishes that the norms that inform gender "are in fact the *effects* of institutions, practices, discourses with multiple and diffuse points of origin" (2006: xxxi). While approaches to the study of gender differ and sometimes contradict, they share a concern with gender identity as central to understanding lived experiences and oppression. An important intervention in gender theory comes from CRITICAL RACE THEORY and entails an INTERSECTIONAL approach to elucidate the structural relation of gendered oppression to different "axes of power" (Cho et al. 2013: 787) such as RACE, CLASS, and NATIONALITY (Crenshaw 1989; Lykke 2011). In COMICS STUDIES considerations of gender also extend to the predominance of male CREATORS and READERS as well as the oversexualised representations of women.

Freija Camps

### *References*

Butler, J. (1990) *Gender Trouble: Feminism and the Subversion of Identity.* Reprint, 2006. Abingdon: Routledge.

Cho, S., Crenshaw, K. W., and McCall, L. (2013) "Towards a Field of Intersectionality Studies: Theory, Applications, and Praxis," *Signs: Journal of Women in Culture and Society* 37(4), pp. 785–810.

Crenshaw, K. (1989) "Demarginalizing the Intersection of Race and Sex: A Black Feminist Critique of Antidiscrimination Doctrine, Feminist Theory and Antiracist Politics," *University of Chicago Legal Forum* 1989(1), pp. 139–167.

Foucault, M. (1976) *The History of Sexuality, Volume 1: An Introduction.* Translated from French by R. Hurley, 1990. New York: Vintage.

Irigaray, L. (1982) *An Ethics of Sexual Difference.* Translated from French by C. Burke and G. C. Gill, 1993. Ithaca, NY: Cornell University Press.

Lykke, N. (2011) "Intersectional Analysis: Black Box or Useful Critical Thinking Technology" in Lutz, H., Vivar, M. T. H., and Supik, L. (eds.) *Framing Intersectionality: Debates on a Multi-Faceted Concept in Gender Studies.* London: Ashgate, pp. 207–220.

## Genealogies

Attempts by twentieth-century scholars to establish a genealogy for comics may be seen as a legitimising strategy, intended to give a "pedigree" to a despised popular ART (Morgan 2003: 26). Gérard Blanchard refers back to cave paintings (1969: 8) and Francis Lacassin to Egyptian books of the dead (1971: 15). David Kunzle, in contrast, embraces comics as POPULAR CULTURE, from the moralistic broadsheets of the post-Gutenberg era to the scurrilous SATIRICAL and political comic strips of the nineteenth century, although he notes the LITERARY tone of Rodolphe Töpffer's works, as well as the Swiss ARTIST'S self-conscious claim, in 1842, to have inaugurated a new art form (1973, 1990). Kunzle conspicuously ends his account in 1896, the starting date for more dominant American genealogies that deem comics to have been born as mass medium in US NEWSPAPERS: the originary moment in this account is Richard F. Outcault's combination of SPEECH BALLOONS with SEQUENTIAL IMAGES in *Hogan's Alley* (1895–1898) (Blackbeard 1995). More recent work has cautioned against the retrospective search for the lineage of a MEDIUM evolving in isolation: Thierry Smolderen (2009) argues that comics has borrowed elements from various sources, including single-image CARTOONS and that its HISTORY has been a process of HYBRIDISATION.

Ann Miller

## *References*

Blackbeard, B. (1995) *R. F. Outcault, the Yellow Kid.* Northampton: Kitchen Sink Press.

Blanchard, G. (1969) *Histoire de la bande dessinée.* Verviers: Marabout Université.

Kunzle, D. (1973) *History of the Comic Strip, Volume 1: The Early Comic Strip 1450–1825.* Berkeley: University of California Press.

Kunzle, D. (1990) *History of the Comic Strip, Volume 2: The Nineteenth Century.* Berkeley: University of California Press.

Lacassin, F. (1971) *Pour un 9e art, la bande dessinée.* Paris: 10/18.

Morgan, H. (2003) *Principes des littératures dessinées.* Angoulême: Éditions de l'an 2.

Smolderen, T. (2000) *The Origins of Comics: From William Hogarth to Winsor McCay.* Translated from French by B. Beaty and N. Nguyen, 2014. Jackson: University Press of Mississippi.

Töpffer, R. (1842) "Essai d'autographie" in Groensteen, T. and Peeters, B. (eds.) *Töpffer, l'inventeur de la bande dessinée.* Reprint 1994. Paris: Hermann.

## Genotext

Genotext (along with PHENOTEXT) is a concept in Julia Kristeva's semanalysis (1980)—SEMIOTICS crossed with, and critiqued by, PSYCHOANALYSIS. It derives from genetics, with its genotype—the genetic material a being contains—and phenotype—the features the being exhibits. But it would be a mistake to make the analogy too strong. The genotext is like the foundation of the signifying process: it makes signification work but is perceptible indirectly outside of structure and signification: "even though it can be seen in language, the genotext is not linguistic (…). It is, rather, a *process*, which tends to articulate structures that are ephemeral (…) and non-signifying" (Kristeva 1980: 121). The genotext is associated with the drives, with deviations from prescribed syntax and sense, eruptions of the poetic and the radical. Hence, the genotext is associated with ARTISTIC LANGUAGE. For COMICS STUDIES, the genotext is important in LINGUISTIC and semiotic interpretations of comics: particularly in the notion of comics as VISUAL LANGUAGE that focuses on the functionality and communicative capacity of such language, rather than its relation to the drives, the psyche, and the body (Grennan 2017; Cohn 2013). The genotext also makes us consider non-functional elements of comics: STYLE, LINE, and other elements that do not signify.

Peter Wilkins

### *References*

Cohn, N. (2013) *The Visual Language of Comics: Introduction to the Structure and Cognition of Sequential Images.* London: Bloomsbury Academic.

Grennan, S. (2017) *A Theory of Narrative Drawing.* London: Palgrave Macmillan.

Kristeva, J. (1969) *Desire in Language: A Semiotic Approach to Literature and Art.* Translated from French by T. Gora and A. Jardine, 1980. Roudiez, L. (ed.) New York: Columbia University Press.

Kristeva, J. (1973) "The System and the Speaking Subject" in Moi, T. (ed.) *The Kristeva Reader.* Translated from French by T. Moi, 1986. New York: Columbia University Press, pp. 24–33.

## Genre

A term shared across the study of LANGUAGE and CULTURE, genre refers to the pre-existing SEMIOTIC structures that underpin the production of meaning (Frow 2006: 10) and organise AFFECT (Berlant 2011: 66). People draw on genres in everyday life (Berlant 2011; Miller 1984) and in NARRATIVE ARTS (Frow 2006). Here is an example of how genre works: if this is the first entry in this collection you READ, as you read it you will infer what you can expect from the other entries—their length, MODE of speaking, the kind of information they offer. If this is not the first entry you have read, you are subtly assessing this entry against others you are familiar with. You may have already worked out *how* to read the entries (how they want to be read, and how you want to read them) and how you feel about them. This fine-grained dynamic relationship between existing expectations (this volume is informational, it should tell you certain kinds of things using the structure of key terms) and individual engagements with those expectations (this particular entry and its meta-commentary on genre) is the work of genre in both its consciously AESTHETIC uses (in SUPERHERO comics, detective novels, or HYBRID works) and its everyday uses (the FORMAL structures that guide, for example, emails between students and professors). Genres are not, however, fixed structures; they evolve over time through use and innovation.

Anna Poletti

### *References*

Berlant, L. (2011) *Cruel Optimism*. Durham: Duke University Press.
Frow, J. (2006) *Genre*. Abingdon: Routledge.
Miller, C. R. (1984) "Genre as Social Action," *Quarterly Journal of Speech* 70, pp. 151–167.

## Gesture

A relationship between the represented gesture of the human body and NARRATIVE DRAWING has existed from the very beginning of the HISTORY of the COMIC STRIP. Smolderen notes that Rodolphe Töpffer's character Monsieur Vieux Bois (1839) adopts specific gestures from ILLUSTRATIONS to Siddons' manual of acting (Siddons 1822), utilising an established melodramatic lexicon of body shapes to represent specific emotions (Smolderen 2014: 36). The idea that visible gesture is non-verbal and meaningful independent of speech continues to frame debates about the DEPICTION of bodies relative to and beyond verbalisation (Lessing 1984; Peeters 1991; Groensteen 1999; Grennan 2017). One hundred and eighty years after Henry Siddons, Will Eisner was able to repeat that the "expression of human emotion is displayed by (...) meaningful postures" (2008: xi). It has significantly impacted ideas of the capacities of drawing (Rosand 2002: 61), in terms of both TRACE and depiction. Current claims that drawn gestures are "independent of propositional content" (Fein and Kasher 1996: 793) and function both METAPHORICALLY (Miers 2015) and through force dynamics (Grennan 2017: 72) are largely underpinned by Mark Johnson's theory of image schemata or the "complex web of non-propositional schematic structures that emerge from our bodily experience" (Johnson 1987: 5).

Simon Grennan

## *References*


Eisner, W. (1985) *Comics and Sequential Art: Principles and Practices from the Legendary Cartoonist.* Reprint 2008. New York: W. W. Norton & Company.

Fein, O. and Kasher, A. (1996) "How to do things with words and gestures in comics," *Journal of Pragmatics* 26(6), pp. 793–808.

Grennan, S. (2017) *A Theory of Narrative Drawing.* London: Palgrave Macmillan.

Groensteen, T. (1999) *The System of Comics.* Translated from French by B. Beaty and N. Nguyen, 2007. Jackson: University Press of Mississippi.

Johnson, M. (1987) *The Body in the Mind: The Bodily Basis of Meaning, Imagination and Reason.* Chicago: University of Chicago Press.

Lessing, G. E. (1767) *Laocoön: An Essay of the Limits of Painting and Poetry.* Translated from German by E. A. McCormick, 1984. Baltimore: Johns Hopkins University Press.

Miers, J. (2015) "Depiction and demarcation in comics: Towards an account of the medium as a drawing practice," *Studies in Comics* 6(1), pp. 145–156.

Peeters, B. (1991) *Case, planche, récit: Comment lire une bande dessinée.* Paris: Casterman.
Rosand, D. (2002) *Drawing Acts: Studies in graphic expression and representation.* Cambridge: Cambridge University Press.
Siddons, H. (1822) *Practical Illustrations of Rhetorical Gesture and Action.* London: Sherwood, Neely and Jones.
Smolderen, T. (2000) *The Origins of Comics: From William Hogarth to Winsor McCay.* Translated from French by B. Beaty and N. Nguyen, 2014. Jackson: University Press of Mississippi.

## Global Manga

Global manga are comics which use similar AESTHETICS, FORMS, and STORYTELLING devices as Japanese MANGA (Brienza 2015). These local manga traditions include Korean or Chinese "manhwa" (Berndt 2012), French "nouvelle manga" (Canário 2015), and Euromanga (Lamerichs 2015). Manga published in English are also referred to as original English language (OEL) manga. Many global manga combine Japanese elements with their own comics traditions, resulting in HYBRID manga (Bainbridge and Norris 2010). Germany, for instance, has a flourishing, local SHŌJO manga tradition (Eckstein 2016). Through INTERMEDIALITY, creators adopt Japanese imagery, storytelling, PANELLING, or GENRES. Global manga can be PUBLISHED at official publishing houses or be self-published online as WEBCOMICS or in PRINT as doujinshi (Kinsella 1998; Noppe 2014). While global manga is often rooted in the creative participatory culture, including its international doujinshi scene, successes such as *Megatokyo* or global anime like *Avatar: The Last Airbender* demonstrate a mainstream interest in these PRODUCTIONS. To understand global manga merely in terms of its production outside of Japan, or as an imitation of Japanese STYLES, simplifies the nature of these comics. Their production and consumption are highly TRANSNATIONAL, a blend of cultures (Kaczuk 2019). Whether this blend is neutral, or contains a certain ORIENTALISM towards Japan (Napier 2007), needs to be examined in further studies.

Nicolle Lamerichs

## *References*

Bainbridge, J. and Norris, C. (2010) "Hybrid Manga: Implications for the Global Knowledge Economy" in Johnson-Woods, T. (ed.) *Manga: An Anthology of Global and Cultural Perspectives*. London: Bloomsbury Academic, pp. 235–252.

Berndt, J. (2012) *Manhwa, Manga, Manhua: East Asian Comics Studies*. Leipzig: Leipziger Universitätsverlag.

Brienza, C. (2015) *Global Manga: Japanese Comics without Japan?* London: Ashgate.

Canário, T. (2015) *On Everyday Life: Frédéric Boilet and the Nouvelle Manga Movement*. Abingdon: Routledge.

Eckstein, K. (2016) *Shojo Manga: Text-Bild-Verhältnisse und Narrationsstrategien im japanischen und deutschen Manga für Mädchen*. Heidelberg: Universitätsverlag Winter.

Kaczuk, Z. (2019) "Re-Examining the 'What is Manga?' Problematic: The Tension and Interrelationship between the 'Style' versus 'Made in Japan' Positions" in Hernández-Pérez, M. (ed.) *Japanese Media Cultures in Japan and Abroad: Transnational Consumption of Manga, Anime, and Media-Mixes*. Basel: MDPI AG.

Kinsella, S. (1998) "Japanese Subculture in the 1990s: Otaku and the Amateur Manga Movement," *Journal of Japanese Studies* 24, pp. 289–316.

Lamerichs, N. (2015) "Euromanga: Hybrid Styles and Stories in Transcultural Manga Production" in Brienza, C. (ed.) *Global Manga: Japanese Comics without Japan?* London: Ashgate, pp. 75–95.

Napier, S. J. (2007) *From Impressionism to Anime: Japan as Fantasy and Fan Cult in the Mind of the West*. London: Palgrave Macmillan.

Noppe, N. (2014) *The Cultural Economy of Fanwork in Japan: Dojinshi Exchange as a Hybrid Economy of Open Source Cultural Goods*. PhD. Catholic University Leuven.

## Grammatology

Grammatology is the study of written LANGUAGE in a scientific way. Originally developed out of LINGUISTICS, grammatology as a science is related to and pursued in disciplines such as anthropology, psychology, language studies, and LITERARY STUDIES. Grammatology considers the MATERIAL, enduring forms of language, including handwritten manuscripts, PRINTED works, and digital texts. Thus, it entails the HISTORIES and TECHNOLOGIES of WRITING, including the tools and materials involved and the developments of SCRIPTS and types. The term grammatology was coined by Ignace Gelb, who suggested it to study how spoken language is represented in scripts, such as the difference between syllabic and alphabetic systems of language. Later grammatologists also considered the impact that developments in written language had on societies and cultures, for example when written texts came to replace oral tradition. This approach was developed by Eric Havelock and developed further by Walter J. Ong, who argued that the development of writing technologies changed the way people think, in part because writing is more MEDIATED than oral language. In comics, grammatology might consider techniques, tools, and TYPES used for LETTERING, whether by hand or digital, as well as the impact letter forms might have on the meaning of the words.

Barbara Postema

## *References*

Gelb, I. (1989) *A Study of Writing: The Foundations of Grammatology*. Chicago: University of Chicago Press.

Havelock, E. (1963) *Preface to Plato*. Cambridge: Harvard University Press.

Ong, W.J. (2009) *Orality and Literacy: The Technologizing of the Word*. Abingdon: Routledge.

## Grapheme

A grapheme is a graphic item in a WRITING system that is inaccessible to further division. The status of any MARK as such an indivisible item derives entirely from its part/part and part/whole relationships with other graphemes in a systemic visual realisation of a LANGUAGE system. This characteristic is definitive, relative to its location in any written graphic array, and is not determined by the shape of the mark, which can appear within the very broadest of parameters (Grennan 2017: 31). Although there is still a tendency to consider graphemes to be scalar formal graphic elements, such as “basic graphical shapes like lines, dots, and shapes” (Cohn 2013: 28), both theoretically and practically, graphemes are visual realisations of letters in the alphabet of a language system, as phonemes are audio items given status by their TEMPORAL correspondence to items in a language system. The distinction between relative topological location (determined by a systematic relationship to a language system) and the shape of the mark is particularly germane to understanding comics, which encompass traditions of utilising radically original mark-shapes for writing, to represent physical effects, such as SOUND (Guynes 2014).

Simon Grennan

## *References*

Grennan, S. (2017) *A Theory of Narrative Drawing*. London: Palgrave Macmillan.

Cohn, N. (2013) *The Visual Language of Comics: Introduction to the Structure and Cognition of Sequential Images*. London: Bloomsbury Academic.

Guynes, S. A. (2014) "Four-Color Sound: A Peircean Semiotics of Comic Book Onomatopoeia," *Public Journal of Semiotics* 6(1), pp. 58–72.

## GRAPHIATION

Coined by Philippe Marion (1993), graphiation, or visual enunciation, is a key term in the description of STYLE in comics. It refers "to the fact that the hand and the body—as well as the whole personality of the artist—is visible in the way he or she gives a visual representation of a certain object, character, setting, or event" (Baetens and Frey 2014: 137). The graphiator's presence, which concerns both the visual and the verbal elements of comics, oscillates on a gliding scale between two extremes: the highly visible presence of the graphiator puts a strong emphasis on individual expression and the personal PERSPECTIVE on STORYTELLING, while a more streamlined and collective style (for instance, when ARTISTS follow a certain studio line or strongly obey GENRE CONVENTIONS) gives priority to the content of the story and STORYWORLD, at the expense of the CREATOR's individuality. There exists a strong link between graphiation and auteur theory, although recent work in and reflections on the notion of style have started to challenge the conventional idea that one work can only have one style, and that unity of style is a prerequisite for the construction of a real AUTHOR position.

Jan Baetens

## *References*

Baetens, J. (2001) "Revealing Traces: A New Theory of Graphic Enunciation" in Varnum, R. and Gibbons, C. T. (eds.) *The Language of Comics: Word and Image*. Jackson: University Press of Mississippi, pp. 145–155.

Baetens, J. and Frey, H. (2014) *The Graphic Novel: An Introduction*. Cambridge: Cambridge University Press.

Gardner, J. (2011) "Storylines," *SubStance* 40(1), pp. 53–69.

Marion, P. (1993) *Traces en cases: Travail graphique, figuration narrative et participation du lecteur. Essai sur la bande dessinée*. Louvain-la-Neuve: Académia.

## Graphic Facilitation

Graphic facilitation involves VISUALISING concepts and discussions for groups, often in real time, through TEXT-IMAGE combination. It is an iterative process requiring dialogue, CARTOONING, and COLLABORATION. Developed in San Francisco in the 1970s, facilitator David Sibbet promoted it as a means for reflecting back, literally helping people to see what they mean (1997). Presence (physically or online), being open about intention, and interacting directly with participants, encourages accountability to those whose PERSPECTIVES are being REPRESENTED. Graphic facilitation is used within public engagement, organisational development, co-production, research design, analysis, and dissemination (Mendonça 2016). It can result in powerful insights, innovation, and "explicit group memory" (Ball 1999), and it can raise significant ETHICAL issues (Mendonça 2019). While DRAWING and WRITING are important, enabling, structuring, and responding to challenging conversations also require contextual knowledge and skilful facilitation (Erfan 2016). Some graphic facilitators are commissioned to design and lead processes, working beyond a single event. Many professionals and students in health and social care, EDUCATION, the arts, and business use graphic facilitation as a tool for reflection, strategic planning, communication, teaching, and learning. Unlike comics workshops, where the primary aim is to produce ARTWORK, the visuals generated here may prove less important than the process of "working out" through graphic facilitation.

Penelope Mendonça

### *References*

Ball, G. (1998) "Graphic Facilitation Focuses a Group's Thoughts: Supporting Effective Agreement." *Mediate*, April 1999. Available at: https://www.mediate.com/articles/ball.cfm [Accessed 5 August 2020].

Erfan, A. (2016) "The Use of Imagery in Conflict Engagement" in Agerbeck, B., Bird, K., Bradd, S., and Shepherd, J. (eds.) *Drawn Together Through Visual Practice.* (Self-Published) Kelvy Bird, p. 141.

Mendonça, P. (2016) "Graphic Facilitation, Sketchnoting, Journalism and 'The Doodle Revolution,'" *New Dimensions in Comics Scholarship. Studies in Comics* 7(1), pp. 127–152.

Mendonça, P. (2019) "Single Mothers Storying the Absent Father and Values-Based Cartooning" in Kearny, K. and Murray, L. (eds.) *Mothers as Keepers and Tellers of Child Origin Stories.* Bradford: Demeter Press, pp. 99–136.

Sibbet, D. (1997) *Group Graphics Workbook: Empowering Through Visual Language.* San Francisco: The Grove Consultants International.

## Graphic Medicine

Coined in 2007 by medical practitioner and comics ARTIST Ian Williams, graphic medicine is a burgeoning area of COMICS STUDIES research and artistic practice that extends the principles of NARRATIVE medicine to comics and "echo[s] calls in the medical humanities for the urgent need for different understandings and expressions of illness and disability than those found in conventional medical discourse" (La Cour and Poletti 2022). Research in the field has largely focused on how comics can uniquely convey information about healthcare issues, treatments, and systems (GraphicMedicine.org "About"), and promotes comics as helpful tools in navigating topics that may be difficult for healthcare workers, patients, and their loved ones to explain or to understand in either verbal or VISUAL LANGUAGE alone. Comics produced as graphic medicine relay fictional or, more often, personal narratives that underscore how communication about healthcare issues is not always easy or straightforward, as it is complicated by a number of factors, including cultural context, language, GENDER, CLASS, and ETHNICITY. For these reasons, graphic medicine research and practice are gaining establishment within both Comics Studies and PATHOGRAPHICS due to their exploration of interactions between individuals and healthcare systems as "scenes of intercultural, interdiscursive, and intergenerational encounter" (La Cour and Poletti 2022; see Czerwiec et al. 2015; Williams 2011 and 2014; Squier and Marks 2014; McNicol 2014; Green and Myers 2010).

Erin La Cour

## *References*

Czerwiec, M. K., Williams, I., Squier, S. M., Green, M. J., Myers, K. R., and Smith, S. T. (2015) *Graphic Medicine Manifesto.* University Park: The Pennsylvania State University Press.

Green, M. J. and Myers K. R. (2010). "Graphic Medicine: The Use of Comics in Medical Education and Patient Care," *BMJ* 13, pp. 573–577.

La Cour, E. and Poletti, A. (2022) "Graphic Medicine's Possible Futures: Reconsidering Poetics and Reading," *Biography: An Interdisciplinary Quarterly* 44(2).

McNicol, S. (2014) "Humanising illness: presenting health information in educational comics," *Medical Humanities* 40(1), pp. 49–55.

Squier, S. M., and Marks, J. R. (2014), guest co-editors. *Configurations* 22(2).

Williams, I. (2011) "Autography as Auto-Therapy: Psychic Pain and the Graphic Memoir," *Journal of Medical Humanities* 32(4), pp. 353–366.

Williams, I. (2014) "Humanising illness: presenting health information in educational comics," *Medical Humanities* 40(1), pp. 49–55.

## Graphic Novel

Coined by Richard Kyle in 1964 (Kunka 2010), the term graphic novel became popularised through the publication of comics ARTIST and scholar Will Eisner's *A Contract with God and Other Tenement Stories* (1978) and his subsequent adamant stance that the MEDIUM of the graphic novel is LITERATURE. Following Eisner, many advocates of the term have made similar claims to its being different from comics based on its "seriousness"—taking the form of comics but the length, packaging, and content of literature—and have welcomed the cultural cachet the term lends to both practice and theory. On the other side of the debate are those who note that the term merely serves to "ingratiate certain comics into the literary canon and perpetuate the denigration of all others" (La

Cour 2016: 79), a clear "reinforce[ment] of the ongoing ghettoization of works deemed unworthy of critical attention" (Labio 2011: 126). Moreover, to a large extent, at least popularly, the term has become conflated with the LITERARY GENRES of MEMOIR and AUTOBIOGRAPHY, despite the fact that many works labelled as graphic novels are fiction and collections of COMIC BOOK series. As Roger Sabin notes, rather than a medium or a genre, the graphic novel can be seen simply as a marketing term aimed at selling comics to an older audience with more money to spend (1993).

Erin La Cour

## *References*

Eisner, W. (2002) "Keynote Address, Will Eisner Symposium," *ImageTexT: Interdisciplinary Comics Studies* 1(1), n.p. Available at http://www.english.ufl.edu/imagetext/archives/v1_1/eisner/index.shtml [Accessed 9 September 2020].

Kunka, A. (2010) "Will Eisner and the 'Graphic Novel.'" Available at http://doctor-k100.blogspot.com/2010/12/will-eisner-and-graphic-novel.html [Accessed 9 September 2020].

La Cour, E. (2016) "Comics as a Minor Literature," *Image [&] Narrative* 17(4), pp. 79–90.

Labio, C. (2011) "What's in a Name? The Academic Study of Comics and 'The Graphic Novel,'" *Cinema Journal* 50(3), pp. 123–126.

Sabin, R. (1993) *Adult Comics: An Introduction*. London: Routledge.

## Graphic Sketchnoting

Graphic sketchnoting is the practice of using IMAGES alongside and in combination with TEXT in one's scholarly notes, typically in conferences and symposia. The practice bears a relationship to sketchnoting in general (Rohde 2012; Mills 2019) but places a greater emphasis on DRAWING rather than LETTERING. In COMICS STUDIES, graphic sketchnoting will typically adopt comics CONVENTIONS to represent the speaker, the acts of speech and thought, and the contents of talk, often using SCHEMATIC or METAPHORICAL images. Unlike GRAPHIC FACILITATION, which is typically done at a board or large sheet visible to an AUDIENCE, and/or conducted for the express purpose of distribution to participants physically or digitally afterwards, graphic sketchnoting is primarily an individual's notes for a conference and reflects the CREATOR'S interests, interpretations, and concerns. However, sketchnotes may be PUBLISHED and distributed during or after a conference (Davies 2017; Mendonça 2017; Davies and Vaughan 2018; "Sketching Graphic Brighton 2019," Miers 2020).

Paul F. Davies

## *References*


Davies, P. F. (2017) "Sketchnotes from Graphic Gothic," *Studies in Comics* 8(2), pp. 265–274.

Davies, P. F. and Vaughan, P. (2018) "Sketchnotes from the 2018 International Graphic Novel and Comics Conference," *Studies in Comics*, 9(2), pp. 349–360.

Mendonça, P. (2017) "How to bring diversity to comics through intersectionality." *The Artful*. Available at: https://www.theartful.co.uk/articles/pen-mendona-how-to-bring-diversity-to-comics-through-intersectionality [Accessed 31 March 2020].

Miers, J. (2020) "Amsterdam Comics," *Digressions* 4(1), pp. 69–74.

Mills, E. (2019) *The Art of Visual Notetaking: An interactive guide to visual communication and sketchnoting*. Mission Viejo: Walter Foster Publishing.

Rohde, M. (2012) *The Sketchnote Handbook: The illustrated guide to visual note taking*. San Francisco: Peachpit Press.

"Sketching Graphic Brighton 2019." (2019) *Graphic Brighton*, 11 May. Available at: https://graphicbrighton.wordpress.com/2019/05/11/sketching-graphic-brighton-2019/ [Accessed 31 March 2020].


## Grid

Standard Western comics' PAGE LAYOUT—traditionally "more rigid" than MANGA layouts (Cao et al. 2012)—has long consisted of SEQUENCES of FRAMED PANELS juxtaposed in STRIPS of constant height. In such a regular setting, the comics FRAME visually creates a grid on the page, which Neil Cohn and Kaitlin Pederson (2016: 8–9) describe as one of the basic panel arrangements in comics' page layouts. This pattern originated in the nineteenth century, in single sheets of popular prints and in chronophotographic plates (Smolderen 2014: 130) before being generalised to early comic strips PUBLISHED in NEWSPAPERS (that were also characterised by a grid-based document layout) and later frequently used in twentieth-century COMIC BOOKS and magazines. It affects the whole READING process, insofar as comics are simultaneously apprehended through the SEQUENTIAL continuum of the panels and through the SPATIAL dimension of the page (Fresnault-Deruelle 2014: 121, Witek 2009: 155). Some scholars even note that "the grid somehow persists in digital comics" (Priego and Wilkins 2018: 17) despite the abandonment of the paper page. This key concept in COMICS STUDIES gave its name, by playing on the meaning of "analysis grid," to *The Comics Grid: Journal of Comics Scholarship*.

Benoît Glaude

## *References*

Cao, Y., Chan, A. B., and Lau, R. W. H. (2012) "Automatic Stylistic Manga Layout," *ACM Transactions on Graphics* 31(6), n.p. Available at: https://dl.acm.org/doi/10.1145/2366145.2366160 [Accessed 30 August 2020].

Cohn, N. and Pederson, K. (2016) "The changing pages of comics: Page layouts across eight decades of American superhero comics," *Studies in Comics* 7(1), pp. 7–28.

Fresnault-Deruelle, P. (2014) "From linear to tabular" in Miller, A. and Beaty, B. (eds.) *The French Comics Theory Reader*. Leuven: Leuven University Press, pp. 121–138.

Priego, E. and Wilkins, P. (2018) "The Question Concerning Comics as Technology: *Gestell* and Grid," *The Comics Grid* 8, pp. 1–26.

Smolderen, T. (2014), *The Origins of Comics. From William Hogarth to Winsor McCay*. Translated from French by B. Beaty and N. Nguyen. Jackson: University Press of Mississippi.

Witek, J. (2009) "The Arrow and the Grid" in Heer, J. and Worcester, K. (eds.) *A Comics Studies Reader*, Jackson: University Press of Mississippi, pp. 149–156.

## Groundlevel

Groundlevel is a term that was coined in the mid-1970s to describe comics that combined features of UNDERGROUND COMIX and mainstream comics (Sherman 1979). The term originates from the idea that groundlevel comics were located between underground comics and aboveground comics, the latter of which was sometimes used as a synonym for mainstream comics (Kennedy 1982: 11, 15). Groundlevel comics injected the adult SEXUAL, social, and spiritual content of underground comix into mainstream GENRES, primarily SCIENCE FICTION and FANTASY. Some of the most influential groundlevel comics were Mike Friedrich's *Star Reach*, the anthology *Heavy Metal*, Wendy and Richard Pini's *Elfquest*, and Dave Sim's *Cerebus*. Although the term fell out of use after the 1980s, PUBLISHERS such as Dark Horse Comics and DC's Vertigo imprint can be seen as continuations of the groundlevel legacy (Singsen 2017: 164–65).

Doug Singsen

### *References*

Kennedy, J. (1982) "Introduction" in Kennedy, J. (ed.) *The Official Underground and Newave Comix Price Guide*. Cambridge: Boatner Norton, pp. 11–15.

Sherman, B. (1979) "Sympathy for the Groundlevel," *The Comics Journal* 51, pp. 70–75.

Singsen, D. (2017) "Critical Perspectives on Mainstream, Groundlevel, and Alternative Comics in *The Comics Journal*, 1977 to 1996," *Journal of Graphic Novels and Comics* 8(2), pp. 156–172.

## Gutter

The gutter refers to the MATERIAL SPACE visible between two juxtaposed comics PANELS. It is part of the monochromatic—often blank—space that surrounds the panels on the comics PAGE. When clearly delimited, the gutter is materialised by a white space and/or by a FRAME that separates the panels. Although it is the place of the off-frame, the intericonic space can sometimes be invaded by DRAWINGS or

TEXT. When there is no clear separation between panels, the gutter only exists through its function (without its materiality), at the risk of being confused with the TEMPORAL and SEMANTIC ellipsis lying between the panels. Scott McCloud (1993: 66–67) popularised a functional understanding of the gutter by describing comics READING as a CLOSURE process in which the READER fills in the gaps between panels. The resulting functional over-determination of the gutter, to the detriment of the visible contents of comics, has been criticised (Groensteen 2007: 112–115). A key concept in COMICS STUDIES, the gutter today retains an undeniable importance, especially as the space of the nonfigurable in nonfiction comics (Chute 2016: 35–36), and has helped to build bridges towards NARRATOLOGY (Berlatsky 2009), poetry studies (McHale 2010), rhetoric (Hilst 2011), and QUEER studies (Chase 2012).

Benoît Glaude

## *References*

Berlatsky, E. (2009) "Lost in the Gutter: Within and Between Frames in Narrative and Narrative Theory," *Narrative* 17(2), pp. 162–187.

Chase, G. (2012) "'In the Gutter': Comix Theory," *Studies in Comics* 3(1), pp. 107–128.

Chute, H. (2016) *Disaster Drawn: Visual Witness, Comics, and Documentary Form*. Cambridge: Harvard University Press.

Groensteen, T. (1999) *The System of Comics*. Translated from French by B. Beaty and N. Nguyen, 2007. Jackson: University Press of Mississippi.

Hilst, J. C. (2011) "Gutter Talk: (An)Other Idiom," *JAC* 31(1–2), pp. 153–176.

McCloud, S. (1993) *Understanding Comics: The Invisible Art*. New York: Harper Perennial.

McHale, B. (2010) "Narrativity and Segmentivity, or, Poetry in the Gutter" in Grishakova, M. and Ryan, M.-L. (eds.) *Intermediality and Storytelling*. Berlin: De Gruyter, pp. 27–48.

## Head Shop

A head shop is a retail storefront that specialises in MERCHANDISE related to drug countercultures. Emerging in the 1960s, "head shops appealed to a new generation of cultural and political rebels eager to purchase products that were purportedly hip or psychedelic, including paraphernalia for enhancing LSD trips or for smoking marijuana" (Davis 2017: 84). UNDERGROUND COMIX were distributed and sold through head shops from the 1960s through the 1970s, though increased scrutiny from law enforcement concerning drug use and obscenity resulted in a decline of the number of head shops and the sale of underground comix in those stores. Yet, the association between head shops and comics would lead to the establishment of some COMIC BOOK shops, such as "the Bay Area's 'Comics & Comix,' by all appearances the first comic book retail chain in the United States (…) Such underground-friendly shops were, arguably, the root of the direct market" (Hatfield 2005: 21). Often independently owned and in close proximity to colleges or universities, head shops helped to establish a distinct and DIRECT MARKET retail system for the circulation and distribution of comics, one that still remains today in the FORM of the COMICS SHOP.

Daniel Worden

### *References*

Arffman, P. (2019) "Comics from the Underground: Publishing Revolutionary Comic Books in the 1960s and Early 1970s," *Journal of Popular Culture* 52(1), pp.169–198.

Davis, J. C. (2017) *From Head Shops to Whole Foods: The Rise and Fall of Activist Entrepreneurs.* New York: Columbia University Press.

Hatfield, C. (2005) *Alternative Comics: An Emerging Literature.* Jackson: University Press of Mississippi.

## Hermeneutics

Hermeneutics is a toolbox of methodologies aimed at solving problems of interpretation of human actions, texts, and other meaningful material. It is an aetiological activity wherein an interpreter (such as a scholar) derives a view with regard to a possible meaning vis-à-vis the subject (such as a comic), which thereafter becomes subject to hermeneutics. Hermeneutics in comics is largely sociological, deriving from Friedrich Schleiermacher who thought interpretation has to be contended through the social and HISTORICAL context in which a work was made. Martin Heidegger further developed this concept of what is known as the hermeneutic circle, which claims that understanding (interpretation) of individual parts of a work is based on understanding the whole work, while the whole work can only be understood through understanding the individual parts. Relayed to comics wherein individual IMAGES juxtaposed (or related in some way) make a whole work of comics, Thierry Groensteen's *The System of Comics* (1999), for example, offers an understanding of the REGISTER through its formal qualia. Interpretations of whole works can come from examination of its parts, which might include verbal, non-verbal, PARATEXTS, and the many actors who had a role in making the work as it appears to be, physical or not.

Bruce Mutard

## *References*

Groensteen, T. (1999) *The System of Comics*. Translated from French by B. Beaty and N. Nguyen, 2007. Jackson: University Press of Mississippi.

Heidegger, M. (1927) *Being and Time*. Translated from German by J. Stambaugh. Reprint 1996. Albany: SUNY Press.

Mantzavinos, C. (2020) "Hermeneutics" in *The Stanford Encyclopedia of Philosophy*. Available at: https://plato.stanford.edu/entries/hermeneutics/ [Accessed 16 June 2020].

Schleiermacher, F. (1838) *Hermeneutics and Criticism: And Other Writings*. Translated from German by A. Bowie (ed.), 2008. Cambridge: Cambridge University Press.

## Hero

In classical terms, a hero is a figure of often otherworldly or supernatural ability and courage who rises to meet danger or right wrongs, and around whom a MYTH or STORY cycle tends to rotate. Joseph Campbell summarises the trajectory of such a character as "[a] hero ventures forth (…) into a region of supernatural wonder: fabulous forces are then encountered and a decisive victory is won: the hero comes back (…) with the power to bestow boons on his fellow man" (1993: 30). In a more modern idiom, the term hero also tends simply to signify the protagonist of a story—Christopher Vogler, for example, has argued that this type of character "is the hero of a journey" (2007: 7) irrespective of what kind of story is being told. Within the idiom of comics, the SUPERHERO has tended to be the most dominant example of the hero figure (this is arguably due to the popularity of Marvel and DC's superhero universes), and in recent years many of the more popular SUPERHEROES have tended to be represented as increasingly morally ambivalent anti-heroes.

Houman Sadri

## *References*

Campbell, J. (1993) *The Hero with a Thousand Faces.* London: Fontana.

Vogler, C. (2007) *The Writer's Journey.* San Francisco: Michael Weise Productions.

## Heteroglossia

Conceived in the 1930s by Russian philosopher and literary critic Mikhail Bakhtin, the idea of varied, multiple LANGUAGES within one single language became known in English as heteroglossia. These different languages are expressed through the socio-cultural, the HISTORICAL, the political, and the contemporaneous, for example, resulting in a range of LITERARY VOICES. Each language thus embodies facets of the socio-cultural through the AUTHOR's choice of, for example, REGISTER, lexemes, and syntax. Within COMICS STUDIES, heteroglossia is identified through a denotation of voices both textually and visually, as the IMAGE-TEXT MEDIUM offers an exceptional space for competing NARRATIVES to find expression. As Bakhtin (1981) writes, "An artistic representation, an image of the object, may be penetrated by this dialogic play of verbal intentions that meet and are interwoven in it; such an image need not stifle these forces, but on the contrary may activate and organize them" (277). In comics the choice of COLOUR palette, the STYLE of LINE work, alongside PAGE LAYOUT and font choices constitute and embody the heteroglossia of the narrative as much as the language is expressed through the choice of register, lexemes, and syntax.

E. Dawson Varughese

### *References*

Bakhtin, M. (1935–1935) "Discourse in the Novel" in Holquist, M. (ed.) *The Dialogic Imagination*. Translated from Russian by C. Emerson and M. Holquist, 1981. Austin: University of Texas Press, pp. 259–422.

## Heterosemiosis

Heterosemiosis is the integrated comprehension of significant REPRESENTATIONS belonging to heterogeneous systems of representation, such as the integrated comprehension of visual DEPICTION and WRITING in the comics REGISTER or the integrated comprehension of music and speech in musical theatre, for example (Martinez 1996). Although literally meaning "other semiosis," referring to the functional differences between SIGN systems, the word also implies either that there are general rules, general conditions, or both, to which all representations conform, regardless of register. As such, heterosemiosis recalls discussions about the specific semiosis of the TEXT/IMAGE relationships in the comics register and, in particular, discussion of either the HYBRIDITY or the singularity of the register (Meskin 2009: 236, Sabin 1993: 9). Elisabeth 'Lisa' El Refaie proposes that the term is a replacement for hybrid, arguing for the overarching importance of discursive functions in integrating heterogeneous sign systems (2014).

Simon Grennan

### *References*

El Refaie, E. L. (2014) "Heterosemiosis: Mixing sign systems in graphic narrative texts," *Semiotica* 202, pp. 21–39.

Martínez, J. M. G. (1996) *Heterosemiosis in musical and literary discourse: Towards an integrated semiotics of music and language*. PhD. University of Murcia.

*Meskin, A. (2009)* "Comics as Literature?" *The British Journal of Aesthetics* 49(3), pp. 219–239.

Sabin, R. (1993) *Adult Comics: An Introduction*. Abingdon: Routledge.

## History

History intersects with comics in three ways. First, comics can serve as sources of history. Scholars can use comics made in a certain period to complement the existing knowledge of that time. Although this is a practice that is not yet applied widely, Chapman et al. have made a convincing case for it (2015). Second, comics themselves can be histories. There are many examples of comic book histories—such as Jack Jackson's *Comanche Moon* (1978) and *Los Tejanos* (1981), Michel de France's (ed.) *Histoire de France en bandes dessinées* (1976–1978), Shigeru Mizuki's *Showa: A History of Japan* (1988–1989), and Shotaro Ishinomori's *Manga Nihon no Rekishi* (1989–1993)—as well as studies thereof, especially in the context of MEMORY STUDIES (Witek 1989; Ahmed and Crucifix 2018; Otmazgin and Suter 2016; Earle 2017; Spanjers 2019). As a GENRE, historical comics have opened borders and often mix with adjacent genres, such as fiction, AUTOBIOGRAPHY, and DOCUMENTARY (El Refaie 2012; Mickwitz 2016; Chute 2016). Finally, comics themselves also have a history, which first was recorded almost exclusively in comics FANDOM and by comics practitioners such as Jim Steranko, and now increasingly is also of interest to academia (Kunzle 1973, 1990; Smolderen 2000; Sabin 1996). In 2012, Fred van Lente and Ryan Dunlavey started PUBLISHING *The Comic Book History of Comics*, combining comics as a subject and MEDIUM for history. Their work is preceded by ARTIST autobiographies that also emphasise the history of the comics medium, such as Yoshihiro Tatsumi's *A Drifting Life* (2008) and Lewis Trondheim's *Approximate Continuum Comics* (2011).

Rik Spanjers

### *References*

Ahmed, M. and Crucifix, B. (eds.) (2018) *Comics Memory: Archives and Styles.* London: Palgrave Macmillan.

Chapman, J., Sherif, A., Hoyles, A., and Kerr, A. (2015) *Comics and the World Wars: A Cultural Record.* London: Palgrave Macmillan.

Chute, H. (2016) *Disaster Drawn: Visual Witness, Comics, and Documentary Form.* Cambridge: Harvard University Press.

Earle, H. E. H. (2017) *Comics, Trauma and the New Art of War.* Jackson: University Press of Mississippi.

El Refaie, E. L. (2012) *Autobiographical Comics: Life Writing in Pictures.* Jackson: University Press of Mississippi.
Kunzle, D. (1973) *History of the Comic Strip, Volume 1: The Early Comic Strip 1450–1825.* Berkeley: University of California Press.
Kunzle, D. (1990) *History of the Comic Strip, Volume 2: The Nineteenth Century.* Berkeley: University of California Press.
Mickwitz, N. (2016) *Documentary Comics: Graphic Truth-telling in a Skeptical Age.* London: Palgrave Macmillan.
Otmazgin, N. and Suter, R. (eds.) (2016) *Rewriting History in Manga: Stories for the Nation.* London: Palgrave Macmillan.
Sabin, R. (1996) *Comics, Comix and Graphic Novels: A History of Comic Art.* London: Phaidon Press.
Smolderen, T. (2000) *The Origins of Comics: From William Hogarth to Winsor McCay.* Translated from French by B. Beaty and N. Nguyen, 2014. Jackson: University Press of Mississippi.
Spanjers, R. (2019) *Comics Realism and the Maus Event: Comics and the Dynamics of World War II Remembrance.* PhD. University of Amsterdam.
Van Lente, F. and Dunlavey, R. (2017) *The Comic Book History of Comics: USA 1898–1972.* London: Penguin Random House.
Witek, J. (1989) *Comic Books as History: The Narrative Art of Jack Jackson, Art Spiegelman and Harvey Pekar.* Jackson: University Press of Mississippi.

## Horror

Horror focuses on PSYCHOLOGICALLY irrational fears of the unknown. ADAPTATIONS from *Classics Illustrated* (1943–onwards) used the gothic TROPES of Percy Bysshe Shelley, Edgar Allan Poe, Bram Stoker and others in their NARRATIVES (Barker 1992; Benton 1992; Gifford 1984). *Eerie #1* (1947) is regarded as the first horror comic with *Adventures into the Unknown* (1948–1967) the MEDIUM'S first ongoing SERIES. Topics included familial madness, decay, ghosts, and (un)death. Luridly black-humoured covers saw women-in-peril, zombies, and headless corpses adorning EC COMICS' *Tales from the Crypt* (1950–1955) (Kurtzman 2019) which in turn led to scrutiny and suggestion by the (1953) Senate Subcommittee on Juvenile Delinquency that content be toned down (Trombetta 2010). Despite EC cancelling their output, reprints and revivals ensured horror's survival, broadening out the GENRE to wider POPULAR CULTURE appeal. Critical reappraisal came with (amongst many other notable examples) Neil Gaiman's *Sandman* (1979–1986), Junji Ito's *Uzumaki* (1998–1999), Charles Burns' *Black Hole* (1995–2005), and Robert Kirkman's *The Walking Dead* (2003–), all of which offered writers and READERS a treatise to explore the *fin de siècle* era. The CANON reflects upon and navigates through, contextual, social, and cultural anxieties, in turn engaging with and reflecting upon the human condition because of their psychological resonances within the individual.

Steven Gerrard

## *References*

Barker, M. (1992) *A Haunt of Fears: The Strange History of the British Horror Comics Campaign*. Jackson: University Press of Mississippi.

Benton, M. (1992) *Horror Comics: The Illustrated History*. Dallas. Taylor Publishing.

Gifford, D. (1984) *The International Book of Comics*. London: Deans International Publishing, pp.180–190.

Goulart, R. (2001) *Great American Comic Books*. Lincolnwood: Publications International, Ltd.

Kurtzman, H. (2019) *Choke Gasp! The Best of 75 Years of EC Comics*. Milwaukee: Dark Horse Books.

Trombetta, J. (2010) *The Horror! The Horror! Comic Books the Government Didn't Want You to Read!* New York: Abrams Books.

## Humour

Humour in comics takes many different forms from the slapstick GAGS of children's comics to the PARODY and SATIRE in UNDERGROUND COMIX and the darker THEMES explored in AUTOBIOGRAPHICAL GRAPHIC NOVELS. The fact that "humour is a crucial element in caricature and satire alike has been recognised in some important work on comics histories" (Mickwitz et al. 2020: 10) and scholars such as Arthur Asa Berger (1970), Jean Lee Cole (2020), David Kunzle (1983), and Roger Sabin (2014) have considered how humour operates in comics by looking at their origins in CARICATURE and CARTOONING. Other aspects of humour have received less attention but recent scholarship has started to address this issue. Nicola Streeten (2020) has examined humour in British FEMINIST cartoons, comics, and graphic novels from the 1960s to the present day, while Christophe J. Thompson (2020) has explored this issue in British children's comics. Ian Gordon (2016) and Alex Valente (2016) have also looked at humour in children's comics but address the issue of TRANSLATION across different LANGUAGES and cultures and what this might mean for the ways in which it operates by examining American, Australian, British, and Italian comics.

Ian Horton

## *References*

Berger, A. A. (1970) *Li'l Abner: A Study in American Satire.* New York: Twayne Publishers.

Cole, J. L. (2020) *How the Other Half Laughs: The Comic Sensibility in American Culture, 1895–1920.* Jackson: University Press of Mississippi.

Gordon, I. (2016) *Kid Comic Strips: A Genre Across Four Continents.* London: Palgrave Macmillan.

Kunzle, D. (1983) "Between Broadsheet Caricature and 'Punch': Cheap Newspaper Cuts for the Lower Classes of the 1830's," *Art Journal* 43(4), pp. 339–346.

Mickwitz, N., Hague, I., and Horton, I. (2020) "Introduction" in Mickwitz, N., Hague, I., and Horton, I. (eds.) *Representing Acts of Violence in Comics.* Abingdon: Routledge, pp. 1–16.

Sabin, R. (2014) "Ally Sloper, Victorian Comic Book Hero: Interpreting a Comedy Type" in Machlin, D. (ed.) *Visual Communication.* Berlin: De Gruyter.

Streeten, N. (2020) *UK Feminist Cartoons and Comics: A Critical Survey.* London: Palgrave Macmillan.

Thompson, C. J. "'Boiled or Fried Dennis?' Violence, Play and Narrative in 'Dennis the Menace and Gnasher'" in Mickwitz, N., Hague, I., and Horton, I. (eds.) *Representing Acts of Violence in Comics.* Abingdon: Routledge, pp. 105–118.

Valente, A. (2016) "'A Fumetto, A Comic and a BD Walk into a Bar…': The Translation of Humour in Comics" in Brienza, C. and Johnston, P. (eds.) *Cultures of Comic Work.* London: Palgrave Macmillan, pp. 265–281.

## Hybrid

While comics are often referred to as a MEDIUM, they are also considered a hybrid FORM and have variously been described as consisting of a mix, blend, combination, or fusion of words and IMAGES (with the exception of IMAGELESS and SILENT COMICS). Miodrag notes that while it is mostly "indisputable that words and images interact in producing comics' narratives," debates have historically arisen when people have attempted to "pin down the precise nature of this interaction" (2013: 83). Thierry Smolderen describes the origin of comics as an "example of graphic hybridisation" (2014: 47) and asserts that it is this hybrid nature that leaves comics open to further hybridisation with other forms (60). This potential for hybridisation can be seen particularly in DIGITAL COMICS which Thierry Groensteen describes as "intrinsically hybrid, cross-fertilizing the comic system" with elements of the World Wide Web, video GAMES, and ANIMATION (2013: 75). Notable digital hybrids include hypercomics, which combine comics with the structures of hypermedia (Goodbrey 2017: 87), game comics which combine comics and video games and MOTION COMICS, which Craig Smith describes a type of "hybrid animation, directly influenced by existing comic book narratives and artwork" (2013: 254). Outside of a digital context, Paul Gravett identifies the format of "gallery comics" (2013: 131) that are MEDIATED by ARCHITECTURE and hybridise comics with aspects of installation ART.

Daniel Merlin Goodbrey

### *References*

Goodbrey, D. (2017) "The Impact of Digital Mediation and Hybridisation on the Form of Comics." PhD. University of Hertfordshire.

Gravett, P. (2013) *Comics Art*. London: Tate Publishing.

Groensteen, T. (2011) *Comics and Narration*. Translated from French by A. Miller, 2013. Jackson: University Press of Mississippi.

Miodrag, H. (2013) *Comics and Language: Reimagining Critical Discourse on the Form*. Jackson: University Press of Mississippi.

Smith, C. (2013) "Motion Comic Poetics: A Study in the Relations between Digital Animation and the Comic Book." PhD. Queen's University Belfast.

Smolderen, T. (2013) "Graphic Hybridization, the Crucible of Comics" in Miller, A. and Beaty, B. (eds.) *The French Comics Theory Reader*. Translated from French by A. Miller and B. Beaty. Reprint 2014. Leuven: Leuven University Press, pp. 47–61.

## Icon

One of the vexing issues in trying to define the concept icon stems from the epistemological difference between the conceptualisation of Peircean SEMIOTICS and Saussurean semiology, both of which employ the same words, but within distinct frameworks. Following Charles Sanders Peirce's definition, an icon is a REPRESENTATION that shares a resemblance with the thing represented (Hoopes 2013). In comics, we recognise in any given depiction, usually DRAWN, our visual experience of instances of those objects, like an "apple," a "table," or "Paul." Engaging with STYLE, an icon can either follow simplified LINES and shapes, in a SCHEMATIC rendition, or use layers of detail and texture in a more naturalistic or even photorealist approach. Scott McCloud uses the term icon in a broader sense, including what he calls "ideas" (1993: 27), and thus encompassing what Peirce deems symbols.

Pedro Moura

### *References*

Hoopes, J. (1991) *Peirce on Signs: Writings on Semiotic by Charles Sanders Peirce.* Chapel Hill: The University of North Carolina Press.

McCloud, S. (1993) *Understanding Comics: The Invisible Art.* New York: Harper Perennial.

## Iconography

An ART historical method, iconography refers to the description and classification of visual motifs and symbols, aimed at situating their meanings in HISTORICAL contexts. Iconography embraces a larger scope of IMAGES than art histories focused on individual ARTISTS. A key attempt in exploring the cultural and anthropological dimensions of iconography was Aby Warburg's study of recurring motifs by means of visual juxtaposition, which he described as an "iconology of the interval" (Michaud 2004: 251–253). Erwin Panofsky famously pushed its cultural symbolism further, refining the term as an "iconography turned interpretative" (1955: 32). This differentiation between iconography and iconology has tended to wane in art history (Gombrich 1972) while raising new INTERDISCIPLINARY questions in studies of VISUAL CULTURE

(Mitchell 1986). If art historical methods have not been the main model for COMICS STUDIES, iconographic approaches have taken a variety of expressions. Katherine Roeder (2014) reads Winsor McCay's work alongside the mass culture of the time, identifying historical motifs. In an exercise of cognitive NARRATOLOGY, Karin Kukkonen (2010) studies how the iconography of SUPERHERO comics helps readers to navigate their complex SERIAL history. Rachel Kunert-Graf (2018) explores the use of a "lynching iconography" and the act of MEDIATED looking it implicates in contemporary works.

Benoît Crucifix

## *References*

Gombrich, E. H. (1972) *Symbolic Images.* London: Phaidon Press.

Kukkonen, K. (2010) "Navigating Infinite Earths: Readers, Mental Models, and the Multiverse of Superhero Comics," *Storyworlds* 2(1), pp. 39–58.

Kunert-Graf, R. (2018) "Lynching Iconography: Looking in Graphic Narrative," *Inks* 2(3), pp. 312–333.

Michaud, P.-A. (2004) *Aby Warburg and the Image in Motion.* New York: Zone Books.

Mitchell, W. J. T. (1986) *Iconology: Image, Text, Ideology.* Chicago: University Press of Chicago.

Panofsky, E. (1955) *Meaning in the Visual Arts.* Garden City: Doubleday.

Roeder, K. (2014) *Wide Awake in Slumberland: Fantasy, Mass Culture, and Modernism in the Art of Winsor McCay.* Jackson: University Press of Mississippi.

## Identity

Judith Butler defines identity as "the internal coherence of the subject, indeed, the self-identical status of the person" (2006: 23). Theorists in the twentieth century have argued that identity is in flux and is always in process or in negotiation with external influences and "social, material, TEMPORAL and spatial contexts" (Edensor 2002: 29). Stuart Hall argues that identities "are produced in specific historical and institutional sites within specific discursive formations and practices, by specific enunciative strategies" (2007: 17). Most importantly for Hall, and for POSTCOLONIAL, FEMINIST, and QUEER scholars, identities are constructed in relation to the Other. Thus, "the 'unities', which identities proclaim, are in fact, constructed within the play of power and exclusion" (ibid.: 18). This view of identity is influenced largely by francophone theory, which draws on various theoretical angles, such as Marxism, Althusserian Marxism, structural LINGUISTICS, and Foucauldian DISCOURSE theory, and also, crucially, PSYCHOANALYSIS (Du Gay et al. 2007: 2). Challenges to this theoretical framework, from, for example, Kleinian theorists, are often based in a critique of its use of psychoanalysis (ibid.: 3–4). Comics' MULTIMODALITY tends to provide opportunities for representations of contrasting intersubjects, often foregrounding contested or mutable identities.

Olivia Hicks

## *References*

Butler, J. (1990) *Gender Trouble: Feminism and the Subversion of Identity.* Reprint, 2006. Abingdon: Routledge.

Du Gay, P., Evans, J., and Redman, P. (2007) "General Introduction" in Du Gay, P., Evans, J., and Redman, P. (eds.) *Identity: A Reader.* London: SAGE, pp. 1–6.

Edensor, T. (2002) *National Identity, Popular Culture and Everyday Life.* Abingdon: Routledge.

Hall, S. (2007) "Who needs 'identity'?" in Du Gay, P., Evans, J., and Redman, P. (eds.) *Identity: A Reader.* London: SAGE, pp.15–30.

## Illness

Illness is an altered human state considered a "malfunction" (Murphy 2020) of biological, psychological, or social processes. Related to duration, illness can be defined as acute or chronic. Illness is often considered a DISABILITY when a normative malfunction becomes chronic and unchangeable or the trajectory of illness is prolonged. Additional "normative judgment" of the perceived suffering by the ill person, caregivers, medical personnel, and the collective society can determine the treatment response. Treatment outcomes are oriented towards cure or a return to optimal functioning. The subjective and social nature of illness inserts a complexity to what is considered a malfunction. Bodily malfunctions may be desirable in the case of a female who takes hormones to interfere with ovulation and possible pregnancy. An illness may also be a product of social values, for example, the classification of homosexuality as a mental illness (Spitzer 1981), which was subsequently declassified amidst much controversy in 1973. The embodied response to illness and their NARRATIVES lend themselves well to the picturing in comics. Kristin Gay (2016) suggests the complexities of illness in its many manifestations can be MEDIATED through comics to "resist totalizing DISCOURSE about illness (that is medical) in favor of subjective accounts" (172). Illness is a subjective, visceral, and social experience.

JoAnn Purcell

## *References*

Gay, K. (2016) "Breaking Up (at/with) Illness Narratives" in Foss, C., Gray, J., and Whalen, Z. (eds.) *Disability in Comic Books and Graphic Narratives.* London: Palgrave Macmillan, pp. 171–186.

Murphy, D. (2020) "Concepts of Disease and Health" in Salta, E. N. (ed.) *The Stanford Encyclopedia of Philosophy. Available at:* https://plato.stanford.edu/entries/health-disease/ *[Accessed 15 July 2020].*

Spitzer, R. L. (1981) "The diagnostic status of homosexuality in DSM-III: A reformulation of the issues," *American Journal of Psychiatry* 138(2) pp. 210–215.

## Illumination

Illumination is traditionally used to refer to the intricate painting of IMAGES or individual letters within a medieval manuscript. Different stages could be involved in the process, including preparing the page with a series of guiding pinpricks, initial sketching, or gilding, for example to add gold leaf, and then the final inclusion of COLOURS and borders. Examples include the Lindisfarne Gospels (London, British Library, Cotton MS Nero D.IV, c. 720, Anglo-Saxon art), the Book of Kells (Dublin, Trinity College Library, MS 58, c. 800, Hiberno-Saxon art), and the Hunterian Psalter (Glasgow, Glasgow University Library, MS Hunter U. 3. 2. (229), c. 1170, Romanesque art). In terms of the proto-HISTORY of comics, illuminated manuscripts can be seen as the first book-FORM image NARRATIVES. The interaction of TEXT and image is also essential, often with illuminated initial letters or *incipits*, which are used to emphasise the start of a section, making an image from the text itself. In contemporary comics a hand-creation process akin to illumination can be used to develop an ARTIST's book that overlaps illustration with GRAPHIC NOVEL, as for example in the case of Dominique Goblet's *Faire semblant c'est mentir* (*Pretending is Lying*, 2007).

Laurence Grove

## *References*

Library of Congress (2010) "Illuminated Manuscripts from Europe" in *World Digital Library*. Available at: https://www.wdl.org/en/sets/illuminated-manuscripts/ [Accessed 3 August 2020].

## ILLUSTRATION

Illustration can be understood as the pictorial element of a comic that interacts and might be contrasted with the TEXT. Although one individual can fulfil the functions of illustrator and scriptwriter—for instance, Hergé for the early *Tintin* stories—increasingly single-AUTHOR PRODUCTION is associated with ALTERNATIVE COMICS, whereas large production houses separate the roles, as in *All Star Superman* (2005–2008) with Grant Morrison as WRITER and Frank Quitely as illustrator. Illustration techniques for comics traditionally start with pencilled outline, to be followed by INKING and COLOURING (again, with these being roles for separate CREATORS in large-scale productions); however, increasingly ARTISTS use software tools. Styles of illustration vary from photo-REALISM to "big nose" simplification, with the overall effect created by means of the *interaction* with the text, for example, through disparity between words and illustration to create HUMOUR. Alternatively, illustration can be stand-alone—such as a discrete watercolour illustration—or can refer to illustrated books. One such example are the editions of A. A. Milne's *Winnie-the-Pooh* bearing E. H. Shepherd's illustration (originally from 1926). However, in such cases, unlike in comics, the IMAGES could be removed, and the story would still function.

Laurence Grove

## Image

An image is a visual construct REPRESENTING something. In its "natural sense," it is "a likeness, a picture, or a simulacrum" (Furbank 1970: 1) where the object of the image could be based upon a real-world person or object, a STORY, or a representation of a more ABSTRACT subject such as an emotion, idea, or concept. W. J. T. Mitchell suggests five branches (graphical, optical, perceptual, mental, and verbal) to categorise the "incredible variety of things" referred to as images. The graphic image is the most pertinent to comics and, when considered in SEQUENCE, the image becomes a key component across various definitions of the comics FORM (Hague 2014: 13–17). The conceptual juxtaposition of the image against the verbal TEXT in COMICS STUDIES can result in the problematic "direct mapping of theorisations of verbal structures onto theorisations of visual phenomena" (Grennan 2017: 24). Resistance to this approach comes from comics' "apparent irreducibility of the image and the story" (Groensteen 2007: 9) created by images in sequence and by the phenomena of "seeing-in" (Grennan 2017: 37, Wollheim 2015: 141–142), which establishes that images, singularly or in sequence, are not equivalent to a word or page of verbal text, but are ultimately balanced against verbal material which may influence further mental imagery or INTERTEXTUAL associations the image evokes (Mitchell 1984: 527).

Geraint D'Arcy

### *References*

Furbank, P. N. (1970) *Reflections on the Word 'Image'*. London: Martin Secker and Warburg, Ltd.

Grennan, S. (2017) *A Theory of Narrative Drawing*. London: Palgrave Macmillan.

Groensteen, T. (1999) *The System of Comics*. Translated from French by B. Beaty and N. Nguyen, 2007. Jackson: University Press of Mississippi.

Hague, I. (2014) *Comics and the Senses: A Multisensory Approach to Comics and Graphic Novels*. London: Taylor and Francis.

Mitchell, W. T. J. (1984) "What is an image?" *New Literary History* 15(3), pp. 503–537.

Wollheim, R. (1968) *Art and its Objects*. Reprint 2015. Cambridge: Cambridge University Press.

## Imageless Comics

Imageless comics, or pictureless comics, are a form of EXPERIMENTAL COMICS that attempt to discard pictorial elements and use only TEXT. If comics are generally a combination of IMAGE and text, imageless comics are the logical extreme on the other end from WORDLESS COMICS (McCloud 2009). In imageless comics, CREATORS often experiment with TYPOGRAPHY and PAGE LAYOUT, making the FORM similar to concrete poetry or graphic DESIGN (Koch 2004). Other examples of pictureless comics focus on PANELS that are either all black, white, or perhaps another flat COLOUR, combining them with CAPTIONS or SPEECH BALLOONS (Badman 2005a-c). In Derik Badman's *A Walking Tour of the MoMA, NYC* (2005), *Best of Nancy* (2005), and *Pictureless Comics* (2005), the single-colour panels are explained as "night sky," "snowstorm," or "monochromatic painting," in which case one can question whether the panels do not become a kind of pictorial REPRESENTATION after all. Similarly, there are pictorial aspects to letters that are graphically manipulated for visual expression, and Holbo even argues, "Letterforms are images. They just aren't pictures" (Holbo 2012: 19). As such, one might question whether imageless comics actually exist, just as in a philosophical argument one might suggest that a novel is the most extreme form of an imageless comic (Holbo 2012; Horrocks 2001).

Barbara Postema

### *References*

Holbo, J. (2012) "Redefining Comics" in Meskin, A. and Cook, R. T. (eds.) *The Art of Comics: A Philosophical Approach.* Hoboken: Wiley-Blackwell, p. 3–30.

Horrocks, D. (2001) *Inventing Comics: Scott McCloud's Definition of Comics.* Wellington: Hicksville Press.

Koch, K. (2004) *The Art of the Possible.* New York: Soft Skull Press.

McCloud, S. (2009) "Comics Without Pictures?" *scottmccloud.com*, 9 October 2009. Available at: http://scottmccloud.com/2009/10/09/comics-without-pictures/ [Accessed 19 August 2020].

## Imagetext

W. J. T. Mitchell coined the term imagetext in his influential *Picture Theory* in order to "reveal the inextricable weaving together of representation and discourse" (1994: 83). Imagetext, he argues, challenges prevailing assumptions and conventions concerning REPRESENTATION in TEXT and IMAGES by signalling their "unstable dialectic" (ibid.). To expose the ways in which texts and images can interact literally and theoretically, he proposes to designate: (1) the (often perceived) gap between image and text as "image/text" and (2) the relations of the visual and the verbal as "image-text," both of which he argues are distinct from (3) the combinations of texts and images, or imagetext (ibid.: 89), distinctions which are also contemplated in INTERMEDIALITY studies. By far the most widespread of these terms, imagetext is often incorrectly assumed to stand for all three (Mitchell 2015). After Mitchell's designation of comics as belonging to the category of imagetext, (1994: 91–94), it has often been used as a synonym for comics, albeit one that stresses a theoretical preoccupation with FORM. The degree to which imagetext has become one of the central theoretical concepts of COMICS STUDIES is reflected by the name of one of the central journals in the field, *ImageTexT: Interdisciplinary Comics Studies* (2004–).

Rik Spanjers

### *References*

Mitchell, W. J. T. (2015) *Image Science: Iconology, Visual Culture, and Media Aesthetics.* Chicago: University of Chicago Press.

Mitchell, W. J. T. (1994) *Picture Theory: Essays on Verbal and Visual Representation.* Chicago: University of Chicago Press.

## Imitation

While somewhat passé in contemporary scholarship, imitation has been a classic notion in rhetoric and ART EDUCATION for centuries. MIMESIS or the "imitation of nature" undergirded particular STYLES, rules, or protocols to follow. Imitation is a key term in Rodolphe Töpffer's (1858) essays on DRAWING, which opposed academic imitation based on mimesis (epitomised by the new daguerreotype) to the expressivity of "simpler" CARICATURE drawings. Thierry Smolderen (2014) expounds this dual meaning of imitation in nineteenth-century graphic culture by identifying its polygraphic HUMOUR based on the imitation and appropriation of visual REGISTERS. Such cases require an imitation "in which the speaker remains fully as an embodied subject recognisably adopting another's subjective position" (Grennan 2017: 248). Imitation relies on the recognition of that which is imitated. Adopting a particular way of drawing can have many reasons: PARODY, SATIRE, admiration, SERIAL continuity, NARRATIVE strategies. A CARTOONIST'S style is always a COLLABORATIVE DIALOGUE with preexisting styles, and graphic choices result from more or less implicit GENEALOGIES and traditions (Baudry et al. 2019). Whether servile or original, imitation always designates a fundamentally social and intersubjective process that involves some form of invention by way of imitation (Tarde 1890).

Benoît Crucifix

## *References*

Baudry, J., Hébert X., and Roger, K. (2019) "Hériter, imiter" in Berthou, B. and Dürrenmatt, J. (eds.) *Style(s) de (la) bande dessinée*. Paris: Classiques Garnier, pp. 53–111.

Grennan, S. (2017) *A Theory of Narrative Drawing*. London: Palgrave Macmillan.

Smolderen, T. (2000) *The Origins of Comics: From William Hogarth to Winsor McCay*. Translated from French by B. Beaty and N. Nguyen, 2014. Jackson: University Press of Mississippi.

Tarde, G. (1890) *Les Lois de l'imitation*. Paris: Félix Alcan.

Töpffer, R. (1858) *Réflexions et menus-propos d'un peintre génevois*. Paris: Dubochet.

## Index

In DRAWING, the MARK is always an indexical SIGN of the activity of its PRODUCTION, following a broad definition of the indexical sign by Charles Sanders Peirce, as a REPRESENTATION that indicates a physical connection with its object (1998: 9). Hence, as an index of a body, a drawn mark has causes (and offers consequences) distinct from the TRACE of a body. Trace is a type of indexical sign produced as a direct remnant of an activity. This distinction is particularly significant relative to descriptions of different mark-making activities and descriptions of different technical processes. Digital imaging TECHNOLOGIES, for example, can index activities of the body without tracing them (i.e. without producing direct remnants), whereas a mark made in the sand with a finger is always both index and trace (Grennan 2017: 15).

Simon Grennan

## *References*

Grennan, S. (2017) *A Theory of Narrative Drawing*. London: Palgrave Macmillan.

Peirce, C. S. (1893–1913) *The Essential Peirce, Volume 2: Selected Philosophical Writings, 1893–1913*. Peirce Edition Project (ed.), 1998. Bloomington: Indiana University Press.

## Influence

Influence designates the capacity to have an effect on someone or something, as in "bad influences" or being "under the influence." It is in these terms that psychiatrists and sociologists inquired into the "impact" of comics on children READERS in the 1950s. Influence—a key term in Fredric Wertham's *Seduction of the Innocent* (1954)—was at the heart of behavioural debates around children and their MEDIA, concerns shared by industry captains and EDUCATORS. This social notion of influence in mass media research presided over the AESTHETIC notion used in HISTORIES of ART and LITERATURE. Harold Bloom's *The Anxiety of Influence* (1973) posits that the "strong poet" has to "swerve" away from their predecessors, and is at odds with the COLLABORATIVE and CONSTRAINED PRODUCTION contexts of the comics industry, in which following influence can be a professional virtue (Hatfield 2012). If the term fell out of favour in literature departments, where it was displaced by INTERTEXTUALITY, recent interest in INTERMEDIAL exchanges, ADAPTATIONS, remixes, circulations, copying—old phenomena accelerated by digital TECHNOLOGIES—have requalified aesthetic influence and its cultural value (Garber 2016). Influence in comics can thus be mapped on a wide range of relationships between objects, social groups, territories, and media (Grennan 2018; Kannenberg 2017).

Benoît Crucifix

## *References*

Bloom, H. (1973) *The Anxiety of Influence: A Theory of Poetry.* Oxford: Oxford University Press.

Garber, M. (2016) "Over the Influence," *Critical Inquiry* 42(4), pp. 731–759.

Grennan, S. (2018) "The Influence of Manga on the Graphic Novel" in Baetens, J., Frey, H., and Tabachnick, S. (eds.) *The Cambridge History of the Graphic Novel.* Cambridge: Cambridge University Press, pp. 320–336.

Hatfield, C. (2012) *Hand of Fire: The Comics Art of Jack Kirby.* Jackson: University Press of Mississippi.

Kannenberg, Jr., G. (2017) "Chips Off the Ol' Blockhead: Evidence of Influence in Peanuts Parodies" in Gardner, J. and Gordon, I. (eds.) *The Comics of Charles Schulz: The Good Grief of Modern Life.* Jackson: University Press of Mississippi, pp. 197–212.

Wertham, F. (1954) *Seduction of the Innocent: The Influence of Comic Books on Today's Youth.* New York: Rinehart.

## Inker

This role is associated with industrialised American COMIC BOOK PRODUCTION methods initiated in the 1930s where the PENCILLER creates PAGE LAYOUTS and the main compositional features within PANELS that are then finished in detail by the inker (Ray Murray 2013: 339–340, Rogers 2006: 509–511). The penciller is usually credited as the main artistic force but when discussing Jack Kirby's work, Charles Hatfield notes the inker has a significant impact, with Joe Sinnott and Mike Royer seen as exemplary in realising Kirby's vision (2012: 182–183). Occasionally, ARTISTS in Europe also inked each other's work mainly due to the pressure of deadlines. In Britain during the 1970s and 1980s Brett Ewins and the McCarthy brothers worked COLLABORATIVELY on a number of COMIC STRIPS for *2000 AD* and Paul Neary was inker on Alan Davies' work for Marvel UK (Klaehn 2014: 10–14, Molcher 2015: 12–18). European artists such as Hergé employed a studio engaged in a range of tasks from tracing original DRAWINGS to inking and COLOURING final pages (Taylor 2010: 200–201). Similarly, in Japan many MANGA artists, such as Masashi Kishimoto, Takao Saito, and Osamu Tezuka, were "supported by a veritable army of artistic assistants who work shoulder-to-shoulder with him, contributing to every imaginable creative task short of adding their own names to the title page" (Brienza 2010: 111).

Ian Horton

## *References*

Brienza, C. (2010) "Producing comics culture: A sociological approach to the study of comics," *Journal of Graphic Novels and Comics* 1(2), pp. 105–119.

Hatfield, C. (2012) *Hand of Fire: The Comics Art of Jack Kirby*. Jackson: University of Mississippi Press.

Klaehn, J. (2014) "The infinite possibilities: An interview with comic book writer/artist Alan Davis," *Studies in Comics* 5(1), pp. 9–14.

Molcher, M. (2015) *2000 AD: The Creator Interviews 02*. Oxford: Rebellion.

Ray Murray, P. (2013) "Behind the Panel: Examining Invisible Labour in the Comics Publishing Industry," *Publishing Research Quarterly* 29(4), pp. 336–343.

Rogers, M. C. (2006) "Understanding Production: The Stylistic Impact of Artisan and Industrial Methods," *International Journal of Comic Art* 8(1), pp. 509–517.

Taylor, R. (2010) "The Artist at Work: Reading Originals in the Musée Hergé," *European Comic Art* 3(2), pp. 190–207.

## Interaction

The longest-lived and most familiar meaning of interaction in COMICS STUDIES denotes the cooperation (or conflict) between word and IMAGE on the page. Philippe Willems uses the term thus to explain

P. J. Hetzel's 1848 *Le Diable à Paris* (2008: 130), and Laurence Grove uses it to suggest an influence of Rodolphe Töpffer and BANDES DESSINÉES on Ferdinand de Saussure (2017: 61). Neil Cohn has also used the term to refer to how READERS connect "multiple interacting systems" to make meaning in comics (2014: 1) in keeping with his larger cognitive-LINGUISTIC understanding of the FORM. Further potential for the concept of interaction lies in its connection to the MEDIA studies theory of interface, a link already made in Branden Hookway's explanation of interface as "the kind of relating across a threshold that is often described as interaction" (2014: 7). Borrowing obliquely from Donald Hoffman (1998), theorists such as Lev Manovich (2001) developed a LANGUAGE for explaining interfaces such as computer screens, and later theorists including Alexander Galloway (2012) explored interface as an action in which form exerts control. Johanna Drucker (2011) has made explicit a link from Comics Studies to cultural studies by grounding an understanding of interface and new media in the frames of comics.

Joe Sutliff Sanders

## *References*

Cohn, N. (2014) "The Architecture of Visual Narrative Comprehension: The Interaction of Narrative Structure and Page Layout in Understanding Comics," *Frontiers in Psychology* 5, pp. 1–9.

Drucker, J. (2011) "Humanities Approaches to Interface Theory," *Culture Machine* 12, pp.1–20.

Galloway, A. (2012) *The Interface Effect*. Cambridge: Polity Press.

Grove, L. (2017) "Ferdinand de Saussure's Unknown 'Bandes Dessinées,'" *Yale French Studies* 131(2), pp. 46–61.

Hoffman, D. (1998) *Visual Intelligence: How We Create What We See*. New York: W. W. Norton.

Hookway, B. (2014) *Interface*. Cambridge: The Massachusetts Institute of Technology Press.

Manovich, L. (2001) *The Language of New Media*. Cambridge: The Massachusetts Institute of Technology Press.

Willems, P. (2008) "'This Strangest of Narrative Forms': Rodolphe Töpffer's Sequential Art," *Mosaic: An Interdisciplinary Critical Journal* 41(2), pp. 127–147.

## Interdisciplinarity

Interdisciplinarity is the application of multiple academic disciplinary strategies to comics analysis, either by one critic who has expertise in multiple disciplines or by at least two critics from different disciplines working COLLABORATIVELY. For instance, a critic might use the terminology and strategies associated with sociology alongside those associated with ART history or theory to produce a nuanced, multifaceted understanding of a comic. Or a sociologist might work with an art historian or theorist to produce the same effect. Interdisciplinarity is common in COMICS STUDIES because comics scholars tend to emerge from disciplines in the humanities and social sciences that, on the face of it, are not specific to comics. These critics apply the theories and stratagems of those disciplines while also using the shared language of comics scholars. Indeed, Charles Hatfield argues Comics Studies can have no particular disciplinary identity "because the heterogeneous nature of comics means (…) comics study has to be at the intersection of various disciplines (…) and (…) because this multidisciplinary nature represents (…) a challenge to the very idea of disciplinarity" (2010: n.p.). Furthermore, as a MULTIMODAL MEDIUM, comics lend themselves to interdisciplinarity.

Peter Wilkins

### *References*

Hatfield, C. (2010) "Indiscipline, or, The Condition of Comics Studies" *Transatlantica* 1, n.p. Available at: https://journals.openedition.org/transatlantica/4933 [Accessed 4 May 2020].

## Intermediality

In 1965, Fluxus ARTIST Dick Higgins introduced the term "intermedia" into contemporary ARTS vernacular with his claim that "[m]uch of the best work being produced today seems to fall between media" (2001: 49). Rather than a call to simply examine various combinations of MEDIA, his impetus was both to critique art DISCOURSE's elitist and capitalistic privileging of the traditional media and to promote intermedia as uniquely capable of interacting with society. In his 1981 article-response, he differentiates intermedia as a "conceptual fusion" as opposed to other media "juxtapositions," which further highlights his problematic inversion of previously held hierarchies (2001: 53). In its current use, intermedia has been reimagined as intermediality studies, which takes as its starting point the definition of MEDIUM across various fields to focus less on the politics of the art MARKET and more on how various media combine and to what effect (Rajewsky 2005; Elleström 2010; Schröter 2011). Intermediality studies has important implications for COMICS STUDIES, especially as it concerns the medium of comics and whether the GRAPHIC NOVEL is a new LITERARY GENRE, a genre of comics, or an altogether new medial combination of comics and LITERATURE (see Baetens 2001; Tan 2001; La Cour 2013 and 2016).

Erin La Cour

## *References*

Baetens, J. (2001) "Introduction: Transatlantic Encounters of the Second Type" in Baetens, J. (ed.) *The Graphic Novel.* Leuven: Leuven University Press, pp. 7–9.

Elleström, L. (2010) "The Modalities of Media: A Model for Understanding Intermedial Relations" in Elleström, L. (ed.) *Media Borders, Multimodality and Intermediality.* London: Palgrave Macmillan, pp. 11–50.

Higgins, D. and Higgins, H. (2001) "Intermedia," *Leonardo* 34(1), pp. 49–54.

La Cour, E. (2013) *The "Graphic Novel": Discourses on the Archive.* PhD. University of Amsterdam.

La Cour, E. (2016) "Comics as a Minor Literature," *Image [&] Narrative* 17(4), pp. 79–90.

Rajewsky, I. (2005) "Intermediality, Intertextuality, and Remediation: A Literary Perspective on Intermediality," *Intermédialités* 6, pp. 43–64.

Schröter, J. (2011) "Discourses and Models of Intermediality," *CLCWeb: Comparative Literature and Culture* 13(3), n.p. Available at: http://docs.lib.purdue.edu/clcweb/vol13/iss3/3 [Accessed 17 September 2019].

Tan, E. S. (2014) "The Telling Face in the Comic Strip and Graphic Novels" in Baetens, J. (ed.) *The Graphic Novel.* Leuven: Leuven University Press, pp. 31–46.

## Intersectionality

The understanding that Black women face a distinct oppression predates Kimberlé Crenshaw's 1989 article "Demarginalizing the Intersection of Race and Sex," which argued that antidiscrimination legislation and antiracist and FEMINIST DISCOURSES defined RACE and GENDER as exclusive categories to the disadvantage of Black women (139). However, it was Crenshaw's publication that named this unique oppression: intersectionality. Since the publication, intersectionality has developed into a theory and academic discipline. Informed by critical studies on IDENTITY such as CRITICAL RACE THEORY, intersectionality challenges discourses that examine identity-based oppression through a "single-issue framework" (ibid.: 152). Instead, it posits that an individual experiences oppression based on their identification with multiple identity groups including ETHNICITY, SEXUALITY, CLASS, and (DIS)ABILITY. These identifications, lived within systems of power that rigidly define identity groups, produce a "unique compoundedness" of discriminations on an individual (ibid.: 150). COMICS STUDIES benefits from an intersectional approach when examining issues of REPRESENTATION, particularly how characters and CREATORS with intersectional identities are represented on the page, and the impact of that representation on a READER or READERSHIP (Galvan 2018; Jiménez 2018).

Rachel A. Davis

### *References*

Crenshaw, K. (1989) "Demarginalizing the Intersection of Race and Sex: A Black Feminist Critique of Antidiscrimination Doctrine, Feminist Theory and Antiracist Politics," *University of Chicago Legal Forum* 1989(1), pp. 139–167.

Galvan, M. (2018) "Making space: Jennifer Camper, LGBTQ anthologies, and queer comics communities," *Journal of Lesbian Studies* 22(4), pp. 373–389.

Jiménez, L. M. (2018) "PoC, LGBTQ, and gender: The intersectionality of America Chavez," *Journal of Lesbian Studies* 22(4), pp. 435–445.

## Intertextuality

Developing the theory of intertextuality, Julia Kristeva argues that a "literary structure does not simply *exist* but is generated in relation to *another* structure" (35–36) and that, therefore, "any text is the absorption and transformation of another" (37). In new texts, we find the TRACES of older ones, and the recognition of this relationship creates a proliferation of meanings. In other words, "intertextual theory argues that texts and signs refer not to the world or even primarily to concepts, but to other texts, other signs" (Allen 2011: 112). Karin Kukkonen writes that intertextuality functions thanks to what she describes as "popular cultural memory" (2008: 261). This MEMORY is made possible through the interplay of three dimensions: the social (between people), the MATERIAL (MEDIA itself), and the mental (the "codes and conventions that facilitate the reading process") (Kukkonen 2008: 261–262). Intertextuality can take place across all three NARRATIVE tracks in comics: they can be traced in "textual clues," such as titles and names; "iconographic references," such as recognisable characters and objects; and "composition and drawing style" (Kukkonen 2013: 55). CARTOONIST and scholar Nick Sousanis has related the deployment of intertextuality in comics to POSTMODERN "sampling and DJ culture" in music (n.d.).

Nicholas Burman

### *References*


Allen, G. (2011) Intertextuality. Abingdon: Routledge.

Kristeva, J. (1969) "Word, Dialogue and Novel" in Moi, T. (ed.) *The Kristeva Reader*. Translated from French by A. Jardine, T. Gora, and L. S. Roudiez, 1986. New York: Columbia University Press, pp. 34–61.

Kukkonen, K. (2008) "Popular Cultural Memory: Comics, Communities and Context Knowledge," *Nordicom Review* 29(2), pp. 261–274.

Kukkonen, K. (2013) *Contemporary Comics Storytelling*. Lincoln: University of Nebraska Press.

Sousanis, N. (n.d.) "Threads: A Spinning Fable." *Spin, Weave, and Cut*. Available at: http://spinweaveandcut.com/threads-a-spinning-fable/ [Accessed 17 June 2020].

## Irony

Irony is a MODE of expression comprising a contradiction or incongruity between what is uttered and what may be implied, and in the case of NARRATIVES, what is expected and what occurs (Colston and Gibbs 2002: 58). It usually conveys an "evaluative attitude other than what is explicitly presented" (Hutcheon 2005: 12), which distinguishes it from other structurally similar forms such as METAPHOR. Dramatic irony is the effect created by the occurrence of actions or dialogue in a narrative that utilises tension generated from the AUDIENCE possessing more information about events in the STORYWORLD than the characters (Milanowicz 2019: 17). Often traced back to Socrates' use in political discussion (Colebrook 2004: 6), irony is frequently used as a vehicle for criticism or SATIRE. The contradictions either draw attention to and disrupt underexamined social and cultural assumptions and beliefs or conversely reinforce norms by unfavourably evaluating alternatives (Hutcheon 2005: 15). Comics have a long history with HUMOUR and satire, and irony is a major part of the repertoire, likely owing to how the polymodal and fragmented visual nature of the REGISTER creates increased and unique opportunities to construct contradictions and incongruity.

Ahmed Jameel

### *References*


Colebrook, C. (2004) *Irony*. Abingdon: Routledge.

Colston, H. L. and Gibbs, Jr., R. (2002) "Are Irony and Metaphor Understood Differently?" *Metaphor and Symbol* 17(1), pp. 57–80.

Hutcheon, L. (1994) *Irony's Edge: The Theory and Politics of Irony*. Digital edition, 2005. London: Taylor and Francis.

Milanowicz, A. (2019) "A short etude on irony in storytelling," *Psychology of Language and Communication* 23(1), pp. 14–26.

## Kitsch

In its earliest conceptions kitsch pointed to a sense of bad taste expressed through a love of mass-produced, cheap, and alluring (POPULAR) CULTURAL products. ART critic Clement Greenberg considered kitsch of a vulgar nature and a danger to high art—and he explicitly labelled comics as kitsch (1939). These negative connotations of kitsch have persisted, as it is still characterised as offering pre-packaged sentiment and reduced complexity (Sturken 2007; Kulka 1996). The concept is closely related to melodrama and camp. Susan Sontag labels Flash Gordon comics and Lynn Ward's woodcuts as fitting the exaggerated and playful artifice of camp (1964). The perceived contrast between kitsch and art, and high and low culture played out in the POP ART appropriations of comics in the 1960s (Beaty 2012). Kitsch has also been used in the context of depictions of mass violence and the Holocaust in comics, for instance, through the term "holokitsch," coined by Art Spiegelman. Recent scholarship views kitsch as a more productive cultural Mode (Noys 2002; Tong 2013). For instance, elements in comics like visual excess and melodramatic storylines can be AFFECTIVE and meaningful and kitsch does not necessarily preclude (SELF-)REFLECTION (in 't Veld 2019).

Laurike in 't Veld

### *References*

Beaty, B. (2012) *Comics versus Art*. Toronto: University of Toronto Press.

Greenberg, C. (1939) "Avant-Garde and Kitsch" in Harrison, C. and Wood, P. (eds.) *Art in Theory, 1900–2000*. 2nd edition. Reprint 2003. Oxford: Blackwell, pp. 539–549.

in 't Veld, L. (2019) *The Representation of Genocide in Graphic Novels: Considering the Role of Kitsch*. London: Palgrave Macmillan.

Kulka, T. (1996) *Kitsch and Art*. University Park: The Pennsylvania State University Press.

Noys, B. (2002) "Fascinating (British) Fascism: David Britton's *Lord Horror*," *Rethinking History* 6(3), pp. 305–318.

Sontag, S. (1964) "Notes on 'Camp'" in Sontag, S. *Against Interpretation and Other Essays*. Reprint 1994. New York: Vintage, pp. 275–292.

Sturken, M. (2007) *Tourists of History: Memory, Kitsch, and Consumerism from Oklahoma City to Ground Zero*. Durham: Duke University Press.

Tong, N. (2013) "Comics and the Indispensability of Kitsch." *Hooded Utilitarian*, 17 July 2013. Available at: www.hoodedutilitarian.com/2013/07/comics-and-the-indispensability-of-kitsch [Accessed 9 March 2021].

## LABOUR

Labour has several related meanings. It describes physical or mental work, refers to exertion when it is difficult, and is part of the process of giving birth. Labour retains its association with this last sense, but the term became more ABSTRACT during the eighteenth century and eventually became part of economic theories of capital. "Work" as a term largely replaced its original sense of any exertion (Williams 1983: 176–179). Adam Smith characterises labour as productive and as part of an exchange for capital. The division of labour is fundamental to free-MARKET capitalism because goods cannot be exchanged without some form of labour specialisation to ensure profit and growth (1976: 13–19). Karl Marx's theory of the COMMODITY holds that in capitalism, workers do not own the means of PRODUCTION and so their labour is obscured within the commodities they make. The exchange value of the commodity becomes more important than its use value, and the result is that workers are alienated from their own labour, as capitalists make a profit from it (2015: 27–60). Other accounts of labour nuance its relation to capital: understanding "women's work" as unpaid labour (Shelton 2006: 375–390) or considering the role of forced labour in world economic growth brings into view who labours, who benefits from labour, and under what conditions it persists (ILO 2014: 45–47).

Julie Rak

### *References*

International Labour Office (2014) *Profits and poverty: The economics of forced labour.* Geneva: International Labour Office.

Marx, K. (1867–1894) *Capital: A Critique of Political Economy.* Translated from German by S. Moore and E. Aveling. Reprint 2015. Engels, F. (ed.) Moscow: Progress Publishers.

Shelton, B. (2006) "Gender and Unpaid Work" in Saltzman-Chafetz, J. (ed.) *Handbook of the Sociology of Gender.* Berlin: Springer, pp. 375–390.

Williams, R. (1976) *Keywords: A Vocabulary of Culture and Society.* Revised edition 1983. Oxford: Oxford University Press.

## Language

Language is a form of human communication that uses spoken or written words to create DISCOURSE based on systems such as grammar. Different countries and communities use different languages, regularly necessitating TRANSLATION between languages. In comics, language is present in the form of written texts included in SPEECH BALLOONS, SOUND effects, or CAPTION BOXES (Varnum and Gibbons 2007; Bramlett 2012). The communication in language in comics is often contrasted with the communication in IMAGES, leading to the perception of comics as IMAGETEXTS that combine language and visuals. Written language can also affect the structure of the comics PAGE: PANELS in a comic are READ in the direction and order the READER of a particular language is accustomed to. Thus, comics in Western languages are usually read from left to right and from top to bottom across the page, while comics from Japan are read from right to left. Some theorists, such as Neil Cohn, contend that the comics FORM is itself a language, a codified VISUAL SYSTEM of communication. However, since the visuals in comics are not ruled by a formal grammar, they may not be systematic enough to constitute an actual language, requiring explanations based on structural, MULTIMODAL, or functional models instead (Miodrag 2013; Davies 2019).

Barbara Postema

### *References*

Bramlett, F. (ed.) (2012) *Linguistics and the Study of Comics.* London: Palgrave Macmillan.

Davies, P. F. (2019) *Comics as Communication: A Functional Approach.* London: Palgrave Macmillan.

Cohn, N. (2013) *The Visual Language of Comics: Introduction to the Structure and Cognition of Sequential Images.* London: Bloomsbury Academic.

Miodrag, H. (2013) *Comics and Language: Reimagining Critical Discourse on the Form.* Jackson: University Press of Mississippi.

Varnum, R., and Gibbons, C. T. (eds.) (2007) *The Language of Comics: Word and Image.* Jackson: University Press of Mississippi.

## Legend

Legend encompasses several SEMANTIC vectors, all of which are relevant to COMICS STUDIES. Scholars approach it as a NARRATIVE GENRE of FOLKLORE, related to rumour and involving an element of belief (Dégh 2001). More commonly, legend refers to a person whose deeds are worth NARRATING, for example, "Stan Lee is a comics legend." Legend is difficult to distinguish from MYTH, though ethnographic study reveals differences such as setting (Bascom 1965). The term originates in hagiography (i.e. *legenda*, a story worth reading, Nicolaisen 1988: 82), but includes such subgenres as local legend, migratory legend, urban legend, and heroic legend, with examples that range from UFO abductions and ghost stories to the feats of athletes and soldiers. CREATORS often ADAPT legends such as King Arthur to the comics MEDIUM (Barr and Bolland 2008). Finally, legend is a term used by PUBLISHERS to lend their characters gravitas and authenticity (Claverie 2019), as in *Batman: Legends of the Dark Knight* (1989–2007).

Daniel Peretti

### *References*

Barr, M. and Bolland, B. (2008) *Camelot 3000.* New York: DC Comics.

Bascom, W. (1965) "The Forms of Folklore: Prose Narratives," *The Journal of American Folklore* 78(307), pp. 3–20.

Claverie, E. (2019) "Folklore, Fakelore, Scholars, and Shills: Superheroes as 'Myth,'" *The Journal of Popular Culture*, 52(5) 976–998.

Dégh, L. (2001) *Legend and Belief: The Dialectics of a Genre.* Bloomington: Indiana University Press.

Nicolaisen, W. F. H. (1988) "German *Sage* and English *Legend:* Terminology and Conceptual Problems" in Bennett, G. and Smith, P. (eds.) *Monsters with Iron Teeth: Perspectives on Contemporary Legend IV.* Sheffield: Sheffield Academic Press, pp. 79–88.

## Letterer

In the comics industry PRODUCTION system, the letterer adds, manually or through computer devices, the textual elements to a comics work, such as dialogues, recitatives, ONOMATOPOEIAS, or PARATEXTS, and

DRAWS and places SPEECH BALLOONS and CAPTIONS. Although often overlooked, lettering plays a central role in STORYTELLING, PAGE LAYOUT, and STYLE. The size, form, and typographic styles of the letters translate verbal contents and their paralanguage modulations. These variations also add to characterisation and NARRATIVE tone. Taken as a whole, lettering contributes to the stylistic and editorial identity of the work and of its CREATOR(S). In that sense, lettering conveys narrative, metanarrative, and extranarrative information (Kannenberg 2001). Thus, lettering is in a constant tension between instrumental and AESTHETIC purposes, between readability and expressivity (Blanchard 1969; Gerbier 2017). Lettering addresses key points for the FORMAL analysis of comics. The "reduction of speech to graphic forms" (Goody 1977) finds some resolution by the "imaging-function" of the lettered TEXT (Fresnault-Deruelle 1970). The MATERIAL heterogeneity of WRITING and drawing is challenged by the drawn letter (Baetens and Lefèvre 1993; Hatfield 2005). The presence of a letterer, distinct from the PENCILLER/ARTIST, specifies the production context of a work. "Large scale production" comics (Bourdieu 1983; Beaty and Woo 2016) usually divide creation between several "support personnel" (Becker 1982). Evolutions in crediting practices, awards, and contracts mark the changing status of the letterer in this assembly-line model.

Jean-Matthieu Méon

## *References*

Baetens, J. and Lefèvre, P. (1993) "Texts and Images" in Miller, A. and Beaty, B. (eds.) *The French Comics Theory Reader.* Translated from French by A. Miller and B. Beaty, 2014. Leuven: Leuven University Press, pp.183–190.

Beaty, B. and Woo, B. (2016) *The Greatest Comic Book of All Time: Symbolic Capital and the Field of American Comic Books.* London: Palgrave Macmillan.

Becker, H. S. (1982) *Art Worlds.* Berkeley: University of California Press.

Blanchard, G. (1969) "Le véritable domaine de la bande dessinée," *Communications et langages* 3, pp. 56–69.

Bourdieu, P. (1983) "The Field of Cultural Production, or: The Economic World Reversed," *Poetics* 12(4–5), pp. 311–356.

Fresnault-Deruelle, P. (1970) "Le verbal dans les bandes dessinées," *Communications* 15, pp. 145–161.

Gerbier, L. (2017), "Lettrage" in Groensteen, T. (ed.) *Dictionnaire esthétique et thématique de la bande dessinée, Neuvième art 2.0.* Available at: http://neuviemeart.citebd.org/spip.php?article1171 [Accessed 30 July 2020].

Goody, J. (1977), *The Domestication of the Savage Mind.* Cambridge: Cambridge University Press.

Hatfield, C. (2005) *Alternative Comics: An Emerging Literature.* Jackson: University Press of Mississippi.

Kannenberg, Jr., G. (2001) "Graphic Text, Graphic Context: Interpreting Custom Fonts and Hands in Contemporary Comics" in Gutjahr, P. C. and Benton, M. L. (eds.) *Illuminating Letters: Typography and Literary Interpretation.* Amherst: University of Massachusetts Press, pp. 165–192.

## Letters Page

The LETTERS PAGE is a feature in the serialised publication format that saw the twentieth-century development of comics before the rise of the self-contained GRAPHIC NOVEL. Although a part of general print newspapers from at least the nineteenth century, in the comics world letters to the editor are often associated with U.S. publications from the 1940s onwards, in particular DC productions, or *Superman* (1958 onwards). Content would generally broach readers' reaction to plot development or characterisation. In Europe *Le Journal de Mickey* (1934–) represents a marker, as the letters page created a community via exchanged ideas, thereby giving a French context to a publication dominated by imports, and allowing assimilation, also leading to the now-famous "Club Mickey" (Grove 2010). The English comic *Viz* (1979–) famously mixes genuine submitted letters and editorial inventions so as to satirise mainstream MEDIA (Donald 2005). A key function of the letters page has been to allow development via fan-based input, a phenomenon that has since blossomed to online fora and blogs, and thereby circumventing traditional gatekeepers (Pustz 1999). The letters page is one of many PARATEXTS associated with comics, others being cover and imprint materials, ADVERTISEMENTS, text-only features, competitions, interviews, and associated events, such as comics CONVENTIONS and COSPLAYING.

Laurence Grove

### *References*

Donald, C. (2004) *Rude Kids: The Unfeasible Story of* Viz. London: HarperCollins.

Grove, L. (2010) "Mickey, Le Journal de Mickey and the Birth of the Popular BD," *Belphégor* 1(1), n.p. Available at https://dalspace.library.dal.ca/bitstream/handle/10222/47641/01_01_Grove_Mickey_cont.pdf?sequence=1&isAllowed=y [Accessed 9 March 2021].

Pustz, M. (1999) *Comic Book Culture: Fanboys and True Believers.* Jackson: University Press of Mississippi.

## LGBTQ+

LGBTQ+ is a shorthand term for the various IDENTITIES that make up the QUEER community: Lesbian, Gay, Bisexual, Transgender, Questioning/Queer. There are other variations of this term such as LGBTQIA, which includes Intersex and Asexual, which, along with other queer identities such as Pansexual, are denoted by the "+." The grouping together of queer communities into one identity is not without its limitations. Brett Beemyn and Mickey Eliason note that "the whole notion of a unitary lesbian, gay, or bisexual identity rests on the assumption that people who share a sexual identity will also have similar attitudes, values and politics," and thus ignores other aspects of an individual's identity, such as RACE, GENDER, or CLASS (1996: 6). Entertainment and POPULAR CULTURE (including comics) have been a primary MODE of queer expression and ACTIVISM (Bronski 2011: XIX). Alexander Doty theorised that the queerness of texts such as comics can be located either in the text's PRODUCTION, in HISTORICALLY and culturally specific READINGS by the queer community, or in adopting a queer position of RECEPTION (Doty 1993: XI). There is a history of explicitly queer comics going back to at least the 1940s, and notably includes the work of Alison Bechdel.

Olivia Hicks

## *References*

Beemyn, B. and Eliason, M. (1996) *Queer Studies: A Lesbian, Gay, Bisexual, and Transgender Anthology.* New York: New York University Press.

Bronski, M. (2011) *A Queer History of the United States.* Boston: Beacon Press.

Doty, A. (1993) *Making Things Perfectly Queer: Interpreting Mass Culture.* Minneapolis: University of Minnesota Press.

## Life Writing

Life writing refers to a very broad range of personal STORYTELLING and forms of communication. These can be private (such as diaries, letters, instant messages, and emails) or public (such as speeches, biopics, AUTOBIOGRAPHICAL comics, DOCUMENTARY FILMS, personal essays, YouTube videos, obituaries, and public social MEDIA posts) (Leader 2015: 1). Like autobiography, life writing is a textual practice that occasions an "intersubjective exchange between narrator and reader aimed at producing a shared understanding of the meaning of a life" (Smith and Watson 2010: 16). Because of its grounding in lived experience, life writing can also provide insight into the forms of subjectivity, ideologies, and NARRATIVE strategies of the period and place in which it is PRODUCED. Therefore, life writing can be approached as HISTORICAL documents used to interpret the past. These can take two forms: ARCHIVAL sources such as diaries and letters; and oral history, where people narrativise their MEMORY of their personal experience and understanding of a specific event. Comics that are autobiography, MEMOIR, or BIOGRAPHY can REMEDIATE forms of life writing as source material, as well as draw on the AUTHOR's own experience directly (see Cvetkovich 2008).

Anna Poletti

## *References*

Cvetkovich, A. (2008) "Drawing the Archive in Alison Bechdel's *Fun Home*," *WSQ: Women's Studies Quarterly* 36(1–2), pp.111–128.

Leader, Z. (ed.) (2015) *On Life-Writing.* Oxford: Oxford University Press.

Smith, S. and Watson, J. (2010) *Reading Autobiography: A Guide for Interpreting Life Narratives.* 2nd edition. Minneapolis: University of Minnesota Press.

## Line

Line is a basic SIGN component used for WRITING and DRAWING. The drawn or graphic line in comics raises three considerations: the physical line as created through effortful movement of the ARTIST; the qualities of line as a constructed STYLE or DESIGN; the scope for line to delineate or imply through either symbol or structure. Philippe Marion's term "graphic enunciation" acknowledges the "trace of gesture" (Ingold 2013: 126), the impact of the unique embodiment of the physiology and training of the CREATOR. The physicality of line therefore is an interaction between the body, the environment, and the MATERIAL elements (Baetens 2001). The line is simultaneously transparent and rendering visible (Sobchack 2008: 258). Marion argues for two aesthetic categories of line: the closed delineative "la ligne-contour" and the open, dynamic "la ligne-expression" (Atkinson 2009: 274). Jared Gardner positions line as style, "impossible to paraphrase" (Gardner 2011: 59). Structural lines delineate PANELS, GUTTERS, CAPTION BOXES, and SPEECH BALLOONS, while PICTORIAL RUNES (Forceville 2011) or CARTOON symbols (McCloud 2006) construct interactional "path lines" such as motion, scopic, and radial lines (Cohn 2013: 38–40). "Comics is a medium that calls attention with every line to its own boundaries, frames, and limitations" (Gardner 2011: 66).

Dona Pursall

### *References*


Atkinson, P. (2009) "Movements within Movements: Following the Line in Animation and Comic Books," *Animation* 4(3), pp. 265–281.

Baetens, J. (2001) "Revealing Traces: A New Theory of Graphic Enunciation" in Varnum, R. and Gibbons, C. T. (eds.) *The Language of Comics: Word and Image*. Jackson: University Press of Mississippi, pp. 145–155.

Cohn, N. (2013) *The Visual Language of Comics: Introduction to the Structure and Cognition of Sequential Images*. London: Bloomsbury Academic.

Forceville, C. (2011) "Pictorial Runes in *Tintin and the Picaros*," *Journal of Pragmatics* 43, pp. 875–890.

Gardner, J. (2011) "Storylines," *SubStance* 40(1), pp. 53–69.

Ingold, T. (2013) *Making: Anthropology, archaeology, art and architecture.* Abingdon: Routledge.
McCloud, S. (2006) *Making Comics. Storytelling Secrets of Comics, Manga and Graphic Novels.* New York: Harper.
Sobchack, V. (2008) "The Line and the Animorph or `Travel Is More than Just A to B,'" *Animation* 3(3), pp. 251–265.

## Linguistics

Researching verbal meaning is enormously facilitated by the fact that languages have a grammar and a vocabulary. Therefore, correct language use is rule-governed. Over the past decades, humanities scholarship has increasingly started to systematically examine non-verbal and partly verbal meaning, for instance, in painting, MUSIC, FILM, and comics. Indeed, it is nowadays generally acknowledged that DISCOURSES and texts are usually MULTIMODAL rather than monomodal—even their presumably purely verbal varieties. Both cognitive linguistics and systemic functional linguistics provide pertinent angles for analysing multimodal MEDIA such as comics, which draw on visuals combined with language. But it is crucial to realise that while visuals have structure, they by and large do not have a grammar (Forceville 1999)—although arguably there are elements *within* comics, such as PICTORIAL RUNES and SPEECH BALLOONS, that have a "micro-vocabulary," and characteristics of a "grammar." Comics scholarship, like research in other non-verbal and multimodal media, can benefit from linguistics but should avoid overextending verbal meaning-making mechanisms to the visual realm and remain optimally open to comics' MEDIUM-specific affordances. Ultimately, a supramodal theory of communication is called for (Forceville 2020).

Charles Forceville

### *References*

Cohn, N. (2013) *The Visual Language of Comics: Introduction to the Structure and Cognition of Sequential Images.* London: Bloomsbury Academic.
Kress, G. and van Leeuwen, T. (1996) *Reading Images: The Grammar of Visual Design.* London: Routledge.

Forceville, C. (1999) "Educating the eye? Kress and Van Leeuwen's *Reading Images: The Grammar of Visual Design* (1996)," *Language and Literature* 8(2), pp. 163–178.
Forceville, C. (2020) *Visual and Multimodal Communication: Applying the Relevance Principle*. Oxford: Oxford University Press.

## Literature

While broadly defined as works of prose, poetry, and drama, what constitutes literature continues to be a subject of great debate both popularly and in academia. In Anglophone use, the term originally encompassed all culturally valued WRITTEN work from philosophy to history to poetry, but with the rise of the novel at the beginning of the eighteenth century, it began to narrow into "'creative' or 'imaginative' writing" (Eagleton 1996: 15). This shift effectively brought GENRE to the fore alongside TASTE ADJUDICATION, which, as Jonathan Culler (1997) has emphasised, has always played a pivotal role in the praise of certain works and the dismissal of others. The demarcation of works as literature depends on several factors including, but not limited to, critical acclaim in POPULAR CULTURE and the establishment and perpetuation of particular works and AUTHORS in the literary CANON in academia, both of which have faced backlash from POSTCOLONIAL-, GENDER-, and CRITICAL RACE THEORY discourses (Mukherjee 2014). The popularisation of the term GRAPHIC NOVEL is an example of such popular and canonical practices, as it has been used to "elevate" certain comics to the status of a sub-genre of literature, perhaps not on par with the "high" literature of the established canon, but good enough to win literary prizes and be taught in university classrooms (La Cour 2021).

Erin La Cour

### *References*

Culler, J. (2009) *Literary Theory: A Brief Insight*. London: Sterling.
Eagleton, T. (1996) *Literary Theory: An Introduction*. 2nd edition. Minneapolis: University of Minnesota Press.

La Cour, E. (2021) "Alison Bechdel: *Dykes to Watch Out For*" Domsch, S., Hassler-Forest, D., and Vanderbeke, D. (eds.) *Handbook on Comics and Graphic Narratives.* Berlin: De Gruyter, pp. 527–541.

Mukherjee, A. (2014) *What is a Classic? Postcolonial Rewriting and Invention of the Canon.* Stanford: Stanford University Press.

## Lithography

Lithography is a technical method for the mass REPRODUCTION of IMAGES that was first developed by Alois Senefelder in Munich in 1796, with details published in his *Vollstandiges Lehrbuch der Steindruckerei* in 1818 (translated into English the following year). Originally, the process involved the application of oil-based DRAWING to the surface of a stone or metal slab, wetting the stone, using ink that will penetrate the drawn areas but not mix with the water, and then applying to paper with a PRINTING press. The process allowed for a more detailed range of image tone than, say, ETCHING, whilst the direct application of the stone and paper within the press made for greater print runs. Lithography is associated with the earliest of modern comics, should mass distribution be considered a pre-requisite, of which the first was the *Glasgow Looking Glass* of 1825. Rodolphe Töpffer used a similar process for his strips, such as his *Histoire de M. Jabot* (1835). An update of the process is offset lithography, often associated with the popular ROMANCE and WAR comics of the 1960s, but in reality not widely used until the 1980s, that became known for inspiring the ARTWORKS of Roy Lichtenstein (1923–1997).

Laurence Grove

### *References*

Senefelder, J. N. F. A. (1818) *A Complete Course of Lithography.* Translated from German by A. Schlichtegroll, 1819. Oxford: Oxford University Press.

## Ludology

Ludology is the study of GAMES and their surrounding contexts. It is often differentiated from NARRATOLOGY (or the study of NARRATIVE) on the basis that the concepts and mechanisms involved in games do not constitute narrative per se, but this differentiation has been disputed by some theorists (Aarseth 2012). A restricted understanding of ludology, which emphasises the FORMAL and mechanical elements of game design and play, has had limited engagement with comics, although works such as Jason Shiga's *Meanwhile* (2010) and Daniel Merlin Goodbrey's *A Duck Has an Adventure* (2012) suggest ways in which this type of READING might be productively employed in comics scholarship (Grennan and Hague 2018). In some cases, alternative terms are used to differentiate between a CONVENTIONAL comic and a more game-like form. Goodbrey, for example, describes *A Duck Has an Adventure* as a hypercomic, in which "the choices made by the reader may influence the sequence of events, the outcome of events or the point of view through which events are seen" (2000–2020: n.p.), gesturing towards concepts of choice and READER (or potentially player) impact. More broadly, there is significant overlap between the cultural contexts of comics and games: they often coexist within the same commercial spaces, environments, and events, and their players/readers and subject matters often crossover as well.

Ian Hague

### *References*

Aarseth, E. (2012) "A Narrative Theory of Games," *Proceedings of the International Conference on the Foundations of Digital Games,* 29 May-1 June 2012, pp. 129–133. Available at: https://dl.acm.org/doi/10.1145/2282338.2282365 [Accessed 12 June 2020].

Goodbrey, D. M. (2000–2020) "Hypercomics." *Daniel Merlin Goodbrey's New Experiments in Fiction.* Available at: http://e-merl.com/hypercomics [Accessed 24 April 2020].

Grennan, S. and Hague, I. (2018) "Medium, knowledge, structure: Capacities for choice and the contradiction of medium-specificity in games and comics," *Image [&] Narrative* 19(1), pp. 73–85.

## Mail Order

Selling back issues of GOLDEN AGE COMIC BOOKS through mail order started in the 1950s and 1960s in America with dealers and store owners, such as Claude Held, Bud Plant, and Howard Rogofsky (Schelly 2010: 40–53). In addition to creating their own catalogues, dealers placed ADVERTISEMENTS in FANZINES, which had from the outset included lists of comics for sale by mail order, usually from the CREATOR's own COLLECTIONS. The most significant of these "adzines" was the *Rocket's Blast-Comicollector* (1964–1983), which was, as its title suggests, a merger of two existing fanzines (ibid. 68–71). Another significant publication for mail order, for both dealers and FANS, was the *Comic Buyer's Guide*, which was formerly known as *The Buyer's Guide* (1971–2013) (Goulart 1991: 316–317). In Britain, the mail order business in dealing comics started through the classified advertising magazine *Exchange and Mart* (1868–2009) before the emergence of fanzines such as the *Fantasy Advertiser* (1965–1991) (Sabin 1993: 63–64). Mail order was also important for the creators of small press comics (sometimes called NEWAVE or MINICOMICS) who would sell copies of their own work by post. Some small press creators would also rely on the services of distributors such as Paul Gravett's *Fast Fiction* (1981–1990) in Britain or Michael Dowers' *Starhead Comix* (1984–1999) in America to sell their work by mail order (Dowers 2010, Sabin 1993, 82–83, 176, 282).

Ian Horton

### *References*

Dowers, M. (ed.) (2010) *Newave!: The Underground Mini Comix of the 1980s*. Seattle: Fantagraphics.

Goulart, R. (1991) *Over 50 Years of American Comic Books*. Lincolnwood: Publications International, Ltd.

Sabin, R. (1993) *Adult Comics: An Introduction*. Abingdon: Routledge.

Schelly, B. (2010) *Founders of Comics Fandom*. Jefferson: McFarland.

## Manga

Manga is the catchall term used in Japan to refer to all forms of SEQUENTIAL ART, from four-PANEL COMIC STRIPS to GRAPHIC NOVELS (although the English loanword "komikkusu" is often applied to American SUPERHERO comics). The majority of NARRATIVE manga are SERIALISED in weekly, monthly, and quarterly magazines (distributed in both PRINT and digital FORMATS) that are marketed and shelved in bookstores according to their demographic GENRE, which include SHŌNEN (targeted at young male READERS) and SHŌJO (targeted at young female readers). Although the word manga can be traced back to the sketchbooks of the "ukiyo-e" ARTIST Katsushika Hokusai (1760–1849), the prolific Osamu Tezuka (1928–1989) is generally considered to be the "godfather of manga" ("manga no kamisama") and a major influence on contemporary formats and STYLISATIONS (Schodt 1996). Since the 1950s, manga have served as the primary source texts driving a corporate marketing strategy known as the MEDIA mix ("media mikkusu"), which involves the creation of TRANSMEDIA franchises that frequently include anime, MERCHANDISE, and video GAMES (Steinberg 2012). Many manga artists begin their careers by SELF-PUBLISHING ZINES and fancomics called "doujinshi" before submitting their work to open competitions sponsored by magazine PUBLISHERS (Prough 2011). The practices of comics subcultures inspired by this fan-driven model of PRODUCTION have spread overseas and become international in the twenty-first century (Beasi 2013).

Kathryn Hemmann

### *References*

Beasi, M. (ed.) (2013) *Manga: Introduction, Challenges, and Best Practices.* Milwaukie: Dark Horse Books.

Prough, J. (2011) *Straight from the Heart: Gender, Intimacy, and the Cultural Production of* Shōjo Manga. Honolulu: University of Hawai'i Press.

Schodt, F. L. (1996) *Dreamland Japan: Writings on modern manga.* Berkeley: Stone Bridge Press.

Steinberg, M. (2012) *Anime's Media Mix: Franchising Toys and Characters in Japan.* Minneapolis: University of Minnesota Press.

## Marcinelle School

Also known as the Charleroi School, the Marcinelle School refers to a group of Belgian CARTOONISTS working for the weekly magazine *Spirou* and gathered around COMIC BOOK artist Jijé (Joseph Gillain). The original "bande à quatre," or gang of four, assembled by Jijé after World War II, consisted of Jijé himself and three younger ARTISTS who started as his assistants: André Franquin, Maurice De Bevere (Morris), and Willy Maltaite (Will). However, the term has also been used to refer to subsequent members and many other artists such as Peyo (Pierre Culliford), Maurice Tillieux, Raymond Macherot, or even Albert Uderzo. The work of the group and its heirs is characterised by its CARICATURE DESIGN with big noses and rounded heads, its dynamism and MOVEMENT, and the HUMOROUS tone of the STORIES (Miller 2007). This STYLE, later dubbed "style atome," soon became the house style of *Spirou*, whose offices were located in the Marcinelle section of Charleroi, Belgium (Huard 2016). The term "École de Marcinelle" was subsequently coined as a counterpart to "École de Bruxelles" (Brussels School), the other main trend of Belgian BANDE DESSINÉE represented by rival magazine *Le Journal Tintin* and commonly associated with the somewhat opposed "ligne claire" (CLEAR LINE) style (Dayez 2001).

Luis Miguel Lus Arana

### *References*

Dayez, H. (2001) *Le duel Tintin-Spirou: Dix-sept témoignages qui donnent un éclairage passionnant sur l'histoire du neuvième art*. Liège: Luc Pire.

Pomier, F. (2005) *Comment lire la bande dessinée?* Paris: Klincksieck.

Miller, A. (2007) *Reading Bande dessinée: Critical Approaches to French-language Comic Strip*. Bristol: Intellect.

Huard, P. (2016) *La parodie dans la bande dessinée franco-belge: Critique ou esthétisme?* Québec: Presses de l'Universite du Québec.

## Mark

A mark is any visual item that reproduces and REPRESENTS those functional aspects of the system of representation that determines its status, such as a WRITING system or any SPATIAL PROJECTION SYSTEM, as an aspect of DEPICTION or from the general ecology in which it is made and seen. The status of a mark usually derives either from its location in a topological system (such as writing or spatial projection systems), relative to other marks and to the rules of the system, or from the experience of VISUALISATION (visual imagining) according to image SCHEMATA, the general potential resources of the body (Grennan 2017: 14–24), what Nigel Thomas describes as the self-perceiving of ideas as phenomena (1999). In addition, marks only gain status if the representational system appears within an encompassing ecology in which they are expected to have this status (Martin 1992, Thibault 2004), such as the TRACE of an action undertaken in the context of an ART studio, where such activities are habitual, for example. Although no specific TECHNOLOGY defines the mark, its theoretical association with a marking body, or DRAWING, produces the idea of autography, or the concept of the representation of a unique SUBJECT by marking (Rosand 2002: 61), of trace and INDEX (Grennan 2017: 15), or of the progress of mark-making as a visual representation of changes in time, in COMICS in particular (Gardner 2011: 64).

Simon Grennan

## *References*


Gardner, J. (2011) "Storylines," *SubStance* 40(1), pp. 53–69.

Grennan, S. (2017) *A Theory of Narrative Drawing*. London: Palgrave Macmillan.

Thomas, N. (1999) "Are theories of imagery theories of imagination? An active perception approach to conscious mental content," *Cognitive Science* 23, pp. 207–245.

Martin, J. (1992) *English Text: System and Structure*. Philadelphia: John Benjamins.

Rosand, D. (2002) *Drawing Acts: Studies in graphic expression and representation*. Cambridge: Cambridge University Press.

Thibault, P. (2004) *Brain, Mind and the Signifying Body: An Ecosocial Semiotic Theory*. New York: Continuum.

## Market

Market refers to a location or gathering where goods are bought and sold. Adam Smith makes the idea of the market a centrepiece of capitalism: the division of LABOUR essential for the flow of capital is affected by the size of the market itself. Markets ensure the division of labour necessary to economic growth. A free-market economy should allow prices for goods to be determined by supply and demand, and should in theory regulate itself (Smith 1976: 31–36). Karl Marx also places the idea of the market at the centre of his analysis, but for him the market is not free because it depends on an unequal relationship between the use value and exchange value of goods, and so obscures, through pricing, the labour that makes commodities (2015: 27, 47–50, 60). Markets therefore have no place in a socialist economy (Engels 1939: 309). Later ideas about the market tend to move between each position. John Maynard Keynes argued that markets in an economic downturn do not automatically reach equilibrium and cannot ensure total employment; therefore, government intervention is needed to stimulate markets when demand for goods is less than their supply (Jahan et al. 2014: 53–54). Joseph Stiglitz also argues that markets are not self-regulating, are prone to failure, and are in need of reform and statement intervention (2013: xii-xv).

Julie Rak

### *References*

Engels, F. (1878) *Anti-Dühring*. Reprint 1939. New York: International Publishers.

Jahan, S., Saber Mahmud, A., and Papageorgiou, C. (2014) "What is Keynesian Economics?" *Finance and Development* 51(3), pp. 53–54.

Marx, K. (1867–1894) *Capital: A Critique of Political Economy*. Translated from German by S. Moore and E. Aveling. Reprint 2015. Engels, F. (ed.) Moscow: Progress Publishers.

Smith, A. (1776) *An Inquiry into the Nature and Causes of the Wealth of Nations*, Volume I. Reprint 1976. Cambell, R.H. and Skinner, A.S. (eds.) Indianapolis: Liberty Classics.

Stiglitz, J. (2013) *Selected Works of Joseph Stiglitz*, Volume 2. Oxford: Oxford University Press.

## Mass Production

Comics originated alongside industrialisation and PRINT culture, so as POPULAR CULTURE it is closely tied to mass production and Noël Carroll's concept of mass ART as one created using industrialised TECHNOLOGIES and dissemination for broad consumption (1998: 3). Within the industry, this has resulted in many practices: a divided creative process employing several roles (WRITER, PENCILLER, INKER, COLOURIST, LETTERER, editor, plate preparers). Moreover, as Ruth-Ellen St. Onge has noted, printing processes employed by PUBLISHERS intrinsically inform the STYLE and MATERIALITY associated with comics (2020). Thus, despite the oft-remarked potential of comics as a FORM, mass production methods have always mandated limitations, as noted by writer Steve Gerber in 1978: "We're working with a limited amount of space.... There is only a certain amount of reproducible detail, due to a really rotten printing process, that can be presented on a comic-book page" (Gerber 2006: 25). Digital PRODUCTION and distribution, however, are radically shifting many of these limitations.

Josh R. Rose

### *References*

Carroll, N. (1998) *A Philosophy of Mass Art.* Oxford: Oxford University Press.

Gerber, S. (2006) "Changing Comics' Course: An interview by Gary Groth" in Spurgeon, T. (ed.) *The Comics Journal Library, Volume 6: The Writers.* Seattle: Fantagraphics Books, pp. 11–44.

St. Onge, R.-E. (2020) "Photoengraving and the Materiality of Twentieth-Century Comic Books," *Sequentials* 1(4), n.p. Available at: https://www.sequentialsjournal.net/issues/issue1.4/stonge.html [Accessed 4 August 2020].

## Materialism

Materialism is a metaphysical philosophical doctrine that holds that everything that exists in the world is of a material nature (Smart 1963). Materialist approaches in LITERARY and ART criticism are loosely connected to this doctrine through the influence of dialectical materialism, Karl Marx's and Friedrich Engel's theory that economic forces determine developments in human history (Gregory 1977). Marxist readings of CULTURE see it as a secondary system built on the basis of—and reflecting—the "natural substratum" of the economic system of every society. For example, Antonio Gramsci's concept of hegemony explains how culture is used to produce consent to economic-political systems, and the Frankfurt School of Critical Theory draws on Marx's theory of fetishism to explain how contemporary culture impedes people from reaching social emancipation (Neyrat 2020: 38–44). Cultural materialism, emerging in the 1970s in Britain, in a context of tensions produced by the social and intellectual movements of the 1960s, reconsiders the orthodox Marxist divide of base and superstructure and tries to avoid the determinism of earlier Marxist approaches to culture, combining a materialist focus with a POSTSTRUCTURALIST trust to the relative AUTONOMY of the SUBJECT, who maintains agency in spite of being constituted within their historical context (Drakakis 2001).

Vasiliki Belia

## *References*

Drakakis, J. (2001) "Cultural Materialism" in Knellwolf, C. and Norris, C. (eds.) *The Cambridge History of Literary Criticism,* Volume 9. Cambridge: Cambridge University Press, pp. 43–58.

Gregory, F. (1977) "Scientific versus Dialectical Materialism: A Clash of Ideologies in Nineteenth-Century German Radicalism," *Isis: History of Science Society*, 68(2), pp. 206–223.

Neyrat, F. (2020) *Literature and Materialisms.* Abingdon: Routledge.

Smart, J. J. C. (1963) "Materialism," *The Journal of Philosophy*, 60(22), pp. 651–662.

## Media

The concept of media developed in the late nineteenth century following the emergence of new TECHNICAL media, marking a shift in the understanding of signification from MIMESIS to communication (Guillory 2010). A behaviourist concern with their effects on AUDIENCES characterises early twentieth-century media theories, exemplified in discussions of comics by Fredric Wertham's (1954) denunciation of their harmful influence on young READERS. In contrast to models such as Claude E. Shannon's (1948), which positions media as a conduit through which messages are transmitted, mid-century MEDIUM theorists emphasised that media themselves are the primary bearers of meaning (McLuhan 1994). This approach in turn was criticised as AHISTORICAL and technologically deterministic, ignoring the ways in which technologies develop in response to societal needs and create change through their implementation rather than their inherent properties (Williams 2003). CULTURAL STUDIES scholars have focused on the reproduction of ideology through media institutions for the purpose of reinforcing political hegemony (Hall 1977) or patriarchal systems (McRobbie 1990). Henry Jenkins countered media theorists' concern that MASS PRODUCED texts invite passive consumption by positioning FAN PRODUCTIONS as "textual poaching" (Jenkins 1988: 85). Common amongst these approaches is a concern with the relationship between the structures of media and the agency they afford their audiences.

John Miers

## *References*

Guillory, J. (2010) "Genesis of the media concept," *Critical inquiry* 36(2), pp. 321–362.

Hall, S. (1977) "Culture, the media and the ideological effect" in Curran, J., Gurevitch, M., and Woollacott, J. (eds.) *Mass Communication and Society*. London: Arnold London.

Jenkins, H. (1988) "Star Trek rerun, reread, rewritten: Fan writing as textual poaching," *Critical Studies in Mass Communication* 5(2), pp. 85–107.

McLuhan, M. (1994) *Understanding media: The extensions of man*. Cambridge: The Massachusetts Institute of Technology Press.

McRobbie, A. (1990) *Feminism and Youth Culture: From 'Jackie' to 'Just Seventeen.'* London: Macmillan International Higher Education.

Shannon, C. E. (1948) "A mathematical theory of communication," *Bell system technical journal* 27(3), pp. 379–423.

Wertham, F. (1954) *Seduction of the Innocent: The Influence of Comic Books on Today's Youth*. New York: Rinehart.

Williams, R. (1974) *Television: Technology and Cultural Form*. Reprint 2003. Abingdon: Routledge.

## Mediation

Mediation refers to "the intervening role that the process of communication plays in the making of meaning" (Couldry 2008: 379). In contradistinction to the Platonic understanding of REPRESENTATION as entities that obscure or enable knowledge of a stable external reality (2008), contemporary uses of the term emphasise that "mediation should be understood not as standing between preformed SUBJECTS, objects, actants, or entities but as the process, action, or event that generates or provides the conditions for the emergence of subjects and objects, for the individuation of entities within the world" (Grusin 2015: 129). As such, COMICS are identified by the unique ways in which they afford reading. Hence, Bruno Latour distinguishes the role of a mediator, which "creates what it translates as well as the entities between which it plays a mediating role" (2012: 78) from that of the intermediary, which "simply transports, transfers, transmits" (ibid. 77). The concept of REMEDIATION was developed to describe the ways in which digital MEDIA "honour, rival and revise" (Bolter and Grusin 2000: 15) established FORMS of communication, but is not limited to digital media: all media respond to and redeploy existing media.

John Miers

### *References*

Bolter, J. D. and Grusin, R. (2000) *Remediation: Understanding New Media*. Cambridge: MIT.

Couldry, N. (2008) "Mediatisation or mediation? Alternative understandings of the emergent space of digital storytelling," *New Media & Society* 10(3), pp. 373–391.

Grusin, R. (2015) "Radical mediation," *Critical Inquiry* 42(1), pp. 124–148.

Latour, B. (1991) *We Have Never Been Modern*. Translated from French by C. Porter, 2012. Cambridge: Harvard University Press.

Plato (c. 375 BC) *Republic*. Translated from Greek by R. Waterfield, 2008. Oxford: Oxford University Press.

## Medium

The parameters for defining what constitutes a medium are most often established by the disciplinary study of particular MEDIA; for example, what comprises the medium of FILM is discussed and debated within the field of film studies. The definition of an individual medium is also generally reliant on the interplay of a medium's FORMAL elements and its content, and to some extent on its specificity—that is, what distinguishes it from other media. COMICS STUDIES, without an established academic disciplinary home, interacts with various fields of study from media studies to LITERATURE, ART, HISTORY, DESIGN, and beyond. While this breadth of approaches makes Comics Studies a dynamic INTERDISCIPLINARY field, it also contributes to conflicting views on the medium of comics as distinct from other media. The rise of the use of the GRAPHIC NOVEL clearly demonstrates this conflict, as within literary studies it points to the appropriation of particular comics as a GENRE of literature, and in INTERMEDIALITY studies as a medium separate from comics that arose from the combination of comics and literature. Such distinctions also highlight the problem of defining media based on their content, which, subject to TASTE ADJUDICATION, problematically often serves to "[strengthen] the distinction between high and low, major and minor" (Labio 2011: 126).

Erin La Cour

### *References*

Labio, C. (2011) "What's in a Name? The Academic Study of Comics and 'The Graphic Novel,'" *Cinema Journal* 50(3), pp. 123–126.

## Memoir

While AUTOBIOGRAPHY has been understood as a LITERARY GENRE that tells the STORY of a life chronologically, memoir is a more flexible form of LIFE WRITING that can focus on a specific event or relationship (Couser 2012: 22–24). In literary and cultural studies, memoir is often positioned as a POPULAR, commercial form of life writing that does not achieve the same level of artistry associated with autobiography (Rak 2004). In the English language context, the turn of the twenty-first century saw a rapid increase in the commercial and cultural significance of memoir. This success has produced a (somewhat predictable) backlash against memoir as the cause of a slide towards narcissism in literary and public DISCOURSE (Yagoda 2007). Yet, as Julie Rak has argued, the increased prominence of memoir indicates the strong connection between the READING and WRITING of stories of personal experience and contemporary forms of citizenship, intimacy, and politics, and indicates larger cultural shifts in the AESTHETIC, social, cultural, and political uses of life writing (2013). The rise of memoir has been tied to the rising prominence of comics, as seen in works such as Alison Bechdel's *Fun Home: A Family Tragicomic*, and *Are You My Mother?*, and Marjane Satrapi's *Persepolis: The Story of a Childhood*.

Anna Poletti

### *References*

Couser, G. T. (2012) *Memoir: An Introduction*. Oxford: Oxford University Press.

Rak, J. (2004) "Are Memoirs Autobiography? A Consideration of Genre and Public Identity," *Genre* 37, 3–4, pp. 483–504.

Rak, J. (2013) *Boom! Manufacturing Memoir for the Popular Market*. Waterloo: Wilfrid Laurier Press.

Yagoda, B. (2007) "A Brief History of Memoir Bashing." *Slate*, 30 March 2007. Available at: http://www.slate.com/articles/news_and_politics/memoir_week/2007/03/a_brief_history_of_memoirbashing.html [Accessed 5 August 2020].

## Memory Studies

Memory studies is a relatively recent research field that studies how cultures and individuals establish connections with the past (Erll 2011). Although the application of memory studies concepts to comics is quite recent (1990s), these concepts are most relevant to comics, since this MEDIUM has been mostly PRODUCED on cheap paper to be thrown away after a quick READ, and consequently, immediately forgotten. The integration of memory studies and comics can be dated to the boom of AUTOBIOGRAPHY as a GENRE in which an individual tells and reflects on her/his past, whether TRAUMATIC (individual, like Alison Bechdel's *Fun Home: A Family Tragicomic*, and/or collective, like Art Spiegelman's *Maus* and Marjane Satrapi's *Persepolis*) or "ordinary" (Aarons 2019, Witek 1989). Even more recently, "comic memory studies" included "remembering comics" (Ahmed and Crucifix 2018), that is, remembering a comic's FORM, since comics are also defined by STYLE, LINE, and COLOUR. These elements are key to memory retention, because they are a type of embodied memory. Having lacked the storage memory of high culture, such as libraries or ARCHIVES, for a very long time, comics relied on "store memory," which has been relayed by comics-specific archives only in the last four decades. More stable archiving practices allow for a more thorough critical DIALOGUE on patrimonial practices, legitimation, and CANON formation (Beaty and Woo 2016). Finally, the 1990s memory boom to which memory studies responded also fostered a huge NOSTALGIA industry (Baetens and Frey 2015), which helped revive comics that had been forgotten because of GENDER (Gibson 2015), RACE, culture, or LINGUISTIC minority.

Chris Reyns-Chikuma

## *References*

Aarons, V. (2019) *Holocaust Graphic Narratives: Generation, Trauma, and Memory*. New Brunswick: Rutgers University Press.

Ahmed, M. and Crucifix, B. (eds.) (2018) *Comics Memory: Archives and Styles*. London: Palgrave Macmillan.

Baetens, J. and Frey, H. (2015) "Nostalgia and the Return of History" in Baetens J. and Frey, H. (eds.) *The Graphic Novel: An Introduction*. Cambridge: Cambridge University Press, pp. 217–245.

Beaty, B. and Woo, B. (2016) *The Greatest Comic Book of All Time: Symbolic Capital and the Field of American Comic Books*. London: Palgrave Macmillan.

Erll, A. (2011) *Memory in Culture*. London: Palgrave Macmillan.

Gibson, M. (2015) *Remembered Reading: Memory, Comics and Post-War Constructions of British Girlhood*. Leuven: Leuven University Press.

Witek, J. (1989) *Comic Books as History: The Narrative Art of Jack Jackson, Art Spiegelman and Harvey Pekar*. Jackson: University Press of Mississippi.

## Merchandise

Merchandise is goods to be sold or bought and, within comics culture, refers to the goods that bear the motifs, COLOURS, or logos of brands or particular comics characters. These goods are typically toys, clothes, bags, mugs, and other household paraphernalia. In addition to the use of logos, merchandise is also marked with IMAGES of specific FILMS, comics, or GAMES, which allows for the continuous PRODUCTION of consumer goods with every new film, COMIC BOOK, or game release. This serves to increase the visibility of brands and comics, which boosts their cultural clout and works to ADVERTISE these brands to non-fans. Comic book merchandise is also defined by its production of limited-edition goods, which appeal to COLLECTORS, who are traditionally associated with comic book FANDOMS. This includes the production of limited-edition comic books throughout the 1990s, as well as old, rare, and seminal comics. These comics are not purchased to be read, but rather are purchased for collection and display. Historically, comics provided advertisement space to various goods, including comics merchandise. In contemporary comics, this advertisement space allows companies to MARKET tie-in toys and other comic book series directly to their READERS. Increasingly, COMICS SHOPS report that the sale of merchandise outstrips the sale of the source material (Resha 2020).

Esther De Dauw

### *References*

Resha, A. (2020) "The Blue Age of Comics Books," *Inks* 4(1), pp. 66–81.

## Metaphor

Aristotle described metaphor as "applying to something a noun that properly applies to something else" (2013: 43). Contemporary theories view it as a cognitive rather than LINGUISTIC phenomenon. I. A. Richards characterised it as "two thoughts of things active together" (1936: 93), a view developed in Max Black's interaction theory (1954, 1993). The most influential theory of metaphor remains George Lakoff and Mark Johnson's conceptual metaphor theory (Lakoff 1993, Lakoff and Johnson 2003), which characterises metaphor use as the mapping of properties from one conceptual domain to another. Common to both theories is the proposal that metaphor involves using the perceived properties of one, usually more concrete concept, to structure the user's understanding of a second, usually more abstract concept. Positioning metaphor as a matter of cognition rather than LANGUAGE allows theorists to identify instances of metaphor in diverse communicative REGISTERS including MUSIC (Zbikowski 2008), GESTURE (Cienki and Müller 2008), and pictures. Charles Forceville (1996) applies Black's interaction theory to the analysis of pictorial and MULTIMODAL METAPHORS and argues (2005) that the presence of metaphors for anger in comics conforming to the mappings described by Lakoff and Johnson supports their theory.

John Miers

## *References*


Aldrich, V. C. (1971) "Form in the Visual Arts," *The British Journal of Aesthetics*, 11(3), pp. 215–226.

Aristotle (c. 335 BC) *Poetics*. Translated from Greek by A. Kenny, 2013. Oxford: Oxford University Press.

Black, M. (1954) "Metaphor," *Proceedings of the Aristotelian Society* 55, pp. 273–294.

Black, M. (1993) "More About Metaphor" in Ortony, A. (ed.) *Metaphor and Thought*. 2nd edition. Cambridge: Cambridge University Press, pp. 19–41.

Cienki, A. J. and Müller, C. (eds.) (2008) *Metaphor and Gesture*. Philadelphia: John Benjamins.

Forceville, C. (1996) *Pictorial Metaphor in Advertising*. Abingdon: Routledge.

Forceville, C. (2005) "Visual Representations of the Idealized Cognitive Model of Anger in the Asterix Album *La Zizanie*," *Journal of Pragmatics* 37, pp. 69–88.

Goodman, N. (1968) *Languages of Art: An Approach to a Theory of Symbols*. Indianapolis: Bobbs-Merrill.

Lakoff, G. (1993) "The Contemporary Theory of Metaphor" in Ortony, A. (ed.) *Metaphor and Thought*. 2nd edition. Cambridge: Cambridge University Press, pp. 202–251.

Lakoff, G. and Johnson, M. (2003) *Metaphors We Live By*. 2nd edition. Chicago: University of Chicago Press.

Rawson, P. (1969) *Drawing*. Oxford: Oxford University Press.
Richards, I. A. (1936) *The Philosophy of Rhetoric*. Oxford: Oxford University Press.
Schier, F. (1986) *Deeper Into Pictures: An Essay on Pictorial Representation*. Cambridge: Cambridge University Press.
Zbikowski, L. M. (2008) "Metaphor and Music" in Gibbs, R. W. (ed.) *The Cambridge Handbook of Metaphor and Thought*. Cambridge: Cambridge University Press, pp. 502–524.

## Migration

Migration refers to people moving and changing their place of residence from one place, region, or country to another with some permanence. A key distinction separates international migration and internal migration within a country (e.g. from rural to urban areas). The reasons for migration are manifold: trade, LABOUR, EDUCATION, family and other group ties, or flight from famine, natural disasters, and aggressors, political and religious persecution, and so on. The reasons for migration are reflected in the terminology used to categorise different groups of migrants (e.g. labour migrants, refugees, and asylum seekers). Migration is, furthermore, divided into voluntary and involuntary or forced displacement, although this division, too, is often blurred. Countries' and regions' histories as areas of origin, transit, and destination for migration vary and entail different social and economic effects. While migration studies, traditionally, has focused on (economic) reasons for migration and incorporation in the host country, there is now significant interest in migrants' diasporas and TRANSNATIONAL connections (Lie 1995, Vertovec 2009) as well as border problematics (Johnson et al. 2011). Migration is a recurring THEME in comics (Marie and Ollivier 2013) and the comics CANON (Marjane Satrapi's *Persepolis* (2000–2003) and Shaun Tan's *The Arrival* (2006)). It has been analysed in, for example, comics LIFE WRITING (Davis 2005, McNicol 2018) and COMICS JOURNALISM (Bumatay 2015, Nabizadeh 2016) and as a tool in education (Boatright 2010, Weber and Moritzen 2017).

Ralf Kauranen

## *References*

Boatright, M. D. (2010) "Graphic Journeys: Graphic Novels' Representations of Immigrant Experiences," *Journal of Adolescent & Adult Literacy* 53(6), pp. 468–476.

Bumatay, M. (2015) "Plural Pathways, Plural Identities: Jean-Philippe Stassen's *Les Visiteurs de Gibraltar*" in Mehta, B. and Mukherji, P. (eds.) *Postcolonial Comics: Texts, Events, Identities.* Abingdon: Routledge, pp. 29–43.

Davis, R. G. (2005) "A Graphic Self: Comics as Autobiography in Marjane Satrapi's *Persepolis*," *Prose Studies* 27(3), pp. 264–279.

Johnson, C., Jones, R., Paasi, A., Amoore, L., Mountz, A., Salter, M. and Rumford, C. (2011) "Interventions on rethinking 'the border' in border studies," *Political Geography* 30(2), pp. 61–69.

Lie, J. (1995) "From International Migration to Transnational Diaspora," *Contemporary Sociology* 24(4), pp. 303–306.

Marie, V. and Ollivier, G. (eds.) (2013) *Albums, bande-dessinée et immigration 1913–2013.* Paris: Futuropolis and Musée de l'histoire de l'immigration.

McNicol, S. (2018) "Telling Migrant Women's Life Stories as Comics," *Journal of Graphic Novels and Comics* 9(4), pp. 279–292.

Nabizadeh, G. (2016) "Comics Online: Detention and White Space in 'A Guard's Story,'" *Ariel* 47(1–2), pp. 337–357.

Vertovec, S. (2009) *Transnationalism.* Abingdon: Routledge.

Weber, A. and Moritzen, K. (eds.) (2017) *Tausend Bilder und eins: Comic als ästhetische Praxis in der postmigrantischen Gesellschaft.* Bielefeld: transcript.

## Mimesis

Since the time of Plato and Aristotle, mimesis has been used in AESTHETIC and ARTISTIC theory to refer to the attempt to imitate or REPRODUCE reality. Largely regarded as dangerous by Plato because it substitutes illusion for truth, which it impersonates and copies (2008), mimesis shows the interior of world as though it were real, imitating the meaning of the thing it wishes to show, but reflecting the limited understanding of it. For comics, this is rhetorical as the displayed intention, cognition, significance, authority, and presence that presents PASTICHE as the IMAGE is "intended to convey information and/or to produce an aesthetic response in the viewer" (McCloud 1992: 9) through an enacted action rather than telling through DIEGESIS and/or a NARRATOR. Further, it is related to proxemics, the examination of "how communication between people changes with shifts in the distance between them and changes in their position," the act of mimicking the quotidian of human communication is meant to elicit a particular sense of understanding from the FORM on the static page but ultimately reveals the assumption of the physical and psychological stance of the text (Levoy 1973: 314).

Eric Atkinson

## *References*

Levoy, R. (1973) "Proxemics," *Australian Journal of Optometry* 56(8), p. 314.

McCloud, S. (1993) *Understanding Comics: The Invisible Art.* New York: Harper Perennial.

Plato (c. 375 BC) *Republic.* Translated from Greek by R. Waterfield, 2008. Oxford: Oxford University Press.

## Minicomics

Minicomics were small, photocopied COMIC BOOKS that were SELF-PUBLISHED in small quantities and distributed by their MAKERS, usually through the mail (Luciano 1985). Sometimes described as NEWAVE comics (Luciano 1985, Dowers 2010) or ALTERNATIVE COMIX (Erling 1982: 36), they were PRODUCED and consumed by a small subculture of dedicated aficionados. Minicomics first emerged in the mid-1970s, reached their high point in the 1980s, and declined thereafter. They avoided mainstream GENRES such as SUPERHEROES and typically displayed an AVANT-GARDE, absurdist STYLE. Minicomics were contemporaries of ALTERNATIVE COMICS but appealed to an even smaller, less mainstream AUDIENCE.

Doug Singsen

### *References*

Dowers, M. (ed.) (2010) *Newave! The Underground Mini Comix of the 1980s*. Seattle: Fantagraphics.

Erling, G. (1982) "Alternative Comix" in Kennedy, J. (ed.) *The Official Underground and Newave Comix Price Guide*. Cambridge: Boatner Norton, pp. 36–38.

Luciano, D. (1985) "Newave Comics Survey," *The Comics Journal* 102, pp. 91–102.

## MINOR LITERATURE

Coined by Gilles Deleuze and Félix Guattari, minor literature illuminates "where the system is coming from and going to, how it becomes, and what element is going to play the role of heterogeneity, a saturating body that makes the whole assembly flow away" (1975: 7). Politically disruptive to conceptions of the ARCHIVE, the CANON, and other problematic promotions of particular ARTISTS, CREATORS, and WRITERS, minor literature can "express another possible community and forge the means for another consciousness and sensibility" (ibid. 17). Minor literature has three characteristics: (1) it is written in a major LANGUAGE, (2) it connects the individual concern to politics, and (3) it is of a collective enunciation. Importantly, the minor is neither necessarily tied to minor communities—every writer can find "his own *patois*"—nor to LITERATURE alone—it can be developed in MUSIC, philosophy, and POPULAR MEDIA (ibid. 17 and 26–27). Comics can be positioned as a minor literature in that the MEDIUM has HISTORICALLY been effectively policed and penned in by various DISCOURSES that maintain that comics exist outside the realms of "real" ART, "real" literature, or "pure" medium qualification, including advocacy for the term GRAPHIC NOVEL (La Cour 2013 and 2016). Moreover, this KITSCH status, as art discourse has it, can be operational: FORM and content analyses can demonstrate how comics can open "new avenues for expression by deterritorializing Art (with a capital *A*) and Literature (with a capital *L*) rather than staking claims to a place within the system of cultural capital" (La Cour 2013: 173).

Erin La Cour

## *References*

Deleuze, G. and Guattari, F. (1975) *Kafka: Toward a Minor Literature.* Translated by D. Polan, 1986. Minneapolis: University of Minnesota Press.

La Cour, E. (2016) "Comics as a Minor Literature," *Image [&] Narrative* 17(4), pp. 79–90.

La Cour, E. (2013) *The "Graphic Novel": Discourses on the Archive.* PhD. University of Amsterdam.

## MISE-EN-PAGE

Mise-en-page (page layout) is the arrangement of graphic items in a tactic relationship with each other on a page (Grennan 2017: 29, Thibault 2007: 134). Arrangements of graphic items that devolve to traditions of use in the comics REGISTER have been identified and generalised by Thierry Groensteen, Benoît Peeters, and Renaud Chavanne (Groensteen 1999: 187, 131–135, Peeters 1991, Chavanne 2015), including GUTTER, PANEL, and types of MARK, among others. A specific relationship between mise-en-page and MISE-EN-SCÈNE (scene-setting) is one of the characteristics of the comics register because the tactic relationship between marks on a page mutually determines the visible arrangement of those aspects of a STORYWORLD that constitute the comics DIEGESIS. As Jan Baetens notes, this relationship between page layout and scene-setting is not simply confined to experiences of DEPICTION in comics, but is rather a function of NARRATION. Hence, non-depictive (abstract) STORIES are also scenes that are set (Baetens 2011: 95).

Simon Grennan

## *References*

Baetens, J. (2011) "Abstraction in Comics," *SubStance* 40(1), pp. 94–113.

Chavanne, R. (2015) "The Composition of Comics," *European Comic Art* 8(1), pp. 111–144.

Grennan, S. (2017) *A Theory of Narrative Drawing.* London: Palgrave Macmillan.

Groensteen, T. (1999) *Systéme de la bande dessinée.* Paris: Presses universitaires de France.

Peeters, B. (1991) *Case, planche, récit: Comment lire une bande dessinée.* Paris: Casterman.

Thibault, P. (2007) "Writing, Graphology and Visual Semiosis" in Royce, T. and Bowcher, W. (eds.) *New Directions in the Analysis of Multimodal Discourse.* Abingdon: Routledge, pp. 111–145.

## Mise-en-Scène

Mise-en-scène (scene-setting) is the visual arrangement and presentation to view of aspects of a STORYWORLD and can refer to both the DESIGN protocol of these arrangements (such as movie cinematography [Martin 2014]) and a single iteration of this protocol (whatever is presented to view in a scene). The design protocols for these arrangements are a significant topic of debate in COMICS STUDIES (Lefèvre 2011, Smith 2012) and lend themselves to comparative MEDIA analysis (Rowe 2016), TRANSMEDIA analysis (Bourdaa 2013), and analysis of ADAPTATION (Toyoura et al. 2012). A specific relationship between mise-en-scène and MISE-EN-PAGE (page layout) is one of the characteristics of the comics REGISTER, because the tactic relationship between MARKS on a page mutually determines the visible arrangement of those aspects of a storyworld that constitute the comics DIEGESIS. As Jan Baetens notes, this relationship between scene-setting and page layout is not simply confined to experiences of DEPICTION in comics, but is rather a function of NARRATION. Hence, non-depictive (abstract) STORIES are also scenes that are set (Baetens 2011: 95).

Simon Grennan

### *References*

Baetens, J. (2011) "Abstraction in Comics," *SubStance* 40(1), pp. 94–113.

Bourdaa, M. (2013) "'Following the Pattern': The Creation of an Encyclopaedic Universe with Transmedia Storytelling," *Adaptation* 6(2), pp. 202–214.

Lefèvre, P. (2011) "Mise-en-scène and Framing: Visual Storytelling in 'Lone Wolf and Cub'" in Smith, M. and Duncan, R. (eds.) *Critical Approaches to Comics: Theories and Methods.* Abingdon: Routledge, pp. 71–83.

Martin, A. (2014) *Mise-en-Scène and Film Style: From Classical Hollywood to New Media Art*. London: Palgrave Macmillan.

Rowe, C. (2016) "Dynamic Drawings and Dilated Time: Framing in Comics and Film," *Journal of Graphic Novels and Comics* 7(4), pp. 348–368.

Smith, C. (2012) "Motion comics: Modes of adaptation and the issue of authenticity," *Animation Practice, Process & Production* 1(2), pp. 357–378.

Toyoura M., Kunihiro, M., and Mao, X. (2012) "Film Comic Reflecting Camera-Works" in Schoeffmann K., Merialdo, B., Hauptmann, A. G., Ngo, C. W., Andreopoulos, Y., and Breiteneder, C. (eds.) *Advances in Multimedia Modelling MMM 2012. Lecture Notes in Computer Science* 7131. Berlin: Springer, pp. 406–417.

## Mode

The word mode is utilised in a number of different ways, according to both the scholarly discipline in which it appears and the topics to which it is applied: in different iterations, it can be synonymous with REGISTER or/and GENRE, or/and refer to traditions of rhetorical use within registers or genres (Biber and Conrad 2009, Howes 2009). Despite this relative permeability of the sense of the word, its use tends towards older traditions of scholarship, shading less readily than its synonyms into analysis of discursive contingencies and more readily into analysis of STYLE (Grennan 2013, 2020). In COMICS STUDIES, the idea of different discursive modes is sometimes used to describe the inclusion of verbal and visual elements. In studies of LANGUAGE, the term "modes of discourse" continues to describe CONVENTIONS emerging in language use, but only within a rhetorical framework encompassed by syntax (or the arrangement of LINGUISTIC items), compared with the pragmatic conventions of use described by register, or those STORY conventions described by genre, for example (Connors 1981).

Simon Grennan

## *References*

Biber, D. and Conrad, S. (2009) *Register, Genre and Style.* Cambridge: Cambridge University Press.

Connors, R. (1981) "The Rise and Fall of the Modes of Discourse," *College Composition and Communication* 32(4), pp. 444–455.

Grennan, S. (2020) "The Enduring Power of Comic Strips" in Chorpening, K. and Fortnum, R. (eds.) *A Companion to Contemporary Drawing: Wiley Blackwell Companions to Art History.* Hoboken: John Wiley & Sons, pp. 513–529.

Grennan, S. (2013) "Register in the guise of genre: Instrumental adaptation in the early comics of Grennan & Sperandio," *Studies in Comics* 4(1), pp. 75–88.

Howes, F. (2009) "Imagining a Multiplicity of Visual Rhetorical Traditions: Comics Lessons from Rhetoric Histories," *ImageText* 5(3), n.p. Available at: http://imagetext.english.ufl.edu/archives/v5_3/howes/ [Accessed 8 May 2020].

## Modernism

Modernism, in ART and LITERARY CRITICISM, is an artistic period that spans from the end of the nineteenth century and through the first half of the twentieth century, although periodisation varies depending on art FORM and geographical location. It encompasses a variety of movements (such as Symbolism, Cubism, Futurism, and Surrealism) that explore or react to the historical condition and human consciousness of modernity. Modernist movements have no cohesive AESTHETIC and do not relate to modernity in the same way but share the tendency to eschew MIMETIC approaches to reality and CONVENTIONS of form (Bradbury and McFarlane 1976: 22–24). Modernism's broad definition indicates a lack of consensus over its meaning: critics produce different theories of Modernism when studying it in relation to other key literary and art history concepts, such as Romanticism and POSTMODERNISM (Eysteinsson 1990: 4). The terminological impasse may also reflect the unresolved contradictions within modernity, which may be seen as either the epitome of or a rupture from the ideologies and aesthetics of the

Enlightenment (Friedman 2001: 499–501). As the emergence of comics coincided with Modernism, their association with commercial culture made them a defining point of contrast to modernist experimentation and expression (Ayres 2016: 111).

Vasiliki Belia

## *References*

Ayres, J. (2016) "Introduction: Comics and Modernism," *Journal of Modern Literature* 39(2), pp. 111–114.

Bradbury, M. and McFarlane, J. W. (eds.) (1976) *Modernism: A Guide to European Literature 1890–1930*. New York: Penguin.

Eysteinsson, A. (1990) *The Concept of Modernism*. Ithaca: Cornell University Press.

Friedman, S. S. (2001) "Definitional Excursions: The Meanings of Modern/ Modernity/ Modernism," *Modernism/modernity* 8(3), pp. 493–513.

## Motion Comics

Motion comics are transpositions of specific comics NARRATIVES onto screen-based audiovisual MEDIA, presenting a HYBRID FORM, the HISTORY of which largely corresponds to the emergence of DIGITAL COMICS (Wershler and Sinervo 2017). Typically, motion comics preserve the majority of the source comic's DRAWINGS and written TEXT (even to the point of including on-screen SPEECH BALLOONS and CAPTION BOXES in many cases), but with the addition of SOUND and MOVEMENT. The soundtracks of motion comics can include spoken dialogue, voiceover NARRATION, MUSIC, and sound effects. The actual motions added can range from camera movements—such as pans across and zooms into and out from the PANEL IMAGES—right up to the movement of select elements of the original drawings of characters and objects to simulate basic actions. To an extent, this manipulation of the two-dimensional drawings resembles certain ANIMATION techniques, such as "paper" or "cutout" animation: the FRAME-by-frame recreation of movement using articulated paper or cardboard figures (Smith 2011). However, motion comics are distinct from ADAPTATIONS of comics into animated FILM, television, or video texts; whereas adaptations employ ARTISTS and animators to REDESIGN the source text to suit a moving-image MEDIUM, motion comics apply such audiovisual effects to the original comics panels. Motion comics have thus met with criticism from both the critical and creative communities for implicitly underlining the "aesthetic incompatibility of comics, animation and film" in such a way that they do a disservice to the original work (Morton 2017: 132).

Christopher Rowe

## *References*

Morton, D. (2017) "'Watched any good books lately?': The Formal Failure of the *Watchmen* Motion Comic," *Cinema Journal* 56 (2), pp. 132–137.

Smith, C. (2012) "Motion comics: Modes of adaptation and the issue of authenticity," *Animation Practice, Process & Production* 1(2), pp. 357–378.

Wershler, D. and Sinervo, K. (2017) "Marvel and the Form of Motion Comics" in Yockey, M. (ed.) *Make Ours Marvel: Media Convergence and a Comics Universe*. Austin: University of Texas Press, pp. 187–206.

## Movement

As Pascal Lefèvre remarks, the reader of comics is not "innocent" and applies cognitive frameworks based on previous experiences (2000). In comics, at least in the Western world, the traditional Z-pattern of reading (left-right, top-bottom) has been inherited from both the READING direction of script and the book FORM (del Rey Cabero 2019), so objects and characters tend to move on a left-to-right axis. A movement from right to left could express setback, retreat, or escape (the opposite applies to MANGA). This has also been observed in paintings (Gross and Bornstein 1978: 36) and was one of the realisations of Hergé (and Rodolphe Töpffer earlier) when he was creating his Tintin series: "from left to right, speed seems greater than from right to left. I use the other direction when a character retraces their steps. If I made the character run from right to left, they would look, in each frame, as if they were going back, chasing themselves" (Peeters 2003: 85). Movement in comics, however, can be multidirectional and does not only occur from PANEL to panel, but also within a panel; the type, trajectory, or origin of the movement (or lack thereof) of characters and objects can be expressed through motion LINES (Cohn and Mahler 2015) and other pictorial resources (Juricevic and Horvath 2016), including position, orientation, and exaggeration.

Enrique del Rey Cabero

## *References*


Cohn, N. and Mahler, S. (2015) "The notion of the motion: The neurocognition of motion lines in visual narratives," *Brain Research* 16(1), pp. 73–84.

del Rey Cabero, E. (2019) "Beyond Linearity: Holistic, Multidirectional, Multilinear and Translinear Reading in Comics," *The Comics Grid: Journal of Comics Scholarship* 9(5),pp. 1–21.

Gross, C. G. and Bornstein, M. H. (1978) "Left and Right in Science and Art," *Leonardo* 1(1), pp. 29–38.

Juricevic, I. and Horvath, A. J. (2016) "Analysis of Motions in Comic Book Cover Art: Using Pictorial Metaphors," *The Comics Grid: Journal of Comics Scholarship* 6, p. 6. Available at: https://www.comicsgrid.com/articles/10.16995/cg.71/ [Accessed 6 July 2020].

Lefèvre, P. (2000) "Narration in Comics," *Image [&] Narrative* 1, n.p. Available at: http://www.imageandnarrative.be/inarchive/narratology/pascallefevre.htm [Accessed 4 July 2020].

Peeters, B. (2003) *Lire la bande dessinée*. Paris: Flammarion.


## Multimodal Metaphor

The study of METAPHOR originated in antiquity, when Aristotle studied its use in poetry as well as in rhetoric. The reputation of the TROPE received a vast boost when George Lakoff and Mark Johnson declared that "the essence of metaphor is understanding and experiencing one kind of thing in terms of another" (1980: 5), thereby claiming that metaphor is primarily a matter of thinking and conceptualising, and only derivatively a matter of LANGUAGE. Taking this assumption seriously led to the study of metaphors in other modes than language, such as visuals, and of metaphors that were expressed MULTIMODALLY. Elisabeth 'Lisa' El Refaie was the first to analyse multimodal metaphors in political CARTOONS (2003), and this has by now become a favourite GENRE in multimodal metaphor scholarship. Eduardo Urios-Aparisi and Forceville compiled the first edited volume on multimodal metaphor, which contains chapters on comics and political cartoons (2009). El Refaie studies multimodal metaphor in what could be called "non-fictional comics" (2019). The study of multimodal metaphor, Forceville (2019) argued, should also be extended to cover other tropes, such as metonymy, symbolism, ALLEGORY, hyperbole, antithesis, and IRONY.

Charles Forceville

## *References*

El Refaie, E. L. (2003) "Understanding visual metaphors: The example of newspaper cartoons," *Visual Communication* 2(1), pp. 75–95.

El Refaie, E. L. (2019) *Visual Metaphor and Embodiment in Graphic Illness Narratives.* Oxford: Oxford University Press.

Forceville, C. and Urios-Aparisi, E. (eds.) (2009) *Multimodal Metaphor.* Berlin: Mouton de Gruyter.

Forceville, C. (2019) "Developments in multimodal metaphor studies: A response to Górska, Coëgnarts, Porto & Romano, and Muelas-Gil" in Navarro i Ferrando, I. (ed.) *Current Approaches to Metaphor Analysis in Discourse.* Berlin: De Gruyter, pp. 367–378.

Lakoff, G. and Johnson, M. (1980) *Metaphors We Live By.* Chicago: University of Chicago Press.

## MULTIMODALITY

Scholarship on non-verbal and partly verbal communication is on the rise, joining LINGUISTICS in investigating meaning-making. Communication drawing on a single SEMIOTIC resource, or MODE, is called monomodal; communication drawing on more than one mode is called multimodal. FILM, for instance, often relies on visuals, spoken language, SOUND, and MUSIC and is thereby a highly multimodal medium. Multimodality is a rapidly growing discipline in the humanities (Jewitt

2014, Klug and Stöckl 2016, Bateman et al. 2017, Wildfeuer et al. 2019). One of the problems of the young discipline is that there is hitherto no general agreement about what should count as a mode (Forceville 2021), which also problematises what is to be considered "monomodality." However, there is no disagreement that (static) visuals and (written) language each deserve mode-status, and indeed this is the most ubiquitous variety of multimodal DISCOURSE—arguably pioneered by Roland Barthes (1985). Comics, depending on these two modes, constitute an excellent MEDIUM for advancing the theorisation of monomodality and multimodality. Notably, these two modes sometimes merge, as in ONOMATOPOEIA. Much non-literal meaning is expressible via MULTIMODAL METAPHOR.

Charles Forceville

## *References*

Barthes, R. (1982) *The Responsibility of Forms: Critical Essays on Music, Art, and Representation.* Translated from French by R. Howard, 1985. Berkeley: University of California Press.

Bateman, J. A., Wildfeuer, J., and Hiippala, T. (2017) *Multimodality: Foundations, Research and Analysis. A Problem-Oriented Introduction.* Berlin: De Gruyter.

Forceville, C. (2021) "Multimodality" in Wen, X. and Taylor, J. R. (eds.) *The Routledge Handbook of Cognitive Linguistics.* London: Routledge, pp. 676–687.

Jewitt, C. (ed.) (2014) *The Routledge Handbook of Multimodal Analysis.* 2nd edition. London: Routledge.

Klug, N.-M. and Stöckl, H. (eds.) (2016) *Handbuch Sprache im multimodalen Kontext.* Berlin: De Gruyter.

Wildfeuer, J., Pflaeging, J., Bateman, J. A., Seizov, O., and Tseng, C. (eds.) (2019) *Multimodality—Towards a New Discipline.* Berlin: De Gruyter.

## Museums

Collaborations between ART museums and comics were initially marked by condescension: single PANELS were wrested from their NARRATIVE context (Couperie 1967: 145, Groensteen 2006) or treated as raw material for "legitimate" ARTISTS (Groensteen 2011: 184, Beaty 2012).

Specialised comics museums have had a consecrating function, although the tension between comics as art and as sociological phenomenon is not always resolved (Groensteen 2006: 142). More recently, art museums have commissioned comics series in democratising initiatives that coincidentally offer MERCHANDISING opportunities to host institutions (Picone 2013, Flinn 2013, Lladó Pol 2021). Participating comics artists have narrativised paintings, sometimes through the device, familiar from previous comics appropriations of high art, of characters climbing into them, or its reversal, as protagonists escape their FRAMES to enjoy INTERTEXTUAL INTERACTIONS with the subjects of other works. They have also recontextualised pictures within different time frames and ideological climates: Catherine Meurisse, for example, contests the spectator's right to fantasy possession of the female model (2014). Elsewhere, there is a REFLEXIVE emphasis on the codes of comics: Marc-Antoine Mathieu stakes its claim as an art form that maximises the potential, latent in the gallery, for relationships between adjacent IMAGES and offers more spectacular mise en abyme than Louvre originals (2006).

Ann Miller

## *References*


Beaty, B. (2012) *Comics versus Art*. Toronto: University of Toronto Press.

Couperie, P. (1967) "Production et diffusion" in Couperie, P. (ed.) *Bande dessinée et narration figurative*. Paris: Musée des arts décoratifs/Palais du Louvre, pp. 129–145.

Flinn, M. C. (2013) "High Comics Art: The Louvre and the *Bande Dessinée*," *European Comic Art* 6(2), pp. 69–94.

Groensteen, T. (2006) *Un objet culturel non identifié*. Angoulême: Éditions de l'an 2.

Groensteen, T. (2011) *Comics and Narration*. Translated from French by A. Miller, 2013. Jackson: University Press of Mississippi.

Lladó Pol, F. (2020) "*El Perdón y la Furia*: José de Ribera's journey from faith to magic. Historical fiction by Altarriba & Keko," *European Comic Art* 13(2).

Mathieu, M. A. (2006) *Les Sous-sols du Révolu*. Paris: Futuropolis/Musée du Louvre Éditions.

Meurisse, C. (2014) *Moderne Olympia*. Paris: Futuropolis/Musée d'Orsay.

Picone, M. (2013) "Comic Art in Museums and Museums in Comic Art," *European Comic Art* 6(2), pp. 40–68.

## Music

Most connections between music and comics include the use of words such as pacing, RHYTHM, and tempo to refer to the TEMPORALITY of comics generally through the variation in and REPETITION of PAGE LAYOUTS and the size and shape of PANELS. Comics can also express musical qualities such as timbre or volume, thanks to their use of TYPOGRAPHY. However, many other approaches are possible, one being the REPRESENTATIONS of music and musicians in comics. This ranges from STORIES of music or musicians (e.g., Robert Crumb's blues, jazz, and country music stories) to more ambitious attempts to borrow, ADAPT, or imitate some of the FORMAL qualities of music in comics: THEMES and leitmotifs, such as in P. Craig Russel's *The Ring of the Nibelung* (2014), POLYPHONY, see Lewis Trondheim and Sergio García's *Les trois Chemins* (2000), or jazz improvisation (Powers and Grimm 2016). As with cinema, music in comics can be DIEGETIC, but also non-diegetic, serving as a soundtrack. Comics can also include musical notation, as in "This Vicious Cabaret," a section of Alan Moore and David Lloyd's *V for Vendetta* (1982–1989) analysed by Kieron Brown (2013: 3–5). Finally, comics can be performed with/as music, as in Cathy Berberian and Roberto Zamarin's *Stripsody* (1966), the famous Angoulême Festival's DRAWN concerts, or Art Spiegelman's show *Wordless!* (2014).

Enrique del Rey Cabero

### *References*

Brown, K. (2013) "Musical Sequences in Comics," *The Comics Grid: Journal of Comics Scholarship* 3(9), pp. 1–6.

Powers, Z. and Grimm, S. (2016) "Playing Together: Analyzing Jazz Improvisation to Improve the Multiframe," *The Comics Grid: Journal of Comics Scholarship* 6, n.p. Available at: https://www.comicsgrid.com/articles/10.16995/cg.76/ [Accessed 4 August 2020].

## Myth

Myths are generally understood to be traditional STORIES that are rooted in ancient or popular belief systems, and often serve as foundational tales. They tend to feature protagonists and HEROES that are ARCHETYPES. To Robert A. Segal, myths can refer to a range of subjects from the literal, often tales of the deities of a specific pantheon or belief system, to the symbolic "such as gods as symbols of natural phenomena, or of human traits" (1999: 2). In this, myths act as ALLEGORIES or FABLES of both human behaviours and natural phenomena. Northrop Frye suggests that myths are "the stories that tell a society what is important for it to know" (1982: 33) and observes that while a distinction is often made between myth and scripture, "there is no consistent structural difference between them" (1982: 33). Laurence Coupe points to the paradigmatic nature of myth, explaining that "[j]ust as one particular story may serve as the paradigm for one kind of myth, so one kind of myth can serve as the paradigm for mythology itself (…) Myth is paradigmatic, but there is no pure paradigm" (1997: 5). SUPERHEROES can often be read as modern updates of mythological figures (e.g., Marvel Comics' Thor and Hercules), and aspects of myth cycles have been used as background for origin stories (Wonder Woman's ties to the Amazons of Greek myth being perhaps the most notable example of this).

Houman Sadri

### *References*

Coupe, L. (1997) *Myth*. Abingdon: Routledge.

Frye, N. (1982) *The Great Code*. Boston: Houghton Mifflin Harcourt.

Segal, R. A. (1999) *Theorizing About Myth*. Amherst: University of Massachusetts Press.

## Narration

Narration is the means through which a STORY is recounted. Peter Hühn and Roy Sommer define it as "a communicative act in which a chain of happenings is meaningfully structured and transmitted in a particular MEDIUM and from a particular point of view" (2013). Different REGISTERS and MEDIA—including fiction, poetry, drama, FILM and television, and comics—have their own STYLISTIC CONVENTIONS for narration. In film and television, narration usually takes the form of a voice-over soundtrack. In comics, it generally appears as TEXT that is presented in a CAPTION BOX or other part of the page outside of a SPEECH BALLOON or THOUGHT BUBBLE. While NARRATIVES can be conveyed through various SENSES, narration only occurs through written, spoken, or sign LANGUAGE. The person(s) or entity(ies) who present narration is/are called (a) NARRATOR(S). Narration is presented from one or more of three POINTS OF VIEW: first-person (I/we), second-person (you), and third-person (he/she/they/it). A given instance of narration will have a limited or omniscient view of events that reflects the narrator's knowledge of the narrative. Narration can be situated in a narrative's timeline through the use of past, present, and/or future tense language (Uspensky 1973: 69–75).

Madeline B. Gangnes

### *References*

Hühn, P. and Sommer, R. (2013) "Narration in Poetry and Drama" in *The Living Handbook of Narratology*. Available at: http://www.lhn.uni-hamburg.de/node/40.html [Accessed 23 April 2020].

Uspensky, B. (1973) *A Poetics of Composition: The Structure of the Artistic Text and Typology of Compositional Form*. Berkeley: University of California Press.

## Narrative

Broadly speaking, a narrative is an account of events, facts, and other information, presented in a logical order and in a way that makes clear the connections between them. In terms of critically approaching STORY-based MEDIA, narrative refers to the part of the text that relays such an account, separate from dialogue, description, and other components of the text. Narratives can be fictional or factional (non-fiction), but due to shifting perceptions of what constitutes fiction, there is no official consensus on where the line between the two categories definitively lies (Schaeffer 2013). Narratives are most commonly told through WRITTEN or spoken LANGUAGE—often through the act of NARRATION by (a) NARRATOR(S)—but they can also be conveyed through IMAGES, audio, and/or tactile means (Kuhn and Schmidt 2014). In comics, narratives are usually conveyed through a combination of verbal/TEXTUAL and visual elements juxtaposed and arranged in deliberate SEQUENCE, though WORDLESS COMICS convey narratives through images alone. Barbara Postema posits that images convey the majority of a comic's narrative content and structure and credits "our culture's regard for the linguistic" for the fact that "the verbal register in comics is so often elevated to equal standing in comics" (2013: 80).

Madeline B. Gangnes

## *References*

Kuhn, M. and Schmidt, J. (2014) "Narration in Film" in *The Living Handbook of Narratology*. Available at: http://www.lhn.uni-hamburg.de/node/64.html [Accessed 23 April 2020].

Postema, B. (2013) *Narrative Structure in Comics: Making Sense of Fragments*. Rochester: Rochester Institute of Technology Press.

Schaeffer, J. (2013) "Fictional vs. Factual Narration" in *The Living Handbook of Narratology*. Available at: http://www.lhn.uni-hamburg.de/node/56.html [Accessed 23 April 2020].

## Narratology

Narratology was initially a branch of SEMIOTICS within the Russian FORMALIST and French STRUCTURALIST tradition. "Classical narratology" was mainly conceived as the study of NARRATIVE structures in WRITTEN, verbal texts. Various expansions have been offered by what has been called a "post-classical narratology," which differs widely in epistemological and methodological orientation (Nünning 2003). Cognitive narratology, for instance, focuses on the intellectual and emotional processing of narrative structures by actual or model READERS (Kukkonen

2013). For some time now, a TRANSMEDIAL narratology (Herman 2014, Ryan and Thon 2014, Thon 2016, Elleström 2019) has compared MEDIA-specific affordances to realise overarching narrative elements—such as STORYWORLDS, NARRATORS, or subjective REPRESENTATIONS—in novels, FILMS, drama, computer GAMES, or comics. As it is uncontested that most comics are narrative forms, there also have been approaches to comic-specific narratologies (Schüwer 2008, Hescher 2016, Mikkonen 2017) that not only apply existing concepts, but revise them through the study of this graphic, DRAWN FORM of media. This might even entail a challenge to the established assumption that single, static pictures cannot also be described in terms of their narrative potential (Grennan 2017).

Lukas R. A. Wilde

## *References*


Elleström, L. (2019) *Transmedial Narration: Narratives and Stories in Different Media*. London: Palgrave Macmillan.

Grennan, S. (2017) *A Theory of Narrative Drawing*. London: Palgrave Macmillan.

Herman, D. (2004) *Story Logic. Problems and Possibilities of Narrative*. Lincoln: University of Nebraska Press.

Kukkonen, K. (2013) *Contemporary Comics Storytelling*. Lincoln: University of Nebraska Press.

Hescher, A. (2016) *Reading Graphic Novels: Genre and Narration*. Berlin: De Gruyter.

Mikkonen, K. (2017) *The Narratology of Comic Art*. Abingdon: Routledge.

Nünning, A. (2003) "Narratology or Narratologies? Taking Stock of Recent Developments, Critique and Modest Proposals for Future Usage of the Term" in Kindt, T. and Müller, H.-H. (eds.) *What is Narratology? Questions and Answers Regarding the Status of a Theory*. Berlin: De Gruyter, pp. 239–275.

Schüwer, M. (2008) *Wie Comics erzählen. Grundriss einer intermedialen Erzähltheorie der grafischen Literatur.* Trier: Wissenschaftlicher Verlag Trier.

Thon, J.-N. (2016) *Transmedial Narratology and Contemporary Media Culture*. Lincoln: University of Nebraska Press.

Ryan, M.-L. and Thon, J.-N. (eds.) (2014) *Storyworlds Across Media: Toward a Media-Conscious Narratology*. Lincoln: University of Nebraska Press.

## Narrator

Although a highly contested concept, a narrator can be defined as a textual entity that is responsible for the selection, organisation, and presentation of STORYWORLD information and is clearly distinct from the AUTHOR. Every story has a narrator—a teller, presenter, or enunciator—that "speaks" either as a character that participates in or is knowledgeable of the storyworld events or as an external observer to and recorder of those storyworld events. In comics, the act of NARRATION occurs in both the verbal track—most often through verbal TEXT appearing in CAPTION BOXES, but also in the GUTTER space or on its own page—and the visual track "as a set of graphic markers evoking the presence of a drawing instance" (Surdiacourt 2012: 174). Comics scholars have proposed several terms to describe this "drawing instance," including "monstrateur" (monstrator) (Baetens 2001, Marion 1993: 193–194, Groensteen 2010, 2013: 96), non-narratorial representation (Thon 2013: 78), and graphic narrator (Mikkonen 2017: 131).

Nancy Pedri

### *References*


Baetens, J. (2001) "Revealing Traces: A New Theory of Graphic Enunciation" in Varnum, R. and Gibbons, C. T. (eds.) *The Language of Comics: Word and Image*. Jackson: University Press of Mississippi, pp. 145–155.

Groensteen, T. (2010) "The Monstrator, the Recitant and the Shadow of the Narrator," *European Comic Art* 3(1), pp. 1–21.

Groensteen, T. (2011) *Comics and Narration*. Translated from French by A. Miller, 2013. Jackson: University Press of Mississippi.

Marion, P. (1993) *Traces en cases: Travail graphique, figuration narrative et participation du lectuer*. Louvain-la-Neuve: Academia.

Mikkonen, K. (2017) *The Narratology of Comic Art*. Abingdon: Routledge.

Surdiacourt, S. (2012) "Can You Hear Me Drawing? 'Voice' and the Graphic Novel" in Baumbach, S., Michaelis, B., and Nünning, A. (eds.) *Telling Concepts, Metaphors, and Narratives: Literary and Cultural Studies in an Age of Interdisciplinary Research*. Trier: Wissenschaftlicher Verlag Trier, pp. 165–178.

Thon, J.-N. (2013) "Who's Telling the Tale? Authors and Narrators in Graphic Narrative" in Stein, D. and Thon, J.-N. (eds.) *From Comic Strips to Graphic Novels: Contributions to the Theory and History of Graphic Narrative*. Berlin: De Gruyter, pp. 67–99.

## Nationalism

Nationalism cannot be discussed without reference to the "nation," a "community of people that (1) share cultural values, norms, and background and (2) believe they, as a group, belong together" (Clott 2017: 1). Nationalism is a form of social and political IDENTIFICATION that positions the nation as a dominant motivation for political action and expression. Further, nations are "imagined communities" because, despite lacking direct connection between each member, individuals imagine themselves sharing norms and values and a sense of common belonging (Anderson 2006). CARTOONING has a long HISTORICAL association with nationalism, and comics have continued this association in a variety of ways (Kunzle 1973, 1990). Since at least the Second World War, for example, many SUPERHEROES have been closely aligned with nationalism (Dittmer 2013), but the range of comics engagement with nationalism range from celebratory to ambiguous to critical. Compare, for example, Marv Wolfman, Mario Ruiz, and William Rubin's *Homeland: The Illustrated History of the State of Israel* (2007) with Sarah Glidden's *How to Understand Israel in 60 Days or Less* (2016) and Harvey Pekar and J.T. Waldman's *Not the Israel My Parents Promised Me* (2012). Comics can serve nationalist social formation by marking who belongs in the nation and who does not (Precup 2015) and are sometimes even policed by the state to ensure that they do not work counter to the state's maintenance of national imaginaries (Rubenstein 1998).

Martin Lund

### *References*

Anderson, B. (1983) *Imagined Communities: Reflections on the Origin and Spread of Nationalism*. Reprint 2006. London: Verso.

Clott, A. (2017) "Nationalism" in Turner, B. S. (ed.) *The Wiley Blackwell Encyclopedia of Social Theory*. Hoboken: John Wiley & Sons. Available at: https://onlinelibrary.wiley.com/doi/abs/10.1002/9781118430873.est0711 [Accessed 1 August 2020].

Dittmer, J. (2013) *Captain America and the Nationalist Superhero*. Philadelphia: Temple University Press.

Kunzle, D. (1973) *History of the Comic Strip, Volume 1: The Early Comic Strip 1450–1825*. Berkeley: University of California Press.

Kunzle, D. (1990) *History of the Comic Strip, Volume 2: The Nineteenth Century*. Berkeley: University of California Press.

Precup, M. (2017), "The Image of the Foreigner in Historical Romanian Comics Under Ceaușescu's Dictatorship" in Ayaka, C. and Hague, I. (ed.) *Representing Multiculturalism in Comics and Graphic Novels.* Abingdon: Routledge, pp. 96–110.

Rubenstein, A. (1998) *Bad Language, Naked Ladies, & Other Threats to the Nation: A Political History of Comic Books in Mexico.* Durham: Duke University Press.

## New Materialism

New materialism refers to a strand of theory that emerged in the late 1990s in FEMINISM, POSTHUMANISM, ECOCRITICISM, and the natural sciences. It is in part a return to the importance of materiality as stressed by MATERIALISM. As noted by philosopher Rosi Braidotti, New Materialism refuses the focus on LANGUAGE and REPRESENTATION that is central to POSTRUCTURALISM by considering the material, or "real," world not as separate from language and meaning, but "stressing instead the concrete yet complex materiality of bodies immersed in social relations of power" (2012: 21). Feminist theorist Karen Barad affirms, "meaning is material. And matter isn't what exists separately from meaning" (2014: 175). In CULTURAL THEORY, New Materialism allows for the emergence of new approaches to studying texts, for example, when the meaning of a text does not merely reside in the READER's perception or in the text alone. Instead, meaning arises from the meeting, encounter, or "intra-action" (Barad 2014) between human and non-human agents. Subsequently, as Stacy Alaimo states, "the producers of various works of literature, art, and activism may themselves grapple with ways to render murky material forces palpable or recognizably 'real'" (2010: 9).

Freija Camps

### *References*

Alaimo, S. (2010) *Bodily Natures: Science, Environment, and the Material Self.* Bloomington: Indiana University Press.

Barad, K. (2014) "Diffracting Diffraction: Cutting Together-Apart," *Parallax* 20(3), pp. 168–187.

Braidotti, R. (2012) "Interview with Rosi Braidotti" in Dolphijn R. and van der Tuin I. (eds.) *New Materialism: Interviews & Cartographies.* Ann Arbor, MI: Open Humanities Press, pp. 19–37.

## Newave

Newave is a term that was used in the 1980s to refer to a wide range of non-mainstream comics. It was a contraction of New Wave, a term that had previously been applied to a number of STYLES in other MEDIA. The first movement to take this label was the French New Wave FILMS of the 1950s and 1960s, which established the term as a way of describing cultural movements that rejected mainstream styles (Biskind 1998: 26–27, Singsen 2017: 168). The term was then applied to countercultural American films of the late 1960s and early 1970s and American post-PUNK MUSIC of the late 1970s and 1980s. In the 1980s the abbreviated version of the term was used to describe MINICOMICS, ALTERNATIVE COMICS, and other post-UNDERGROUND comics (Kennedy 1982, Dowers 2010).

Doug Singsen

### *References*

Biskind, P. (1998) *Easy Riders, Raging Bulls: How the Sex-Drugs-and-Rock 'n' Roll Generation Saved Hollywood.* New York: Simon and Schuster.

Dowers, M. (ed.) (2010) *Newave! The Underground Mini Comix of the 1980s.* Seattle: Fantagraphics.

Kennedy, J. (1982) "Introduction" in Kennedy, J. (ed.) *The Official Underground and Newave Comix Price Guide.* Cambridge: Boatner Norton, pp. 11–15.

Singsen, D. (2017) "Critical Perspectives on Mainstream, Groundlevel, and Alternative Comics in *The Comics Journal*, 1977 to 1996," *Journal of Graphic Novels and Comics* 8(2), pp. 156–172.

## Newspaper Strips

Originating during the 1890s' "newspaper wars" between Pulitzer and Hearst in New York, newspaper strips are assumed to be an American invention. Encompassing FORMATS as diverse as daily and Sunday multipanel comics, single-panel GAGS, and political CARTOONS, all COMIC STRIPS are intimately tied to the business, circulation, and

PRODUCTION of newspapers, as Coulton Waugh noted in 1947. Brian Walker describes their rapid NATIONAL expansion: within two decades strips were included in 75 per cent of American Sunday newspapers (2004: 22). Donald Phelps notes the parallels between strips and their publication source: "[C]omic strips are among the most parasitic of forms and of subjects; feeding themselves continually, voraciously, from contemporary social, artistic, political phenomena, usually from aspects and highlights" (Phelps 2001: viii). Strip SYNDICATES were established to aid this expansion, mandating professional control into the twenty-first century, although their dominance has lessened in tandem with PRINT JOURNALISM. Related practices include strips PUBLISHED in "alternative" weekly newspapers and WEBCOMICS, which often emulate newspaper strip structures and release schedules.

Josh R. Rose

## *References*

Phelps, D. (2001) *Reading the Funnies: Essays on Comic Strips.* Seattle: Fantagraphics.

Walker, B. (2004) *The Comics: Before 1945.* New York: Harry N. Abrams.

Waugh, C. (1947) *The Comics.* London: Macmillan.

## Ninth Art

Comics are frequently referred to as the ninth art in France and Belgium, which indicates the high level of cultural esteem accorded comics in those countries (Duncan and Smith 2009: 297). The term was coined by the French critic Claude Beylie in 1964, as part of his argument that comics should be considered a legitimate ART FORM and not mere POP CULTURE ephemera. The practice of enumerating the arts dates back to ancient Greece, where the Muses served as patron deities of various art forms. Beylie's argument built on the work of Ricciotto Canudo, a seminal FILM theorist who published *The Birth of the Sixth Art* in 1911 and *Reflections on the Seventh Art* in 1923 to argue for the legitimacy of film as an artistic MEDIUM. The identification of comics as the ninth art became commonplace, thanks to a column by Maurice De Bevere, known as Morris, which ran in the *Journal de Spirou* from 1964 to 1967, and a 1971 book by Francis Lacassin, both of which used the term in their titles. Today, the nine arts are usually listed as ARCHITECTURE, sculpture, painting, MUSIC, dance, poetry, film, television, and comics, but in both ancient and modern times the number and exact identity of the arts fluctuates from AUTHOR to author.

Doug Singsen

## *References*

Beylie, C. (1964) "La bande dessinée, est-elle un art?" *Lettres et Médecins*, January 1964, pp. 9–14.

Canudo, R. (1911) "The Birth of the Sixth Art" in Simpson, P., Utterson, A., and Shepherdson, K. (eds.) *Film Theory: Critical Concepts in Media and Cultural Studies.* Translated from Italian by B. Gibson, D. Ranvaus, S. Sokota, and D. Young, 2004. Abingdon: Routledge, pp. 25–33.

Duncan, R. and Smith, M. (2009) *The Power of Comics: History, Form and Culture.* New York: Continuum.

Grove, L. (2010) *Comics in French: The European Bande Dessinée in Context.* New York: Berghahn Books.

Lacassin, F. (1982) *Pour un Neuvième Art: La Bande Dessinée.* Paris: Slatkine.

Morris (1964–1967) "Neuvième Art, Musée de la Bande Dessinée." *Journal de Spirou*, December 1964–July 1967.

## Nostalgia

Nostalgia as a concept was first used in 1688 by Johannes Hofer, a Swiss physician, to describe the longing for a return to one's homeland (Su 2005: 180, Boym 2002: 3). Over the course of the twentieth century, nostalgia became a commonly used concept that denotes a sense of longing for a past. Nostalgia is a common THEME in comics, as well as of contemporary culture as a whole (Baetens and Frey 2015: 217, Cremins 2018: 3). Many comics CREATORS, such as Chris Ware and Seth, can be called nostalgic in their choice of thematics and/or treatment of the past

(Busi Rizzi 2018: 16). Besides being nostalgic or thematising nostalgia as their subject matter, comics themselves, seeing as how the MEDIUM is often associated with childhood and adolescence, are frequently the object of nostalgia (see Cremins 2018). READERS and COLLECTORS are nostalgic for the SERIES they associate with their past. Comics FANDOM thus has nostalgic tendencies, which PUBLISHERS are more than happy to exploit. Seeing as how the connotations of nostalgia are almost completely negative, critics have also attempted to show how certain comics creators have attempted to interrogate the nostalgia with which contemporary (comics) culture is so entwined (Baetens and Frey 2015, Busi Rizzi 2018).

Jos van Waterschoot

## *References*

Baetens, J. and Frey, H. (2015) "Nostalgia and the Return of History" in Baetens J. and Frey, H. *The Graphic Novel: An Introduction*. New York: Cambridge University Press, pp. 217–245.

Boym, S. (2002) *The Future of Nostalgia*. New York: Basic Books.

Busi Rizzi, G. (2018) "Portrait of the Artist as a Nostalgic: Seth's *It's a Good Life if You Don't Weaken*" in Ahmed, M. and Crucifix, B. (eds.) *Comics Memory: Archives and Styles*. London: Palgrave Macmillan, pp. 15–36.

Cremins, B. (2018) *Captain Marvel and the Art of Nostalgia*. Jackson: University Press of Mississippi.

Su, J. J. (2005) *Ethics and Nostalgia in the Contemporary Novel*. Cambridge: Cambridge University Press.

## Novelisation

In the strictest sense, novelisation designates both a LITERARY GENRE (Baetens 2018) and its most common occurrence (Mahlknecht 2012): a novel ADAPTED from the SCRIPT of a movie blockbuster and sold, along with other tie-in products, during the FILM'S theatrical distribution period. In the broadest sense, novelisation is a literary process that consists of adapting into a novel a work that has appeared in a non-literary MEDIUM (film, video GAME, comics, etc.). Since *Voyages et aventures du Docteur Festus*, self-novelised by Rodolphe Töpffer in 1840 (Kunzle 2007: 74–82), Big Little Books and American SUPERHERO universes have been the main providers of novels based on comics (Lowery 2007, Weiner 2008: 257–281), some of which fall into adaptation and others into TRANSMEDIA STORYTELLING. By extension, the term novelisation has sometimes been used in COMICS STUDIES to refer to the literarisation at work in the GRAPHIC NOVEL (Williams 2020: 6–8).

Benoît Glaude

## *References*

Baetens, J. (2008) *Novelization: From Film to Novel.* Translated from French by M. Feeney, 2018. Columbus: The Ohio State University Press.

Kunzle, D. (2007) *Father of the Comic Strip: Rodolphe Töpffer.* Jackson: University Press of Mississippi.

Lowery, L. F. (2007) *The Golden Age of Big Little Books.* Danville: Educational Research and Applications, LLC.

Mahlknecht, J. (2012) "The Hollywood Novelization: Film as Literature or Literature as Film Promotion?" *Poetics Today* 33(2), pp. 137–168.

Weiner, R. G. (2008) *Marvel Graphic Novels and Related Publications: An Annotated Guide to Comics, Prose Novels, Children's Books, Articles, Criticism and Reference Works, 1965–2005.* Jefferson: McFarland.

Williams, P. (2020) *Dreaming the Graphic Novel: The Novelization of Comics.* New Brunswick: Rutgers University Press.

## Onomatopoeia

Onomatopoeia (from Greek, meaning "creation of words") are SOUND words that imitate the sound of objects (a clock's "tick tock"), animals (a pig's "oink"), and even humans' emotional and bodily expressions (sneezing's "achoo"). It is IRONIC that comics, a SILENT MEDIUM, is often identified with onomatopoeias, even if it is far from being used systematically (Hague 2014). The transcription of sound in pictures goes at least as far back as the ninth century (Deyzieux 2019). Onomatopoeias have been used creatively, including in ways that do not imitate the sound but instead CONVENTIONALLY explain the action, which reinforces the AESTHETIC effect and emotion (HUMOROUSLY or dramatically). Contrary to other types of TEXT that are contained (in SPEECH BALLOONS and CAPTION BOXES), they are often blended in the SPACE that is usually reserved for IMAGES. Visual aspects like size, shape, font, and COLOUR greatly contribute to indicate the quality of the sound, such as the intensity, pitch, and crescendo (see e.g. Kurtzman and Wood 1955). American onomatopoeias had a strong influence on several comic traditions, such as the French one. Because the Japanese language is particularly rich in onomatopoeias, MANGA abounds in them and they cover many FRAMES and PAGES. Their overwhelming presence and the fact that they are arbitrary sounds make them difficult to TRANSLATE from one LANGUAGE to another (e.g. "kaboom" in English, "boum" in French, and "dokkan" in Japanese for an explosion) (Reyns-Chikuma and Tarif 2016).

Chris Reyns-Chikuma

### *References*


Deyzieux, A. (2019) "Onomatopée et Son" in Groensteen, T. (ed.) *Dictionnaire esthétique et thématique de la bande dessinée, Neuvième art 2.0.* Available at: http://neuviemeart.citebd.org/spip.php?article1235 [Accessed 14 May 2020].

Hague, I. (2014) *Comics and the Senses: A Multisensory Approach to Comics and Graphic Novels.* Abingdon: Routledge.

Kurtzman, H. and Wallace, W. (1955) "Sounds effects!" *Mad* #20. New York: EC Comics. Available at: https://from-dusk-till-drawn.com/2016/05/03/sound-effects-by-harvey-kurtzman-wlly-wood-usa-1955/ [Accessed 14 May 2020].

Reyns-Chikuma, C. and Tarif, J. (eds.) (2016) "Translation and Comics," *TranscUlturAl* 8(2).

## Orientalism

According to Edward W. Said, Orientalism is "a style of thought based upon [a] distinction made between 'the Orient' and (most of the time) 'the Occident'" (2003: 2). European colonial ventures in Asia have resulted in a conceptual divide between the East and the West that is maintained through Western REPRESENTATIONS of the Eastern Other. "Everyone who writes about the Orient," argues Said, "must locate himself vis-à-vis the Orient" (ibid. 20), a practice that has both created and continues to perpetuate such RACIAL STEREOTYPES as "Arabic sensuality, sloth, fatalism, cruelty, degradation and splendor" (ibid. 345). Since the bulk of these representations issue from the West, which often positions itself in opposition to the East, Orientalism may also be discussed "as a Western style for dominating, restructuring, and having authority over the Orient" (ibid. 3). Contemporary examples of the pervasiveness of Orientalism in the comics field are the continued Othering of Arab characters in seemingly inclusive American SUPERHERO comics (Strömberg 2011) and the emergent complexities of appropriating, TRANSLATING, and categorising traditionally Japanese MANGA in an American cultural context (Brienza 2009).

Camilla Prytz

## *References*

Brienza, C. E. (2009) "Books, Not Comics: Publishing Fields, Globalization, and Japanese Manga in the United States," *Publishing Research Quarterly* 2, pp. 101–117.

Said, E. W. (1978) *Orientalism*. Reprint 2003. London: Penguin.

Strömberg, F. (2011) "'Yo, rag-head!': Arab and Muslim Superheroes in American Comic Books after 9/11," *Amerikastudien / American Studies* 56(4), pp. 573–601.

## Page

Although COMICS are to a certain extent MEDIUM-insensitive (a NEWSPAPER STRIP can be reproduced as a poster, shown on a banner, copied in a digital format, etc.), most comics are works in print and as such they are in most cases inseparable from the notion of page, which as a spatial unity involves three major and strongly interconnected dimensions. First, page refers to the surface that hosts the DRAWINGS, not always in an exclusive way. A newspaper comic, for instance—typically a "strip," not a "book"—had to compete with other comics and non-comics material (Smolderen 2013). Second, page can also refer to a certain size and format: horizontal or vertical, on the one hand, smaller or larger, on the other hand. Third, it also has to do with the number of pages a work can or must occupy. Generally speaking, the rules that govern the use and choice of these page features vary according to the type of comic. The more industrialised a comic is, the more all choices will pre-exist the actual making of the comic. When there is more freedom for the individual CREATOR, one immediately notices more variety (Menu 2010). However, even strongly predetermined formats are open to creative uses (and vice versa).

Jan Baetens

### *References*

Menu, J.-C (2010) *La bande dessinée et son double.* Paris: L'Association.

Smolderen, T. (2013) *The Origin of Comics.* Jackson: The University of Mississippi Press.

## Page Layout

A comics page juxtaposes multiple IMAGES, which are usually FRAMED. It is "a site of contiguity even more than a site of continuity" (Peeters 1990: 33). To describe this compartmentalised SPACE, Henri Van Lier proposed the concept of "multiframe" ("*multicadre*," 1988: 5). The page layout is both the operation that determines the place, the shape, and the size of each of the images, and the result of that operation. It ensures the compatibility of the frames and gives the page its general organisation. The Belgian comics ARTIST André Franquin used the term "waffle iron" ("*gaufrier*") to denote a comics page based on a regular pattern in which all frames are identical. This model makes every deviation conspicuous: a non-standard frame becomes *ipso facto* a special effect. Not all pages adhere to a strict orthogonal configuration. Some are decorative, ostentatious, or simply eccentric. However, the most frequent model is the one that Benoît Peeters calls *rhetorical*. It takes advantage of the possibility, for the artist, of constantly redefining the size of the "screen" and adapting it to the content: a narrow frame for a CLOSE-UP shot or a standing character, and a large one for a vast landscape or a crowd scene.

Thierry Groensteen

## *References*

Peeters, B. (1990) "Un inventeur du dimanche" in Groensteen, T. (ed.) *Little Nemo au pays de Winsor McCay*. Toulouse: Milan, pp. 28–35.

van Lier, H. (1988), "La bande dessinée, une cosmogonie dure" in Groensteen, T. (ed.) *Bande dessinée, récit et modernité*. Paris: Futuropolis, pp. 5–24.

## Panel

Comics PAGES are usually made up of panels, which are individual FRAMES following one another, with the exceptions of single panel pages and full-page drawings. Single panel comics pages can be distinguished from full-page drawings because they mostly utilise clearly distinctive panel borders, even if the page only consists of one panel. However, some scholars consider full-page drawings to function as whole-page panels or monoframes (Groensteen 2011). Panels are traditionally separated by an empty GUTTER space and consist of a single moment in TIME, with the consecutive panel indicating another moment in time, so constructing a NARRATIVE. Barbara Postema (2013), following Thierry Groensteen (2011), considers meaning in comics to be constructed through the negotiation of elements out of which a specific comics consists. From this point of view, the size and number of panels on the page, their appearance, and the size of the gutters that separate them have a meaning-making function within the MEDIUM of comics. Conversely, Scott McCloud (1994) considers the gutter to be the primary force that constructs meaning in comics. While panels are most often used to construct a linear narrative, many comics ARTISTS experiment with panel and page layout in order to create non-linear narratives.

Esther De Dauw

## *References*

Eisner, W. (1985) *Comics and Sequential Art: Principles and Practices from the Legendary Cartoonist.* Reprint 2008. New York: W. W. Norton & Company.

Groensteen, T. (2011) *Comics and Narration.* Translated from French by A. Miller, 2013. Jackson: University Press of Mississippi.

McCloud, S. (1993) *Understanding Comics: The Invisible Art.* New York: Harper Perennial.

Postema, B. (2013) *Narrative Structure in Comics: Making Sense of Fragments.* Rochester: Rochester Institute of Technology Press.

## PARATEXT

Paratext is defined by Gérard Genette as the threshold, or the "undefined zone," between text and off-text (1997: 2). Jan Baetens and Pascal Lefèvre favour the term perigraphy, which they describe as "all those elements of the book that surround the actual work without being part of it" (2014: 191). Paratext can be subdivided in peritext, which includes elements that are located in the vicinity of the text, and epitext, which is located outside of the text. Paratextual elements include, but are not limited to, the title, name, and biography of the AUTHOR; epigraphs; blurbs; dedications; pre- and postfaces; LETTERS PAGES; and interviews. Paratext can, however, also encompass many more elements, like FANZINES, trailers, posters, and other promotional texts. Paratext plays an important role in MARKETING the text and ensuring it is READ (and read in the right way). Paratext is characterised by its heterogeneity and therefore encompasses a range of DISCOURSES and practices that are subject to change over time. In response to Genette, issues around SERIALITY, visual paratext, authorship, PRODUCTION, and the influence of GENRE are often a focus of comics and MEDIA scholarship (Brienza 2009, Stein 2013, Brookey and Gray 2017, in 't Veld 2019).

Laurike in 't Veld

## *References*

Baetens, J. and Lefèvre, P. (1993) "The Work and its Surround" in Miller, A. and Beaty, B. (eds.) *The French Comics Theory Reader.* Translated from French by A. Miller and B. Beaty, 2014. Leuven: Leuven University Press, pp. 191–202.

Brienza, C. E. (2009) "Paratexts in Translation: Reinterpreting 'Manga' for the United States," *International Journal of the Book* 6(2), pp. 13–20.

Brookey, R. and Gray, J. (2017) "'Not Merely Para': Continuing Steps in Paratextual Research," *Critical Studies in Media Communication* 34(2), pp. 101–110.

in 't Veld, L. (2019) *The Representation of Genocide in Graphic Novels: Considering the Role of Kitsch.* London: Palgrave Macmillan.

Stein, D. (2013) "Superhero Comics and the Authorizing Functions of the Comic Book Paratext" in Stein, D. and Thon, J.-N. (eds.) *From Comic Strips to Graphic Novels: Contributions to the Theory and History of Graphic Narrative.* Berlin: De Gruyter, pp. 155–189.

## Parody

Parody (closely related to burlesque and travesty*)* is ART that imitates in STYLE or content a different artistic instance, usually well known, for purposes ranging from open hostility to either original and target, or both, down to benign/amused respect for the original and/or the target. In art William Hogarth was the first NARRATIVE ARTIST to base his SATIRE on parody—of the action in the contemporary stage play and the taste for old master styles in painting. Scenes from William Hogarth's *Marriage A-la-mode* (1745) were parodied in *Punch* in 1855, as political critiques (Leech 1845, 1852). Swiss Rodolphe Töpffer's picture STORIES are absurdist versions of the current fictional ROMANCE (Kunzle 2007). The French cartoonist Cham (Charles Amédée de Noé) made a staple of parodic or burlesque travel tales (Kunzle 2019). In England Richard Doyle was the first to parody (in 1848) a famous work of art, *The Bayeux Tapestry* (Doyle 1848). Gustave Doré's monumental *Histoire de la Sainte Russie* (1854) is parodic both in its Rabelaisian LANGUAGE and in its ILLUSTRATION of bloody Russian HISTORY. The first parody of a major contemporary novel was Cham's of Victor Hugo's *Les Misérables,* in 241 DRAWINGS (1862–1863) (Kunzle 2019: 18).

David Kunzle

## *References*

Doyle, R. (1848) "The Bayeux Tapestry," *Punch* #14, pp. 33–38.
Kunzle, D. (2007) *Rodolphe Töpffer: The Complete Comic Strips.* Jackson: University Press of Mississippi.
Kunzle, D. (2019) *Cham.* Jackson: University Press of Mississippi.
Leech, D. (1845) "Untitled," *Punch* #15, p. 181.
Leech, D. (1852) "Untitled," *Punch* #22, p. 37.

## Pastiche

Pastiche is an acknowledged and INTERTEXTUAL relation between two texts (or between a text and a series of pre-existing texts), in which salient FORMAL features of a hypotext are replicated, in an imitative relationship: "In pastiche and cliché, difference can be said to be reduced to similarity" (Hutcheon 1985: 38). Pastiche exists in tension with PARODY, on one hand, and with plagiarism, on the other, and is not always readily distinguishable from either. While parody "proceed[s] through a transformation of the text, and [pastiche] through an imitation of style" (Genette 1997: 25), the fact that meaning-making processes are shaped by STYLE—and indeed by styles for multimodal texts such as comics—creates an abundance of ambiguous cases, especially when the pastiche or parody does not refer to a single text but to an entire GENRE. Similarly, the distinction between pastiche and plagiarism rests on a matter of auctorial intent and potentially judicial determination, which cannot be adjudicated at the text level and requires contextual analysis. In contemporary comics, pastiche (and associated practices, such as SWIPING) has emerged as a key way to critically engage with the HISTORY of the MEDIUM and with shared cultural MEMORIES (Pizzino 2016).

Nicolas Labarre

## *References*

Groensteen, T. (2010) *Parodies: La bande dessinée au second degré.* Paris: Skira/Flammarion.
Hutcheon, L. (1985) *A Theory of Parody. The Teachings of Twentieth-Century Art Forms.* London: Methuen.
Pizzino, C. (2016) *Arresting Development: Comics at the Boundaries of Literature.* Austin: University of Texas Press.

## Pathographics

Pathography, first coined by Anne Hunsaker Hawkins in 1998, has been defined as "a narrative of illness" by Susan M. Squier (2015). The history of this GENRE, embedded in LITERATURE and the medical humanities, is laid out further by Squier, with scholarship from physician Rita Charon and MEDIA studies scholar Kirsten Ostherr. These NARRATIVES are written by patients, their caregivers, and medical personnel, and provide a source of first-hand knowledge of the experience of living with, beside, or treating ILLNESS and impairments. Some provide a cathartic purpose for the experience, others a DOCUMENTING and/or making visible an encounter with illness or impairment, which often includes subsequent treatment. GRAPHIC MEDICINE, coined by British physician and comics ARTIST Ian Williams, is the sub-genre graphic side of pathographics, which uses the comics MEDIUM as the STORYTELLING vehicle. Prior to the coining of these terms, sociologist Arthur W. Frank (1995) wrote the groundbreaking book, *The Wounded Storyteller*, which outlined different approaches to telling illness narratives. Audre Lorde's work is often referenced, in particular her refusal to be silenced or make others comfortable with her illness. Frank foregrounds the power of illness testimony by the patient or the caregivers and he also includes the READER because once these stories are known, there is no unknowing.

JoAnn Purcell

### *References*

Charon, R. (2006) *Narrative Medicine*. Oxford: Oxford University Press.

Frank, A. W. (1995) *The Wounded Storyteller: Body, Illness, and Ethics*. Chicago: The University of Chicago Press.

Hawkins, A. H. (1999) "Pathography: patient narratives of illness," *The Western Journal of Medicine* 171(2), pp. 127–129.

Lorde, A. (1980) *The Cancer Journals*. San Francisco: spinsters/*aunt lute*.

Ostherr, K. (2013) *Medical Visions: Producing the Patient Through Film, Television, and Imaging Technologies*. Oxford: Oxford University Press.

Squier, S. (2015) "The Uses of Graphic Medicine for Engaged Scholarship" in Czerwiec, M. K., Williams, I., Squier, S., Green, M., Myers, K., and Smith, S. (eds.) *Graphic Medicine Manifesto*. University Park: The Pennsylvania State University Press, pp. 41–66.

## Pedagogy

Pedagogy refers to the method and practice of teaching, as either an academic subject or a theoretical concept. In COMICS STUDIES, pedagogy can refer to the use of EDUCATIONAL comics to explain or teach various other subjects, or to the use of comics in the classroom to teach secondary skills. According to David D. Seelow, comics can help with "sparking student creativity, [and] building students' critical thinking and multimodal literacy skills" (2019: 10). This is because, Dale Jacobs argues, "reading comics involves a complex, multimodal literacy" (2013: 3) that asks READERS to interpret TEXT and IMAGE simultaneously while also considering such other elements of the comic as the DESIGN and PAGE LAYOUT. In addition, Nick Sousanis suggests that the combination of text and image involved in both READING and DRAWING comics may inspire creativity, and Susan E. Kirtley, Antero Garcia, and Peter E. Carlson argue that "teaching through producing comics introduces the FORM and mechanics of the medium in order to offer a communicative outlet for students alternative to text structures more traditionally used in classroom settings" (2020: 12). Consequently, many approaches to comics pedagogy involve an element of practical comics-making as a form of hands-on learning experience for students.

Frederik Byrn Køhlert

### *References*

Jacobs, D. (2013) *Graphic Encounters: Comics and the Sponsorship of Multimodal Literacy.* London: Bloomsbury Academic.

Kirtley, S. E., Garcia, A., and Carlson, P. E. (2020) "Introduction: A Once and Future Pedagogy" in Kirtley, S. E., Garcia, A., and Carlson, P. E. (eds.) *With Great Power Comes Great Pedagogy: Teaching, Learning, and Comics.* Jackson: University of Mississippi Press, pp. 3–20.

Seelow, D. D. (2019) "Introduction: Enjoyment and Learning" in Seelow, D. D. (ed.) *Lessons Drawn: Essays on the Pedagogy of Comics and Graphic Novels.* Jefferson: McFarland, pp. 5–11.

Sousanis, N. (2015) *Unflattening.* Cambridge: Harvard University Press.

## Penciller

The penciller is in charge of several dimensions of the graphic and NARRATIVE CREATION of comics. S/he chiefly PRODUCES the pencil DRAWINGS—in a more or less finished manner ("loose" or "tight" pencils)—to be INKED, LETTERED, and/or COLOURED, but s/he may also contribute to the preliminary work (sketches, thumbnails, rough) and to the narrative construction of the STORY (breakdown of the story, PAGE LAYOUTS). Through his/her "GRAPHIATION" (Marion 1993), the idiosyncratic nature of the LINE (Gardner 2011), s/he is a central agent of NARRATION. The term penciller locates the creator in a specific context of production based on division of LABOUR in an assembly-line fashion, with writers, pencillers, inkers, letterers, and COLOURISTS working under editorial supervision. The division of tasks between these producers is fluid and varies according to the context and the working procedures (Brienza and Johnston 2016). This division has STYLISTIC and narrative implications since the "graphiation" of the penciller is CONSTRAINED by cooperation and by possible editorial directives (such as following a house style) and necessarily becomes POLYPHONIC (Baetens 1996). The division also has symbolic and material consequences: authorship attribution (Ahmed 2017), economic retribution (Gordon 2013), and prestige distribution (Beaty and Woo 2016) may be altered by the COLLABORATIVE nature of the work, which thus affects the recognition of the penciller (as of other contributors).

Jean-Matthieu Méon

### *References*

Ahmed, M. (2017) "Comics and authorship: An introduction," *Authorship* 6(2), n.p. Available at: https://www.authorship.ugent.be/article/view/7702 [Accessed 3 August 2020].

Baetens, J. (1996) "Sur la graphiation. Une lecture de *Traces en cases*," *Recherches en communication* 5, pp. 223–235.

Beaty, B. and Woo, B. (2016) *The Greatest Comic Book of All Time: Symbolic Capital and the Field of American Comic Books*. London: Palgrave Macmillan.

Brienza, C. and Johnston, P. (eds.) (2016) *Cultures of Comics Work*. London: Palgrave Macmillan.

Gardner, J. (2011) "Storylines," *SubStance* 40(1), pp. 53–69.

Gordon, I. (2013) "Comics, Creators and Copyright: On the Ownership of Serial Narratives by Multiple Authors" in Johnson, D. and Gray, J. (eds.) *A Companion to Media Authorship*. Hoboken: Wiley-Blackwell, pp. 221–236.

Marion, P. (1993) *Traces en cases: Travail graphique, figuration narrative et participation du lecteur. Essai sur la bande dessinée*. Louvain-la-Neuve: Académia.

## Periphery

The term periphery can acquire different meanings in relation to comics. In its geographical sense, it concerns the distribution of comics PRODUCTION and its cultural implications: peripheral comics are those beyond the main MARKETS (Anglo-American, Franco-Belgian, and Japanese). Since most READERS are unaccustomed to other LANGUAGES, this calls into question matters of CANON construction, cultural ADAPTATION, and TRANSLATION policies. Furthermore, a periphery logically entails a centre that it opposes: an implied hierarchy that should always be problematised (e.g. in a TRANSNATIONAL perspective, Stein et al. 2013). If we transpose this spatial perspective to the DIEGESIS, REPRESENTING the periphery usually aims at deconstructing the above-mentioned centre/fringes dichotomy, aiming to give voice to marginalised SUBJECTS, or it may involve setting the events in the suburbs (a TROPE especially prominent in North American independent works). If we focus instead on the MATERIAL aspect, we may consider comics periphery to be its PARATEXT—namely, everything that surrounds the NARRATIVE, literally or METAPHORICALLY. Finally, if we accept a working definition of comics as a MULTIMODAL combination of TEXT and IMAGES, usually with narrative purposes, we can regard as peripheral any instance deviating from this core: ABSTRACT COMICS, IMAGELESS COMICS, SILENT COMICS, DIGITAL COMICS, and so on.

Giorgio Busi Rizzi

## *References*

Apter, E. (2006) *The Translation Zone: A New Comparative Literature*. Princeton: Princeton University Press.

Brienza, C. (2016) *Manga in America: Transnational Book Publishing and the Domestication of Japanese Comics*. London: Bloomsbury Academic.

Genette, G. (1987) *Paratexts: Thresholds of Interpretation*. Translated from French by J. Lewin, 1997. Cambridge: Cambridge University Press.

Leerssen, J. (2007) "Centre/periphery" in Beller, M. and Leerssen, J. T. (eds.) *Imagology: The cultural construction and literary representation of national characters. A critical survey*. Amsterdam: Rodopi, pp. 278–281.

Malone, P. M. (2020) "A Periphery surrounded by centres: The German-Language comics market, transnational relationships, and graphic novels," *Journal of Graphic Novels and Comics* 11(1), pp. 10–30.

Stein, D., Denson, S., and Meyer, C. (eds.) (2013) *Transnational Perspectives on Graphic Narratives: Comics at the Crossroads*. London: Bloomsbury Academic.

Zanettin, F. (2008) *Comics in Translation*. Abingdon: Routledge.

## Perspective

The term perspective is generally employed as a broad synonym of POINT OF VIEW or way of regarding something, and is mostly applied to three distinct aspects of composition and NARRATION: REPRESENTATIONAL skills (as in the painterly tradition, the techniques "responsible for creating an illusion of space" [Schneider 2012: 67]), the subjective stance of an AUTHOR or a character on a given issue, or NARRATIVE FOCALISATION. All three meanings of perspective are often employed in the same text, although the latter is likely the most adopted in COMICS STUDIES. Scholarly writing on NARRATOLOGICAL perspective in comics tends to identify and analyse the TEXTUAL and visual elements that allow the READER to understand through whose eyes he or she is apprehending the DIEGESIS, or to explain how perspective can be blurred by opaque STORYTELLING. Nicholas Hetrick exemplifies this in his analysis of Wilfred Santiago's *In My Darkest Hour* (2004): "Such complicated patterns of representation might suggest that we cannot tell whose perspective and voice control this novel" (2010: 196), as Henry Jenkins does when writing on Art Spiegelman's *In the Shadow of No Towers* (2004): "This instability of perspective is suggested by his shifting pronouns" (2013: 313).

David Pinho Barros

## *References*

Hetrick, N. (2010) "Chronology, Country, and Consciousness in Wilfred Santiago's *In My Darkest Hour*" in Aldama, F. L. (ed.) *Multicultural Comics: From Zap to Blue Beetle*. Austin: University of Texas Press, pp. 189–201.

Jenkins, H. (2013) "Archival, Ephemeral, and Residual: The Functions of Early Comics in Art Spiegelman's *In the Shadow of No Towers*" in Stein, D. and Thon, J.-N. (eds.) *From Comic Strips to Graphic Novels: Contributions to the Theory and History of Graphic Narrative*. Berlin: De Gruyter, pp. 301–322.

Schneider, G. (2012) "Lost Gazes, Detached Minds: Strategies of Disengagement in the Work of Adrian Tomine," *Scandinavian Journal of Comic Art* 1(2), pp. 58–81.

## PHENOTEXT

Phenotext belongs with GENOTEXT in Julia Kristeva's semanalysis system (1980, 1986). While genotext is slippery, phenotext is straightforward—LANGUAGE as it functions as a regular code of communication: "We shall use the term *phenotext* to denote language that serves to communicate, which linguistics describes in terms of 'competence' and 'performance'" (Kristeva 1986: 121). The PSYCHOANALYTIC dimension of Kristeva's system identifies the phenotext with consciousness and ego—it is "constantly split up and divided"—and the genotext with the drives, the unconscious, and the pre-symbolic, where the SUBJECT is unaware of their split (1986: 121). In comics, phenotext is problematic, given its LINGUISTIC nature. It can function only if comics is a linguistic phenomenon or at least analogous to language. If so, the phenotext of comics is DRAWING as it signifies, when a picture of a house signifies a house, when MOVEMENT LINES signify movement (Juricevic and Horvath

2016), and when SPEECH BALLOONS and THOUGHT BUBBLES indicate that characters are speaking or thinking (McCloud 2008). The phenotext in comics is everything that works to produce a particular understanding between the enunciating subject and the addressee, while the genotext is everything that escapes functionality and signification but that nevertheless makes it possible.

Peter Wilkins

## *References*

Juricevic, I. and Horvath, A. J. (2016) "Analysis of Motions in Comic Book Cover Art: Using Pictorial Metaphors," *The Comics Grid: Journal of Comics Scholarship* 6, p. 6. Available at: https://www.comicsgrid.com/articles/10.16995/cg.71/ [Accessed 6 July 2020].

Kristeva, J. (1969) *Desire in Language: A Semiotic Approach to Literature and Art*. Translated from French by T. Gora and A. Jardine, 1980. Roudiez, L. (ed.) New York: Columbia University Press.

Kristeva, J. (1973) "The System and the Speaking Subject" in Moi, T. (ed.) *The Kristeva Reader*. Translated from French by T. Moi, 1986. New York: Columbia University Press, pp. 24–33.

Kristeva, J. (1974) "Revolution in Poetic Language" in Moi, T. (ed.) *The Kristeva Reader*. Translated from French by M. Waller, 1986. New York: Columbia University Press, pp. 89–136.

McCloud, S. (1993) *Understanding Comics: The Invisible Art*. New York: Harper Perennial.

## Photography

Since its invention in 1839, photography has at once been promoted for its truthfulness and REALISM and understood to be a REPRESENTATION that is meaningful because of subjective choices made at all stages of the photographic process and because of the cultural codes and CONVENTIONS that inform it. CARTOONING and photography have often been theorised as opposite types of IMAGES in relation to how closely they resemble their real-life counterparts. Unlike photographic images that are said to have a necessary "relationship to objective reality," cartoon images have a "relationship to the subjectivity of the artist" (Woo

2010: 175). This type of binary thinking has informed studies that understand photography in comics as serving a DOCUMENTARY function (Cook 2012, El Refaie 2012: 158). It has also been challenged by studies that argue that cartooning can dismantle belief in the photograph's superior evidential force (Cook 2015, Pedri 2011, Pedri 2012), that the factual and the subjective work together to inform truth or authenticity in graphic memoir (Ernst 2015, Pedri 2017), or that photographs in WORDLESS COMICS fulfil an expository function and thus are stand-ins for TEXT (Postema 2015). Both stances accentuate the complex questions raised when photography is introduced into the cartoon universe of comics.

Nancy Pedri

## *References*

Cook, R. (2012) "Drawings of Photographs in Comics," *Journal of Aesthetics and Art Criticism* 70(1), pp. 129–138.

Cook, R. (2015) "Judging a Comic Book by its Cover: Marvel Comics, Photo-covers, and the Objectivity of Photography," *Image [&] Narrative* 16(2), pp. 14–27.

El Refaie, E. L. (2012) *Autobiographical Comics: Life Writing in Pictures.* Jackson: University Press of Mississippi.

Ernst, N. (2015) "Authenticity in Graphic Memoir: Two Nordic Examples," *Image [&] Narrative* 16(2), pp. 65–83.

Pedri, N. (2011) "When Photographs Aren't Quite Enough: Reflections on Photography and Cartooning in 'Le Photographe,'" *ImageText* 6(1), n.p. Available at: http://imagetext.english.ufl.edu/archives/v6_1/pedri/ [Accessed 1 August 2020].

Pedri, N. (2012) "Cartooning Ex-Posing Photography in Graphic Memoir," *Literature & Aesthetics* 22(2), pp. 248–266.

Pedri, N. (2017) "Photography and the Layering of Perspective in Graphic Memoir," *ImageText* 9(2), n.p. Available at: http://imagetext.english.ufl.edu/archives/v9_2/pedri/ [Accessed 10 July 2020].

Postema, B. (2015) "Establishing Relations: Photography in Wordless Comics," *Image [&] Narrative* 16(2), pp. 84–95.

Woo, B. (2010) "Reconsidering Comics Journalism: Information and Experience in Joe Sacco's 'Palestine'" in Goggin, J. and Hassler-Forest, D. (eds.) *The Rise and Reason of Comics and Graphic Literature: Critical Essays on the Form.* Jefferson: McFarland, pp. 166–177.

## Photonovel

Curiously often called FUMETTI in the US, the photonovel is a particular kind of VISUAL NARRATIVE born in the immediate post-World War II years that was immensely POPULAR in the 1950s, the pre-television era in Europe (mainly France and Italy). From a CULTURAL-INDUSTRIAL point of view, the photonovel is a REMEDIATION of the "drawn novel," a new type of romance comics in a photorealistic style strongly indebted to the glamour of Hollywood cinema. From a technical point of view, the photonovel is at the same time similar to and different from comics. The LAYOUT principles of both comics and photonovels are comparable, but the strong focus on melodrama, the countless references to FILM settings, the exclusive publication in women's magazines, as well as the practical, that is financial and technical difficulties of showing nonrealistic IMAGES (there is definitely a link with Italian Neo-REALISM), make the photonovel a very idiosyncratic format and MEDIUM. Although the heydays of the photonovel as a POPULAR CULTURAL form have been superseded by television formats (the best example being the Brazilian telenovela, a direct successor of the photonovel), modern ARTISTS are rediscovering the GENRE both offline and online (Plissart and Derrida 1998).

Jan Baetens

### *References*

Baetens, J. (2012) "The Photo-Novel: A Minor Medium?" *NECSUS Journal for Media Studies* 1(1), n.p. Available at: https://necsus-ejms.org/the-photo-novel-a-minor-medium-by-jan-baetens/ [Accessed 1 August 2020].

Baetens, J. (2019) *The Film Photonovel: A Cultural History of Forgotten Adaptations.* Austin: Texas University Press.

Plissart, M.-F. and Derrida, J. (1985) *Right of Inspection.* Translated from French by D. Willis, 1998. New York: Monacelli Press.

## Pictorial Runes

Pictorial runes, a term introduced by John M. Kennedy (1982), are "non-mimetic graphic elements that contribute narratively salient information" (Forceville 2011: 875, 2005), such as "flourishes" surrounding characters or objects. There are a very limited number of pictorial runes, whose meaning moreover appears to be highly coded, so that they constitute a kind of "micro-language." Forceville (2011) distinguishes five types in Hergé's *Tintin and the Picaros* (1976): MOVEMENT/speed LINES, spirals, droplets, twirls, and spikes. In addition, Kazuko Shinohara and Yoshihiro Matsunaka (2009) found the "popped-up vein" rune in MANGA. Depending on the type and their location, pictorial runes have different meanings. When they appear behind a character or object, they suggest movement ("motion lines"); when they appear above or around a character's head, they suggest emotion ("emotion lines"). Sometimes the "spike" type of rune occurs around a person or object only as an attention-drawing device. Pictorial runes are also known under different names, including "indicia" (Walker 2000) and "upfixes" (Cohn 2013). Variables pertaining to pictorial runes are their FORM, location, and orientation. Pictorial runes can be distinguished from pictograms (Forceville et al. 2014), although the border between the two is fuzzy. Both await further in-depth theoretical and HISTORICAL analysis in comics.

Charles Forceville

## *References*

Cohn, N. (2013) *The Visual Language of Comics: Introduction to the Structure and Cognition of Sequential Images.* London: Bloomsbury Academic.

Forceville, C. (2005) "Visual representations of the Idealized Cognitive Model of *anger* in the Asterix album *La Zizanie*," *Journal of Pragmatics* 37, pp. 69–88.

Forceville, C. (2011) "Pictorial runes in *Tintin and the Picaros*," *Journal of Pragmatics* 43, pp. 875–890.

Forceville, C., El Refaie, E. L., and Meesters, G. (2014) "Stylistics and Comics" in Burke, M. (ed.) *The Routledge Handbook of Stylistics.* London: Routledge, pp. 485–499.

Kennedy, J. M. (1982) "Metaphor in pictures," *Perception* 11, pp. 589–605.

Shinohara, K. and Matsunaka, Y. (2009) "Pictorial metaphors of emotion in Japanese comics" in Forceville, C. and Urios-Aparisi, E. (eds.) *Multimodal Metaphor.* Berlin: Mouton de Gruyter, pp. 265–293.

Walker, M. (1980) *The Lexicon of Comicana.* Reprint 2000. Lincoln: iUniverse.

## Picture Book

Picture book is a permeable term that describes an IMAGETEXT in which IMAGES play a significant or dominant role in showing and telling a STORY (Whalley and Chester 1988: 216, Alderson 1988), crossing contingencies of use determined by the age of READERS and appearing across GENRES (Lewes 1995a: 100). The term evolved in the late nineteenth century to describe the novelty of the text/image balance in books by Randolph Caldecott (*The Three Jovial Huntsmen*, 1880) or Kate Greenaway (*Under the Window*, 1880), for example, and still occupies a niche in children's LITERATURE in particular (such as Carle's *The Very Hungry Caterpillar*, 1969), subsequently sometimes describing ARTIST'S books and ILLUSTRATED books for adult readers (Albero, Hafenbrak, and Partzel 2013). Although David Lewis notes the HISTORIC relationship between children's toys and picture books, specifically the similarity of the UNMEDIATED relationship between child readers of picture books and between children's play and toys (Lewis 1995a: 185), more recently, Joe Sutliff Sanders has noted the role of "those adults who stand between children and the books they read" (ibid. 100), identifying the picture book as the occasion for a unique READING relationship between adults and children, which he terms CHAPERONED READING (Sanders 2013).

Simon Grennan

### *References*

Albero, A., Hafenbrak, T., and Partzel, P. (2013) *Biograpfiktion*. London: Nobrow.

Alderson, B. (1986) *Sing a Song for Sixpence: The English Picture Book Tradition and Randolph Caldecott*. Cambridge: Cambridge University Press.

Lewis, D. (1995a) "The Picture Book: A Form Awaiting Its History," *Signal* 77, pp. 99–113.

Lewis, D. (1995b) "The Jolly Postman's Long Ride, or, Sketching a Picture-Book History," *Signal* 78, pp. 178–192.

Sanders, J. S. (2013) "Chaperoning Words: Meaning-Making in Comics and Picture Books," *Children's Literature* 41, pp. 57–90.

Whalley, J. and Chester, T. (1988) *A History of Children's Book Illustration*. London: John Murray.

## Poetics

Poetics addresses the correlation between three main axes: the making of works of ART, the TEXT itself, and the effects it produces in its AUDIENCE. Its first occurrence dates from Aristotle's treatise *Poetics* (c. 335 BC), in which he considered each type of poetry from the perspective of the effects they have on the audience, identifying the strategies and resources used to achieve them. Although Aristotle was concerned with lyrical drama, the idea influenced the way we face objects of art in general. A study of poetics investigates how texts are activated by READERS and which effects and MODES of COMPOSITION are typical to each GENRE. The main contribution of this concept lies in its pragmatic dimension, which has had a great influence on the AESTHETICS of RECEPTION, as it takes into account the cooperative role of the reader (Iser 1978, Valery 1989). Classic poetics was recovered by LITERARY STUDIES, conceived of as a discipline devoted to a systematic understanding of texts and their strategies to produce meaning (Todorov 1981). Contemporary uses of classic poetics are not confined to verbal texts, but widely applied to other MEDIA (Gomes 2004, Bordwell 2007), including several attempts to explore a poetics of comics (Fresnault-Deruelle and Samson 2007, Baetens 1991, Picado 2012, Crucifix, Dozo, and Rommens 2017).

Greice Schneider

### *References*

Aristotle (c. 335 BC) *Poetics.* Translated from Greek by A. Kenny, 2013. Oxford: Oxford University Press.

Baetens, J. (1991) "Pour une poétique de la gouttière," *Word & Image* 7(4), pp. 365–376.

Bordwell, D. (2007) *Poetics of Cinema.* Abingdon: Routledge.

Crucifix, B., Dozo, B.-O., and Rommens, A. (eds.) (2017) "Special Collection: Poetics of Digital Comics," *Comics Grid: Journal of Comics Scholarship.* Available at: https://www.comicsgrid.com/collections/special/poetics-of-digital-comics/ [Accessed 25 June 2020].

Fresnault-Deruelle, P. and Samson, J. (2007) *Poétiques de la bande dessinée.* Paris: Éditions L'Harmattan.

Gomes, W. (2004) "La poética del cine y la cuestión del método en el análisis fílmico," *Significação: Revista de Cultura Audiovisual* 31(21), pp. 85–105.
Iser, W. (1978) *The Act of Reading: A Theory of Aesthetic Response.* London: Routledge and Kegan Paul.
Picado, B. (2012) "Retórica e Poética do Traço: O estilo na caricatura e a estrutura episódica do humor gráfico" in Dalcastagnè, R. (ed.) *História em quadrinhos: diante da experiência dos outros.* Vinhedo: Horizonte, pp. 149–162.
Todorov, T. (1981) *Introduction to Poetics.* Brighton: Harvester Press.
Valéry, P. (1989) *The Art of Poetry.* Princeton: Princeton University Press.

## Point of View

Point of view has been used as a synonym of FOCALISATION and PERSPECTIVE (Horstkotte and Pedri 2011). However, it can differ theoretically from both, first in proposing the dominance of vision—what is seen/who is seeing (Herman 2009, Simpson 1993, Mikkonen 2012: 72)—setting aside cognition and judgement and, in a broader sense, describing the range of central or peripheral positions we imagine and adopt relative to what is shown or told, in the process of PRODUCING REPRESENTATIONS (Pouillon 1946, McNeill 1992: 92, Johnson 1987: 36). Point of view also structures VISUALISATION, or visual imagining, in that it is the orientation of the SUBJECT, relative to the visualisation, that organises the subsequent mental IMAGE (Grennan 2017: 88).

Simon Grennan

### *References*

Herman, D. (2009) "Beyond Voice and Vision: Cognitive Grammar and Focalisation Theory" in Hühn, P., Schmid, W., and Schönert, J. (eds.) *Point of View, Perspective, Focalization: Modeling Mediacy.* Berlin: De Gruyter, pp. 119–142.
Horstkotte, S. and Pedri, N. (2011) "Focalisation in Graphic Narrative," *Narrative* 19(3), pp. 330–357.

Johnson, M. (1987) *The Body in the Mind: The Bodily Basis of Meaning, Imagination and Reason*. Chicago: University of Chicago Press.
McNeill, D. (1992) *Hand and Mind: What Gestures Reveal About Thought*. Chicago: University of Chicago Press.
Mikkonen, K. (2012) "Focalisation in Comics. From the specificities of the medium to conceptual reformulation," *Scandinavian Journal of Comic Art* 1(1), pp. 70–95.
Pouillon, J. (1946) *Temps et roman*. Paris: Gallimard.
Simpson, P. (1993) *Language, Ideology and Point of View*. Abingdon: Routledge.

## Polygraphy

Polygraphy is described by Thierry Smolderen as a "prominent feature" (2014: 51) of the engraved ART of eighteenth- and nineteenth-century ARTISTS and ILLUSTRATORS such as William Hogarth and Rodolphe Töpffer. Citing Hogarth as an early pioneer of SEQUENTIAL art, Smolderen concedes that the complexity of his presentation, "replete with incidents, allusions and secondary (…) plots" (2014: 8), is, for contemporary AUDIENCES, difficult to READ. The READER is invited to "lose [themselves] in the details," to "generate comparisons, inferences and endless paraphrases" (ibid.). Employing an approach Smolderen describes as HUMOROUS and largely "unsystematic," illustrators of this era engaged in "productive exchanges" with emerging MEDIA (ibid.). Thus emerged an INTERTEXTUAL overlapping of visual imagery, which Smolderen equates with the POLYPHONY—or multiple voices—of Mikhail Bakhtin's LINGUISTIC philosophy (Baetens and Surdiacourt 2011: 595). This early work bridges the gap between the eccentric novel and modern PANEL comic art, through the introduction of sequence to single IMAGES. Smolderen's innovation is to reject the notion of "the drawing as a single field," and to "redefine it as a set of items and signs to be deciphered" (ibid.). As the COMIC STRIP moved away from its original setting of NEWSPAPERS and journals, this polygraphic, intertextual DISCOURSE was slowly abandoned.

Paul Jackson

## *References*

Baetens, J. and Surdiacourt, S. (2012) "How to 'Read' Images with Texts: The Graphic Novel Case" in Margolis, E. and Pauwels, L. (eds.) *The SAGE Handbook of Visual Research Methods*. London: SAGE, pp. 590–600.

Smolderen, T. (2000) *The Origins of Comics: From William Hogarth to Winsor McCay*. Translated from French by B. Beaty and N. Nguyen, 2014. Jackson: University Press of Mississippi.

## POLYPHONY

Mikhail Bakhtin introduced the term polyphony to LITERARY STUDIES in his *Problems of Dostoevsky's Poetics* in 1929 (Renfrew 2015). For Bakhtin, a piece of writing can tend towards either monologism or polyphony. Monologism, which Bakhtin associates with Leo Tolstoy, is writing in which a definitive dominant meaning is present in the text (Bakhtin 1984: 203–204). Polyphonic writing, conversely, is characterised by a co-presence of different VOICES that are not subsumed under an all-defining final meaning. For Bakhtin, polyphony is thus connected to notions like "freedom" and "AUTONOMY" (Pearce 1994: 225). In COMICS STUDIES, the term polyphony is used outside of the strict LINGUISTIC context that Bakhtin had in mind. Here, Bakhtin's notion of polyphony transcends the purely written word and can be found as a way to understand the INTERACTION between different kinds of TEXTS and IMAGES in comics. It is somewhat confusing, however, to use a sonorous metaphor that was originally used to explain an ability of literary LANGUAGE in a visual-verbal context. For a way of dealing with this issue, see POLYGRAPHY.

Rik Spanjers

## *References*

Bakhtin, M. (1929) *Problems of Dostoevsky's Poetics*. Translated from Russian by C. Emerson (ed.), 1984. Minneapolis: University of Minnesota Press.

Pearce, L. (1994) *Reading Dialogics*. London: Edward Arnold.

Renfrew, A. (2015) *Bakhtin*. Abingdon: Routledge.

## Polysemy

Polysemy is a concept from LINGUISTICS that indicates that a word has several related meanings. In their introduction to the subject, Ingrid Lossius Falkum and Agustin Vicente (2015: 1) illustrate this by using the lexeme "line" in the collocations "draw a line," "read a line," "a line of bad decisions," and "wait in a line." Sometimes, these multiple meanings are systematic, resulting from metonymic relations between a container and its contents ("glass"). On other occasions, they depend on the individual lexemes. The relatedness of the meanings distinguishes polysemy from homonymy, for example, "bat" as an animal and sports equipment. The term is useful in the analysis of the LITERARY aspects of written TEXT in comics, which Hannah Miodrag (2013) amongst others has strongly advocated. In the wake of theories inspired by cognitive science that stress the resemblance of the visual codes in comics with aspects of LANGUAGES, such as Neil Cohn (2013), polysemy is also occasionally employed to indicate systematic ambiguity in visual REPRESENTATION (Grennan 2017: 22–23), especially when explaining the diverse but related meanings emanata/PICTORIAL RUNES may have (Miodrag 2013: 182–183). Hergé, for example, used a twirl to indicate a movement or a dizziness (Forceville et al. 2014: 492–493).

Gert Meesters

### *References*

Cohn, N. (2013) *The Visual Language of Comics: Introduction to the Structure and Cognition of Sequential Images.* London: Bloomsbury Academic.

Forceville, C., El Refaie, E. L., and Meesters, G. (2014) "Stylistics and Comics" in Burke, M. (ed.) *The Routledge Handbook of Stylistics.* Abingdon: Routledge, pp. 485–499.

Grennan, S. (2017) *A Theory of Narrative Drawing.* London: Palgrave Macmillan.

Lossius Falkum, I. and Vicente, A. (2015) "Polysemy: Current perspectives and approaches," *Lingua* 157, pp. 1–16.

Miodrag, H. (2013) *Comics and Language: Reimagining Critical Discourse on the Form.* Jackson: University Press of Mississippi.

## Pop Art

The Pop Art movement of the 1960s used comics as an important source of subject matter alongside other motifs drawn from POPULAR CULTURE (Varnedoe and Gopnik 1990: 187–212, Crow 2014: 119–34). Roy Lichtenstein, the Pop ARTIST who drew most heavily on comics, is best known for his paintings of blown-up COMIC BOOK PANELS. The Pop artists sought to inject popular imagery from mass MEDIA into the realm of fine ART with the aim of eradicating the cultural hierarchy between high art and popular culture (Crow 2014: vii–ix). However, Lichtenstein's SWIPING of panels drawn by Russ Heath and others has drawn criticism for appropriating their work without crediting them or paying ROYALTIES (Panko 2017). It is also important to note that the Pop artists did not necessarily see comics or other works of popular culture as achieving a level of quality equal to that of high culture. Rather, they tended to oppose the whole notion of quality in the traditional sense (Buchloh 2002). This contrasts with the position of many advocates of comics as an art FORM, such as Art Spiegelman, who want comics to receive respect as an artistic MEDIUM on par with more established media such as LITERATURE and FILM (Spiegelman 1988).

Doug Singsen

### *References*

Buchloh, B. (2002) "Andy Warhol's One-Dimensional Art" in Michelson, A. (ed.) *Andy Warhol*. Cambridge: MIT, pp. 1–46.

Crow, T. (2014) *The Long March of Pop: Art, Music and Design 1930–1995*. New Haven: Yale University Press.

Panko, B. (2017) "The Comic Artists Who Inspired Roy Lichtenstein Aren't Too Thrilled About It," *Smithsonian Magazine*, 27 October 2017. Available at: https://www.smithsonianmag.com/smart-news/comics-behind-roy-lichtenstein-180966994/ [Accessed 10 July 2020].

Spiegelman, A. (1988) "Commix: An Idiosyncratic Historical and Aesthetic Overview," *Print* 42(6), pp. 61–73, 195–196.

Varnedoe, K., and Gopnik, A. (1990) *High and Low: Modern Art and Popular Culture*. New York: Museum of Modern Art.

## Popular Culture

Popular culture, sometimes called "low" culture, is a way of understanding everyday ways of life, cultural forms (such as MEDIA, MUSIC, or ART) liked by many people, and as a description of tastes of non-elite people (Williams 1976: 80–82). The term emerged in the twentieth century as a non-judgemental way of understanding mass culture in its own right, particularly in the wake of scholars studying working-class traditions and Marxist approaches (Thompson 1963: 12–13, Hoggart 1957), in opposition to fears of mass culture as empty entertainment, false consciousness, or spectacle (Arnold 1993: 53–54, DeBord 1967: 7–9). Theodor Adorno and Max Horkheimer of the Frankfurt School were suspicious of popular culture and characterised it as deceptive (2020: 94–136). Members of the Birmingham School in the UK took a different approach within CULTURAL STUDIES and characterised popular culture as the environment of working-class tactics, to explain how institutionalised forms of culture can be opposed, and to provide meaning for those who are disrespected by elites or institutionally educated people (Hebdige 1979, Hall 1981, McRobbie 2000: 126–34). Later work on popular culture understands it more broadly within the activities of subcultures that oppose dominant ways of being, from a broadly leftist perspective (Grossberg 2010) and as a complex of meanings, practices, and responses to mass media and new media (Storey 2015, Hesmondalgh 2019).

Julie Rak

### *References*


Adorno, T. and Horkheimer, M. (1947) "The Culture Industry: Enlightenment as Mass Deception" in Schmid Norr, G. (ed.) *Dialectic of Enlightenment: Philosophical Fragments.* Translated from German by E. Jephcott, 2002. Stanford: Stanford University Press. 94–136.

Arnold, M. (1867) "Culture and Anarchy: an Essay in Political and Social Criticism (1867–69)" in Collini, S. (ed.) *Arnold: Culture and Anarchy and Other Writings.* Reprint 1993. Cambridge: Cambridge University Press, pp. 53–54.

DeBord, G. (1967) *The Society of the Spectacle.* London: Rebel Press.

Grossberg, L. (2020) *Cultural Studies in the Future Tense.* Durham: Duke University Press.

Hall, S. (1981) "Notes on Deconstructing the Popular" in Samuel, R. (ed.) *People's History and Socialist Theory*. Abingdon: Routledge, pp. 227–240.
Hebdige, D. (1979) *Subculture and the Meaning of Style*. Abingdon: Routledge.
Hesmondalgh, D. (2019) *The Cultural Industries*. 4th edition. London: SAGE.
Hoggart, R. (1957) *The Uses of Literacy: Aspects of Working-class Life*. London: Chatto and Windus.
McRobbie, A. (2000) *Feminism and Youth Culture: From 'Jackie' to 'Just Seventeen.'* 2nd edition. London: Palgrave Macmillan.
Storey, J. (2015) *Cultural theory and popular culture: An introduction*. 7th edition. Abingdon: Routledge.
Thompson, E. P. (1963) *The Making of the English Working Class*. New York: Vintage.
Williams, R. (1976) *Keywords: A Vocabulary of Culture and Society*. London: Croom Helm.

## Pornography

Conventionally, pornography describes representations made for the purpose of eliciting SEXUAL arousal. However, it is the arousal response to a REPRESENTATION that defines pornography, rather than the intention of a maker, any CONVENTIONS of use, or the properties of the representation. That is, when a description or DEPICTION is used by a READER or viewer to become sexually aroused, that relation between user and object is pornographic. Hence, any GENRE can become pornographic, which has given rise to specific subgenres such as erotica, as well as social distinctions between high and low culture, relative to sexual arousal. Comics, throughout their HISTORY, have been intended to arouse and have been used as objects of arousal. Famous study objects within the field of comics pornography are the TIJUANA BIBLES, which were small format comics popular in the US in the first half of the twentieth century (Adelman 1997). From the perspective of critical porn studies, comics are a study object because they allow for FEMINIST critiques of the depiction of female bodies (Peppard 2020 and Aldama 2020) because they can challenge the existing power structures of much mainstream pornography (Sandifer et al. 2007) and because they offer insights into the social contingencies and cultural specificities of porn PRODUCTION and consumption. Here, much discussed examples are UNDERGROUND

COMIX specifically made for female audiences (Shamoon 2004 and Roberts 2015), and various MANGA genres (Levi et al. 2010 and Galbraith 2011).

Rik Spanjers

## *References*

Aldama, F. L. (ed.) (2020) *The Routledge Companion to Gender and Sexuality in Comic Book Studies*. London: Routledge.

Adelman, B. (1997) *Tijuana Bibles: Art and wit in America's forbidden funnies, 1930s–1950s*. New York: Simon & Schuster.

Galbraith, P. W. (2011) "Lolicon: The Reality of 'Virtual Child Pornography' in Japan," *Image [&] Narrative* 12(1), pp. 83–119.

Levi, A., McHarry, M., and Pagliassotti, D. (eds.) (2010) *Boys' Love Manga: Essays on the Sexual Ambiguity and Cross-Cultural Fandom of the Genre*. Jefferson: McFarland.

Peppard, A. F. (ed.) (2020) *Supersex: Sexuality, Fantasy, and the Superhero*. Austin: University of Texas Press.

Roberts, J. (2015) "Girly porno comics. Contemporary US pornographic comics for women," *Journal of Graphic Novels and Comics* 6(3), pp. 214–229.

Sandifer, P., Kidd K., Eklund, C., Hatfield, C., and Collins, M. (2007) "ImageSexT: A Roundtable on *Lost Girls*," *ImageTexT* 3(3), n.p. Available at http://imagetext.english.ufl.edu/archives/v3_3/lost_girls/index.shtml [Accessed 5 March 2021].

Shamoon, Deborah: "Office Sluts and Rebel Flowers. The Pleasures of Japanese Pornographic Comics for Women" in Williams, L (ed.) *Porn Studies*. Durham: Duke University Press, pp. 77–103.

## Postcolonialism

Postcolonial studies thematises power relations between dominant and suppressed groups, identity politics, and space theories. The term "subaltern," writes C. L. Innes, "signifies those who are not part of the ruling group, and subaltern history refers to the history of those groups—those who are subordinated by the dominant class, which is usually author and subject in history" (Innes 2007: 11). Postcolonial comics, therefore, "seek to redefine and recreate identity out of a violent and often obliterated past" (Knowles et al. 2016: 382) and use HYBRIDITY to deconstruct the colonial remnants through PARODY, hyperbole when appropriating RACIAL STEREOTYPES, and, most importantly, retell colonial HISTORY from a postcolonial lens. Examples of postcolonial comics are Marjane Satrapi's *Persepolis* (2003), the graphic journalism of Joe Sacco, as well as *Black Panther* (1966–). The latter features a series, "A Nation Under Our Feet," which is characterised by its hybridity inasmuch as its writer, Ta-Nehisi Coates, draws on the original story but bestows it with fresh characteristics like the incorporation of African American LITERATURE and cultural references from Malcolm X to black poetry by Henry Dumas. Thereby, Coates contributes to a self-fashioning of the formerly oppressed African Americans in the US and gives them the chance to represent themselves rather than being represented by the dominant group.

Andrea Schlosser

## *References*

Knowles, S., Peacock, J., and Earle, H. (2016) "Introduction: Trans/formation and the Graphic Novel," *Journal of Postcolonial Writing*, 52(4), pp. 378–384.

Newkirk, V. R. (2018) "The Provocation and Power of Black Panther." *The Atlantic*, 14 February 2018. Available at: https://www.theatlantic.com/entertainment/archive/2018/02/the-provocation-and-power-of-black-panther/553226/ [Accessed 26 May 2020].

Innes, C. (2007) *The Cambridge Introduction to Postcolonial Literatures in English*. Cambridge: Cambridge University Press.

Spivak, G. (1988) "Can the Subaltern Speak? Speculations on Widow Sacrifice" in Nelson, C. and Grossberg, L. (eds.) *Marxism and the Interpretation of Culture*. Urbana: University of Illinois Press, pp. 271–313.

## Posthumanism

The application of posthumanism across different fields of study "focuses on the critique of the humanist ideal of 'Man' as the universal representative of the human" (Braidotti and Hlavajova 2018: 1). Rosi Braidotti elucidates that "posthuman theory is a generative tool to help us re-think the basic unit of reference for the human in the bio-genetic age known as 'anthropocene,' the historical moment when the Human has become a geological force capable of affecting all life on this planet" (2013: 5). Posthumanism thereby offers theoretical ground to investigate and challenge the concept of the human as well as to critically engage with the various realms where human and non-human matters converge, such as in, but not limited to, TECHNOLOGY, MEDICINE, and ECOLOGY. Thus, posthumanism, "[b]y extension, (…) can also help us re-think the basic tenets of our interaction with both human and non-human agents on a planetary scale" (Braidotti 2013: 5–6). As noted by Lisa Diedrich, comics may "render this [posthuman] condition through various formal practices, including radical juxtaposition and assemblage as method, as well as through the articulation of a concept of the subject as always in the process of becoming in relation to both human and nonhuman others" (2016: 96).

Freija Camps

### *References*

Braidotti, R. (2013) *The Posthuman*. Cambridge: Polity Press.

Braidotti, R. and Hlavajova, M. (2018) "Introduction" in Braidotti, R. and Hlavajova, M. (eds.) *Posthuman Glossary*. London: Bloomsbury Academic, pp. 1–14.

Diedrich, L. (2016) "Comics and Graphic Narratives" in Clarke, B. and Rossini, M. (eds.) *The Cambridge Companion to Literature and the Posthuman*. Cambridge: Cambridge University Press, pp. 96–108.

## Postmodernism

Postmodernism, a theoretical and AESTHETIC response to postmodernity, the cultural-historical condition of late capitalism, is an intellectual movement that emerged in the cross-pollination between

POSTSTRUCTURALIST philosophy and the radical movements of the 1960s (Butler 2002, DeKoven 2004). Postmodernist theory is characterised by an incredulity towards grand NARRATIVES of Western humanism (Lyotard 1984), a critical epistemology that doubts the accessibility of truth and a distrust to the ability of LANGUAGE to refer to the external world (Butler 2002: 29). Postmodernist ART and LITERATURE maintains the SELF-REFLEXIVITY and STYLISTICS of MODERNISM but breaks down the distinction between "high" and "mass" culture that characterised the latter (DeKoven 2004: 15, Hassan 1982: 267). Postmodern fiction is, moreover, characterised by an ontological uncertainty about the separateness between the fictional and the real world (McHale 1987). HISTORIOGRAPHIC metafiction is thus the GENRE par excellence of postmodernism, as it problematises the MIMETIC relation between reality and REPRESENTATION (Hutcheon 1988). Comics like Art Spiegelman's *Maus* (1980–1991) and Alison Bechdel's *Fun Home: A Family Tragicomic* (2006) belong to this genre. The MEDIUM of comics in general can be called postmodern as it often brings "features of high visual and literary modernism," to the field of POPULAR CULTURE (Chute 2011: 375).

Vasiliki Belia

## *References*

Butler, C. (2002) *Postmodernism: A Very Short Introduction*. Oxford: Oxford University Press.

Chute, H. (2011) "The Popularity of Postmodernism," *Twentieth Century Literature*, 57(3–4), pp. 354–363.

DeKoven, M. (2004) *Utopia Limited: The Sixties and the Emergence of the Postmodern*. Durham: Duke University Press.

Hassan, I. (1982) *The Dismemberment of Orpheus: Toward a Postmodern Literature*. Madison: The University of Wisconsin Press.

Hutcheon, L. (1988) *A Poetics of Postmodernism: History, Theory, Fiction*. London: Routledge.

Lyotard, J.-F. (1979) *The Postmodern Condition: A Report on Knowledge*. Translated from French by G. Bennington and B. Massumi, 1984. Minneapolis: University of Minnesota Press.

McHale, B. (1987) *Postmodernist Fiction*. Abingdon: Routledge.

## Poststructuralism

Poststructuralism relies on the premise that meaning is unstable. Whereas STRUCTURALISM proposes an understanding of meaning as reliant on the arbitrary SIGN, consisting of a signifier and signified, poststructuralism builds on the notion that the signifier incites "the indefinite referral of signifier to signifier" (Derrida 2002: 29). It follows that "the play of meaning has no necessary closure, no transcendental justification" (Silverman 1983: 41). A cultural text can thus be understood as "a multi-dimensional space in which a variety of writings, none of them original, blend and clash" (Barthes 1977: 146). In turn, "a text's unity" is only achieved by the reader (ibid. 148). This insistence on the openness of meaning informs the study of culture and ideology, for it allows a revealing of "the claims of totality and universality (...) that implicitly operate to quell the insistent ambiguity and openness of linguistic and cultural signification" (Butler 2006: 54). Poststructuralism has informed the study of comics by considering the relationship between ideology, the text, and the reader. Such approaches "go against the idea of the passive reader and thereby opened for the idea of popular culture being polysemic" (Christiansen and Magnussen 2000: 21).

Freija Camps

### *References*

Barthes, R. (1961–1973) *Image, Music, Text.* Translated from French by S. Heath (ed.), 1977. London: Fontana.

Butler, J. (1990) *Gender Trouble: Feminism and the Subversion of Identity.* Reprint 2006. Abingdon: Routledge.

Christiansen, H.-C. and Magnussen, A. (2000) "Introduction" in Magnussen, A. and Christiansen, H.-C. (eds.) *Comics and Culture: Analytical and Theoretical Approaches to Comics.* Copenhagen: Museum Tusculanum Press, pp. 7–28.

Derrida, J. (1967) *Writing and Difference.* Translated from French by A. Bass, 2002. Abingdon: Routledge.

Silverman, K. (1983) *The Subject of Semiotics.* Oxford: Oxford University Press.

## Print

Comics can now be PRODUCED and consumed onscreen, without using paper for ARTWORK or printing. Art Spiegelman, contemplating this digital revolution, said that "the history of comics has up to now been the history of printing" (Mitchell and Spiegelman 2014: 30). For centuries, the visual syntax of pictorial NARRATIVE was not that of the ARTIST, but was MEDIATED by the handcrafting of, for example, mediaeval woodcuts, or William Hogarth's eighteenth-century engravings (Ivins 1969: 61–70, Kunzle 1973). Rodolphe Töpffer found an autographic (self-DRAWN and LETTERED) printing method, transfer LITHOGRAPHY, for his 1830s picture STORIES (Twyman 1990: 186–190), but reached a wide AUDIENCE only when his *M. Cryptogame* was wood-engraved by other hands for magazine printing, with TYPE-set TEXT (Kunzle 2007: 95–100). Photoengraving of autographic LINE drawings directly to printing plates began to displace wood engraving from 1872 (Gillot 1898), reaching newspapers in 1880s New York (Juergens 1966: 97). From 1893, hand-crafted printing plates using Ben Day dots added COLOUR to photoengraved black artwork in Sunday editions. In the Sunday papers, already selling hundreds of thousands of copies, the COMIC STRIP first became a mass entertainment MEDIUM (Gordon 1998: 24–36). Similar "letterpress" printing dominated US comics until the 1980s. European publishers exploited higher quality techniques decades earlier—gravure (*Journal de Mickey* 1934), offset lithography (*Tintin* 1946)—reflecting international differences in the cultural value of the medium, and contributing to its development (Sabin 1993: 184–190).

Guy Lawley

### *References*

Gillot, C. (1898) "La Photogravure" in Bayard, E. (ed.) *L'Illustration et les Illustrateurs.* Paris: Librairie Ch. Delagrave, 358–359.

Gordon, I. (1998) *Comic Strips and Consumer Culture 1890–1945.* Washington: Smithsonian Institution Press.

Ivins, Jr., W. M. (1969) *Prints and Visual Communication.* Cambridge: The Massachusetts Institute of Technology Press.

Juergens, G. (1966) *Joseph Pulitzer and the New York World.* Princeton: Princeton University Press.

Kunzle, D. (1973) *The Early Comic Strip*. Berkeley: University of California Press.

Kunzle, D. (2007) *Father of the Comic Strip: Rodolphe Töpffer*. Jackson: University Press of Mississippi.

Mitchell, W. J. T. and Spiegelman, A. (2014) "Public Conversation: What the %$#! Happened to Comics? May 19, 2012," *Critical Inquiry* 40(3), pp. 20–35.

Sabin, R. (1993) *Adult Comics: An Introduction*. Abingdon: Routledge.

Twyman, M. (1990) *Early Lithographed Books*. London: Farrand Press.

## Production

Despite arguments that comics extend back to ancient civilisations, the FORM is intrinsically linked to PRINT culture (McCloud 1994). Hence, production is closely related to MASS PRODUCTION, including industrial creative practices, the economics of PRINTING methods and circulation, and RECEPTION as POPULAR CULTURE. HISTORICALLY, comics and CARTOON CREATION is indirect, involving a division of LABOUR between WRITERS, PENCILLERS, background ARTISTS, INKERS, COLOURISTS, LETTERERS, and editors (although these vary across specific practices and regions). For example, early American COMIC BOOKS utilised a Fordian assembly-line method within independent studios (the "shop system") whose finished product was purchased by PUBLISHERS (Harvey and Eisner 2002). Jean-Paul Gabilliet has distinguished between this early "studio" era and the later "contracts" era of freelance artists working directly for specific publishers like Marvel and DC (Gabilliet 2010). Alternatively, MANGA typically consolidates the American process with lead artists and assistants (Schodt 1983: 138).

Josh R. Rose

### *References*

Gabilliet, J.-P. (2005) *Of Comics and Men: A Cultural History of American Comic Books*. Translated from French by B. Beaty and N. Nguyen, 2010. Jackson: University Press of Mississippi.

Harvey, R. C. and Eisner, W. (2002) "The Shop System I: Will Eisner," *The Comics Journal* 1, pp. 62–69.

Schodt, F. L. (1983) *Manga! Manga!: The world of Japanese comics*. Tokyo: Kodansha International.

## Propaganda

Propaganda encompasses attempts to systematically spread sponsored information, usually through mass MEDIA (Snow 2019)—consisting of facts, rumours, lies, and symbols—often appealing to emotions, with the aim of influencing receivers by adjusting and manipulating their perceptions, attitudes, and behaviour, as desired by the producer of such selective NARRATIVES. The origin of the term dates back to 1622 when the Catholic Church founded the "Congregatio de Propaganda Fide" (Congregation for Propagating the Faith) to spread Catholicism among non-believers (Lilleker 2006: 162). Despite these roots, propaganda came to be seen as a political method of social control across societies, manipulating views of the collective self and other. With the rise of mass media in the late nineteenth and early twentieth centuries, propaganda became increasingly widespread (Jowett and O'Donnell 2018: 151–152), using various popular media, including COMIC STRIPS, which were regarded as inexpensive, accessible, and appealing because of their mixed visual and TEXTUAL elements. This resulted in a vast PRODUCTION of comics propaganda mobilising entire populations especially during WARS, although propaganda is applied as well in peacetime, in totalitarian and democratic societies. Initiatives for propagandistic expressions do not lie exclusively with governmental or political institutions. Not always equally conscious of its nature or intention, comics CREATORS have also initiated propaganda, creating and reinforcing partisan-motivated REPRESENTATIONS of friend and foe (Strömberg 2020: 38–59).

Kees Ribbens

### *References*


Jowett, G. S. and O'Donnell, V. (2018) *Propaganda and Persuasion*. 7th edition. London: SAGE.

Lilleker, D. G. (2006) *Key Concepts in Political Communication*. London: SAGE.

Snow, N. (2019) "Propaganda" in Vos, T.P. and Hanusch, F. (eds.) *The International Encyclopedia of Journalism Studies*. Hoboken: John Wiley & Sons, Inc.

Strömberg, F. (2010) *Comic Art Propaganda: A Graphic History*. Lewes: Ilex Press, Ltd.

## Psychoanalysis

The founder of psychoanalysis as a system of thought was Sigmund Freud (1856–1939), a Vienna-based neurologist who proposed to treat mental suffering through dialogue between patient and analyst. Around the turn of the century, he developed the first of his two conceptual schemes of the human psyche, dividing it into the unconscious, preconscious, and conscious (Freud 1963). Later in his career, he proposed a second scheme, this time consisting of the id, ego, and superego (Freud 1964). Together with these two maps of the psyche, he introduced a host of concepts that are being contested to this day, including castration anxiety, the death drive, defence mechanisms, libido, melancholia, mourning, the Oedipus complex, penis envy, phallic imagery, repression, transference, and the uncanny. Freud's thinking was taken up and expanded on by various influential thinkers, including among others Carl Jung, Melanie Klein, and Jacques Lacan. In COMICS STUDIES, as in CULTURAL analysis overall, psychoanalysis functions in three ways, the first two of which have been controversial; psychoanalytical insights are applied to: (1) fictional characters as if they are patients; (2) comics CREATORS whose oeuvre is treated as a patient's speech in a therapy setting; and (3) comics texts that draw on psychoanalytical concepts.

Roel van den Oever

### *References*

Freud, S. (1915–1917) *The Standard Edition of the Complete Psychological Works of Sigmund Freud, Volumes 15 (1915–1916) and 16 (1916–1917): Introductory Lectures on Psycho-Analysis.* Translated from German by J Strachey, 1963. London: Hogarth Press.

Freud, S. (1932–1936) *The Standard Edition of the Complete Psychological Works of Sigmund Freud, Volume 22 (1932–1936): New Introductory Lectures on Psycho-Analysis and Other Works.* Translated from German by J. Strachey, 1964. London: Hogarth Press.

## Publishing

Originally, comics were directly linked to NEWSPAPER and magazine publishing. From the 1890s, American SUNDAY FUNNIES were published as newspaper inserts and in the UK the foremost publisher of COMIC BOOKS, Amalgamated Press (later Fleetway Publications then International Publishing Corporation), mainly PRODUCED newspapers and magazines (Sabin 1996: 18–19, 27–33). In the 1930s, companies like Detective Comics (later DC Comics) were founded to publish only comic books but others, such as Timely Comics (later Marvel Comics), continued to publish pulp fiction and magazines. Such publishers were responsible for CREATION, PRINTING, and packaging but generally not distribution (Lee 2002: 22–32, 98–110, Simon 2011: 90–98). The UNDERGROUND COMIX of the 1960s saw a shift towards SELF-PUBLISHING which continued with the emergence of ALTERNATIVE COMICS in the late 1970s, though in both cases new publishing firms such as Last Gasp and Fantagraphics emerged to take advantage of these new MARKETS (Sabin 1996: 107, 178). The most vocal advocate for self-publishing in this period was Dave Sim, the creator of *Cerebus*, who also led key debates about creators' rights (Beaty and Woo 2016: 121–131). With the emergence of the GRAPHIC NOVEL, new players entered the field in the form of books publishers and most recently WEBCOMICS have created new publishing models.

Ian Horton

### *References*

Beaty, B. and Woo, B. (2016) *The Greatest Comic Book of All Time: Symbolic Capital and the Field of American Comic Books.* London: Palgrave Macmillan.

Lee, S. and Mair, G. (2002) *Excelsior! The Amazing Life of Stan Lee.* London: Boxtree.

Sabin, R. (1996) *Comics, Comix and Graphic Novels: A History of Comic Art.* London: Phaidon Press.

Simon, J. (2011) *Joe Simon: My Life in Comics.* London: Titan Books.

## PUNK

While punk is usually associated with rock MUSIC, it is also a larger cluster of AESTHETIC, political, and social movements that emerged in the UK and the US in the mid-1970s. The New York-based magazine *Punk* featured CARTOONS and comics, and in series like *Anarchy Comics* and *Raw* magazine, ARTISTS would experiment with the do-it-yourself, intentionally amateurish, nihilistic, and raucous STYLES associated with punk subcultures. Prominent artists associated with the punk movement include Peter Bagge, Julie Doucet, Gilbert Hernandez, Jaime Hernandez, Gary Panter, and John Porcellino, among many others, as well as contemporary comics artists associated with the Fort Thunder group in Rhode Island. While differing in artistic style and social critique from the earlier UNDERGROUND COMIX largely associated with the 1960s counterculture, punk comics nonetheless resemble their predecessors through their emphasis on individual artistry and expression, and their publication outside of traditional or mainstream venues. Many artists committed to the do-it-yourself philosophy common to punk subcultures SELF-PUBLISH ZINES and MINICOMICS, and a wide variety of artistic and NARRATIVE styles have emerged out of punk. In mainstream comics such as *Transmetropolitan* and *Watchmen*, punk characters and philosophies are prevalent, as well as in the subgenres of cyberpunk and steampunk. Contemporary, independent comics PUBLISHERS such as Ad Astra Comix and Silver Sprocket continue to publish work that participates in punk subcultures.

Daniel Worden

### *References*

Lawley, G. (1999) "'I like Hate and I hate everything else': The Influence of Punk on Comics" in Sabin, R. (ed.) *Punk Rock: So What?* Abingdon: Routledge, pp. 100–119.

Noys, B. (2018) "No Future: Punk and the Underground Graphic Novel" in Baetens, J., Frey, H., and Tabachnick, S. (eds.) *The Cambridge History of the Graphic Novel.* Cambridge: Cambridge University Press, pp. 235–250.

Spurgeon, T. (2003) "Fort Thunder Forever." *The Comics Reporter*, 21 December 2003. Available at: https://www.comicsreporter.com/index.php/briefings/commentary/1863/ [Accessed 16 June 2020].

## Puzzle Comics

Puzzle comics problematise or play with NARRATIVE path expectations, sometimes confounding what Thierry Groensteen calls the ARTHROLOGY of comics (1999). Early examples include Gustave Verbeek's COMIC STRIP *Upside Downs* (1903–1905), which was designed to be READ normally and then turned upside down to finish the STORY. Recent examples have been more complex and EXPERIMENTAL, such as Richard McGuire's *Here* (1989), which shows the same corner of a room with continual shifts in time, revealing, achronologically, the different events that have taken place there. Much of the work of Chris Ware plays with narrative CONVENTIONS, in particular *Building Stories* (2012), which consists of 14 separate PRINTED items that can be read in any order, and thus, as Benoît Crucifix argues, "does not rely on models of digital seriality" (2018). Others, like Joe Sacco's *The Great War,* a 24-foot long panorama, challenge whether they are narrative comics at all, and DIGITAL COMICS obviously offer many complex possibilities. Another type of puzzle comic introduces a three-dimensional element. An early version was Harvey Kurtzman's hexaflexagon for *Trump* (1957), which he DESIGNED an adjustable folded paper narrative. More recent examples of this include the work of Jason Shiga in a GENRE that Aaron Kashtan describes as "origami comics" (2018).

Dave Huxley

### *References*

Crucifix, B. (2018) "From loose to boxed fragments and back again: Seriality and archive in Chris Ware's *Building Stories,*" *Journal of Graphic Novels and Comics* 9(1), pp. 3–22.

Groensteen, T. (1999) *The System of Comics.* Translated from French by B. Beaty and N. Nguyen, 2007. Jackson: University Press of Mississippi.

Kashtan, A. (2018) *Between Pen and Pixel: Comics, Materiality, and the Book of the Future.* Columbus: The Ohio State University Press.

## Queer Comics

Queer comics are comics which foreground queer characters and/or NARRATIVES. Stephen Neale writes that GENRES function through processes of REPETITION and difference, which interact on three levels: "the level of expectation, the level of the generic corpus, and the level of the 'rules' or 'norms' that govern both" (1990: 56). The expectation of a queer comic is not of a specific STORY pattern, but that queerness will be foregrounded in the narrative and/or the characters. Queer comics thus also contain a range of genres such as AUTOBIOGRAPHICAL (Tillie Walden's *Spinning*), HORROR (Emily Carroll's *When I Arrived at the Castle*), and SCIENCE-FICTION (iggy craig's *Sad Girl Space Lizard*). The marginalisation of queer creators in mainstream PUBLISHING, in particular those with marginalised gender identities and people of colour, has led to CREATORS establishing "a strong presence through online comics and zines" (Earle 2019: 4). These alternative methods of dissemination allow for unusual stories and generic fusion, further complicating and denying the categorisation of queer narratives into a single genre. A uniquely queer genre is that of the coming-out story, where a character recognises and embraces their queerness. Nicki Hastie argued that this genre has its roots in the *Bildungsroman* (1993: 68).

Olivia Hicks

### *References*

Hastie, N. (1993) "Lesbian BiblioMythography" in Griffin, G. (ed.) *Outwrite: Lesbianism and Popular Culture.* London: Pluto Press, pp. 68–85.

Earle, M. (2019) *Writing Queer Women of Color: Representation and Misdirection in Contemporary Fiction and Graphic Narratives.* Jefferson: McFarland.

Neale, S. (1990) "Questions of Genre," *Screen* 31(1), pp. 45–66.

## Race

Prior to the Age of Exploration, race existed to differentiate humans from animal species (Walton and Caliendo 2011: 3). During the seventeenth century, Europeans developed race into a social categorisation system to differentiate between humans (ibid.). From these enterprising origins came the modern understanding of race where individuals are given a social IDENTITY and are grouped based on physical characteristics such as skin tone and facial features. Race conjures assumptions "that subconsciously affect our thoughts and behaviors and which have been incorporated into our social and political institutions" (ibid. 5). Mass MEDIA, including the comics MEDIUM, is such an institution; as comics scholar Marc Singer notes, "(c)omics rely upon visually codified representations in which characters are continually reduced to their appearances" (107). This codification creates STEREOTYPES, and these unrealistic portrayals (or, just as unrealistically, lack of portrayals) reaffirm any negative assumptions towards certain racial groups (ibid.). As such, it is important for comics scholars to identify the racial ideology of a comics text using theoretical frameworks such as CRITICAL RACE THEORY and INTERSECTIONALITY, comparing race to other social identities such as GENDER, CLASS, ETHNICITY, and SEXUALITY.

Rachel A. Davis

### *References*

Singer, M. (2002)" 'Black Skins' and White Masks: Comic Books and the Secret of Race," *African American Review* 36(1), pp. 107–119.

Walton, F. C. and Caliendo, S. M. (2011) "Origins of the Concept of Race" in Caliendo, S. M. and McIlwain, C. D. (eds.) *The Routledge Companion to Race and Ethnicity*. Abingdon: Routledge, pp. 3–11.

## Readers

A reader is one who reads, but being a comics reader implies more than literacy. Early research in mass communications and education could fairly be described as studying the COMIC BOOK reader in general (Zorbaugh 1944; Heisler 1944; Karp 1954; Blakely 1957; see also Gibson 2015).

Following the creation of the DIRECT MARKET, however, comics reading became a largely SUBCULTURAL practice. According to market research, the audience of mainstream comics in the United States is mostly middle-aged, middle-class white men. Contemporary studies of comic book culture tend to conflate these fans with readers (Cedeira Serantes 2019: 19; see also Brown 1997; Tankel and Murphy 1998; Pustz 1999), but not every reader describes themselves as a fan and not every fan actually reads comics (Burke 2015: 120). Within FANDOM, the social identity of reader may signal distinct motivations from "fan" or "collector" (Woo 2018). Such distinctions are often tied to hierarchies of authenticity (Scott 2013, 2019). Yet, comics' resurgence as reading material for young people, their legitimation as literature and expansion into schools and libraries, and the discovery of "applied cartooning" (Bennett and Sturm 2015) by fields like journalism and health communication all point to the growing relevance of the reader-in-general.

Benjamin Woo

## *References*

Bennett, M. and Sturm, J. (2015, March 20) "TCJ Roundtable Discussion ~ APPLIED CARTOONING," *The Comics Journal*, http://www.tcj.com/tcj-roundtable-discussion-applied-cartooning/.

Blakely, W.P. (1957) *A Study of Seventh Grade Children's Reading of Comics Books as Related to Certain Other Variables*. University of Iowa, PhD dissertation.

Brown, J.A. (1997) "Comic Book Fandom and Cultural Capital," *Journal of Popular Culture* 30(4), pp. 13–31.

Burke, L. (2015) *The Comic Book Film Adaptation: Exploring Modern Hollywood's Leading Genre*. Jackson: University Press of Mississippi.

Cedeira Serantes, L. (2019) *Young People, Comics, and Reading: Exploring a Complex Reading Experience*. Cambridge: Cambridge University Press.

Gibson, M. (2015) *Remembered Reading: Memory, Comics and Post-War Constructions of British Girlhood*. Leuven: Leuven University Press.

Heisler, F.A. (1944) *Characteristics of Elementary-School Children Who Read Comic Books, Attend the Movies, and Prefer Serial Radio Programs*. New York University, PhD dissertation.

Karp, E.E. (1954) *Crime Comic Book Role Preferences.* New York University, PhD dissertation.

Pustz, M. (1999) *Comic Book Culture: Fanboys and True Believers.* Jackson: University Press of Mississippi.

Scott, S. (2013) "Fangirls in Refrigerators: The Politics of (In)Visibility in Comic Book Culture," *Transformative Works and Cultures* 13, http://journal.transformativeworks.org/index.php/twc/article/view/460.

Scott, S. (2019) *Fake Geek Girls: Fandom, Gender, and the Convergence Culture Industry.* New York: NYU Press.

Tankel, J.D. and Murphy, K. (1998) "Collecting Comic Books: A Study of the Fan and Curatorial Consumption" in Harris, C. and Alexander, A. (eds.) *Theorizing Fandom: Fans, Subculture and Identity.* Cresskill, NJ: Hampton Press, pp. 55–68.

Woo, B. (2012) "Understanding Understandings of Comics: Reading and Collecting as Media-Oriented Practices," *Participations: Journal of Audience & Reception Studies* 9(2), pp. 180–199.

Zorbaugh, H. (1944) "The Comics—There They Stand!" *Journal of Educational Sociology* 18(4), pp. 196–203.

## Reading

Reading is the process of making sense of MARKS on a page. Inhabiting the space between looking and understanding, reading is both an individual and a social process: individual because we each use our own combinations of references to decode a given text (Hall 1973, Kristeva 1974), and social because it is through the social and cultural construct of LANGUAGE, expressed in verbal and visual FORMS, that we share meaning (Vygotsky 1935). Making sense of a text also involves navigating multiple possible meanings for a given word or other unit within a text in relation to the whole (Bakhtin 1981). For this reason, while eye-tracking TECHNOLOGY can offer insights into where on a page and for how long a person looks, it alone cannot uncover why they linger on particular parts of the page or what they understand from it. Specific considerations for reading comics as IMAGETEXTS relate to their MULTIMODALITY and SEQUENTIALITY, which often necessitate active reading. As multimodal works the TEXTS and IMAGES of a comic can offer consistent or divergent meanings, and as sequential texts comics require the READER to combine static PANELS and GUTTERS into a NARRATIVE, whether as specific features or in consideration of comics as a system or grammar (Groensteen 2007).

Lydia Wysocki

## *References*

Bakhtin, M. (1935–1935) "Discourse in the Novel" in Holquist, M. (ed.) *The Dialogic Imagination*. Translated from Russian by C. Emerson and M. Holquist, 1981. Austin: University of Texas Press, pp. 259–422.

Groensteen, T. (1999) *The System of Comics*. Translated from French by B. Beaty and N. Nguyen, 2007. Jackson: University Press of Mississippi.

Hall, S. (1973) "Encoding/Decoding" in During, S. (ed.) *The Cultural Studies Reader*. 2nd edition. Reprint 1993. Abingdon: Routledge, pp. 507–517.

Kristeva, J. (1974) "Revolution in Poetic Language" in Moi, T. (ed.) *The Kristeva Reader*. Translated from French by M. Waller, 1986. New York: Columbia University Press, pp. 89–136.

Vygotsky, L. (1935) "The Problem of the Environment" in van der Veer, R. and Valsiner, J. (eds.) *The Vygotsky Reader*. Translated from Russian by T. Prout, 1994. Oxford: Blackwell, pp. 338–354.

## Realism

Although the term realism is frequently used in the RECEPTION of comics, scholarship avoids it. Already in 1922, Roman Jakobson criticised the confusion that accompanies the concept (1987: 20). Going through only a short HISTORY of LITERARY or ART criticism is enough to show that a wide range of different REPRESENTATIONAL procedures have claimed realism or have been called realistic (Auerbach 1953, Gombrich 2002, Jameson 2013). With POSTMODERNISM, academic critique of both claims on realism as well as the use of the term in scholarship intensified (Barthes 1989). For postmodernists, the reality to which realism refers is illusory because humans can only access it through representation. In COMICS STUDIES, accordingly, realism is not a concept that can be used unapologetically, especially because historically, comics DRAWING STYLES have often been defined in opposition to various realisms (McCloud 1993: 28, Smolderen 2014: 28). Comics, however, are not limited to the CARTOONESQUE with which they are primarily associated. In fact, traditions exist within comics that aim for and approximate more CONVENTIONAL FORMS of realistic representation (Spanjers 2019: 33). There are also comics that combine different styles, such as the work in the CLEAR LINE tradition.

Rik Spanjers

## *References*

Auerbach, E. (1946) *Mimesis: The Representation of Reality in Western Literature*. Translated from German by W. R. Trask, 1953. Princeton: Princeton University Press.

Barthes, R. (1968) "The Reality Effect" in Barthes, R. *The Rustle of Language*. Translated from French by R. Howard, 1989. Berkeley: University of California Press, pp. 141–148.

Gombrich, E. H. (2002) *The Preference for the Primitive: Episodes in the History of Western Taste and Art*. London: Phaidon Press.

Jacobson, R. (1922) "On Realism in Art" in Pomorska, K. and Rudy, S. (eds.) *Language in Literature*. Reprint 1987. Cambridge: Harvard University Press, pp. 19–27.

Jameson, F. (2013) *The Antinomies of Realism*. New York: Verso.

McCloud, S. (1993) *Understanding Comics: The Invisible Art*. New York: Harper Perennial.

Smolderen, T. (2000) *The Origins of Comics: From William Hogarth to Winsor McCay*. Translated from French by B. Beaty and N. Nguyen, 2014. Jackson: University Press of Mississippi.

Spanjers, R. (2019) *Comics Realism and the Maus Event: Comics and the Dynamics of World War II Remembrance*. PhD. University of Amsterdam.

## Reception

Reception theory considers how individual READERS construct meaning from a given text or IMAGETEXT. This aspect of LITERARY THEORY and AUDIENCE studies reflects the complexity of how we make sense of the world around us and contrasts with claims to a single correct READING of a comic. Stuart Hall's work on Encoding/Decoding explored the potential mismatch between the writer's intended meaning and the meaning constructed by the reader of a text. This allows that meaning is culturally dependent: what is normal in one context may be unfamiliar in another. Reception theory could yet be taken further in studying and making comics. As an inherently MULTIMODAL MEDIUM, comics can intentionally use IMAGES and TEXT to communicate clearly but can also introduce deliberate or inadvertent misunderstandings between what is WRITTEN and what is DRAWN.

Lydia Wysocki

## *References*

Hall, S. (1973) "Encoding/Decoding" in During, S. (ed.) *The Cultural Studies Reader*. 2nd edition. Reprint 1993. Abingdon: Routledge, pp. 507–517.

## Referent

A referent is the actual person or object in the real world to which a SIGN may refer. Although Ferdinand de Saussure considered the referent (the thing signified) to be beyond the scope of LINGUISTIC pursuits, linguists and LITERARY scholars continue to consider the referent paramount "for all reflective, intellectual use of language" (Ogden and Richards 1923: 10). The role of the referent in the process of meaning-making has also garnered much discussion from scholars who study visual MODES of signification. The PHOTOGRAPHIC IMAGE, for instance, has been theorised as "not *immediately* or *generally* distinguished from its referent" (Barthes 1980: 5) and as an image whose meaning has nothing at all to do with the pre-photographic referent (Tagg 1988: 3). Considerations of how verbal and VISUAL LANGUAGES refer to a referent feature prominently in comics scholarship, from studies that accentuate the hand-DRAWN quality of CARTOONING (Groensteen 2007: 42, Wolk 2007: 120) to those that examine the MEDIUM's relationship to accuracy and truth (Chute 2016, Mickwitz 2016, El Refaie 2012).

Nancy Pedri

## *References*

Barthes, R. (1980) *Camera Lucida: Reflections on Photograph.* Translated from French by R. Howard, 1981. New York: Hill and Wang.

Chute, H. (2016) *Disaster Drawn: Visual Witness, Comics, and Documentary Form.* Cambridge: The Belknap Press.

El Refaie, E. L. (2012) *Autobiographical Comics: Life Writing in Pictures.* Jackson: University Press of Mississippi.

Groensteen, T. (1999) *The System of Comics.* Translated from French by B. Beaty and N. Nguyen, 2007. Jackson: University Press of Mississippi.

Mickwitz, N. (2016) *Documentary Comics: Graphic Truth-telling in a Skeptical Age.* London: Palgrave Macmillan.

Ogden, C. K. and Richards, I. A. (1923) *The Meaning of Meaning: A Study of the Influence of Language upon Thought and of the Science of Symbolism.* New York: A Harvest Book.

Tagg, J. (1988) *The Burden of Representation: Essays on Photographies and Histories.* Minneapolis: University of Minnesota Press.

Wolk, D. (2007) *Reading Comics: How Graphic Novels Work.* Cambridge: Da Capo.

## Register

A register may be characterised as a set of CONVENTIONS that is used to make meanings in a given situation. The register will normally reflect the MODE that is being used, the field of meaning the CREATOR is REPRESENTING, and the tenor of the relationship between creator(s) and READER(S) or AUDIENCE(S). It is characterised by a set of default, unmarked STYLISTIC choices that develop a relatively stable identity (Halliday and Matthiessen 2014: 28–29, 71–72). A register may be typical for a given mode of PRODUCTION, but is not identical with it. Likewise, some writers may use GENRE with meanings overlapping with register; genre is typically used to refer to norms of content and, for some WRITERS, their supporting formal TROPES. Experiments with comics registers include those by Matt Madden in *99 Ways to Tell a Story* (2005), R. Sikoryak's *Masterpiece Comics* (2009), and oppositional/SATIRICAL texts such as *The Adventures of Tintin: Breaking Free* (Daniels 1989).

Paul F. Davies

## *References*

Halliday, M. A. K. and Matthiessen, C. (2014) *Halliday's Introduction to Functional Grammar*. Abingdon: Routledge.

## Religious Comics

Religious comics comprise graphic narratives that interpret and communicate spiritual philosophies of world religions: Baha'i, Buddhism, Christianity, Confucianism, Hinduism, Islam, Jainism, Judaism, Sikhism, Shinto, Taoism, Zoroastrianism, exerting a phenomenological reader affect particularly in celebratory or devotional consumption (Kandhari 2020). Evangelism is examined as an effective function of Christian comics (Nuss 2015), whilst adaptations of sacred texts and epics in graphic narratives are posited as educational in reading the sacred in new, creative ways through the unique multimodal form (Gamzou and Koltun-Fromm 2018), demonstrated by *Amar Chitra Katha's* adaptation of the Hindu epic, *Mahabharata* (McLain 2009). Simplified production styles of religious figures in hagiographic narratives, rendering illustrations in bold, clear lines facilitates narrative flow of panel texts and comprehension of religious themes and philosophies, exemplified by Classics Illustrated *Jesus* comic and *Amar Chitra Katha* comics representing Indian deities, prophets and gurus. Drawing upon Scott McCloud's theories on reader identification of iconic imagery (Orcutt 2010), religious figurative representations adopt iconographic elements derived from painting and sculptural traditions to present recognisable figurative forms in comics such as Guru Nanak rendered in the master of modern Sikh Art's paintings, Sobha Singh and the symbols of Buddhist enlightenment, 'lakshana' portrayed in Tezuka's *Buddha* (Kandhari 2022).

Jasleen Kandhari

## *References*

Gamzou, A. and K. Koltun-Fromm (eds.) (2018) *Comics and Sacred Texts: Reimagining Religion and Graphic Narratives*. University Press of Mississippi.

Kandhari, J. (2020) "Graphic Narratives in Sikh Comics: Iconography and Religiosity as a Critical Art Historical Enquiry of the Sikh Comics Art Form," *International Journal of Comics Art* 22(1), pp. 170–186.

Kandhari, J. (2022) "Introducing Sikh Comics: A Critical Study in Canon Formation," *International Journal of Comics Art* 23 (2) n.p.

McLain, K. (2009) *India's Immortal Comic Books: Gods, Kings and Other Heroes.* Bloomington: Indiana University Press.

Nuss, C. (2015) "Christian Ministry in a Comic Book Culture: 'Parabolic Evangelism' and the Use of Stories in Evangelistic Ministry," *Canadian Journal for Scholarship and the Christian Faith*, n.p.

Orcutt, D. (2010) "Comics and Religion: Theoretical Connections" In Lewis, A. D. and C. H. Kraemer (eds.) *Graven Images: Religion in Comic Books and Graphic Novels.* New York: Continuum Publishing, pp. 93–106.

## Remediation

Remediation is a relationship between MEDIA FORMS that relies on a double logic: "Our culture wants both to multiply its media and to erase all traces of mediation: ideally, it wants to erase its media in the very act of multiplying them" (Bolter and Grusin 1998: 5). On the one hand, remediation involves reproducing the experience of one media form in the frame of another. For example, when we leaf through the "pages" of a "book" on the screen of a computer, there is an attempt in the use of skeuomorphic DESIGN techniques and INTERACTION design to give a sense of immediacy and replicate the experience of reading a PRINTED object. On the other, we have the inescapable reality that this is *not* the experience of reading a printed book, and the techniques used to reproduce that experience only serve to emphasise what is missing in the digital experience, highlighting the act and nature of (re)mediation. Remediation plays an important role in the experience of comics READING, particularly in terms of reprints, reissues, facsimiles, and digital versions of texts, which often attempt to reproduce a form that is both absent and a source of specific NOSTALGIA for READERS.

Ian Hague

## *References*

Bolter, J. D. and Grusin, R. (2000) *Remediation: Understanding New Media*. Cambridge: MIT.

## Repetition

Repetition refers to the reappearance of something that has already been represented. Repetition in comics is both a necessity for creating an effective NARRATIVE and a creative device that comics ARTISTS may choose to deploy. Pierre Masson labelled comics the "stuttering art ('art du bégaiement')" in light of the frequent repetition of images, which enables a narrative to form (1985:72). For a comics READER to follow a SEQUENCE of events as occurring in the same SPACE and TIME and with the same characters, elements within a sequence of PANELS must be repeated. Beyond narrative necessity, repetition also exists as a way for comics artists to manipulate a readers' sense of time. As Thierry Groensteen observes, "By repeating the same framing over and over again, the artist emphasizes a key moment within the narrative and prolongs it not in the mode of 'and then' but rather of 'and still...and still...'" (2013: 144). Repetition can thereby emphasise key moments or draw out narrative time. In addition to this, repetition in comics can be used as a motivic device to foreground key objects as thematically significant. This is similar to the way key phrases in music can signal particular characters or ideas (Addis, 2017: pp. 11–12).

Victoria Addis

## *References*

Addis, V. (2017) "The Musicalization of Graphic Narratives," *Studies in Comics* 8(1), pp. 7–28.

Groensteen, T. (2011) *Comics and Narration*. Translated from French by A. Miller, 2013. Jackson: University Press of Mississippi.

Masson, P. (1985) *Lire la bande dessinée*. Lyon: Presses Universitaires de Lyon.

## Representation

Representation is the process by which one entity comes to stand for or SIGNIFY another. Accounts of how this is achieved have historically emphasised that representations stand for their SUBJECTS either by virtue of a likeness or through an arbitrary symbolic connection. Plato held a MIMETIC view and in his ALLEGORY of the cave positioned representations as illusions that MEDIATE individuals' access to the real. The referential view became dominant following Ferdinand de Saussure's (1916) development of a SEMIOLOGICAL LINGUISTICS and its subsequent extension across the humanities by STRUCTURALIST thinkers. Theories of representation overlap significantly with theories of MEDIATION, focussing upon the relationships between the subject and the means of representation. As such, COMICS are identified by the unique ways in which they afford these relationships. Roland Barthes (1957) described a second level of representation, connotation, in which the objects denoted by first-order signs are placed in wider MYTHICAL SEMANTIC fields, and through which ideological concepts such as "Englishness" or "imperialism" are depoliticised. Although representation is now seen as consisting in relationships between signs or the construction of discursive structures (Foucault 1982), W. J. T. Mitchell's assertion that "representation (in memory, in verbal descriptions, in images) not only 'mediates' our knowledge (…) but obstructs, fragments and negates that knowledge" (1995: 188) suggests that concerns about its obfuscatory power remain salient for contemporary theorists.

John Miers

### *References*

Barthes, R. (1957) *Mythologies.* Paris: Seuil.

de Saussure, F. (1916) *Course in General Linguistics.* Translated from French by W. Baskin, 1959. New York: Philosophical Library.

Foucault, M. (1969) *The Archaeology of Knowledge and the Discourse on Language.* Translated from French by A. M. Sheridan Smith, 1982. New York: Vintage.

Mitchell, W. J. T. (1994) *Picture Theory: Essays on Verbal and Visual Representation.* Chicago: University of Chicago Press.

Plato (c. 375 BC) *Republic.* Translated from Greek by R. Waterfield, 2008. Oxford: Oxford University Press.

## Reproduction

Most comics are made to be shared as multiples of the same IMAGETEXT. Even comics made as one-offs using specialist ART and craft techniques (such as embroidery, oil painting, or graffiti) might be shared by scans or PHOTOGRAPHS of the original work. Making a comic that is intended to be reproduced raises practical issues that can influence the comics CREATOR'S choices of art STYLE, COLOUR, page count, and more, as they consider how TECHNOLOGIES influence not only the READING but the making process. Walter Benjamin (1955) explored how mass duplication of a work of art differs from its authentic original. Developments in PRINTING technology changed how people react to originals and copies. In COMICS STUDIES and FANDOM both the original artwork and the large print-run version of a comic can become desirable items for scholars, READERS, and COLLECTORS. Moreover, contemporary DIGITAL artwork and PUBLICATION processes can mean there is no physical original or no discernible difference between original and copy. In terms of copyright, there are limits to the reproducibility of comics as legislation prohibits the reproduction of a comic without the copyright owner's explicit consent. Yet, unauthorised scans or reprints can help comics reach new AUDIENCES and ensure that out of print comics are not lost. Comics also has rich traditions of learning by imitation, through SWIPING, doujinshi, and PARODY.

Lydia Wysocki

### *References*

Benjamin, W. (1955) *Illuminations.* Translated from German by H. Zohn, 1992. Arendt, H. (ed.) London: Fontana.

## Retcon

Retcon is the popularised and abbreviated form of "retroactive continuity." The term was first coined by E. Frank Tupper in *The Theology of Wolfhart Pannenberg*, who describes it as "history flow[ing] fundamentally from the future into the past" (100). This concept was later refined in its application to comics by Andrew J. Friedenthal in *Retcon Game:*

*Retroactive Continuity and the Hyperlinking of America*. Friedenthal defines retcon as “a revision of the fictional universe in order to make the universe fresh and exciting for contemporary readers” (10–11). In other words, retcon—which may be used as either a noun or a verb—happens when a previously established element of a fictional WORLD is changed, whether to right a past political fault, to allow new STORYLINES to make sense, or to bring back characters from the dead. Retcon is a frequent occurrence in SERIAL texts with multiple CREATORS, such as SUPERHERO comics, where keeping a decades-long NARRATIVE error-free is nearly impossible. Changing the past of a fictional world allows new futures to flourish.

Jasmine Palmer

## *References*

Friedenthal, A. J. (2017) *Retcon Game: Retroactive Continuity and the Hyperlinking of America*. Jackson: University Press of Mississippi.

Tupper, E. F. (1974) *The Theology of Wolfhart Pannenberg*. London: S. C. M. Press.

## Rhythm

Rhythm describes the pattern of the pulse or beat of a work as it moves through TIME. Rhythm in comics is experienced both visually as a pattern of MOVEMENT across the PAGE, and aurally, as the pattern of SOUNDS in their LITERARY aspect. The POETIC elements of comics WRITING, the cadences and figurative LANGUAGE, are particularly emphasised in non-NARRATIVE works: EXPERIMENTAL COMICS, ABSTRACT COMICS, and the HYBRID of comics poetry. As Tamryn Bennett has observed, comics WRITERS, like poets, employ various techniques that create a sense of rhythm, including the manipulation of metre, line breaks, and enjambment (2014: 108). In terms of the visual aspect of comics, the multiframe has been described by Thierry Groensteen as representing the underlying beat of comics PAGE LAYOUT. As Groensteen explains, “On a page consisting of two large images one above the other, the beat is slow and steady (…) in a page containing numerous rows of small panels, it is faster" (2013: 136). This core beat can be manipulated by, for example, varying the size and shape of the PANELS. As Joseph Witek states, "Like slight variations in poetic meter and rhyme, even this relatively small change in the regularity of the grid mitigates the visual sing-song of identically shaped and sized panels" (2009: 153).

Victoria Addis

## *References*

Bennet, T. (2014) "Comics Poetry: Beyond Sequential Art," *Image [&] Narrative* 15(2), pp. 106–123.

Groensteen, T. (2011) *Comics and Narration*. Translated from French by A. Miller, 2013. Jackson: University Press of Mississippi.

Witek, J. (2009) "The Arrow and the Grid" in Heer, J. and Worcester, K. (eds.) *A Comics Studies Reader*. Jackson: University Press of Mississippi, pp. 149–156.

## ROMANCE

Romance comics emerged simultaneously in the late 1940s in America and Europe from women's magazines, novels, and confessional magazines. They had an extensive, mainly female, READERSHIP up to the 1970s when the emergence of COMICS SHOPS changed distribution practices (Nolan 2008).

In America, the first romance comic *Young Romance* (1947) led to a boom (ibid.). American comics featured three to four stories often in confessional MODE with salacious titles but tame content (ibid.). Romance comics were published in Italy from 1947 as PHOTONOVELLAS ("Il mio sogno") and magazines (*Grand Hotel* [1946–present]) ADAPTED from novels and FILMS and SYNDICATED throughout Europe. British comics FORMATS were a blend of magazine and comic, the most influential being *Jackie* (DC Thomson 1964–1993). WRITINGS on romance comics fall into five main areas: HISTORIES (Nolan 2008, Robbins 1999, Benson 2007); critiques of their REPRESENTATIONS and effects on girls (McRobbie 1978, 1991); READER negotiation and consumption

(Gibson 2016, Frazer 1987); research methods and analysis (Barker 1989); and constructing girlhood (Gibson 2016, Tinkler 1995, 2014, Kidd and Tebbutt 2017, Ormrod 2018).

Joan Ormrod

## *References*


Barker, M. (1989) *Comics: Ideology, Power, and the Critics.* Manchester: Manchester University Press.

Benson, J. (2007) *Confessions, Romances, Secrets and Temptations: Archer St. John and the St. John Romance Comics.* Seattle: Fantagraphics.

Gibson, M. (2015) *Remembered Reading: Memory, Comics and Post-War Constructions of British Girlhood.* Leuven: Leuven University Press.

Kidd, A. and Tebbutt, M. (2017) "From 'marriage bureau' to 'points of view': Changing patterns of advice in teenage magazines: *Mirabelle*, 1956–1977" in Kidd, A. and Tebbutt, M. (eds.) *People, Places and Identities.* Manchester: Manchester University Press, 180–201.

McRobbie, A. (1978) *'Jackie': An Ideology of Adolescent Femininity.* Discussion paper. Birmingham: Birmingham Centre for Contemporary Cultural Studies.

McRobbie, A. (1990) *Feminism and Youth Culture: From 'Jackie' to 'Just Seventeen.'* London: Macmillan International Higher Education.

Nolan, M. (2008) *Love on the Racks.* Jefferson: McFarland.

Ormrod, J. (2018) "Reading Production and Culture UK Teen Girl Comics from 1955 to 1960," *Girlhood Studies: An Interdisciplinary Journal* 1(3), pp. 18–33.

Robbins, T. (1999) *From Girls to Grrrlz: A History of Female Comics from Teens to Zines.* San Francisco: Chronicle Books.

Tinkler, P. (1995) *Constructing girlhood: Popular magazines for girls growing up in England, 1920–1950.* London: Taylor and Francis.

Tinkler, P. (2014) "'Are You Really Living?' If Not, 'Get with It!': The Teenage Self and Lifestyle in Young Women's Magazines, Britain 1957–70," *The Journal of the Social History Society* 11(4), 597–619.

## Royalty Payment

The royalty is the percentage amount a publisher pays to a CREATOR based on the income generated by their work (Sergi 2015). Press SYNDICATES, since the late nineteenth century, have remunerated CARTOONISTS through diverse contractual royalty systems based on the number of newspapers carrying their COMIC STRIPS and the MERCHANDISING revenue, if any. By contrast, the COMIC BOOK industry born in the late 1930s relied for decades upon work-made-for-hire, treating creators as freelancers PRODUCING corporate-owned MATERIAL with no right to any extra income beyond the page rate paid on delivery, even for the characters and concepts they authored. Creator-owned comics and the intellectual property rights attached to them appeared in the 1960s' UNDERGROUND PUBLISHING and subsequently became the norm among alternative publishers. Only in 1982 did Marvel and DC start paying royalties to their bestselling creators for fear of losing talent to non-mainstream comics (Gabilliet 2010: 116–121). Nowadays, except for the "stars" that can negotiate generous contracts, a creator authoring a work not to be SERIALISED before publication will receive an advance that is a guaranteed minimum royalty payment, although it is not necessarily sufficient to cover living expenses throughout the time required to complete a work (Rhoades 2007: 171–208).

Jean-Paul Gabilliet

### *References*

Gabilliet, J.-P. (2005) *Of Comics and Men: A Cultural History of American Comic Books.* Translated from French by B. Beaty and N. Nguyen, 2010. Jackson: University Press of Mississippi.

Rhoades, S. (2007) *Comic Books: How the Industry Works.* New York: Peter Lang.

Sergi, J. (2015) *The Law for Comic Book Creators: Essential Concepts and Applications.* Jefferson: McFarland.

## Satire

Satire is a sub-GENRE of multiple artistic disciplines, in which public figures, organisations, governments, societies, and ideologies are held up to ridicule and criticism, often via the use of METAPHOR or ALLEGORY. While HUMOUR is often derived from satirical texts, this does not have to be the case. There are three principal forms of satire: Menippean, Horatian, and Juvenalian, each named for a specific Greek or Roman practitioner. Menippean satire tends to focus on attitudes and approaches to life and society, as opposed to ridiculing individuals and "thus resembles the confession in its ability to handle abstract ideas and theories," approaching "evil and folly (…) as a kind of maddened pedantry" (Frye 1990: 309). Horatian satire is gentler, tending to wryly mock human absurdity in a warm fashion, designed to encourage the AUDIENCE to also recognise, and laugh at, its own behaviour and foibles. By contrast, Juvenalian satire is harsher, and more apt to attack and ridicule both individuals and groups that are seen by the satirist as malign, in a way designed to damage their reputations and influence in order to attempt to raise awareness or even bring about some form of lasting change. While satire can often provoke anger or cause offence, it is often privileged or protected by law as a means of speaking truth to power. Satirical comics often take the form of political cartoons or underground COMIX, but mainstream publications such as *Mad Magazine* or Marvel's defunct *Not Brand Echh* are also examples of the genre.

Houman Sadri

### *References*

Frye, N. (1957) *Anatomy of Criticism*. Reprint 1990. Princeton: Princeton University Press.

## Schematism

The concept of schematism originates from Immanuel Kant's *Critique of Pure Reason* (1781), in which he argues that a transcendental schema is that which makes possible the application of "pure concepts of the understanding to appearances in general" (1998: 272). Kant's schemata are thus MEDIATING instances that relate to pure concepts, on the one hand,

and to empirical reality on the other. Schematism refers to the procedure of understanding that occurs through schemata (ibid. 273). In ART theory, the term schematism is used to refer to visual shorthands that are based on social and/or cultural CONVENTIONS (Gombrich 1984: 18). It thus denotes a move away from empirically based REALISM and towards standardisation. As such, schematism is often associated with CARICATURE, CARTOONING, and other simplified pictorial STYLES and opposed to photorealism. In COMICS STUDIES, the term diagrammatic is often used as a synonym for schematism (Smolderen 2014: 113). The philosophical origins of the concept of schematism allow proponents of caricature and cartooning to argue that the perceived simplicity of such graphic styles in fact draw their strength from the way they make use of a conceptual shorthand to efficiently convey a wealth of information in a few well-placed MARKS.

Rik Spanjers

## *References*

Gombrich, E. H. (1960) *Art and Illusion: A Study in the Psychology of Pictorial. Representation.* Reprint 1984. London: Phaidon Press.

Kant, I. (1781) *Critique of Pure Reason.* Translated from German by P. Guyer and A. W. Wood, 1998. Cambridge: Cambridge University Press.

Smolderen, T. (2000) *The Origins of Comics: From William Hogarth to Winsor McCay.* Translated from French by B. Beaty and N. Nguyen, 2014. Jackson: University Press of Mississippi.

## Science Fiction

Science fiction (SF) is a broadly defined GENRE encompassing adventure STORIES featuring futuristic and/or extraterrestrial elements and settings ("soft" SF), as well as idea-driven NARRATIVES exploring the consequences of scientific discoveries or other paradigm-shifting events ("hard" SF or "speculative fiction"). The most succinct, and perhaps best-known, academic definition of the genre was made by Darko Suvin, who called SF "the literature of cognitive estrangement" (372). SF is one of the dominant genres in comics, particularly in consideration of the fact that SUPERHERO comics can, to a significant extent, be considered a sub-genre of SF. Many of the prototypical superhero narratives were directly derived from pulp SF literature; for example, Jerry Siegel and Joe Shuster's character Superman (1938) owes a clear debt to Edgar Rice Burroughs' popular *John Carter of Mars* SERIES and other contemporary SF novels (1912–1964). The earliest popular ongoing SF comics narratives, however, were newspaper serials such as *Buck Rogers*, which began publication in 1929 and was joined by *Flash Gordon* five years later (Horn 1976). These and other SF comics entered a series of TRANSMEDIA exchanges with FILM, radio, and LITERATURE, and thereby contributed in an essential way to the visual ICONOGRAPHY and narrative TROPES of science fiction in modern POPULAR CULTURE at large (Wasielewski 2009).

Christopher Rowe

## *References*

Horn, M. (1976) "Buck Rogers" in Horn, M. (ed.) *The World Encyclopedia of Comics*. New York: Chelsea House, pp. 137–138.

Suvin, D. (1972) "On the Poetics of the Science Fiction Genre," *College English* 34(3), pp. 372–382.

Wasielewski, M. (2009) "Golden Age Comics" in Bould, M., Butler, A., Roberts, A., and Vint, J. (eds.) *The Routledge Companion to Science Fiction*. New York: Routledge, pp. 62–70.

## Script

A script is a written document that plans a comics text, before being DRAWN, INKED, COLOURED, LETTERED, edited, and finally PUBLISHED. Often provided by a scriptwriter, some ARTISTS create their own scripts. Besides entailing decisions on plot, character development, and dialogue, it can also "[spark] the desire of the image in the artist" (Peeters 1993: 94). There are two major common practices, with numerous variants, and in which the control exerted by the WRITER is a matter of degree. In the English-speaking world, the first is known as The "Marvel Method," predating but retrospectively associated with Stan Lee and the artists he COLLABORATED with in the 1960s. It consists of an outline of the plot, with dialogue added later. It is synonymous with a back-and-forth collaboration between writer and artist. Then there's the

"Full Script": a detailed description of what happens in each PANEL, sometimes down to colour and ONOMATOPOEIA. Alan Moore's work is a major example of obsessively detailed scripts (*From Hell: The Compleat Scripts Book One*, 1995). Scripts in the form of rough thumbnails to be re-drawn by the final artist or other peculiar methods also deserve mention. Some scripts are published either as appendices to collections and "director's cuts" editions or in book FORM.

Pedro Moura

## *References*

Peeters, B. (1993) *La Bande Dessinée. Un Exposé pour Comprendre, un Essai pour Réfléchir.* Paris: Flammarion.

## Self-Publishing

AUTHORS self-publish when they fund the REPRODUCTION, marketing, and distribution of their own work. Associated with DIY culture, self-published authors may also be, but are not always, involved in the LABOUR of PRINTING, DESIGNING, and distributing their work. Self-published work is often distributed through DIRECT TO CONSUMER CHANNELS, secures CREATOR ownership of characters and STORYLINES, and thus can be seen as the procurement of AUTONOMY, measured by "the degree to which the decision-making process (…) is free from intervention by any other agent" (Barber and Martin 2000: 345). In North America in the 1980s, the success of self-published comics such as Wendy and Richard Pini's *Elfquest* and Kevin Eastman and Peter Laird's *Teenage Mutant Ninja Turtles* during the so-called BLACK-AND-WHITE Boom gave authors the confidence to protest what was perceived as exploitative contracts provided by major PUBLISHERS. This led to the Creator's Bill of Rights in 1988, drafted by cartoonist Scott McCloud (McCloud, n.d.). The decline of the direct sales MARKET in the mid-1990s made self-publishing less viable (Bissette 2005). However, the direct to consumer possibilities of CONVENTIONS and online retail continue to sustain self-published comics and WEBCOMICS, as have, since the late 2000s, crowdfunding platforms (Valenti 2019: 129).

Nicholas Burman

## *References*

Barber, K. S. and Martin C. E. (2000) "Autonomy as Decision-Making Control" in Castelfranchi, C. and Lespérance, Y. (eds.) *Intelligent Agents VII: Agent Theories Architectures and Languages.* Berlin: Springer, pp. 343–345.

Bissette, S. (2005) "The Creator's Bill of Rights: A Chat with Steve Bissette." Interviewed by A. Nickerson for *Ya Can't Erase Ink*, 8 March 2005. Available at: http://albert.nickerson.tripod.com/creatorsbillofrightsbsette.html. [Accessed 16 June 2020].

McCloud, S. (1988) "The Creator's Bill of Rights." *Scott McCloud.* Available at: http://scottmccloud.com/4-inventions/bill/ [Accessed 16 June 2020].

Valenti, K. (2019) "How We Got Here: A Distribution Overview 1996–2019," *The Comics Journal* 303, pp. 120–136.

## Self-Reflexivity

ART critic Clement Greenberg's oft-cited 1939 article "Avant-Garde and Kitsch" not only reified MEDIAL differences based on their presumed affordances and limitations, but firmly established the boundary between what he terms the high art mediums of the AVANT-GARDE and the low or non-art KITSCH of cultural objects (2003: 533). Once "common currency in the art world," Greenberg's insistence on the "purity" of MEDIUM-specificity was famously critiqued by art critic Rosalind Krauss as an antiquated notion that promotes an "essentialist reduction of painting to 'flatness'" (1999: 6). While Krauss agrees with both Greenberg and Walter Benjamin in considering PHOTOGRAPHY the end of the traditional media due to its use of TECHNICAL support, she asserts that in the "post-medium condition" the parameters for medium must be reconceived. To this end, she argues for the criterion of self-reflexivity in art. Adding to art critic Stanley Cavell's insistence that a work of art must reflect its own internal plurality, Krauss asserts that if a technical support is used in a manner that exploits it, criticises it, or subverts it, and is thereby self-reflexive, it can at once avoid being labelled as kitsch and be viewed as its own new post-medium (ibid.). In COMICS STUDIES inquiries into self-reflexivity largely focus on the FORM and/or content of particular works, groups of works, or in terms of the medium's operational potential as a "post-medium."

Erin La Cour

## *References*

Greenberg, C. (1939) "Avant-Garde and Kitsch" in Harrison, C. and Wood, P. (eds.) *Art in Theory, 1900–2000*. 2nd edition. Reprint 2003. Oxford: Blackwell, pp. 539–549.

Krauss, R. (1999) *"A Voyage on the North Sea": Art in the Age of the Post-Medium Condition*. London: Thames and Hudson.

## SEMANTICS

If we consider semantics as "the study of meaning, of the structural ways in which it is realised in natural language" (Aloni and Dekker 2016: 11), we should look into the LINGUISTIC approaches believing comics to be a proper LANGUAGE (Varnum and Gibbons 2007, Miodrag 2013, Cohn 2013, Davies 2019, Cohn 2020). If we assume instead (slightly simplistically) that semantics is the study of meaning at large, then we should ask ourselves what produces meaning in comics. Mostly, the STORY recounted, and the way the verbal NARRATOR shapes it (perhaps filtered through IRONY or unreliably depicted). But meaning is also created through the way a story is visually FRAMED and plotted, by the AUTHOR or the "meganarrator" (Marion 1993). In this perspective, (almost) everything becomes meaningful: the PAGE LAYOUT, the POINT OF VIEW, the FOCALISATION, the COLOUR palette, the individual choices and characteristics concerning one's DRAWING STYLE, and the montage (Peeters 1991, McCloud 1993, Groensteen 2007, Baetens and Frey 2015, Mikkonen 2017, Grennan 2017). Finally, meaning often comes from the connections between elements, on several levels (thematic, stylistic, or structural); those links may be intra-textual (e.g. ARTHROLOGICAL), INTERTEXTUAL, or INTERMEDIAL.

Giorgio Busi Rizzi

## *References*

Aloni, M. and Dekker, P. (eds.) (2016) *The Cambridge Handbook of Formal Semantics*. Cambridge: Cambridge University Press.

Baetens, J. and Frey, H. (2015) *The Graphic Novel: An Introduction*. Cambridge: Cambridge University Press.

Cohn, N. (2013) *The Visual Language of Comics: Introduction to the Structure and Cognition of Sequential Images.* London: Bloomsbury Academic.
Cohn, N. (2020) *Who Understands Comics?: Questioning the Universality of Visual Language Comprehension.* London: Bloomsbury Academic.
Davies, P. F. (2019) *Comics as Communication: A Functional Approach.* London: Palgrave Macmillan.
Grennan, S. (2017) *A Theory of Narrative Drawing.* London: Palgrave Macmillan.
Groensteen, T. (1999) *The System of Comics.* Translated from French by B. Beaty and N. Nguyen, 2007. Jackson: University Press of Mississippi.
Marion, P. (1993) *Traces en cases: Travail graphique, figuration narrative et participation du lecteur. Essai sur la bande dessinée.* Louvain-la-Neuve: Académia.
McCloud, S. (1993) *Understanding Comics: The Invisible Art.* New York: Harper Perennial.
Mikkonen, K. (2017) *The Narratology of Comic Art.* Abingdon: Routledge.
Miodrag, H. (2013) *Comics and Language: Reimagining Critical Discourse on the Form.* Jackson: University Press of Mississippi.
Peeters, B. (1991) *Case, planche, récit: Comment lire une bande dessinée.* Paris: Casterman.
Varnum, R., and Gibbons, C. (2007) *The Language of Comics: Word and Image.* Jackson: University Press of Mississippi.

## Semiotics

A semiotic approach to comics seeks to identify the SIGNS that constitute the comic as a signifying text. Its roots are in Ferdinand de Saussure's model of LANGUAGE as a system of signs which consist of a signifier, its audio or visual MATERIAL manifestation, and a signified, its meaning, as proposed in the *Course in General Linguistics* of 1916 (1959). This may be generalised, as in the work of Charles Sanders Peirce (1998), into broader categories of meaningful phenomena, including INDEXICAL (material or physical TRACES of a meant event), symbolic (conventionally determined meanings), and ICONIC (meaning by resemblance). Michael Halliday, Robert Hodge, and Gunther Kress further distinguish a social semiotics (Halliday 1978, Hodge and Kress 1988), which treats meaning-making through semiosis as a negotiated and evolving social activity, rather than signs as elements of an agreed code. Semiotician Umberto Eco produced seminal analyses of comics, including "The Myth of Superman" (1972) and "A Reading of Steve Canyon" (Eco 1965). The READING of comics as texts made of signs, selected from a paradigm of possibilities and laid out in SEQUENCE according to coded syntagms, following de Saussure's account, is foundational to treatments of comics as parallel to language (Cohn 2013, Bramlett 2019). This approach is subject to criticism on the basis that comics texts cannot be broken down into isolatable signs in this way (Miodrag 2013).

Paul F. Davies

## *References*

Bramlett, F. (2019) 'Why There Is No "Language of Comics"' in F. L. Aldama (ed.) *The Oxford Handbook of Comic Book Studies.* Oxford: Oxford University Press. Available at: https://www.oxfordhandbooks.com/view/10.1093/oxfordhb/9780190917944.001.0001/oxfordhb-9780190917944-e-2 [Accessed 10 August 2020].

Cohn, N. (2013) *The Visual Language of Comics: Introduction to the Structure and Cognition of Sequential Images.* London: Bloomsbury Academic.

Eco, U. (1972) "The Myth of Superman," *Diacritics* 2(1), pp. 14–22.

Eco, U. (1965) "A Reading of Steve Canyon." Reprint 1976. *Twentieth Century Studies* 15–16, pp. 19–33.

Halliday, M. A. K. (1978) *Language as Social Semiotic: The Social Interpretation of Language and Meaning.* Baltimore: University Park Press.

Hodge, B. and Kress, G. R. (1988) *Social Semiotics.* Ithaca: Cornell University Press.

Miodrag, H. (2013) *Comics and Language: Reimagining Critical Discourse on the Form.* Jackson: University Press of Mississippi.

Peirce, C. S. (1893–1913) *The Essential Peirce, Volume 2: Selected Philosophical Writings, 1893–1913.* Peirce Edition Project (ed.), 1998. Bloomington: Indiana University Press.

de Saussure, F. (1916) *Course in General Linguistics.* Translated from French by W. Baskin, 1959. New York: Philosophical Library.

## Senses

Senses can be understood as physiological systems enabling living beings to experience their bodies and environment through the processing of stimuli. HISTORICALLY a five-sense model incorporating sight, hearing, touch, taste, and smell has been dominant in culture, but science has long accepted that there are more than five senses and (depending on the model) includes senses such as pain, mechanoreception (e.g. balance), and blood pressure (Howes 2009: 24). The senses play a role in various philosophies, most notably phenomenology (e.g. Merleau-Ponty 2002: 240–282), which is concerned with perception and experience, but they also connect to MATERIALITY, PRODUCTION, and RECEPTION. COMICS STUDIES is generally ocularcentric, understanding the senses other than sight only as metaphorical and implicit in a *visual* presentation (McCloud 1994: 118–137). The physical senses are rarely addressed in Comics Studies (Hague 2014, Lord 2016), but do appear in some studies of reception, in which READERS often remark on "the comic as a physical object – an object experienced" (Gibson 2015: 102). An increasing focus on comics' materiality in comic studies since the mid-2010s and the development of sensory studies as a more coherent grouping at the intersection of various disciplines suggest a route by which the senses might be more substantively incorporated into the study of comics in the longer term.

Ian Hague

### *References*

Gibson, M. (2015) *Remembered Reading: Memory, Comics and Post-War Constructions of British Girlhood.* Leuven: Leuven University Press.

Hague, I. (2014) *Comics and the Senses: A Multisensory Approach to Comics and Graphic Novels.* Abingdon: Routledge.

Lord, L. (2016) *Comics: The (Not Only) Visual Medium.* MSc. Massachusetts Institute of Technology. Available at: http://hdl.handle.net/1721.1/106761 [Accessed 30 April 2020].

McCloud, S. (1993) *Understanding Comics: The Invisible Art.* New York: Harper Perennial.

Merleau-Ponty, M. (1945) *Phenomenology of Perception.* Translated from French by Colin Smith, 2002. Abingdon: Routledge.

## SEQUENCE

The sequence in comics is a series of consecutive PANELS displaying coherent or related contents, a part of the FORMAL apparatus of comics. Sequences often form NARRATIVE progressions, though in ABSTRACT COMICS they may be held together by visual coherence and dynamics instead, as Andrei Molotiu argues (2012). The sequence of panels is a central principle in many definitions of comics, inspiring Will Eisner to label comics "sequential art" (1985), and leading to Scott McCloud's elaboration of comics as "juxtaposed pictorial and other images in deliberate sequence" (1994: 9). Thierry Groensteen is one of the foremost theorists of the sequence in comics, suggesting the key concept of "iconic solidarity" as the condition that provides the sequence of IMAGES with its signifying potential (2007: 18). The condition of ICONIC solidarity, with images being both co-present on the PAGE ('in praesentia'), yet separated from one another (by FRAMES and GUTTERS), is what allows panels in a sequence to take on syntagmatic meaning that requires the panels to be READ in relation to one another in order to be fully understood (Postema 2013: 57). The sequence of panels is the main means by which comics represent the passing of TIME, and thus the action of events taking place.

Barbara Postema

### *References*

Eisner, W. (1985) *Comics and Sequential Art.* Tamarac: Poorhouse Press.

Groensteen, T. (1999) *The System of Comics.* Translated from French by B. Beaty and N. Nguyen, 2007. Jackson: University Press of Mississippi.

McCloud, S. (1993) *Understanding Comics: The Invisible Art.* New York: Harper Perennial.

Molotiu, A. (2012) "Abstract Form: Sequential Dynamism and Iconostasis in Abstract Comics and in Steve Ditko's *Amazing Spider-Man*" in Smith, M. J. and Duncan, R. (eds.) *Critical Approaches to Comics: Theories and Methods.* Abingdon: Routledge, pp. 84–100.

Postema, B. (2013) *Narrative Structure in Comics: Making Sense of Fragments.* Rochester: Rochester Institute of Technology Press.

## Serialisation

Serialisation is a way of PUBLISHING long-form works in short instalments over a period of time, common since the Victorian era (Gordon 1998, Meyer 2019). As a publishing practice, serialisation is often chosen for economic reasons, as it spreads the cost of publication across multiple, cheaper issues, while the CREATOR or publisher of the work can get paid for these issues even if the work as a whole is not yet complete. Another reason for serialisation is to create interest from READERS and test the popularity of a work as it is still in progress. Jennifer Hayward discusses the influence of letters from readers on Milt Caniff's continuity strip *Terry and the Pirates*, for example. Serial NARRATIVE can be found in most narrative MEDIA, including PRINT, FILM, radio, and television, as well as TRANSMEDIALITY (Allen and van den Berg 2014). Individual instalments in serials may be able to stand alone, but more often they require the previous and following instalments to be successful in their narrative and entertainment. Many serials rely on short-term storylines and long ongoing narrative arcs, often with the ending forever deferred. In comics, serialisation occurs in NEWSPAPER STRIPS, COMIC BOOKS, comics magazines, and WEBCOMICS. Previously serialised narratives may be collected into ALBUMS, trade paperbacks, and marketed as GRAPHIC NOVELS.

Barbara Postema

### *References*

Allen, R. and van den Berg, T. (2014) *Serialization in Popular Culture.* Abingdon: Routledge.

Gordon, I. (1998) *Comics Strips and Consumer Culture, 1890–1945.* Washington: Smithsonian Institution Press.

Hayward, J. (1997) *Consuming Pleasures: Active Audiences and Serial Fictions From Dickens to Soap Opera.* Lexington: University Press of Kentucky.

Meyer, C. (2019) *Producing Mass Entertainment: The Serial Life of the Yellow Kid.* Columbus: The Ohio State University Press.

## SEXUALITY

Sexuality is the interplay of sexual behaviour, orientations, and IDENTITIES. Robert A. Padgug describes it as "a group of social relations, of human interactions" (2007: 23). Sexuality is often considered on an individual, "fixed" level, that is constructed within "private" spheres (i.e. the home, the family, the bedroom), rather than on a wider, "public" socio-economic level (ibid. 20). This individualistic, private view of sexuality was, in Western society, a development of the seventeenth century (Foucault 1978: 3). However, sexuality is an intrinsic part of society, and cannot be disengaged from CLASS and politics (Padgug 2007: 19). As sexuality is tied to society and social constructions, sexual reality "changes within individuals, within genders, and within societies, just as it differs from gender to gender, from class to class, and from society to society (...) the history of sexuality is therefore the history of a subject whose meaning and contents are in a continual process of change" (ibid. 22–23). QUEER theory argues that a sexual "norm" can only be defined in society by reference to anti-normative, queer sexualities (Goldman 1996: 169). Meg-John Barker and Jules Scheele's comic *Sexuality: A Graphic Guide* (2021), a follow-up to their *Queer: A Graphic History* (2016), offers an exploration of sexuality in comics FORM.

Olivia Hicks

### *References*

Foucault, M. (1976) *The History of Sexuality, Volume 1: An Introduction.* Translated from French by R. Hurley, 1990. New York: Vintage.

Goldman, R. (1996) "Who Is That *Queer* Queer? Exploring Norms around Sexuality, Race, and Class in Queer Theory" in Beemyn, B. and Eliason, M. (eds.) *Queer Studies: A Lesbian, Gay, Bisexual, and Transgender Anthology.* New York: New York University Press, pp. 169–182.

Padgug, R. A. (2007) "Sexual matters: On conceptualizing sexuality in history" in Parker, R. and Aggleton, P. (eds.) *Culture, Society and Sexuality: A Reader.* Abingdon: Routledge, pp. 17–30.

## Shapereader

At the crossroads of DISABILITY STUDIES, DESIGN, and COMICS STUDIES, Shapereader is a system of tactile storytelling that was initially conceptualised for READERS and makers of comics with visual impairment. Initially funded by the Kone Foundation in Helsinki and designed by ARTIST and researcher Ilan Manouach, Shapereader is a trans-disciplinary, inclusive project that challenges able-body assumptions within the visual predominance ethos of comics; it promotes an embodied, non-retinal, NARRATIVE experience by transposing SEMANTIC cognition to the reader's fingertips. Its design is based on a growing repertoire of tactile ideograms (tactigrams) intended to provide haptic equivalents for all the semantic features, the conceptual functions, and textual attributes of a narrative (Kartalopoulos 2016). *Arctic Circle*, the first narrative work built on tactigrams, is an original novel of fifty-seven content pages and six communication boards, allowing the reader to get acquainted with the narrative's semantic content, conveniently sorted in elementary categories: characters, objects, settings, actions, affections, graphic, and textual devices (Dunne 2016). Since 2016, Shapereader has been developing an international outreach through artist conferences, workshops, and exhibitions unfolding in a variety of FORMATS and COLLABORATIONS situated in diverse fields of expertise and contexts. In 2019 the project's resources have also found application in MUSICAL notation under the titles *Tangible Natives* ("Ilan Manouach & Maria Arnal" 2020) and *Coro Shapereader* ("Coro Shapereader" 2019).

Ilan Manouach

## *References*

"Coro Shapereader." (2019) *Tabakalera*, June 2019. Available at: https://www.tabakalera.eu/es/coro-shapereader [Accessed 5 May 2020].

Dunne, C. (2016) "A Conceptual Artist Designs Tactile Comic Books for Blind Readers." *Hyperallergic*, 5 August 2016. Available at: https://hyperallergic.com/312333/a-conceptual-artist-designs-tactile-comic-books-for-blind-readers/ [Accessed 5 May 2020].

"Ilan Manouach & Maria Arnal, 'Tangible Natives.'" (2020) *Vooruit*, 7 March 2020. Available at: https://www.vooruit.be/en/

agenda/2549/_Tangible_Natives_/Ilan_Manouach_Maria_Arnal/ [Accessed 5 May 2020].

Kartalopoulos, B. (2016) "Ilan Manouach: Defamiliarising Comics." *World Literature Today*, March 2016. Available at: https://www.worldliteraturetoday.org/2016/march/ilan-manouach-defamiliarizing-comics-bill-kartalopoulos [Accessed 8 May 2020].

## Shōjo

Shōjo (girls) ostensibly indicates Japanese comics created for an AUDIENCE of elementary to high school-aged female READERS (Schodt 1983). Like SHŌNEN MANGA, however, this division often merely indicates the intended demographics of the magazine in which the comic originally appeared. Also like shōnen manga, shōjo manga often has a READERSHIP that expands beyond the purported readership of the magazines to include older women as well as boys and men (Schodt 1996). Although shōjo is not a term that indicates GENRE per se (and can encompass all types of STORIES including sports and SCIENCE FICTION), there are STEREOTYPICAL ARTISTIC (soft LINES, expressively large eyes) and storytelling (an emphasis on friendship and ROMANCE) CONVENTIONS common to many shōjo manga. These types of stories first appeared in the early twentieth century and continued through the post-World War II years, with particularly revolutionary changes occurring in the 1970s by female artists associated with the informal Nijūyo-nen Gumi (Year 24 Group, named because many of them were born in or around Showa 24 (1949)) (Thorn 2005: 130). This change in AUTHORSHIP also reflected a change in the subjects and THEMES of shōjo stories, sometimes questioning and pushing back on the received and accepted GENDER roles of earlier shōjo works. Additionally, these works introduced male homosexual elements, which would go on to create the foundation for boys' love (BL) and "yaoi" comics (McLelland 2015).

Brian Ruh

## *References*

McLelland, M., Nagaike, K., Suganuma, K. and Welker, J. (eds.) (2015) *Boys Love Manga and Beyond: History, Culture, and Community in Japan*. Jackson: University Press of Mississippi.

Schodt, F. L. (1983) *Manga! Manga!: The world of Japanese comics*. Tokyo: Kodansha International.

Schodt, F. L. (1996) *Dreamland Japan: Writings on modern manga*. Berkeley: Stone Bridge Press.

Thorn, R. (2005) "The Magnificent Forty-Niners," *The Comics Journal* 269, pp. 130–133.

## Shōnen

Termed comics "for boys" in the Japanese MANGA landscape (often contrasted with comics "for girls," or SHŌJO), shōnen manga encompass some of the best-selling comics in Japan. The flagship *Weekly Shōnen Jump* has long been one of the top-selling magazines in the world, as well as the most popular manga magazine among Japanese girls as well as boys (Schodt 1996). These comic magazines grew out of pre-war magazines for children, although the FORM and content changed in the post-war years as demand for mass entertainment increased (Thorn 2006: 28). Some early shōnen titles featured activities that were considered antisocial, such as an emphasis on eroticism, drinking, and fighting, making them unpopular with parents. Over time, many of shōnen manga's rough edges were filed off and the form became more acceptable, with thematic emphasis on friendship, hard work, and victory (Zoth 2011). Many of these THEMES are present to a greater or lesser degree whether the actual GENRE of the title is sports, SCIENCE FICTION, or ROMANCE (Drummond-Matthews 2010: 64–70). Once a READER ages out of shōnen manga titles, they can move on to "seinen" (youth) comics, aimed at young adult men, whose titles may be somewhat more serious in tone and may deal with more risqué or mature themes (Schodt 1983).

Brian Ruh

### *References*

Drummond-Mathews, A. (2010) "What Boys Will Be: A Study of Shōnen Manga" in Johnson-Woods, T. (ed.) *Manga: An Anthology of Global and Cultural Perspectives.* New York: Continuum.

Schodt, F. L. (1983) *Manga! Manga!: The world of Japanese comics.* Tokyo: Kodansha International.

Schodt, F. L. (1996) *Dreamland Japan: Writings on modern manga.* Berkeley: Stone Bridge Press.

Thorn, R. (2006) "Japan: The Hollywood of Manga," *Japan Echo* 33(2), pp. 28–31.

Zoth, T. (2011) "The Politics of One Piece: Political Critique in Oda's Water Seven," *Forum For World Literature Studies* 3(1), pp. 107–117.

## Sign

Charles Sanders Peirce classifies signs as (1) INDEXICAL, signifying by a physical connection between the signifier as a TRACE of what it signifies; (2) ICONIC, signifying by resemblance between the signifier and that which it signifies; and (3) Symbolic, signifying only via a learned set of CONVENTIONS, or code, which associates one arbitrary signifier to a signified of any kind (Peirce 1998, Atkin 2013). There are limits on the extent to which any sign is truly arbitrary, and a sign may share in more than one of these features. Indeed, Peirce proposed extended ranges of classification during the development of this theory, but these three are the most commonly used. Note that these categories do not match those used by Scott McCloud in *Understanding Comics* (1993), where he takes non-MIMETIC "symbols" to be a subcategory of "icon."

Paul F. Davies

### *References*

Atkin, A. (2013) "Peirce's Theory of Signs" in Zalta, E. N. (ed.) *The Stanford Encyclopedia of Philosophy.* Summer 2013 edition. Available at: https://plato.stanford.edu/archives/sum2013/entries/peirce-semiotics/ [Accessed 19 February 2020].

McCloud, S. (1993) *Understanding Comics: The Invisible Art*. New York: Harper Perennial.

Peirce, C. S. (1893–1913) *The Essential Peirce, Volume 2: Selected Philosophical Writings, 1893–1913*. Peirce Edition Project (ed.), 1998. Bloomington: Indiana University Press.

## Silent Comics

Silent comics are a FORMALLY defined sub-GENRE of comics: these are comics that forego verbal TEXT in CAPTION BOXES and SPEECH BALLOONS, relying only on IMAGES, PANELS, and PAGE LAYOUT to convey their NARRATIVE. ABSTRACT COMICS, which are not narrative, also tend to be WORDLESS (Postema 2019: 288), but silent comics can certainly be used to tell STORIES. Silent comics are not IMAGETEXTS and thus take an interesting theoretical position within the comics form, as they do not demonstrate one of the basic formal definitions of comics: the combination of image and text. Silent comics demonstrate the importance of SEQUENTIAL images in creating visual narrative, as well as numerous types of visual signification (Beronä 2002: 38). During the nineteenth century, silent comics developed amongst the many formal variations of comics narrative (Smolderen 2014: 113–117, Kunzle 2001: 5). Throughout the twentieth century they were a small but constant part of comics PRODUCTION, particularly in NEWSPAPERS STRIPS, woodcut novels, and small press or EXPERIMENTAL COMICS (Groensteen 1997). Into the twenty-first century, silent comics have become increasingly visible, both in GRAPHIC NOVELS and in children's comics. The types of stories in silent comics span the spectrum from visual GAGS (Mordillo, *Mordillo Cartoons Opus 1,* 1980, and Vandenbroucke, *White Cube,* 2014), to psychological explorations (Castrée, *Die Fabrik*, 2000, and Sacco, *Josephine*, 2017), to narratives addressing contemporary social issues (Kuper, *The System,* 1997, and Ma, *Leaf*, 2015) and beyond.

Barbara Postema

## *References*

Beronä, D. A. (2002) "Pictures Speak in Comics without Words: Pictorial Principles in the Work of Milt Gross, Hendrik Dorgathen, Eric Drooker, and Peter Kuper" in Varnum, R. and Gibbons, C. T. (eds.) *The Language of Comics: Word and Image*. Jackson: University Press of Mississippi, pp. 19–39.

Groensteen, T. (1997) "Histoire de la bande dessinée muette, deuxième partie," *9e Art* 3, pp. 92–105.

Kunzle, D. (2001) "The Voices of Silence: Willette, Steinlen, and the Introduction of the Silent Strip in the *Chat Noir*, with a German Coda" in Varnum, R., and Gibbons, C. T. (eds.) *The Language of Comics: Word and Image*. Jackson: University Press of Mississippi, pp. 3–18.

Postema, B. (2019) "Adding up to What? Degrees of Narrative in Wordless Abstract Comics" in Rommens, A., Crucifix, B., Dozo, B., Dejasse, E., and Turnes, P. (eds.) *Abstraction and Comics / Bande dessinée et abstraction*, Volume 1. Liège: La Cinquième *Couche* / Presses Universitaires de Liège, pp. 285–298.

Smolderen, T. (2000) *The Origins of Comics: From William Hogarth to Winsor McCay*. Translated from French by B. Beaty and N. Nguyen, 2014. Jackson: University Press of Mississippi.

## Situationism

Situationism was a cultural, political, and philosophical movement that was devoted to a revolutionary critique of capitalist society and contemporary culture. Led by Guy Debord, the movement was launched in 1957 out of a split from the LITERARY movement of Lettrism, which had in turn evolved out of Surrealism. The Situationists critiqued what they saw as Western society's wholesale absorption by MEDIA and COMMODITY consumption and the consequent loss of freedom and humanity (Ford 2005, Knabb 2006, Zacarias and Hemmens 2020). One technique used by the Situationists to break through this dystopian condition was DÉTOURNEMENT, which altered existing TEXTS or IMAGES to insert a political critique into them (Zacarias 2020). The Situationists influenced the May 1968 uprising in Paris and many subsequent cultural and political movements but dissolved themselves as an organisation in 1972.

Doug Singsen

## *References*

Ford, S. (2005) *The Situationist International: A User's Guide*. Revised and expanded edition. London: Black Dog.

Knabb, K. (ed.) (2006) *Situationist International Anthology*. Berkeley: Bureau of Public Secrets.

Zacarias, G. (2020) "Détournement in Language and the Visual Arts" in Zacarias, G. and Hemmens, A. (eds.) *The Situationist International: A Critical Handbook*. London: Pluto, pp. 214–235.

Zacarias, G. and Hemmens, A. (eds.) (2020) *The Situationist International: A Critical Handbook*. London: Pluto.

## SLASH

Slash is a ROMANTIC GENRE of FAN FICTION or fan ART usually featuring male-male pairings. It is primarily created by and for straight women (Thorn 2003: 169–170). The first known instance originated in *Star Trek* fandom and featured a Kirk/Spock pairing, and the term itself comes from the slash between the two names (Jenkins 1992). The pairings usually are from a known piece of MEDIA, including comics, but are known to extend to CELEBRITIES and sports figures (Waysdorf 2015: n.p.). English language slash fiction usually takes the FORM of LITERATURE or art, and more rarely the form of a comic. Genres similar in type have independently developed in Sinophone countries with "danmei," which similarly takes mostly a literary format and sometimes is behind a paywall (Madill, Zhao, and Fan 2018: 418–419), and in Japan with the BL genre, which is primarily comics (Thorn 2003: 169–170).

Zu Dominiak.

## *References*

Jenkins, H. (1992) *Textual Poachers: Television Fans and Participatory Culture*. Abingdon: Routledge.

Madill, A., Zhao, Y. and Fan, L. (2018) "Male-male marriage in Sinophone and Anglophone Harry Potter danmei and slash," *Journal of Graphic Novels and Comics* 9(5), pp. 418–434.

Thorn, R. M. (2003) "Girls And Women Getting Out Of Hand: The Pleasure and Politics of Japan's Amateur Comics Community" in Kelly, W. W. (ed.) *Fanning the Flames: Fandoms and Consumer Culture in Contemporary Japan*. New York: State University of New York Press, pp. 169–187.

Waysdorf, A. (2015) "The creation of football slash fan fiction," *Transformative Works and Cultures* 19, n.p. Available at: https://journal.transformativeworks.org/index.php/twc/article/view/588/489 [Accessed 1 August 2020].

## Somaesthetics

A branch of philosophy coined by Richard Shusterman, somaesthetics means to displace the mind/body hierarchy as it "can be provisionally defined as the critical, meliorative study of the experience and use of one's body as a locus of sensory-aesthetic appreciation ('aisthesis') and creative self-fashioning" (Shusterman 1999: 302). Built on the phenomenological work of Charles Sanders Peirce, somaesthetics is "aimed at creating disruptive effects in DISCOURSE that allow embodied subjects to confront normalisation" (Jolles 2012: 309). For comics, it is a critical line of inquiry that confronts the notion that the depicted IMAGE is largely imitative of the natural and an obviously suggestive means for rhetorical, dramatic, and poetic effect. Somaesthetics, then, emphasises that the lexical and graphic work can challenge the relationship between what is seen, the viewer's perception, and its meaning. In this sense, the depicted image signals its own uncanny valley—not merely in the traditional sense in which a synthetic depiction of human or humanness generates an unsettling quality of the missing "humanness," but in that a "pragmatic dimension will always presuppose that analytic dimension. But it transcends mere analysis not simply by evaluating the facts that analysis describes, but by proposing various methods to improve certain facts by remaking the body and society" (Shusterman 1999: 305).

Eric Atkinson

## *References*

Jolles, M. (2012) "Between Embodied Subjects and Objects: Narrative Somaesthetics," *Hypatia* 27(2), pp. 301–318.

Shusterman, R. (1999) "Somaesthetics: A Disciplinary Proposal," *The Journal of Aesthetics and Art Criticism* 57(3), pp. 299–313.

## Sound

Sound in comics is usually REPRESENTED by either visual IMAGERY or TEXT-based sound effects. Due to the limits of available COMPOSITIONAL SPACE, only sounds that serve as significant AESTHETIC or NARRATIVE elements are typically represented on the page, representations that involve written text will often display "a high level of phonetic realism. A car … [emits] … a 'roooaaar' or a 'vroom vroom'" (Lacassin 2014: 40). The visual DESIGN of these textual elements can also be used to evoke the audible qualities of the sounds being DEPICTED. SPEECH BALLOONS are another common visual device used to represent audible elements within a narrative. While comics are primarily discussed in terms of their representational use of sound, some comics formats may also involve elements of audible sound. Ian Hague asserts that in PRINTED COMIC BOOKS, "the sound of a turning page emphasises the 'objectness' of the comic" (2014: 72). While often considered "incidental," such sounds can potentially "tell the reader certain things about the progression of the text and modification of the comic as an object" (65). Some types of DIGITAL COMICS have also been described as "audible comics" due to their incorporation of audible sound effects and MUSICAL elements (Goodbrey 2017: 145).

Daniel Merlin Goodbrey

## *References*

Goodbrey, D. (2017) "The Impact of Digital Mediation and Hybridisation on the Form of Comics." PhD. University of Hertfordshire.

Hague, I. (2014) *Comics and the Senses: A Multisensory Approach to Comics and Graphic Novels*. Abingdon: Routledge.

Lacassin, F. (1971) "Dictionary Definition" in Miller, A. and Beaty, B. (eds.) *The French Comics Theory Reader.* Translated from French by A. Miller and B. Beaty. Reprint 2014. Leuven: Leuven University Press, pp. 39–46.

## Space

Space in comics is central to the MEDIUM'S practice and definition since comics are a visual ART (Lessing 1984, Groensteen 2018). Contrary to other visual mediums such as painting, TIME is also essential in comics because comics are also a NARRATIVE art. Space plays a role on various levels: inside the PANEL; in the size and shape of the panels; in the ordering, PAGE LAYOUT, or COMPOSITION of panels; in their distribution on the page; and in their inter-connections. Like a painter does with a painting, a comics ARTIST plays with space first in a single-FRAME comic, although time can also be expressed in a single frame (McCloud 1999, 95). Comics traditionally use multiple, consecutive panels, but their order and distribution on the page is meaningful. The frames are usually rectangular, but artists have creatively manipulated frame shapes since the beginnings of comics in order to reinforce the content. See, for example, the works of comics pioneer Rodolphe Töpffer and Winsor McCay's *Little Sammy Sneeze* (1904–1906). It is worth noting that just as there are WORDLESS COMICS, there are also frameless comics, for example, Will Eisner's *A Contract with God* (1978). Typically, Western readers are expected to first face the page or even spread as a whole, and then transverse it from left to right and top to bottom (Groensteen 2007). Furthermore, Thierry Groensteen demonstrates how the medium also allows for the creation of virtual spaces when connections are established across the whole COMIC BOOK, through BRAIDING. Finally, DIGITAL COMICS open a new type of space—the "infinite canvas" (McCloud 2000).

Chris Reyns-Chikuma

### *References*

Groensteen, T. (1999) *The System of Comics.* Translated from French by B. Beaty and N. Nguyen, 2007. Jackson: University Press of Mississippi.

Groensteen, T. (2018) *L'excellence de chaque art.* Tours: Presses Universitaires François Rabelais.

Lessing, G. E. (1767) *Laocoön: An Essay of the Limits of Painting and Poetry*. Translated from German by E. A. McCormick, 1984. Baltimore: Johns Hopkins University Press.

McCloud, S. (1993) *Understanding Comics: The Invisible Art*. New York: Harper Perennial.

McCloud, S. (2000) *Reinventing Comics: How Imagination and Technology are Revolutionising an Artform*. New York: Paradox Press.

## Spatial Projection System

A spatial projection system is a closed system of visual REPRESENTATION in which, for example, the topological location of MARKS on a two-dimensional surface systematically corresponds to the relative proximities between three-dimensional coordinates found in the object of representation (Grennan 2017: 36). Systematic equivalence of the location of two-dimensional marks and three-dimensional coordinates governs all such spatial projection systems, including those that calculate and produce the location of a horizon and horizon lines, VANISHING POINT, and POINT OF VIEW (Andersen 2007, Jarombek 1990). John Willats defines these as "systems that map the spatial relations between features of the scene into corresponding relations on the picture surface" (Willats 2006: n.p.). Patrick Maynard notes that spatial projection systems guide the location of marks independently from the shape of the marks themselves (Maynard 2005: 19–52).

Simon Grennan

### *References*

Andersen, K. (2007) *The Geometry of an Art: The History of the Mathematical Theory of Perspective from Alberti to Monge*. Berlin: Springer.

Jarombek, M. (1990) "The Structural Problematic of Leon Battista Alberti's De picture," *Renaissance Studies* 4(3), pp. 273–285.

Maynard, P. (2005) *Drawing Distinctions: The Varieties of Graphic Expression*. Ithaca: Cornell University Press.

Willats, J. (2006) "Ambiguity in Drawing," *Tracey*, n.p. Available at: https://www.lboro.ac.uk/microsites/sota/tracey/journal/ambi/images/Willats.pdf [Accessed 14 August 2020].

## Spatio-Topia

Spatio-topia is a concept in Thierry Groensteen's comics-specific semiotics. Rather than trying to identify "minimal signifying units," Groensteen approaches comics at "the level of grand articulations" (2007: 5). His starting point is the COMIC BOOK, as a collection of IMAGES that are separate from one another, and which create meaning through a co-presentation of elements (ibid. 18). Spatio-topia is the organisation of the different elements of the comics page (ibid. 21). For Groensteen, the spatio-topical organisation and development of the space of the comics page is not subordinate to an intended, pre-existing NARRATIVE in the mind of the CREATOR. Rather, "from the instant that an author begins the comics story (…), he thinks of this story, and his work still to be born, within a given mental form [the spatio-topia] with which he must negotiate" (ibid.). In practice, a comics ARTIST's spatio-topic decisions appear most visibly as PAGE LAYOUT (ibid. 91).

Rik Spanjers

### *References*

Groensteen, T. (1999) *The System of Comics*. Translated from French by B. Beaty and N. Nguyen, 2007. Jackson: University Press of Mississippi.

## Speech Balloons

Speech balloons are one of the most recognisable characteristics of comics. The by now CONVENTIONAL form of the speech balloon is a circular LINE DRAWN around dialogue, with a tail that points towards the speaking character. If no tail is present, the speech balloon is ascribed to the character standing closest to it or to someone standing outside of the PANEL. Here, however, it is important to distinguish between the circular speech balloon, which indicates dialogue, and the square CAPTION BOX, which conventionally indicates external and/or internal NARRATION. In his documentation of the HISTORY of the speech balloon, Thierry Smolderen traces its origin in graphic SATIRE years before it became a common staple of the comics MEDIUM. Initially, comics did not provide dialogue between characters and only included labels with captions. The speech balloon's lines are usually smooth, but can be used to indicate mood or tone by a double outline, dashed lines, or spikier and jagged lines (Eisner 2008). The COLOUR, shape, and boldness of the LETTERING inside the speech balloon can also serve to indicate the mood and MODE of the character's speech. The speech balloon is also distinct from the THOUGHT BUBBLE, which indicates a character's thoughts. Neil Cohn considers the speech balloon to be indicative of "the integration of text and image into a meaningful whole" (Cohn 2013: 37).

Esther De Dauw

## *References*

Cohn, N. (2013) "Beyond word balloons and thought bubbles: The integration of text and image," *Semiotica* 197, pp. 35–63.

Eisner, W. (1985) *Comics and Sequential Art: Principles and Practices from the Legendary Cartoonist.* Reprint 2008. New York: W. W. Norton & Company.

Smolderen, T. (2000) *The Origins of Comics: From William Hogarth to Winsor McCay.* Translated from French by B. Beaty and N. Nguyen, 2014. Jackson: University Press of Mississippi.

## Splash

Splash is often used interchangeably with "full page," "full page panel," or in the combination "splash panel" or "splash page," meaning a PANEL that takes up a whole comics PAGE (Duncan and Smith 2009). Often this splash page is used as a title page in the beginning of a STORY to draw the READER in, to set the scene in terms of time and space, or to focus the reader's attention on a character. Splash is sometimes also used to describe several pages: "One variation of the complex polyptych panel are 'splash' pages and the use of large panels as spreads. Typically, a splash panel evokes movement or a series of actions in static form" (Mikkonen 2016: 57). Because every panel balances between its linear and tabular qualities, caught between being embedded in a SERIES and being read as part of a whole page (Fresnault-Deruelle 1976), the splash presents a particular example that tones down the panel's linear connection and can emphasise its momentous TEMPORALITY (Cortsen 2014) as well as underline a shock effect or action.

Rikke Platz Cortsen

## *References*

Cortsen, R. P. (2014) "Full Page Insight: The Apocalyptic Moment in Comics Written by Alan Moore," *Journal of Graphic Novels and Comics* 5(4), pp. 397–410.

Duncan, R. and Smith, M. J. (eds.) (2009) "Glossary" in Duncan, R. and Smith, M. J. (eds.) *The Power of Comics: History, Form and Culture*. New York: Continuum, pp. 315–320.

Fresnault-Deruelle, P. (1976) "Du linéaire au tabulaire," *Communications* 24(1), pp. 7–23.

Mikkonen, K. (2017) *The Narratology of Comic Art. Abingdon:* Routledge.

## Stereotypes

Richard Dyer (2002) usefully distinguishes between typing and stereotyping. Typing is a SEMIOTIC activity necessary to make sense of the world: we need classifications in order to recognise individual objects. For instance, walking into a room for the first time, we can still recognise a particular object as a table. Stereotyping, in contrast, "reduces people to a few, simple, essential characteristics, which are represented as fixed by Nature" (Hall 1997), and functions to uphold power inequalities between social groups. For example, women are stereotyped as emotional, an assignment that is ascribed to their biological make-up. Supposedly, consequently, women are considered less fit to hold positions of authority, which keeps the power inequality between the sexes in place. As such, stereotypes work to maintain divisions between an unmarked dominant group and a marked, because stereotyped, "Other." Think of whiteness operating as an unspecified norm from which stereotyped people of colour deviate (i.e. the distinction between a lawyer and a black lawyer) (Dyer 1997). COMICS STUDIES can scrutinise REPRESENTATIONS that either uphold existing stereotypes or attempt to undermine them (Ayaka and Hague 2015, Gateward and Jennings 2015).

Roel van den Oever

## *References*

Ayaka, C. and Hague, I. (eds.) (2015) *Representing Multiculturalism in Comics and Graphic Novels.* Abingdon: Routledge.

Dyer, R. (1997) *White.* Abingdon: Routledge.

Dyer, R. (1979) "The Role of Stereotypes" in Dyer, R. (ed.) *The Matter of Images: Essays on Representation.* 2nd edition. Reprint 2002. Abingdon: Routledge, pp. 11–18.

Foss, C., Gray, J., and Whalen, Z. (eds.) (2016) *Disability in Comic Books and Graphic Narratives.* London: Palgrave Macmillan.

Gateward, F. and Jennings, J. (eds.) (2015) *The Blacker the Ink: Constructions of Black Identity in Comics and Sequential Art.* New Brunswick: Rutgers University Press.

Hall, S. (1997) *Representation: Cultural Representations and Signifying Practices.* London: SAGE.

## Story

Although there is a wide range of theoretical terminology describing story, according to different theories of NARRATIVE, these theories broadly share the foundational concept that story encompasses what is told or shown, as structurally and functionally distinct from the activities of telling or showing, following, among others, Harald Weinrich's or Émile Benveniste's identification of story ("erzählte welt," "histoire") and its discursive means ("besprochene welt," "discours"), extrapolated by Seymour Chatman as two distinct TEMPORAL INDICES (Weinrich 1964, Benveniste 1971, Chatman 1978). A number of other influential ideas complicate this relationship, as a definition of narrative, such as the distinction between the constitutive elements of the world of a story, which are known only in the telling or showing of the story, or FABULA and the way in which these elements are arranged as an individual iteration of incidents, plot, or *SJUŽET (*Shklovsky 2012). Theoretical distinctions between the functions of telling and showing, described by Plato as DIEGESIS and MIMESIS (Plato 2008: 3.392c–398b), further complicate definitions of story in cases of visual REPRESENTATION. Historically excluded from narration due to logocentric definitions of UTTERANCE and NARRATOR, these have only recently been challenged by

TRANSMEDIA theories, for example, or MEDIA-specific NARRATOLOGICAL concepts, in which the unique affordances of specific media themselves define narrative functions, as in Marion's concept of the "GRAPHIATEUR" (Baetens 2001).

Simon Grennan

## *References*

Baetens, J. (2001) "Revealing Traces: A New Theory of Graphic Enunciation" in Varnum, R. and Gibbons, C. T. (eds.) *The Language of Comics: Word and Image*. Jackson: University Press of Mississippi, pp. 145–155.

Benveniste, É. (1971) *Problems in General Linguistics*. Coral Gables: University of Miami Press.

Chatman, S. (1978) *Story and Discourse: Narrative Structure in Fiction and Film*. Ithaca: Cornell University Press.

Plato (c. 375 BC) *Republic*. Translated from Greek by R. Waterfield, 2008. Oxford: Oxford University Press.

Shklovsky, V. (1917) "Art as Technique" in Lemon, L. T. and Reis, J. R. (eds.) *Russian Formalist Criticism*. 2nd edition. Reprint 2012. Lincoln: University of Nebraska Press, pp. 3–24.

Weinrich, H. (1964) T*empus – Besprochene und erzählte Welt*. Stuttgart: Kohlhammer.

## Storyworld

Marie-Laure Ryan defines a storyworld as "the world of the characters" (Ryan 2014: 32). In both factual and fictional WRITING, a storyworld extends the DISCOURSE held within the framework of the NARRATIVE, to a place beyond itself; through the collusion of the READER (for it is the reader on whom a storyworld must depend), a "global mental construction" can be formed (Herman 2002: 5). Ryan notes that any multimodal storyworld can be "constantly expand[ed and revised]" by "creators and fans alike" (Ryan & Thon 2014: 1). The reference points for this extended world will fall to the reader: a so-called real world will often suffice, unless the reader is told otherwise (Ryan 2014: 35). Thus, when a character within a story refers to some distant time or place (such as the Wild West) the reader has a set of HISTORICAL, social, and cultural references on which to draw. In COMIC BOOKS, both intradiegetic and extradiegetic elements are at play; the former is the text within the SPEECH BALLOONS representing the mental world of a character. But its presentation—the balloon or FRAME itself—is extradiegetic, with the NARRATOR framing the boundaries of the storyworld. A storyworld is that which is referred to, but unexplained: a moment in the past, a place beyond the horizon.

Paul Jackson

## *References*

Ryan, M.-L. (2014) "Story/Worlds/Media: Tuning the Instruments of a Media-Conscious Narratology" in Ryan, M.-L. and Thon, J.-N. (eds.) *Storyworlds Across Media: Toward a Media-Conscious Narratology.* Lincoln: University of Nebraska Press, pp. 25–49.

Ryan, M.-L. and Thon, J.-N. (2014) "Introduction" in Ryan, M.-L. and Thon, J.-N. (eds.) *Storyworlds Across Media: Toward a Media-Conscious Narratology.* Lincoln: University of Nebraska Press, pp. 1–23.

Herman, D. (2002) *Story Logic: Problems and Possibilities of Narrative.* Lincoln: University of Nebraska Press.

## Structuralism

The underlying principles of structuralism rely on the work of LINGUIST Ferdinand de Saussure, who proposes to study LANGUAGE synchronically, as a closed "system of [linguistic] signs that express ideas" (1959: 16). For de Saussure, the SIGN is composed of a signifier, the "*sound-image*," and the signified, the "*concept*" (1959: 67). As explored by LITERARY critic Roland Barthes, de Saussure's linguistic principles can similarly be applied to the study of cultural texts, as Barthes poses that any text can be understood as a composition of signs that convey culturally specific and dominant ideology through signification (1972a: 113). The structuralist notion that to study a cultural object should reveal "the rules of functioning (the 'functions') of this object" (Barthes 1972b: 214) informed a broad scope of literary and CULTURAL STUDIES research in the 1960s. For the study of comics, structuralism entails a focus not on the meaning, value, or context of a single comic, but on the codes and CONVENTIONS that underlie the structure and meaning of the FORM. Various early theoretical works on the study of comics, primarily in the Franco-Belgian context, build on structuralism, including "the study of comics narrative, often analysed as mythological systems, and (...) the study of comics as graphic language system" (Christiansen and Magnussen 2000: 12).

Freija Camps

## *References*

Barthes, R. (1957) *Mythologies.* Translated from French by A. Lavers, 1972a. New York: Farrar, Straus and Giroux.

Barthes, R. (1964) "The Structuralist Activity" in *Critical Essays.* Translated from French by R. Howard, 1972b. Evanston: Northwestern University Press, pp. 213–220.

Christiansen, H.-C. and Magnussen, A. (2000) "Introduction" in Magnussen, A. and Christiansen, H.-C. (eds.) *Comics and Culture: Analytical and Theoretical Approaches to Comics.* Copenhagen: Museum Tusculanum Press, pp. 7–28.

de Saussure, F. (1916) *Course in General Linguistics.* Translated from French by W. Baskin, 1959. New York: Philosophical Library.

## Style

Style refers to the particular qualities of a comic's visual dimension, most often in terms of such components of the IMAGE as the DRAWING, LAYOUT, and SPEECH BALLOON. According to Kai Mikkonen, "graphic style [functions] as a kind of signature of the story's creation, the image bearing the signs of its making" (2013: 101), which suggests that a TRACE of the ARTIST's subjectivity can be inferred from the drawing. As such, visual style is similar to the auteur theory from FILM studies, in which an artist is considered to imprint their work with an individual and recognisable sensibility. Style may also refer to various NATIONAL traditions of comics art, as well as to the "house style" of individual PUBLISHING companies. Although Gert Meesters has noted that "unity of style" is often considered a "fundamental law of comic art" (qtd. in Groensteen 2013: 113), style may also evolve and change over time, or be varied for effect, as demonstrated by Matt Madden (*99 Ways to Tell a Story: Exercises in Style*, 2005). Crucially, as Anna F. Peppard notes, "in comics, where even the text is drawn and action is abstracted into symbols and iconic fragments, content is especially inseparable from style" (2018: 2), and any responsible analysis ought therefore to consider the two in unison.

Frederik Byrn Køhlert

## *References*

Groensteen, T. (2011) *Comics and Narration*. Translated from French by A. Miller, 2013. Jackson: University Press of Mississippi.

Mikkonen, K. (2013) "Subjectivity and Style in Graphic Narratives" in Stein, D. and Thon, J.-N. (eds.) *From Comic Strips to Graphic Novels: Contributions to the Theory and History of Graphic Narrative*. Berlin: De Gruyter, pp. 101–123.

Peppard, A. F. (2018) "The Power of the Marvel(ous) Image: Reading Excess in the Styles of Todd McFarlane, Jim Lee, and Rob Liefeld," *Journal of Graphic Novels and Comics* 10(3), pp. 1–22.

## Stylistics

Stylistics looks at what is "going on" with a maker's use of LANGUAGE in a work using LINGUISTIC tools to explain the choices they made to express themselves. It may examine character development, dialogue, internal thoughts, FORM, structure, pacing, mood, use of colloquialisms, and/or jargon, among other features. In comics, stylistics must contend with verbal as well visual UTTERANCES, howsoever they appear. In the article *Stylistics in Comics*, Charles Forceville, Elisabeth 'Lisa' El Refaie, and Gert Meesters list features for examination: PAGE, PANEL arrangements, body types and postures, SPEECH BALLOONS, and ONOMATOPOEIA, among many others. Paul F. Davies provided a list of questions to bring to the text in *Comics and Communication*, including: how and what type of processes (verbal, mental, behavioural) are represented, and "what does the reader have to do to make sense of the text?" (2019: 285–287). Consideration could also be given to GRAPHIATION—"the specific enunciative act made by the author or agent when he or she makes the drawings" (Baetens 2001: 147). This may reflect in AUTOBIOGRAPHICAL comics, which "draw attention to the specific conjunctions of visual and verbal text in this genre of autobiography, and also to the subject positions that narrators negotiate in and through comics" (Whitlock 2006: 966).

Bruce Mutard

## *References*

Baetens, J. (2001) "Revealing Traces: A New Theory of Graphic Enunciation" in Varnum, R. and Gibbons, C. T. (eds.) *The Language of Comics: Word and Image*. Jackson: University Press of Mississippi, pp. 145–155.

Davies, P. F. (2019) *Comics as Communication: A Functional Approach*. London: Palgrave Macmillan.

Forceville, C., El Refaie, E. L., and Meesters, G. (2014) "Stylistics and Comics" in Burke, M. (ed.) *The Routledge Handbook of Stylistics*. Abingdon: Routledge, pp. 485–499.

Wales, K. (2014) *A Dictionary of Stylistics*. Abingdon: Routledge.

Whitlock, G. (2006) "Autographics: The Seeing "I" of the Comics," *MFS Modern Fiction Studies* 52(4), pp. 965–979.

## SUBJECT

The subject is a central concept in philosophy, PSYCHOANALYSIS, and law. Michel Foucault was interested in the human subject proscribed by LANGUAGE, economic productivity, and biology (1982), and Jacques Lacan in how the infant subject sought meaning in the pre-existing social structures and IMAGES presented to it (Lacan 2014). In LITERATURE, subject positions are construed differently depending on the critical theory brought to bear on their analysis. Liberal humanism has it that we are essentially free and the sum of our experiences. In Marxist and (POST) STRUCTURALIST readings, however, the subject is mostly "subject to" the prevailing ideology of its culture (Bertens 2017: 5–22). Cultural products including literature, FILM, and comics can provide a vehicle for, or offer a critique of, hegemonic indoctrination. The comics theorist can add the problem of visual REPRESENTATION of the subject. Graphic showing and STYLE invite the READER to attribute particular visual choices to the consciousness of a character (Mikkonen 2013: 114). At the same time, visual representation risks turning the subject into an object, for visual consumption. Accordingly, representations of ETHNICITY,

SEXUALITY, and GENDER are scrutinised in COMICS STUDIES (El Refaie 2012: 72), as are the levels of representation and creative control afforded by the comics industry (Brown 2001: 27).

Stuart Medley

## *References*

Bertens, H. (2017) *Literary Theory: The Basics.* Abingdon: Routledge.

Brown, J. A. (2001) *Black Superheroes, Milestone Comics, and their Fans.* Jackson: University Press of Mississippi.

El Refaie, E. L. (2012) *Autobiographical Comics: Life Writing in Pictures.* Jackson: University Press of Mississippi.

Foucault, M. (1982) "The Subject and Power," *Critical inquiry* 8(4), pp. 777–795.

Lacan, J. (1949) "The Mirror Stage as Formative of the Function of the I as Revealed in Psychoanalytic Experience" in Birksted-Breen, D., Flanders, S., and Gibeault, A. (eds.), 2014. *Reading French Psychoanalysis.* Abingdon: Routledge, pp. 97–104.

Mikkonen, K. (2013) "Subjectivity and style in graphic narratives" in Stein, D. and Thon, J.-N. (eds.) *From Comic Strips to Graphic Novels: Contributions to the Theory and History of Graphic Narrative.* Berlin: De Gruyter, pp. 101–123.

## Sunday Funnies

The Sunday Funnies in American NEWSPAPERS developed from earlier, more general, HUMOROUS sections that included text and graphic material. The New York *World's* 1889 page of this material carried the label *The World's Funny Side* (Gordon 1998: 24). In 1893 the *World* published a COLOUR supplement and by October 1896 this became the *Comic Weekly* (West 2012: 11). The words "funny" and "comic" were used somewhat interchangeably to describe these supplements, as in a 1908 article entitled "In Defense of Comic Supplement" that discussed the content as "funnies" (Stranathan 1908: 234). By 1908 the Sunday comic supplements were mostly made up of COMIC STRIPS and daily comic strips had begun. The funnies became an all-encompassing term for the sections and the strips to the point that a 1921 *Saturday Evening Post* story described a character as looking like one of the funnies (Lowe 1921: 36). In a prescient 1925 article on American global soft power the *New*

*York Times* listed the funnies as one of its constituents (Wilson 1925: 7). In their heyday from the 1920s to the early 1960s the Sunday Funnies in major newspapers consisted of eight pages or so of regularly appearing full or half page colour comic strips.

Ian Lewis Gordon

## *References*

Gordon, I. (1998) *Comic Strips and Consumer Culture 1890–1945.* Washington: Smithsonian Institution Press.

Lowe, C. (1921) "Psycho-Anne." *Saturday Evening Post*, 21 May 1921, pp. 10–11, 36.

Stranathan, M (1908) "In Defense of Comic Supplement." *National Magazine*, May 1908, pp. 234–235.

West, R. S. (2013) "Secret Origins of the Sunday Funnies: How the Comics Supplement Was Born" in Maresca P. (ed.) *Society Is Nix: Gleeful Anarchy of the Dawn of the American Comic Strip 1895–1915.* Palo Alto: Sunday Press Books, p. 11.

Wilson, P. W. (1925) "Few Worlds Left For Us To Conquer." *New York Times*, 4 January 1925, pp. SM7.

## SUPERHERO

The word "superhero" commonly signifies a shifting generic figure and a loose generic designation HISTORICALLY associated primarily with COMIC BOOKS, but increasingly common in other MEDIA (primarily FILM, cartoons, and television). Most superheroes exist within shared, present-oriented STORYWORLDS (the two largest being DC and Marvel) and are published in SERIALISED monthly FORMATS. Many have special powers, costumes, secret IDENTITIES, character-displaying origin stories, and fight SUPERVILLAINS, while others lack one or several of these characteristics. The GENRE allows much variation in, for example, power sets and character types, but is largely dominated by characters conforming to prevailing US social norms, the superhero's main MARKET (i.e. white, cisgender male, straight, and able-bodied). Many definitions of the superhero exist, but none is definitive or universally accepted; the common assumption seems to be that we know them when we see them. Consequently, two major strands of study exist that can be labelled "formalist" and "historical-contextual" studies. The former is concerned with capturing what constitutes a superhero, and often does not consider the figure as political (Coogan 2006, Bahlmann 2016), while the latter is interested in what figures identified as superheroes say and do in a given context, and sees the figure and genre as inherently political, often conservatively so (Dittmer 2013, De Dauw 2021).

Martin Lund

## *References*

Bahlmann, A. R. (2016) *The Mythology of the Superhero.* Jefferson: McFarland.

Coogan, P. (2006) *Superhero: The Secret Origin of a Genre.* Austin: MonkeyBrain Books.

De Dauw, E. (2021) *Hot Pants and Spandex Suits: Gender Representation in American Superhero Comic Books.* New Brunswick: Rutgers University Press.

Dittmer, J. (2013) *Captain America and the Nationalist Superhero.* Philadelphia: Temple University Press.

## Suspense

Suspense can be defined as an emotion that emerges from a partial uncertainty about the progression of an action (Prince 2003: 1993). It is a type of narrative tension (Baroni 2007) aroused by a temporary indetermination in the plot, encouraging the READER to wait for a resolution (Sternberg 1992). The discussion of suspense in comics has to take into account the particular tension between linear and tabular READINGS (Fresnault-Deruelle 1976), since suspense could be affected by a synoptical view of the full PAGE, that occurs along with the SEQUENTIAL reading (Baetens 2011, Boillat and Revaz 2016, Schneider 2017). There are different types of suspense that vary according to how distant events in time are presented. A "short" type depends on the visual REPRESENTATION of immediate actions, and a "long" type occurs in prolonged intervals and depends less on visual cues (Baroni 2007: 338). Suspense in comics can be preserved by strategically hiding information on the page or controlling the progressive reading along pages and volumes. A popular form of producing suspense is the cliffhanger, widely used in SERIALISED fiction to interrupt the action in a crucial moment of the STORY, moving the reader's expectations towards future instalments (Baroni 2016).

Greice Schneider

## *References*


Baetens, J. (2011) "Hommage à Pierre Fresnault-Deruelle: Pour relire 'Du Linéaire au tabulaire,'" *Les Cahiers du Grit* 1(1), pp. 110–116.

Boillat, A. and Revaz, F. (2016) "Intrigue, Suspense, and Sequentiality in Comic Strips" in Baroni, E. and Revaz, F. (eds.) *Narrative Sequence in Contemporary Narratology*. Columbus: The Ohio State University Press, pp. 107–129.

Baroni, R. (2007) *La Tension Narrative*. Paris: Éditions du Seuil.

Baroni, R. (2016) "Le cliffhanger: Un révélateur des fonctions du récit mimétique," *Cahiers de narratologie* 31, pp. 1–15.

Baroni, R. (2007) "Le suspense dans le feuilleton littéraire et dans la bande dessinée" in Kaenel, P. and Lugrin, G. (eds.) *Bédé, ciné, pub et art: D'un média à l'autre*. Gollion: Les Éditions Infolio, pp. 141–165.

Fresnault-Deruelle, P. (1976) "Du linéaire au tabulaire," *Communications* 24(1), pp. 7–23.

Prince, G. (2003) *A Dictionary of Narratology*. Lincoln: University of Nebraska Press.

Schneider, G. (2017) "Suspensão do suspense nos quadrinhos contemporâneos," *Esferas* 9, pp. 23–31.

Sternberg, M. (1992) "Telling in Time (II): Chronology, Teleology, Narrativity," *Poetics Today* 13(3), pp. 463–541.


## Swiping

Swiping is comics jargon for the practice of redrawing, tracing, or otherwise appropriating IMAGES. A synonym for stealing, swiping became a trade term in North American COMIC BOOK culture and has circulated widely in FANDOM, where it is used to identify and evaluate the process and PRODUCT of redrawing (Wertham 1973: 109). CARTOONISTS routinely assembled "swipe files" with fragments that could be used for reference in a variety of contexts and narrative opportunities, or as a way of learning to DRAW in a certain house STYLE. In fan DISCOURSES, swiping regularly contributes to authorising graphic styles, and identifying and distinguishing "idiographic peculiarities" (Hatfield 2012: 50) and their copied versions. It engages an evaluative process, valorising citational referentiality or condemning the copy as camouflaged plagiarism, based on criteria that have changed through comics HISTORY (Witek 2016). Although the term has no legal value as such, swipes can be gathered in a court case as evidences of copyright infringement. While swiping is often wrongly seen as a token of incompetence, the practice intersects with the contemporary interest for unoriginality (Crucifix 2017). Today, swiping is more likely to refer to the physical gesture of READING comics on digital devices.

Benoît Crucifix

## *References*

Crucifix, B. (2017) "Cut-Up and Redrawn: Reading Charles Burns's Swipe Files," *Inks* 1(3), pp. 309–333.

Feiffer, J. (1965) *The Great Comic Book Heroes.* New York: The Dial Press.

Hatfield, C. (2012) *Hand of Fire: The Comics Art of Jack Kirby.* Jackson: University Press of Mississippi.

Wertham, F. (1973) *The World of Fanzines: A Special Form of Communication.* Carbondale: Southern Illinois University Press.

Witek, J. (2016) "If a Way to the Better There Be: Excellence, Mere Competence, and The Worst Comics Ever Made," *Image [&] Narrative* 17(4), pp. 26–42.

## Syndicates

Syndicates are organisations that sell, and usually own, COMIC STRIPS that are sold for publication in NEWSPAPERS and magazines. HISTORICALLY, syndicates consist of two main types: the dominant FORM linked to newspaper empires and the independents with no affiliation within the PUBLISHING industry ("The Funny Papers" 1933: 45–46). Many syndicates, such as newspaper magnate William Randolph Hearst's King Features Syndicate, were founded in America in the first decades of the twentieth century before going on to syndicate comic strips such as *Krazy Kat* and *The Katzenjammer Kids* internationally (Gravett 2013: 13). This international reach was further developed by the emergence of local agents for American syndicates such as the Yaffa Syndicate in Australia and Bulls Press serving the Nordic region (Patrick 2017: 62–64, Scholz 2020: 82, 90). Until the mid-1930s, syndicates were content to sell publication rights of their newspaper strips to entrepreneurial publishers for repackaging in COMIC BOOK form. As the comic books boomed, syndicates went into the business themselves. One of the first was United Features Syndicate which PRODUCED *Tip Top Comics* in 1936 featuring characters such as Tarzan and Li'l Abner (Goulart 1991: 7–37). The 1960s saw syndicates merge and absorbed by MEDIA conglomerates, a process that has accelerated in subsequent years resulting in an industry now consisting of a few powerful players.

Ian Horton

## *References*

Goulart, R. (1991) *Over 50 Years of American Comic Books.* Lincolnwood: Publications International, Ltd.

Gravett, P. (2013) *Comics Art.* London; Tate Publishing.

"The Funny Papers," *Fortune*, April 1933.

Patrick, K. (2017) *The Phantom Unmasked: America's First Superhero.* Iowa City: University of Iowa Press.

Scholz, M. (2020) "In a Growing Violent Temper: The Swedish Comic Market during the Second World War" in Hague, I., Horton, I. and Mickwitz, N. (eds.) *Contexts of Violence in Comics.* Abingdon: Routledge, pp. 81–96.

## Syuzhet

Transliterated from the Russian, syuzhet is most frequently translated as plot, "the process which falls between story and discourse" (Kukkonen 2013: 36), and is frequently assigned an ALLUSION to the French definition for plot, "intrigue"—that which makes the STORY interesting. Syuzhet is a LITERARY focus upon the key NARRATIVE events of a work in the chronological order in which they occur in the work. The order of these events, which emphasise or make a work's THEMES emotionally resonant to its AUDIENCE, is important because this is what is considered the "true" literary ART (Tomashevsky 2012: 47, 49, Selden, Widdowson, and Brooker 1997: 35, Gaudreault and Marion 2004). Often the English word plot is used interchangeably, and its definition conflated with other uses of the word. To use the transliterated term syuzhet is, however, to flag an affiliation with the tenets of Russian formalism (Tomashevsky 2004: 124–132, Tomashevsky 2012: 46–64) via twentieth-century FILM analysis and NARRATOLOGY (Bordwell 1985: 49–57). Comics-specific models of narrative, such as Grennan's "epistemological system of discourse characterised as narrative" or Marion's GRAPHIATION, allocate the functions of STORY differently (Grennan 2015: 146–56, Baetens 2001). The use of syuzhet implies a focus upon the internal structures of a work rather than external contexts. This approach makes each syuzhet individual to a work and to the FORM of that work, making it MEDIUM-specific to the work within which it operates (Gaudreault and Marion 63–64).

Geraint D'Arcy

## *References*

Baetens, J. (2001) "Revealing Traces: A New Theory of Graphic Enunciation" in Varnum, R. and Gibbons, C. T. (eds.) *The Language of Comics: Word and Image*. Jackson: University Press of Mississippi, pp. 145–155.

Bordwell, D. (1985) *Narrative in the Fiction Film*. Madison: University of Wisconsin Press.

Gaudreault, A. and Marion, P. (2004) "Transécriture and Narrative Mediatics: The Stakes of Intermediality" in Stam, R. and Raengo, A. (eds.) *A Companion to Literature and Film*. Oxford: Blackwell, 58–70.

Grennan, S. (2017) *A Theory of Narrative Drawing*. London: Palgrave Macmillan.

Kukkonen, K. (2013) *Studying Comics and Graphic Novels*. Hoboken: John Wiley & Sons.

Selden, R., Widdowson, P., and Brooker, P. (1997) *A Reader's Guide to Contemporary Literary Theory*. London: Prentice Hall.

Tomashevsky, B. (2004) "The New School of Literary History in Russia," *PMLA* 119(1), pp. 120–132.

Tomashevsky, B. (2012) "Thematics" in Lemon, L. T., Reis, M. J., and Morson, G. S. (eds.) *Russian Formalist Criticism: Four Essays*. Lincoln: University of Nebraska, pp. 46–64.

## Taste Adjudication

Commercial success, critical praise, and word-of-mouth can all drive a comic to be widely READ and liked, or to be derided or ignored. As in fields such as LITERARY studies, COMICS STUDIES and its CANON privilege certain texts (*Maus*, *Persepolis*), AUTHORS (Art Spiegelman, Alan Moore), and GENRES (SUPERHEROES, AUTOBIOGRAPHY) with limited concern for how REPRESENTATIVE these examples are of the field as a whole. Such decisions are driven by taste and perceptions of importance that may have been imported wholesale from other fields of study. Taste adjudicators may appear to be in conflict with each other: commercial success and critical praise, for example, are often seen as contradictory. In recent years, scholars have argued that this approach to comics does not produce useful outcomes. In 2015, Bart Beaty asserted that work on popular but critically ignored comics like *Archie* would help correct "a long history of misunderstanding and misrepresenting the past, particularly when those contributions can be found in genres that are out of favour—such as the children's humor comic" (2015: 6). In this and other works (Beaty 2012, Beaty and Woo 2016), Beaty and other scholars have explored how taste and symbolic capital work in comics, and how taste adjudication has formed both our understandings of comics and the shape of Comics Studies as a field.

Ian Hague

### *References*

Beaty, B. (2015) *Twelve Cent Archie.* New Brunswick: Rutgers University Press.

Beaty, B. (2012) *Comics versus Art.* Toronto: University of Toronto Press.

Beaty, B. and Woo, B. (2016) *The Greatest Comic Book of All Time: Symbolic Capital and the Field of American Comic Books.* London: Palgrave Macmillan.

## Technology

Most comics depend for their existence on some means of mechanical reproduction for words and IMAGES. Woodblock PRINTING in the 1400s produced what David Kunzle (1973, 1990) has called the early comic strip. After 1776, wood engraving, then metal plates and PHOTOGRAPHIC techniques saw ILLUSTRATIONS become widely reproduced in magazines and comics. Printing method, paper quality, and dimensions all affect the nature of a given comic. Hand or "pochoir" COLOURING became prevalent, particularly in early French comics of the nineteenth century. Printed colour increased the impact of NEWSPAPER STRIPS, and offset LITHOGRAPHY and the use of the Ben-Day system of coloured dots dominated the look of the American COMIC BOOK. A PARODY of this colouring was a feature of Roy Lichtenstein's POP ART paintings of the 1960s. Limitations of these reproduction systems and cheap newsprint also affected DRAWING STYLES, whilst European photogravure printing sometimes allowed more lavish full colour artwork. Photocopying in the 1960s and 1970s fuelled the growth of SELF-PUBLISHED comics, as has the digital age. The latter has impacted all publications, where, as Gary Spencer Millidge comments, "comics rarely rarely make it to the page (…) without being touched (…) by computer applications." Changes in technology continue to affect the AESTHETICS of comics. In terms of reception, Wilde notes that digital technology has intensified debates about the COMICS MEDIUM, arguing that the visual/verbal mix that the medium affords is made more complex and less easy to identify, by digital interfaces (2015).

Dave Huxley

## *References*

Kunzle, D. (1973) *History of the Comic Strip, Volume 1: The Early Comic Strip 1450–1825*. Berkeley: University of California Press.

Kunzle, D. (1990) *History of the Comic Strip, Volume 2: The Nineteenth Century*. Berkeley: University of California Press.

Millidge, G. S. (2009) *Comic Book Design*. Lewes: Ilex.

Wilde, L. (2015) "Distinguishing Mediality: The Problem of Identifying Forms and Features of Digital Comics." *Media, Communication and Cultural Studies Association,* Volume 8, Number 4, 2005. Available at: https://ojs.meccsa.org.uk/index.php/netknow/article/view/386 [Accessed 8 January 2021].

## TEMPORALITY

Temporality in NARRATIVE is often analysed as the relationship between STORY time (the chronology of the story) and DISCOURSE time (the arrangement of the elements of the story for the READER) (Genette 1980). In comics this connection is expressed as a SPATIALISATION of TIME in that the correlation between PANEL, SEQUENCE, and PAGE LAYOUT expresses story time (Mikkonen 2017). Time in comics has been said to be the same as space (McCloud 1993), panels being "boxes of time" (Chute and DeKoven 2006: 769) or an instance where the structure of panels create an illusion of time (Eisner 1985). Because of temporal affordances of TEXT and IMAGE in combination, and the way comics can manipulate time through spatial organisation of fragments, their potential for expressing subjective time has been deemed essential in AUTOBIOGRAPHICAL and TRAUMA comics (El Refaie 2012) as well as GRAPHIC MEDICINE. The figure of the SUPERHERO has been described as caught in a temporal paradox between the perpetual forward motion of the SERIALISED format and the demand for an unchanging hero (Eco 1972), emphasising how the format of comics can impact temporality, just as WEBCOMICS can offer alternative ways of structuring temporality (McCloud 2000).

Rikke Platz Cortsen

### *References*

Chute, H. L. and DeKoven, M. (2006) "Introduction: Graphic Narrative," *MFS Modern Fiction Studies* 52(4), pp. 767–782.

Eco, U. (1972) "The Myth of Superman," *Diacritics* 2(1), pp. 14–22.

Eisner, W. (1985) *Comics and Sequential Art.* Tamarac: Poorhouse Press.

El Refaie, E. L. (2012) *Autobiographical Comics: Life Writing in Pictures.* Jackson: University Press of Mississippi.

Genette, G. (1979) *Narrative Discourse: An Essay in Method.* Translated from French by J. E. Lewin, 1980. Ithaca: Cornell University Press.

McCloud, S. (1993) *Understanding Comics: The Invisible Art.* New York: Harper Perennial.

McCloud, S. (2000) *Reinventing Comics: How Imagination and Technology are Revolutionizing an Art Form.* New York: Paradox Press.

Mikkonen, K. (2017) *The Narratology of Comic Art.* Abingdon: Routledge.

## Text

Text in comics and COMIC STUDIES can refer to the pre-text or the SCRIPT, as it was laid out by (usually) one writer, before being entrusted to one or more ARTISTS. More narrowly, text can then designate the actual words on a page as they can be found within SPEECH BALLOONS and CAPTION BOXES, or as ONOMATOPOEIA (Miodrag 2013). They are opposed to the IMAGES in comics, usually with a presumed "predominance of image over text" (Kunzle 1973: 2). However, as Charles Hatfield has pointed out, "comics continually work to destabilise this very distinction" (2009: 133). The sum of the MULTIMODAL resources of comics (words and pictures) that can be read as a meaningful structure due to its textuality (de Beaugrande and Dressler 1981) is also addressed as text—or as IMAGETEXT (Davies 2019: 169–202). Its coherence, however, is often undermined by the fact that verbal and pictorial signs in comics frequently PARODY the assumption of a consistent, unified STORYWORLD (Frahm 2000). Text finally serves to exclude various PARATEXTS (such as LETTER COLUMNS or back material) from the actual work (Baetens and Lefèvre 2014).

Lukas R. A. Wilde

### *References*

Baetens, J. and Lefèvre, P. (1993) "The Work and its Surround" in Miller, A. and Beaty, B. (eds.) *The French Comics Theory Reader.* Translated from French by A. Miller and B. Beaty, 2014. Leuven: Leuven University Press, pp. 191–202.

de Beaugrande, R. and Dressler, W. U. (1981) *Introduction to Text Linguistics.* London: Longman.

Davies, P. F. (2019) *Comics as Communication: A Functional Approach.* London: Palgrave Macmillan.

Frahm, O. (2000) "Weird Signs: Comics as Means of Parody" in Magnussen, A. and Christiansen, H.-C. (eds.) *Comics and Culture: Analytical and Theoretical Approaches to Comics.* Copenhagen: Museum Tusculanum Press, pp. 107–121.

Hatfield, C. (2009) "An Art of Tensions" in Heer, J. and Worcester, K. (eds.) *A Comics Studies Reader.* Jackson: University Press of Mississippi, pp. 132–148.

Kunzle, D. (1973) *History of the Comic Strip, Volume 1: The Early Comic Strip 1450–1825*. Berkeley: University of California Press.

Miodrag, H. (2013) *Comics and Language: Reimagining Critical Discourse on the Form*. Jackson: University Press of Mississippi.

## Theme

Theme, in the sense used by functional LINGUISTICS, is the initial element of a clause, usually an adverbial or subject (Halliday and Matthiessen 2014: 88–92). It typically contains "given" information, framing and marking a "jumping-off point" for the clause, before new information is introduced in the rheme. Patterns of thematic REPETITION or development can be traced in a text to expose the line of argument or preoccupations across the text's structure. Gunther Kress and Theo van Leeuwen (1996) have used "given-and-new" as part of their account of information structure in single-IMAGE texts, mapping given to the left and new to the right of the image. Mario Saraceni (2000, 2016) has used the concept to account for progression in comics from PANEL to panel. Paul F. Davies (2019) proposes that a thematic position is found to the top and left of a composition in comics, at the level of both panel and PAGE: the upper tier tending to be thematic, and the upper left of a panel tending to be the space for thematising functions such as adverbials of TIME and place. This implies a rheme area to the centre, bottom, and right, with the lower right especially as a "tonic" area, preparatory to revealing new information.

Paul F. Davies

### *References*

Davies, P. F. (2019) *Comics as Communication: A Functional Approach*. London: Palgrave Macmillan.

Halliday, M. A. K. and Matthiessen, C. (2014) *Halliday's Introduction to Functional Grammar*. Abingdon: Routledge.

Kress, G. and van Leeuwen, T. (1996) *Reading Images: The Grammar of Visual Design*. Abingdon: Routledge.

Saraceni, M. (2000) *Language Beyond Language: Comics as Verbo-visual Texts*. PhD. University of Nottingham.

Saraceni, M. (2016) "Relatedness: Aspects of textual connectivity in comics" in Cohn, N. (ed.) *The Visual Narrative Reader*. London: Bloomsbury Academic, pp. 115–127.

## Thought Bubble

A thought bubble is graphical device to indicate thought, somewhat analogous to using italics rather than quotation marks (usually reserved for speech) in TEXT. Its shape is generally similar to a SPEECH BALLOON, except for appearing more "puffy" (with scalloped bulges around the edges) and with the tail replaced by a series of circles (bubbles). Like other forms of word balloons, thought bubbles remain separate from the DIEGETIC worlds on view: "They display no materiality" (Postema 2013: 83). The use of thought bubbles can assist in creating complex characterisations, such as in situations where a character may have ulterior motives for an utterance or an action. Alternatively, they can indicate a character's emotional state or non-verbal reaction to a situation through the use of simple punctuation (e.g. "?") or non-textual symbols instead of LANGUAGE, thus rendering the balloon itself ICONIC (Groensteen 2007: 85). In the past few decades, many commercial comics CREATORS have eschewed the use of thought bubbles, substituting interior monologues divided into short CAPTIONS across PANELS or entire PAGES. This practice was an anomaly in SUPERHERO comics when writer Alan Moore used it in his and Dave Gibbons' *Watchmen* (1986–1987). However, the ubiquity of thought bubbles and speech balloons in broader POPULAR CULTURE testifies to their central place as indicators of communication beyond the comics page.

Gene Kannenberg Jr

### *References*

Groensteen, T. (1999) *The System of Comics*. Translated from French by B. Beaty and N. Nguyen, 2007. Jackson: University Press of Mississippi.

Postema, B. (2013) *Narrative Structure in Comics: Making Sense of Fragments*. Rochester: Rochester Institute of Technology Press.

## Tijuana Bible

The name Tijuana Bible originated in California in the 1940s, to describe small (2.5 × 4 inch) eight-page pornographic comics, featuring the unauthorised use of characters from contemporary NEWSPAPER STRIPS, movie and CELEBRITY culture, current from the end of the First World War to the 1960s (Cray 1962, Adelman 1997). The name referred to the idea that the books were smuggled as contraband into the US across the border from the Mexican town of Tijuana, although there is no evidence for this and Tijuana Bibles were PRODUCED across the US. Due to their illegality (their pornographic content and lack of copyright), the AUTHORS, ARTISTS, and PUBLISHERS are largely unknown or pseudonymous ("Mr Prolific," "Elmer Zilch," "La France Publishing"). Tijuana Bibles share characteristics with later UNDERGROUND COMIX, focusing on refiguring commercial POPULAR CULTURE and establishing self-distribution networks, although their very large scale of production and distribution in the 1930s somewhat contradicts this (Danky and Kitchen 2009). They also belong to the wider MEDIA GENRE now known as FIC or fan fiction.

Simon Grennan

### *References*

Adelman, B. (1997) *Tijuana Bibles: Art and wit in America's forbidden funnies, 1930s–1950s.* New York: Simon & Schuster.

Cray, E. (1962) "Ethnic Place Names and Derisive Adjectives," *Western Folklore* 21, pp. 27–34.

Danky, J. and Kitchen, D. (2009) *Underground Classics: The Transformation of Comics into Comix.* New York: Abrams.

## Time

Time in comics is the result of its narrativity. Time can be expressed in words, through visual REPRESENTATIONS of time, such as clocks or a rising sun, and by way of SIGNS suggesting speed. Also, as is the case with all narratives, time is expressed through the order of events, either given chronologically or in disorder. The number and shape of the PANELS can also suggest the speed at which time passes (McCloud 2000). Ellipsis is a fundamental concept for the structuring of times in comics. Ellipsis indicates the passage of time between each panel, which can vary tremendously from a very long interval to less than a second, even expressing simultaneity when the ellipsis expresses change of SPACE rather than time. Certain dispositions of panels on the PAGE might suggest fast READING. MANGA has particularly excelled in suggesting speed, which prompted critics to suggest that this reflects the place where they are often read (public transportation) or reflects the influence of Japanese television ANIMATION. Different comics cultures might emphasise different kinds of TEMPORALITY, for example, Scott McCloud's discussion of transition types in manga in *Understanding Comics* (1993: 83–85) and Neil Cohn's DISCOURSE on visual language (2013). The reader's time is also to be considered, since most comics are "read" more quickly than a full page of TEXT. Comics, therefore, have often been thought of as a MEDIUM fit for quick reading. However, some comics, such as *Watchmen* (1986–1987), defy this reading model by enforcing, through, for example, visual and narrative complexity, a slower reading experience.

Chris Reyns-Chikuma

## *References*

Cohn, N. (2013) *The Visual Language of Comics: Introduction to the Structure and Cognition of Sequential Images.* London: Bloomsbury Academic.

Genette, G. (1972) *Figures III.* Reprint 1987. Paris: Seuil.

Groensteen, T. (2011) *Bande dessinée et narration: Système de la bande dessinée*, Volume 2. Paris: PUF.

McCloud, S. (1993) *Understanding Comics: The Invisible Art.* New York: Harper Perennial.

## TRACE

Trace is a subcategory of INDEXICAL SIGNS, following a broad definition of the indexical sign by Charles Sanders Peirce as a REPRESENTATION that indicates a physical connection with its object (1998: 9). Trace is a type of indexical sign produced as a direct remnant of an activity and, as such, has causes (and offers consequences) distinct from index itself. For example, digital imaging TECHNOLOGIES can index activities of the body without tracing them (i.e. without producing direct remnants), whereas a MARK made in the sand with a finger is always both index and trace (Grennan 2017: 15). The traces of COMICS DRAWING activities have been discussed as autographic (Gardner 2011: 64) and theorised as an essential characteristic of comics MEDIATION (Baetens 2001).

Simon Grennan

## *References*

Baetens, J. (2001) "Revealing Traces: A New Theory of Graphic Enunciation" in Varnum, R. and Gibbons, C. T. (eds.) *The Language of Comics: Word and Image*. Jackson: University Press of Mississippi, pp. 145–155.

Gardner, J. (2011) "Storylines," *SubStance* 40(1), pp. 53–69.

Grennan, S. (2017) *A Theory of Narrative Drawing*. London: Palgrave Macmillan.

Peirce, C. S. (1893–1913) *The Essential Peirce, Volume 2: Selected Philosophical Writings, 1893–1913*. Peirce Edition Project (ed.), 1998. Bloomington: Indiana University Press.

## Tragedy

Tragedy is a SUB-GENRE within fiction wherein a protagonist comes to ruin as a result of intrinsic flaws within his or her own character, a process that invokes catharsis in AUDIENCES or READERS. To some extent, the sub-genre can be said to have its basis in MYTH, in as much as the Athenian tragedies of the fifth century BC, which are rooted in Greek mythological tales, are the oldest surviving dramatic texts in existence (though the tales upon which they are based are far older) (Alaux 2011: 141). Aristotle's *Poetics* states that the structure of tragedy dictates that the tragic HERO be seen to dramatically fall from a position of power, influence, or success and that this fall cannot be blamed on external forces, such as misfortune or divine intervention (2018: 17). Arguably the most common contributing tragic flaw is hubris, which in mythological terms results in the hero being "blasted from within and without" (Campbell 1993: 37), though this is not the only such flaw. Joseph Carroll observes that tragedy causes "sexual and familial bonds [to] become pathological, and social bonds [to] disintegrate" (2011: 112), while Northrop Frye points to the primacy of tragedy coming from the fall of a figure of "properly heroic size (…) with a sense of his relation to society and with a sense of the supremacy of natural law" (1990: 37). Under these criteria, Neil Gaiman's *The Sandman* is an example of a long-form tragedy within the comics idiom.

Houman Sadri

## *References*

Alaux, J. (2011) "Acting Myth: Athenian Drama" in Dowden, K. and Livingstone, N. (eds.) *A Companion to Greek Mythology.* Oxford: Blackwell, pp. 141–156.

Aristotle (c. 335 BC) *Poetics.* Translated from Greek by M. Zerba and D. Gorman (eds.), 2018. New York: W. W. Norton & Company.

Campbell, J. (1993) *The Hero with a Thousand Faces.* London: Fontana.

Carroll, J. (2011) *Reading Human Nature.* Albany: State University of New York Press.

Frye, N. (1957) *Anatomy of Criticism.* Reprint 1990. Princeton: Princeton University Press.

## Transitions

Transitions, as characterised by Scott McCloud (1993, 2006), are the intermediate events or concepts that are taken by a READER to occur between adjacent pairs of PANELS in comics texts, the GUTTER. McCloud identifies six transition types, ordered by the amount of CLOSURE each demands of the reader: moment-to-moment, in which very little change is to be inferred and a relatively short amount of TIME passed; action-to-action, in which more substantial events are to have been performed by depicted characters; SUBJECT-to-subject, which switches focus between characters; scene-to-scene, wherein location and time are understood to have changed; aspect-to-aspect, in which there is no change of place, and little or none of time, nor indeed action, but different elements of MISE-EN-SCENE are focused upon; and finally non-sequitur, which is attributed to the "alchemy" of comics the reader's willingness to interpret any paired panels, even when no other connection is apparent (1993: 70–74) These transitions depend upon NARRATIVE categories, and imply that adjacency of delineated panels, forming a gutter, is at the heart of comics meaning-making. Jessica Abel and Matt Madden (2008, 2012) have expanded the categories to include metaphorical transitions, which make meaning by invoking a TROPE or prompt an interpretation of one or other image as non-literal. McCloud's account has been challenged, for example, by Thierry Groensteen (1999), Neil Cohn (2013), and Paul F. Davies (2019), by calling into question (a) the linearity of panel READING, (b) the practices readers undertake in making sense of panel relationships, even when not adjacent, and (c) McCloud's grounds for classifying panel types and groupings.

Paul F. Davies

## References

Abel, J. and Madden, M. (2008) *Drawing Words and Writing Pictures.* New York: First Second.

Abel, J. and Madden, M. (2012) *Mastering Comics: Drawing Words & Writing Pictures, Continued.* New York: First Second.

Cohn, N. (2013) *The Visual Language of Comics: Introduction to the Structure and Cognition of Sequential Images.* London: Bloomsbury Academic.

Davies, P. F. (2019) *Comics as Communication: A Functional Approach.* London: Palgrave Macmillan.

Groensteen, T. (1999) *The System of Comics.* Translated from French by B. Beaty and N. Nguyen, 2007. Jackson: University Press of Mississippi.

McCloud, S. (1993) *Understanding Comics: The Invisible Art.* New York: Harper Perennial.

McCloud, S. (2006) *Making Comics. Storytelling Secrets of Comics, Manga and Graphic Novels.* New York: Harper.

## Translation

Translation is the process of translating words from one LANGUAGE to another. Because comics are MULTIMODAL their translation involves both TEXT and IMAGE (Zanettin 2008). Comics have several types of texts: (1) speech (traditionally in SPEECH BALLOONS), (2) NARRATION (often in CAPTION BOXES), and (3) sounds (usually ONOMATOPOEIAS). While translating speech and narration is similar to traditional translation methods, the text usually has to be placed within the space originally allocated to avoid obscuring the image (Borodo 2016), which can lead to textual legibility issues. Onomatopoeias pose different challenges: they are often difficult to equivocally translate and are usually spread over the image. Similar to other text in the image, like the name of a restaurant, the translator must decide what can and should be translated. Visual elements might also need "translation"; for example, the thumbs-up signals approval in many cultures, but connotes obscenity in others (Frias 2011). Because these visual elements, like text in the image, are not easy to change, they may require a footnote instead. With globalisation, comics translations have exponentially increased over the last few decades, but they are often conducted by non-professionals, especially for MANGA, where scanlation, the translation of scanned manga, is a common practice (Johnson-Woods 2010).

Chris Reyns-Chikuma

## *References*

Borodo, M. (2016) "Exploring the Links Between Comics Translation and AVT," *Transcultural* 8(2), pp. 68–85.

Frias, J. Y. (2011) "Traduire l'image dans les albums d'Astérix: À la recherche du pouce perdu en Hispanie" in Richet, B. (ed.) *Le Tour du monde d'Astérix*. Paris: Presses Sorbonne Nouvelle, pp. 255–271.

Johnson-Woods, T. (ed.) (2010) *Manga: An anthology of global and cultural perspectives*. Abingdon: Routledge.

Zanettin, F. (2008) *Comics in Translation*. Abingdon: Routledge.

## Transmedia

Originally coined by Marsha Kinder (1991), this term gained wider traction with Henry Jenkins' (2003) analysis of MEDIA plurality and CONVERGENCE in the digital era. For Jenkins, transmedia STORYTELLING describes the "integration of multiple texts to create a narrative so large that it cannot be contained within a single medium" (Jenkins 2006: 95). Cinematic franchises and television SERIALS alike rely on PRINT and WEBCOMICS, podcasts, online videos, CARTOONS, and GAMES to achieve these aims. DC and Marvel offer prime examples of narrative expansion and AUDIENCE engagement using a range of platforms and media. For purposes of transmedia analysis, CULTURAL INDUSTRIES approaches (Proctor 2018) and consideration of user-generated content (Scolari, Bertetti and Freeman 2014) usefully complement more text-based NARRATOLOGICAL approaches (Kukkonen 2011).

Bearing in mind that the distinction between transmedia storytelling and ADAPTATION remains contested (Ryan 2016: 40–41), comics offer ample opportunity to apply the term retrospectively. Approaching "transmedia storytelling as a social narrative practice" (Scolari 2014: 2384) could include crossovers between late nineteenth-century print comics and MUSIC hall performance (Sabin 2009), transferences between twentieth-century print comics and radio serials, or approaching POPULAR CULTURE ICONS such as the Lone Ranger (Santo 2015) as transmedia characters.

Nina Mickwitz

## *References*

Jenkins, H. (2006) *Convergence Culture: Where Old and New Media Collide*. New York: New York University Press.

Jenkins, H. (2003) "Transmedia Storytelling." *MIT Technology Review*, 15 January 2003. Available at: https://www.technologyreview.com/2003/01/15/234540/transmedia-storytelling/ [Accessed 1 August 2020].

Kinder, M. (1991) *Playing with Power in Movies, Television, and Video Games: From Muppet Babies to Teenage Mutant Ninja Turtles*. Berkeley: University of California Press.

Kukkonen, K. (2011) "Comics as a test case for transmedial narratology," *SubStance* 40(1), pp. 34–52.

Proctor, W. (2018) "Transmedia comics: Seriality, sequentiality, and the shifting economies of franchise licensing" in Freeman, M. and Gambarato, R. (eds.) *The Routledge Companion to Transmedia Studies*. Abingdon: Routledge, pp. 52–61.

Ryan, M.-L. (2016) Transmedia narratology and transmedia storytelling," *Artnodes* 18, pp. 37–46.

Sabin, R. (2009) "Ally Sloper on stage," *European Comic Art* 2(2), pp. 205–125.

Santo, A. (2015) *Selling the Silver Bullet: The Lone Ranger and Transmedia Brand Licensing*. Austin: University of Texas Press.

Scolari, C., Bertetti, P., and Freeman, M. (2014) *Transmedia Archaeology: Storytelling in the Borderlines of Science Fiction, Comics and Pulp Magazine*. London: Palgrave Macmillan.

Scolari, C. (2014) "*Don Quixote of La Mancha*: Transmedia Storytelling in the Grey Zone," *International Journal of Communication* 8, pp. 2382–2405.

## Transnationalism

Transnationalism refers to activities, networks, flows, and relationships across national borders, between different locations and actors, in more than one national context or nation-state. Whereas the parallel term "international" refers to interstate relations, "transnational" describes the connections of non-state actors such as individuals, families, corporations, NGOs, religious institutions, and criminal and terrorist networks. Intensified cross-border flows of people, capital, and information form the basis for transnational social formations as well as for globalisation (Hannerz 1992: 46, Levin 2002). In addition to a historical phenomenon, transnationalism may also be defined as an alternative analytical perspective to "methodological nationalism," the postulation that society equals, and social phenomena are bound, to the nation-state (Chernilo 2006, Amelina et al. 2012). In COMICS STUDIES, a transnational perspective on comics has highlighted, for example, transnational AESTHETICS (Beaty 2006, Bragard 2016) and transnational comics PRODUCTION (Brienza 2016). Bart Beaty shows how a "shared, transnational, aesthetic disposition" (2006: 128) was maintained in the 1990s European comics culture through different transnational connections: travel, festivals, face-to-face contacts, and anthologies, and so on. Casey Brienza (2016) describes MANGA in the US as the result of many forms of labour in a process of transnational cultural production and domestication. In addition, the transnational perspective applied on national comics cultures in two collections, a book (Stein et al. 2013) and a journal issue (Kraenzle and Ludewig 2020), show how nationally defined fields, the US and Germany respectively, are thoroughly transnational.

Ralf Kauranen

### *References*

Amelina, A., Faist, T., Glick Schiller, N., and Nergiz, D. D. (2012) "Methodological Predicaments of Cross-Border Studies" in Amelina, A., Nergiz, D. D., Faist, T., and Glick Schiller, N. (eds.) *Beyond Methodological Nationalism: Research Methodologies for Cross-Border Studies.* Abingdon: Routledge, pp. 1–19.

Beaty, B. (2007) *Unpopular Culture: Transforming the European Comic Book in the 1990s.* Toronto: University of Toronto Press.

Bragard, V. (2016) "Belgo-Congolese Transnational Comics Esthetics: Transcolonial Labor from Mongo Sisse's *Bingo en Belgique* to Cassiau-Haurie & Baruti's *Madame Livingstone: Congo, la Grande Guerre* (2014)," *Literature Compass* 13(5), pp. 332–340.

Brienza, C. (2016) *Manga in America: Transnational Book Publishing and the Domestication of Japanese Comics.* London: Bloomsbury Academic.

Chernilo, D. (2006) "Methodological Nationalism and Its Critique" in Delanty, G. and Kumar, K. (eds.) *The SAGE Handbook of Nations and Nationalism.* London: SAGE, pp. 129–140.

Stein, D., Denson, S., and Meyer, C. (eds.) (2013) *Transnational Perspectives on Graphic Narratives: Comics at the Crossroads.* London: Bloomsbury Academic.

Hannerz, U. (1992) *Cultural Complexity.* New York: Columbia University Press.

Kraenzle, C. and Ludewig, J. (eds.) (2020) "Transnationalism in German Comics," *Journal of Graphic Novels and Comics* 11(1).

Levin, M. D. (2002) "Flow and Place: Transnationalism in Four Cases," *Anthropologica* 44(1), pp. 3–12.

## TRANSTEXTUALITY

According to Gérard Genette, transtextuality signifies "all that sets the text in a relationship (...) with other texts" (1997: 1). He divides transtextuality into five categories: INTERTEXTUALITY, "a relationship of copresence between two or more texts," which includes quotations, allusion, and plagiarism (Genette 1997b: xviii); paratextuality, which contains all the texts that "surround" the original text (Genette 1997a: 3) (e.g. Don Rosa uses paratextual prefaces in his Disney comics to explain his intertextual references (Kontturi 2015: 92–93)); metatextuality, which provides a commentary that unites a text to another without citing it (Genette 1997: 4); hypertextuality, which signifies any kind of relationship which unites "a text B (hypertext) to an earlier text A (hypothext)," such as imitations, parodies, pastiches, and travesties (Genette 1997: 5–6, 9); and architextuality, which links the text to the "various kinds of discourse of which it is a representative" (Genette 1997b: xix) (e.g. Alison Bechdel's *Fun Home: A Family Tragicomic* provides its GENRE in its title). Transtextuality is typical for postmodern texts. Considering comics, the term intervisuality describes the relationship between images (Nikolajeva and Scott 2006: 228), thus making it considerable alternative for the concept.

Katja Kontturi

## *References*

Genette, G. (1987) *Paratexts: Thresholds of Interpretation.* Translated from French by J. Lewin, 1997. Cambridge: Cambridge University Press.

Genette, G. (1982) *Palimpsests. Literature in the Second Degree.* Translated from French by J. Lewin, 1997. Cambridge: Cambridge University Press.

Kontturi, K. (2015) "'Shades of Conan Doyle! A lost world!' Fantasy and Intertextuality in Don Rosa's 'Escape from Forbidden Valley'" in Cortsen, R. P., La Cour, E., and Magnussen, A. (eds.) *Comics and Power: Representing and Questioning Culture, Subjects and Communities.* Cambridge: Cambridge Scholars, pp. 89–109.

Nikolajeva, M. and Scott, C. (2006) *How Picturebooks Work.* Abingdon: Routledge.

## TRAUMA

Trauma once simply meant "wound," but with the early work of Jean-Martin Charcot, Sigmund Freud, and others it gained a psychological modern sense, and can now also be defined as a haunting psychological phenomenon triggered by an overwhelming external event that is not perceived in the moment through the normal structures of MEMORY but returns out of place. Trauma has had a contested history of expansion of its criteria and symptomatology (Luckhurst 2008) and trauma theory has thus undergone significant critical revisions. FEMINISM considers traumas that were "outside the range of usual human experience" (Brown 1995: 111) to engage with culturally and socially embedded processes that enable traumatogenic settings. POSTCOLONIALISM allows a movement past the Western CANON of trauma, recognising collective experiences such as slavery, genocide, RACIAL violence, and forms of socio-economic aggression (Craps 2013). As a MODE of REPRESENTATION, comics "intervenes against the trauma-driven discourse of the unrepresentable and the ineffable" (Chute 2016: 178). Critically successful texts such as Art Spiegelman's *Maus* (1980–1991), Justin Green's *Binky Brown* (1972), Alissa Torres' *American Widow* (2009), Debbie Dreschler's *Daddy's Girl* (1996), and Alison Bechdel's *Fun Home* (2006) reinforce the classical perspective of trauma. One can also engage with trauma theory to READ AUTHORS such as Gabrielle Bell or Mattt Konture, the political-economic essays of Pasquale Squarzoni, or even comics-specific psychological pressures as presented in Lewis Trondheim's *Désoeuvré*.

Pedro Moura

## *References*

Brown, L. S. (1995) "Not Outside the Range: One Feminist Perspective on Psychic Trauma" in Caruth, C. (ed.) *Trauma: Explorations in Memory*. Baltimore: The Johns Hopkins University Press, pp. 100–112.

Caruth, C. (1996) *Unclaimed Experience. Trauma, Narrative, and History*. Baltimore: The Johns Hopkins University Press.

Chute, H. (2016) *Disaster Drawn Visual Witness, Comics, and Documentary Form*. Cambridge: Harvard University Press.

Craps, S. (2013) *Postcolonial Witnessing: Trauma Out of Bounds*. London: Palgrave Macmillan.

Luckhurst, R. (2008) *The Trauma Question*. Abingdon: Routledge.

## Trope

A trope is an established figure of speech in works of LITERATURE, such as ALLEGORY, hyperbole, IRONY, and so forth. Kevin Burke identifies METAPHOR, metonymy, synecdoche, and irony as the "four master tropes" in literature (1969: 503–517). With reference to cinema, Michael Rizzo defines a trope as "a universally identified image imbued with several layers of contextual meaning creating a new visual metaphor" (Rizzo 2014: 513). Comics, as IMAGETEXTUAL cultural artefacts, may contain both LITERARY and visual tropes, as well as tropes that are particular to the REGISTER (McCloud 1993). The term is commonly used to describe established NARRATIVE and generic CONVENTIONS, such as familiar plot elements and ARCHETYPICAL characters. For example, Christopher Booker identifies seven basic plots common to most narratives (2004), and screenwriter Frank Gruber describes seven basic plots for STORIES from the American Western GENERIC tradition (1967). The crowd-sourced encyclopaedic web resource TVTropes.org maintains an expansive database of common tropes in television, FILM, literature, and other narrative MEDIA.

Madeline B. Gangnes

## *References*

Booker, C. (2004) *The Seven Basic Plots: Why We Tell Stories.* New York: Continuum.

Burke, K. (1969) *A Grammar of Motives.* Berkeley: University of California Press.

Gruber, F. (1967) *The Pulp Jungle.* Los Angeles: Sherbourne Press.

McCloud, S. (1993) *Understanding Comics: The Invisible Art.* New York: Harper Perennial.

Rizzo, M. (2014) *The Art Direction Handbook for Film.* Waltham: Focal Press.

## Typography

The TEXT in most COMIC BOOKS was hand-DRAWN by the LETTERER or ARTIST and typography was rarely used for CAPTION BOXES or SPEECH BALLOONS. Although not strictly typography, the Leroy template system, designed for lettering ARCHITECTURAL and engineering drawings, was used in EC COMICS such as *Tales from the Crypt* in the 1950s (Kannenberg 2001: 183, Brownstein 2010: 91). In 1950, the *Eagle* employed the typographer Ruari McLean to DESIGN the

LAYOUT of the first issue and typography was used for captions. Berthold Wolpe created the *Eagle* masthead based on his Tempest typeface, which demonstrates the close links between typography and lettering (Morris 1977: 8, Morris and Hallwood 1998: 128). The British newspaper and magazine PUBLISHER DC Thomson used typography for all text in their comic books, initially hot-metal typesetting before switching to the IBM "Golfball" electronic typewriter and a wide range of phototypesetting systems in the 1960s (Laird 2020). Gil Kane employed typography to mixed critical reactions in his proto-GRAPHIC NOVELS *My Name is … Savage* (1968) and *Blackmark* (1971), which foreshadowed the graphic novel boom and an increased use of typography (Brownstein 2010: 91, Thomas 2017: 6–7). By the mid-1990s, award-winning letterers such as Todd Klein were using digital typography for most of their work, often CREATING fonts based on their own lettering. The 1990s saw the formation of digital foundries like Comicraft with the result that the majority of lettering in comic books is now technically typography (Kannenberg 2001: 183–90, Klein n.d.).

Ian Horton

## *References*

Brownstein, C. (2010) "The Walk Through the Rain: Excerpt from *Eisner/Miller*" in Schwartz, B. (ed.) *The Best American Comics Criticism*. Seattle: Fantagraphics, pp. 86–91.

Kannenberg, Jr., G. (2001) "Graphic Text, Graphic Context: Interpreting Custom Fonts and Hands in Contemporary Comics" in Gutjahr, P. C. and Benton, M. L. (eds.) *Illuminating Letters: Typography and Literary Interpretation*. Amherst: University of Massachusetts Press, pp. 165–192.

Klein, T. (n.d.) "Computer Lettering." *Todd Klein: Lettering, Logos, Design. Letters.* Available at: http://kleinletters.com/ComputerLettering.html [Accessed 7 May 2020].

Laird, C. (2020) Email to Ian Horton, 27 April 2020.

Morris, M. (1977) *The Best of The Eagle*. London: Ebury Press.

Morris, S. and Hallwood, J. (1998) *Living With Eagles: Marcus Morris, Priest and Publisher*. Cambridge: The Lutterworth Press.

Thomas, R. (ed.) (2017) *Alter Ego* #149. Raleigh: Twomorrows.

## Underground

Underground COMIX emerged in the US in the 1960s and provided a format through which comics ARTISTS could PUBLISH work outside of the restrictions that the COMICS CODE Authority (CCA) placed on newsstand COMIC BOOKS. In general, underground comix were staple-bound, comic book pamphlets, typically with BLACK AND WHITE interiors, and circulated through HEAD SHOPS. Some of the best-known underground comix artists, such as Robert Crumb, Kim Deitch, Jack Jackson, Trina Robbins, Spain Rodriguez, Gilbert Sheldon, and S. Clay Wilson, dealt with overtly countercultural, political, or sexual THEMES in their work, often with a satirical slant towards mainstream social norms. A number of publishers would PRODUCE underground comix during their heyday from the 1960s through the 1970s, including Kitchen Sink Press, Last Gasp, and Rip Off Press, and other underground comix were SELF-PUBLISHED by their CREATORS. Underground comix dealt with adult themes, such as drug use and SEXUALITY, and often contained profanity, thus expanding the kinds of NARRATIVES and content possible in US comics, the mainstream version of which had been regulated by the CCA since the 1950s. Stemming from earlier, pornographic TIJUANA BIBLE comic pamphlets and the SATIRICAL CARTOONING of *MAD Magazine*, underground comix would usher in the AUTOBIOGRAPHICAL forms of comics storytelling that would establish later ALTERNATIVE COMICS and the GRAPHIC NOVEL as ARTISTIC and LITERARY FORMS.

Daniel Worden

### *References*

Danky, J. and Kitchen, D. (2009) *Underground Classics: The Transformation of Comics into Comix.* New York: Abrams.

Hatfield, C. (2005) *Alternative Comics: An Emerging Literature.* Jackson: University Press of Mississippi.

Rosenkranz, P. (2002) *Rebel Visions: The Underground Comix Revolution, 1963–1975.* Seattle: Fantagraphics.

## Utterance

Mikhail Bakhtin's four conditions of utterance are MEDIA-specific. He defines utterance exclusively as a unit of co-present speech, characterised by a habituation to the circumstances in which an utterance is made, boundaries to the form of utterance, either responsiveness to other utterances or generating dialogue and encompassed by a change in the "speaking subjects." The last of these conditions is especially cogent, because Bakhtin also states that these conditions are structured by the general relationship between participating SUBJECTS, rather than by a LANGUAGE system (Bakhtin 1986: 60 and 71, Olson 1977). This has opened the way for a theoretical REMEDIATION of the concept of utterance, to include types of visual REPRESENTATION, in the case of GESTURE and DRAWING, for example (Kendon 2004, Krčma 2007: 92), and wholesale theorisation of both the capacities of the body (Johnson 1987) and MEDIUM-specific NARRATOLOGY, such as Philippe Marion's theory of GRAPHIATION (Baetens 2001).

Simon Grennan

### *References*

Baetens, J. (2001) "Revealing Traces: A New Theory of Graphic Enunciation" in Varnum, R. and Gibbons, C. T. (eds.) *The Language of Comics: Word and Image*. Jackson: University Press of Mississippi, pp. 145–155.

Bakhtin, M. (1952–1953) "The Problem of Speech Genres" in Emerson, C. and Holquist, M. (eds.) *Speech Genres and Other Late Essays*. Translated from Russian by V. W. McGee, 1986. Austin: University of Texas Press, pp. 60–102.

Johnson, M. (1987) *The Body in the Mind: The Bodily Basis of Meaning, Imagination and Reason*. Chicago: University of Chicago Press.

Kendon, A. (2004) *Gesture: Visible Action as Utterance*. Cambridge: Cambridge University Press.

Krčma, J. (2007) *Trace, Materiality and the Body in Drawing after 1940*. PhD. University College London.

Olson, D. (1977) "From Utterance to Text: The Bias of Language in Speech and Writing," *Harvard Educational Review* 47(3), pp. 257–281.

## Vanishing Point

Vanishing point, a fundamental concept of PERSPECTIVE DRAWING, refers to the point in an IMAGE where two-dimensional projections of parallel lines seem to converge. In COMICS STUDIES, the expression is mostly used in analyses of graphic perspective, but particularly when vanishing points lose their natural invisibility—that is, when they are visually or narratively conceived in an unnatural way, defying classical Renaissance perspective. One such case is Marc-Antoine Mathieu's *La 2,333e Dimension*, whose plot is based on "a malfunction of the code which normally enables a three-dimensional world to be represented in a two-dimensional medium" (Miller 2007: 133). The ALBUM'S main character "loses a vanishing point, which affects the confined world of his comic" (Suhr 2010: 235), and its last PAGE presents "an inwardly moving spiral for which the vanishing point cannot be defined" (Bridgeman 2010: 130). The vanishing point has also been considered as a culturally specific element, of European origin. In MANGA studies, for instance, it is often used as a proof of the HISTORICAL TRANSNATIONALISM of Japanese comics, as Adam L. Kern does when examining an eighteenth-century "kibyōshi": "[it] sported one of the earliest scenes of Western vanishing point perspective published in Asia" (Kern 2017: 110).

David Pinho Barros

### *References*

Bridgeman, T. (2010) "Figuration and configuration: Mapping imaginary worlds in BD" in Forsdick, C., Grove, L. and McQuillan, L. (eds.) *The Francophone Bande Dessinée*. Amsterdam: Rodopi, pp. 115–136.

Kern, A. L. (2017) "East Asian Comix: Intermingling Japanese Manga and Euro-American Comics" in Bramlett, F., Cook, R. T., and Meskin, A. (eds.) *The Routledge Companion to Comics.* Abingdon: Routledge, 106–115.

Miller, A. (2007) *Reading Bande dessinée: Critical Approaches to French-language Comic Strip*. Bristol: Intellect.

Suhr, A. (2010) "Seeing the City through a Frame: Marc-Antoine Mathieu's Acquefacques Comics" in Ahrens, J. and Meteling, A. (eds.) *Comics and the City: Urban Space in Print, Picture and Sequence.* New York: Continuum, 231–246.

## Verisimilitude

VERISIMILITUDE refers to the "lifelikeness" of a work of fiction. It assists the reader's engagement with the story-world. According to Todorov, there are two types of verisimilitude: generic and social or cultural. He writes of the first type "is what we call rules of the genre: for a work to be said to have verisimilitude, it must conform to these rules" (Todorov 1981: 118). Of the second type, Todorov calls back to the origins of verisimilitude in the ancient Greek dramatic theory of mimesis (the imitation of nature), writing "Aristotle (…) has already perceived that the verisimilar is not a relation between discourse and its referent (the relation of truth), but between discourse and what readers believe is true. The relation is here established between the work and a scattered discourse that in part belongs to each of the individuals of a society but of which none may claim ownership; in other words to public opinion" (Todorov 1981:118–119). In COMICS STUDIES, this idea has underpinned theoretical distinctions between STYLES of DRAWING, distinguishing between REALISM and CARTOONS (Smolderen 2014: 28). Steve Neale adds that "neither [type] equates in any direct sense with 'reality' or 'truth'" (Neale 2000: 28). Some scholars suggest that cultural verisimilitude is a moot point and that stories should be adjudicated as realistic based on their own internal logic (see Sparshott 1967).

Harriet E. H. Earle

### *References*

Neale, S. (2000) *Genre and Hollywood.* Abingdon: Routledge.

Smolderen, T. (2000) *The Origins of Comics: From William Hogarth to Winsor McCay.* Translated from French by B. Beaty and N. Nguyen, 2014. Jackson: University Press of Mississippi.

Sparshott, F. (1967) "Truth in Fiction," *The Journal of Aesthetics and Art Criticism* 26(1), p. 3.

Todorov, T. (1981) *Introduction to Poetics.* Brighton: Harvester Press.

## Vernacular

Vernacular refers to informal, common, or popular knowledge as opposed to the theoretical and critical knowledge developed through scientific study. Vernacular knowledge of any particular subject arises out of various social contexts and differs depending on the context in which it was obtained. Within fields of academic study, vernacular knowledge may refer to MYTHS that are widely distributed and REPRODUCED through publication, but lack substantiation or thorough examination. In LANGUAGE or LINGUISTIC studies, vernacular also refers to the native or colloquial language spoken by ordinary people, and sometimes to the subject-specific language created by a specific group. Vernacular comics, then, refer to comics that focus on regional language or dialect as well as comics made by autodidactic CREATORS who do not identify as ARTISTS. These comics are homemade and provide an avenue of knowledge exchange and communication outside of institutional or formal knowledge production. A famous example are the UNDERGROUND COMIX of the 1960s and 1970s, which were SELF-PUBLISHED and dealt with taboo subjects banned by the COMICS CODE Authority. As such, vernacular comics often become a viable site of research for those interested in radical, subversive, or unconventional knowledge production.

Esther De Dauw

### *References*

Wagner, W. (2007) "Vernacular science knowledge: Its role in everyday life communication," *Public Understanding of Science* 16(1), pp. 7–22.

Buhle, P. (2006) "Toward the Understanding of the Visual Vernacular: Radicalism in Comics and Cartoons," *Rethinking Marxism* 18(3), pp. 367–368.

## Viewing

POINT OF VIEW in NARRATIVE is termed FOCALISATION by Gérard Genette (1979) and was adapted for COMICS STUDIES by David Herman (2010). Focalisation is the narrative as revealed through the consciousness of its characters. Herman also borrowed for comics "viewing arrangement," from Ronald Langacker's METAPHOR embodying "viewing" as a shared understanding within LINGUISTIC expressions (Langacker 2008: 73). With visual REGISTERS, such as FILM, François Jost found it necessary to distinguish between focalisation and ocularisation (2004: 74), with the latter being more literally what the camera presents. Comics may exhibit these distinctions or blur them:

subjects DRAWN in a way that veers towards the SCHEMATIC or expressionistic may align more closely with Genette's focalisation, at the same time being presented from an impersonal viewpoint (Mikkonen 2013: 104–105). This issue is further complicated in comics through application of multiple graphic STYLES with the intention of manipulating the AFFECT of the READER, and direction of the viewer's focus through which key moments of the STORY can be aligned with placements of "natural privilege" on the PAGE (Groensteen 2011: 32). The MULTIMODAL nature of comics, including the verbal track, methods of DEPICTION and FRAMING may all contribute to, or call into question, the reader's understanding of whose viewpoint is being shown (Horstkotte and Pedri 2011: 338–339).

Stuart Medley

## *References*

Genette, G. (1979) *Narrative Discourse: An Essay in Method.* Translated from French by J. E. Lewin, 1980. Ithaca: Cornell University Press.

Groensteen, T. (1999) *The System of Comics.* Translated from French by B. Beaty and N. Nguyen, 2007. Jackson: University Press of Mississippi.

Herman, D. (2010) "Multimodal storytelling and identity construction in graphic narratives" in Schiffrin, D., De Fina, A., and Nylund, A. (eds.) *Telling Stories: Language, Narrative, and Social Life.* Washington: Georgetown University Press, pp.195–208.

Horstkotte, S. and Pedri, N. (2011) "Focalisation in graphic narrative," *Narrative* 19(3), pp. 330–357.

Jost, F. (2004) "The Look: From Film to Novel: An Essay in Comparative Narratology" in Stam, R. and Raengo, A. (eds.) *A Companion to Literature and Film.* Hoboken: Wiley-Blackwell, pp. 71–80.

Langacker, R. W. and Langacker, R. (2008) *Cognitive grammar: A basic introduction.* Oxford: Oxford University Press.

Mikkonen, K. (2013) "Subjectivity and Style in Graphic Narratives" in Stein, D. and Thon, J.-N. (eds.) *From Comic Strips to Graphic Novels: Contributions to the Theory and History of Graphic Narrative.* Berlin: De Gruyter, pp. 101–123.

## Villain

A villain (not to be confused with an ANTI-HERO) is a HERO's antagonist, often a criminal, or figure of evil (though if the tale's protagonist is such a character, the more traditional hero figure may be seen in a villainous light). According to Vladimir Propp, the role of the villain in a STORY is to "create [the] possibility of occurrence" (2009: 31), and as such is the axis upon which any plot must pivot. A villain often stands in as a dark mirror of a hero, in as much as they lack "the ability to feel for others, to see themselves as part of a larger whole" (Alsford 2006: 120), and as a result the heroic character can be defined in contrast to the figure he or she must oppose. This in turn corresponds to PSYCHOANALYST Carl Gustav Jung's definition of the shadow, or id, as a "moral problem that challenges the whole ego-personality" (1976: 145). Further, Joseph Campbell frames the hero's confrontation with a dark adversary in terms of a necessary atonement with a father figure that leads inexorably to the character's apotheosis (1993: 126–149). The line between villain and anti-hero can often be blurred when a villainous character proves popular enough to recur regularly, or when the character's origins or motivations are elucidated in a way that piques the AUDIENCE's sympathy (examples of this include Magneto, Deathstroke the Terminator, and Doctor Doom, characters who were initially presented as unequivocally evil, but have become increasingly sympathetic in more recent years).

Houman Sadri

### *References*

Alsford, M. (2006) *Heroes and Villains.* London: Darton, Longman and Todd.

Campbell, J. (1993) *The Hero with a Thousand Faces.* London: Fontana.

Jung, C. G. (1951) "Aion: Phenomenology of the Self" in Campbell, J. (ed.) *The Portable Jung.* Translated from German by R. F. C. Hull. Reprint 1976. New York: Penguin Books, pp. 139–162.

Propp, V. (1928) *Morphology of the Folktale.* Translated from Russian by L. Scott, 2009. Austin: University of Texas Press.

## Visual Culture

This term refers to the sociology of the whole panoply of pictures, SIGNS, IMAGES, and other REPRESENTATIONS that circulate in the modern world (or for that matter in earlier periods). It asserts an open analytical frame that is not prescribed by any one kind of visual material as its exclusive subject. Among early exponents one need first and foremost consider Roland Barthes (1957); whereas for a more global historical reach, Edward Said (1978). Visual culture transcends out-dated predecessors: Art history, MEDIA studies, FILM studies, graphic DESIGN, and ADVERTISING, that artificially circumscribed fields into limited segments. COMICS STUDIES has developed this self-isolating tendency, with scholars defining their interests very narrowly. Yet, from within creative practice and HISTORICAL experience, no such boundaries ever existed. This was pointed out by Lawrence Alloway (1969). The borders are porous and indeterminate. Comics are ADAPTED into film and film is advertised with posters and PHOTOGRAPHY, re-adapted into novels, supported by graphic design (Buono and Eco 1966). Untrained ARTISTS collage this material or re-DRAW it for their pleasure. The old disciplinary lines not only ignore these feedback loops, they actively conceal them precisely when claiming scholarly authority.

Hugo Frey

### *References*

Alloway, L. (1969) "Popular Culture and Pop Art" in Crossman, R. H. S., Alloway, L., and Chambers, P. (eds.) *Three Studies in Modern Communication*. London: Panther Record.

Barthes, R. (1957) *Mythologies*. Paris: Seuil.

del Buono, O. and Eco, U. (eds.) (1966) *The Bond Affair*. London: Macdonald.

Said, E. (1978) *Orientalism*. New York: Pantheon.

## Visual Language Theory

The assertion that there is a special "visual language" of comics has been CANONISED amongst scholars and practitioners of comics alike (Saraceni 2003, Varnum and Gibbons 2001). Initially derived from related attempts within French FILM studies (Metz 1971), comic scholars from text

LINGUISTICS and SEMIOTICS began to investigate verbal and pictorial SIGNS as components of a unified, overarching structure (Gauthier 1976, Krafft 1978). Often these approaches were concerned with potential minimal units ("visual morphemes") and with established Saussurean distinctions such as signifier versus signified or *langue* versus *parole* (Nöth 1990). Recent linguistic approaches to comics have broadened significantly (Bramlett 2012). Neil Cohn, especially, broke away from the STRUCTURALIST tradition to introduce psychology and neuroscience to the empirical study of comics (Dunst, Laubrock, and Wildfeuer 2018). To him, comics as "social objects" (Cohn 2013: 1) are not a visual language but they employ one (a "system of communication" (ibid. 2)) that can also be traced in other domains of MULTIMODAL expressions (Cohn 2016). Cohn thus posits a cognitive—not social—visual grammar necessary to impose hierarchical, recursive structural regularities of interpretation. A more dynamic model of meaning-making has been proposed by the interrelated field of multimodal DISCOURSE SEMANTICS, working on similar problems (Bateman and Wildfeuer 2014).

Lukas R. A. Wilde

## *References*

Bateman, J. A. and Wildfeuer, J. (2014) "A Multimodal Discourse Theory of Visual Narrative," *Journal of Pragmatics* 74, pp. 180–208.

Bramlett, F. (ed.) (2012) *Linguistics and the Study of Comics.* London: Palgrave Macmillan.

Cohn, N. (2013) *The Visual Language of Comics: Introduction to the Structure and Cognition of Sequential Images.* London: Bloomsbury Academic.

Cohn, N. (ed.) (2016) *The Visual Narrative Reader.* London: Bloomsbury Academic.

Dunst, A., Laubrock, L., and Wildfeuer, J. (eds.) (2018) *Empirical Comics Research: Digital Multimodal and Cognitive Methods.* Abingdon: Routledge.

Gauthier, G. (1976) "Les Peanuts: Un graphisme idiomatique," *Communications* 24, pp. 108–139.

Krafft, U. (1978) *Comics lesen. Untersuchungen zur Textualität von Comics.* Stuttgart: Klett-Cotta.

Metz, C. (1971) *Langage et cinema.* Paris: Larousse.

Nöth, W. (1990) *Handbook of Semiotics.* Indianapolis: University of Indiana Press.
Saraceni, M. (2003) *The Language of Comics.* Abingdon: Routledge.
Varnum, R., and Gibbons, C. (2007) *The Language of Comics: Word and Image.* Jackson: University Press of Mississippi.

## Visualisation

Visualisation, or visual imagining, is a type of mental REPRESENTATION. Whilst not requiring exteroceptive experience, such as vision, visualisations are themselves perceived. As such, visualisations conform in structure and function to perceptions, even if they are fictions. (Grennan 2017: 89–91, Slezak 1995, Reisberg and Chamber 1995, Walton 1990). Three theoretical approaches aim to explain visualisation relative to perception: two cognitive approaches ("pictorial" and "propositional") and an embodied approach ("perceptual activity"). Pictorial theories explain visualisation as the generation of cognitive copies of visual perceptions (Kosslyn 1994). Propositional models require no cognitive regress, no "mind's eye" cognition of a distinct experience of interoceptive perception. Rather, perceptions are propositional in themselves, in that they are structures of cognition and types of knowledge (Pylyshyn 1984). In perceptual activity theories, visualisations are not "IMAGES," but cognitive processes, the structures of which themselves continuously realise the structures of recalled schemata as present-time cognitive experiences (Thomas 1999). The activity of viewing the DRAWINGS and WRITING that constitute COMICS provides a MEDIUM-specific experience, characterised by the inference of the drafter's body (Grennan 2017: 28–37). Visualisation is structured according to POINT OF VIEW, so that it is the orientation of the SUBJECT, relative to the perception, that organises the subsequent mental image (Grennan 2017: 88).

Simon Grennan

### *References*

Grennan, S. (2017) *A Theory of Narrative Drawing.* London: Palgrave Macmillan.
Kosslyn, S. (1994) *Image and Brain: The Resolution of the Imagery Debate.* Cambridge: Harvard University Press.

Pylyshyn, Z. (1984) *Computation and Cognition*. Cambridge: The Massachusetts Institute of Technology Press.

Reisberg, D. and Chambers, D. (1995) "Neither pictures nor propositions: What can we learn from a mental image?" *Canadian Journal of Psychology* 45, pp. 336–352.

Slezak, P. (1995) "The 'Philosophical' Case Against Visual Imagery" in Slezak, P., Caelli, T., and Clark, R. (eds.) *Perspectives on Cognitive Sciences: Theories, Experiments and Foundations*. Norwood: Ablex, pp. 237–271.

Thomas, N. (1999) "Are theories of imagery theories of imagination? An active perception approach to conscious mental content," *Cognitive Science* 23, pp. 207–245.

Walton, K. (1990) *Mimesis as Make-Believe: On the Foundations of the Representational Arts*. Cambridge: Harvard University Press, pp. 21–24, 72.

## Voice

A distinct element of fiction, voice was first introduced by Gérard Genette to distinguish who speaks or narrates the STORY (NARRATION) from who sees or adopts a perspective on the STORYWORLD information (FOCALISATION). Accordingly, voice designates a defining discursive function of the NARRATOR, namely, the expression of tone, mood, POINT OF VIEW, attitude, emotion, and experience across STYLISTIC choices. Voice is also used to designate a character's thought and speech or the enunciative act of a collective that shares social and rhetorical properties, as in female voices or minority voices. In comics, narrative voice is usually confined to CAPTION BOXES, whereas character voice is presented in SPEECH BALLOONS or THOUGHT BUBBLES. In addition, LETTERING can be used to suggest the pitch or tone of voice. Through these techniques and devices, comics invite READERS to not only READ SOUND, but see sound "so as to recreate narrative atmospheres throughout which readers can form in their minds particular voices, timbres, or even auditory effects" (Pelletteri 2019: 516).

Nancy Pedri

## *References*

Pelletteri, M. (2019) "The Aural Dimension in Comic Art" in Grimshaw-Aagaard, M., Walther-Hansen, M., and Knakkergaard, M. (eds.) *The Oxford Handbook of Sound and Imagination*. Volume 1. Oxford: Oxford University Press, pp. 511–547.

## WAR

War has been represented in sequences of images long before the emergence of the COMIC STRIP (Chute 2016). During World War I, newspapers and magazines for children and adults contained war NARRATIVES in comics FORM, combining a patriotic undertone with a humorous approach to make the topic fit into an entertainment MEDIUM. Fictional stories about real wars became popular in American COMIC BOOKS shortly before World War II. These comics selectively depicted "a clear goal, a clear enemy, and a clear victory" (Scott 2014: 52), reinforcing racial stereotyping of the enemy (Conroy 2009: 70), while focusing on heroic masculine military combat. In the 1950s and 1960s, *Two-Fisted Tales*, *Frontline Combat*, and *Blazing Combat* presented less sanitised representations of brutal warfare, introducing antiwar sentiments (Chute 2019: 313). Still, many war comics in Europe and North America featured conventional stories glorifying war, though the enemy was depicted with more nuance (Ribbens 2010). More recently, Art Spiegelman's *Maus*, Keiji Nakazawa's *Barefoot Gen*, and Joe Sacco's *Safe Area Goražde*, which all represent personal experiences of wartime atrocities, helped war comics move beyond the traditional frame of the GENRE. Aiming at a more realistic representation—supported by a shift in readership towards adults—they express individual voices, with an eye for the position of civilians in the era of total war and do not shun chaos and complexity, immediacy of violence, and moral and political ambiguity (Scott 2014: 135–137).

Kees Ribbens

## *References*

Chapman, J., Sherif, A., Hoyles, A., and Kerr, A. (2015) *Comics and the World Wars: A Cultural Record*. London: Palgrave Macmillan.

Chute, H. (2016) *Disaster Drawn: Visual Witness, Comics, and Documentary Form.* Cambridge: Harvard University Press.
Chute, H. (2017) *Why Comics? From Underground to Everywhere.* New York: Harper Perennial.
Conroy, M. (2009) *War Comics: A Graphic History.* Lewes: Ilex Press, Ltd.
Ribbens, K. (2010) "World *War* II in European Comics: National Representations of Global Conflict in Popular Historical Culture," *International Journal of Comic Art* 12(1), pp. 1–33.
Scott, C. A. (2014) *Comics and Conflict. Patriotism and Propaganda from WWII through Operation Iraqi Freedom.* Annapolis: Naval Institute Press.

## Webcomics

Webcomics are some of the most recognisable manifestations of the MEDIUM of comics on digital devices. Although the term is sometimes used as a synonym for DIGITAL COMICS, the prefix "web" suggests that webcomics refers to a subcategory of digital comics that primarily exist and are distributed on internet web pages. They are usually born digital, but this does not necessarily need to be the case; a lot of PRINT original comics now exist digitally as webcomics (e.g. Jim Davis' *Garfield* or, for that matter, Dan Walsh's *Garfield Minus Garfield*). However, they are more than just digitised scans—webcomics are structurally ADAPTED to the browser window and they make use of the inherent elements of a web page in order to enrich their presentation. They are often SERIALISED, much like NEWSPAPER STRIPS, but their digital nature allows them to be accessed and ARCHIVED much more conveniently. Such comics call for a MEDIA-specific analysis (Hayles 2004, Carroll 2008), as the criteria for READING and analysing print comics cannot be applied in the same way to webcomics found online.

Josip Batinić

### *References*

Carroll, N. (2008) *The Philosophy of Motion Pictures.* Oxford: Blackwell.
Hayles, Katherine. (2004) "Print Is Flat, Code Is Deep: The Importance of Media-Specific Analysis," *Poetics Today* 25(1), pp. 67–90.

## Western

The Western comic derives from the nineteenth-century dime novel, popular Wild West shows, and nineteenth-century pulp magazines (Grady 2016: 685). The ART FORM draws on formulaic elements constituting the GENRE. The classical Western repertoire consists of "stagecoach robberies, bank holdups, cattle rustlings, heroic rescues of defrauded widows, and illegal land take-overs" (Zan 2010: 688). Typical places of action are saloons, huts, railroad stations, military forts, and Native American villages. The STORIES usually take place in the nineteenth century, a period in which the Western frontier still "had to be tamed" (ibid. 686). With regard to characters, Martha Zan suggests five types of the Western hero: "the cowboy, the lone rider/reformed outlaw, the lawman, the (ex-) military man, and the Indian" (ibid.). Native Americans are most often represented as "antagonists of the Cavalry" and savages (ibid. 688). Similarly, female characters often occupy subordinate roles as objects of desire. While the Western experienced its heyday from the 1940s to the 1960s, the 1970s contributed to an anti-Western sentiment caused by the Vietnam War. Hence, what followed was the direct reversal of the plot in Western comics. Jack Jackson's comic book *Comanche Moon*, for instance, represents the disenfranchisement of Native Americans and the consequences of American expansionism in the late nineteenth century. In recent years, however, the genre experienced a rejuvenation, albeit as an amalgamation with other genres such as HORROR.

Andrea Schlosser

### *References*

Grady, W. (2016) "Western Comics" in Bamlett, F., Cook, R., and Meskin, A. (eds.) *Routledge Companion to Comics.* Abingdon: Routledge, pp. 164–173.

Zan, M. (2010) "Western Comics" in Booker, M. K. (ed.) *Encyclopedia of Comic Books and Graphic Novels.* Santa Barbara: Greenwood, pp. 685–692.

## Witness

To witness involves both seeing and saying (Durham Peters 2009: 26). Significant in religious and juridical contexts, witnessing gained prominence in LITERATURE following World War II (Durham Peters 2009: 30). To experience an event can potentially make one a witness to it, but witnessing exceeds observation. It is underwritten by bodily presence and vulnerability, and the act of bearing witness (telling another/others who were not present) solicits a heightened and ETHICAL response that is predicated on empathy (la Capra 2004: 76–7). Witness is therefore a salient term for COMICS JOURNALISM and DOCUMENTARY, as well as AUTOBIOGRAPHY (Chute 2016). Whether a comics CREATOR relays their own experiences or the working process has included occupying a position of secondary witness (or s/he combines these methods), the MEDIATED testimony and resulting text will in turn perform an act of bearing witness (Frosh 2009: 60). Signalling their witnessing intentions through GENRE and PARATEXTS, such texts make available the position of secondary witnessing. Witness accounts and REPRESENTATIONAL IMAGES share the staging of absence; "[a] witness is the paradigm case of a medium: the means by which experience is supplied to others who lack the original" (Durham Peters 2009: 26, Guerin and Hallas 2007).

Nina Mickwitz

### *References*

Chute, H. (2016) *Disaster Drawn: Visual Witness, Comics, and Documentary Form.* Cambridge: Harvard University Press.

Durham Peters, J. (2009) "Witnessing" in Frosh, P. and Pinchevski, A. (eds.) *Media Witnessing: Testimony in the Age of Mass Communication.* London: Palgrave Macmillan, pp. 23–41.

Frosh, P. (2009) "Telling Presences: Witnessing, Mass Media, and the Lives of Strangers" in Frosh, P. and Pinchevski, A. (eds.) *Media Witnessing: Testimony in the Age of Mass Communication.* London: Palgrave Macmillan, pp. 49–72.

Guerin, F. and Hallas, R. (eds.) (2007) *The Image and the Witness: Trauma, Memory and Visual Culture.* London: Wallflower Press.

La Capra, D. (2004) *History in Transit: Experience, Psychoanalysis, Critical Theory.* Ithaca: Cornell University Press.

## Wordless Comics

Wordless comics are SEQUENTIAL NARRATIVES that eschew the use of TEXT to convey any amount of meaning, instead relying on the visual aspects of the comics REGISTER. They are distinct from storyboards in that wordless comics are end products rather than operational material—such as SCRIPTS—PRODUCED for the purpose of planning another FORM of work and are at best "an oblique part of the form of expression itself" (Grennan 2017: 177). Distinguishing between a wordless comic and a PICTURE BOOK is more ambiguous, and largely a matter of the degree to which the comics apparatus is recognisably exploited (Postema 2014: 312–313). Wordless comics have existed since at least the 1890s (ibid. 312) and still feature prominently in more contemporary small press and experimental milieux, while extended wordless sequences that can serve as entire scenes or acts are not uncommon in mainstream comics narratives. The existence and frequency of wordless comics are instrumental not only in highlighting how the uniquely visual elements of comics (Lefèvre 2011: 29) define the register but also in developing conversations about the relationships between comics and other forms of VISUAL narrative.

Ahmed Jameel

### *References*

Grennan, S. (2017) *A Theory of Narrative Drawing*. London: Palgrave Macmillan.

Lefèvre, P. (2011) "Some Medium-Specific Qualities of Graphic Sequence," *Substance* #124, 40(1), pp. 26–30.

Postema, B. (2014) "Following the pictures: Wordless comics for children," *Journal of Graphic Novels and Comics* 5(3), pp. 311–322.

## Worldbuilding

Worldbuilding is the act of creating a WORLD in which a STORY happens and gives a story a sense of both time and place. The world created may resemble reality or may be entirely imaginary. Worldbuilding thus facilitates storytelling, but also often includes details and events that are not designed to help the story along but rather to add depth, richness, and

REALISM to the world in which the story is told. Worldbuilding is often "transnarrative and transmedial in form" (Wolf 2012: 3): multiple stories can happen in a single world (or, as is often the case, universe) and span across different kinds of MEDIA such as comics, novels, FILM, television, and reference works like glossaries, maps, and encyclopaedias. One of the most well-known examples of worldbuilding in comics is the Marvel Universe (or Multiverse, as it extends into parallel universes), which has been created over the course of nearly seven decades. The stories of hundreds of characters—whether SUPERHEROES, VILLAINS, or somewhere in between—exist within this Multiverse where the CREATORS "strive to stress realism in every panel" (Lee 9). The "realism" of Marvel means that its worlds are believable, despite not always resembling our own world. Convincing worldbuilding acts as stage that allows story to stand in the limelight.

Jasmine Palmer

## *References*

Lee, S. (1991) "Introduction" in Daniels, L. *Marvel: Five Fabulous Decades of the World's Greatest Comics.* New York: Harry N. Abrams.

Wolf, M. J. P. (2012) *Building Imaginary Worlds.* Abingdon: Routledge.

## WRITER

Bringing a story to life is often a collaborative process between writers (also referred to as SCRIPTERS or plotters), ARTISTS, PENCILLERS, COLOURISTS, and others. Maaheen Ahmed casts this process in relational terms when she points out that "collaboration and mediation (through the medium of comics in general but also its individual components and devices) are (…) inextricable components of comics authorship" (2017: 7). Storytelling devices such as SPEECH BALLOONS and THOUGHT BUBBLES, and the artist's renderings of the writer's ideas, add depth to the storyline. Yet as Moore advises, "the writer should have a clear picture of the imagined world in all its detail inside his or her head at all times" (21). Philosophical frameworks may also influence the writer's style, such as Dela Cruz's application of Ricoeur's hermeneutical phenomenology to the COMICS FORM that "takes heed of the sociocognitive complexity involved in understanding the motivations of characters, which may entail careful attention to the subtext of word-image juxtapositions" (2015: 10). Writers also script WORDLESS comics that rely solely on

IMAGES to communicate complex ideas. As an auteur, their "VOICE" is communicated through the artist. These MULTIMODAL approaches allow writers to infuse comics with layered meaning, complexity, and versatility.

Monalesia Earle

## *References*

Ahmed, M. (2017) "Comics and Authorship: An Introduction." *Authorship* 6, pp. 1–13.

Dela Cruz, N. (2015) "Surviving Hiroshima: An Hermeneutical Phenomenology of *Barefoot Gen* by Keiji Nakazawa." Discussion paper. National Conference of the Philosophical Association of the Philippines.

Moore, A. (2003) *Alan Moore's Writing for Comics.* Illinois: Avatar Press.

## Writing

Writing is defined by a single principle. Without being tied to any MEDIUM, in writing, the time-based relationships between items in a LANGUAGE system (e.g. between sequences of imagined words or sounds) determine the visible relationships between marks in an array, such as musical notation or a written sentence (Grennan 2017: 31). The meaning of writing is also influenced, if not functionally defined, by both potential variations in the shapes of marks and discursive factors from outside the system, constituting the ecology in which writing is made and seen (Harris 2002: 96–97, Halliday 1985: 225–241). However, of themselves, the specific graphic marks and visual systems of writing are independent of their SEMIOTIC function, because semiotic values and functions are assigned to these graphic marks according to their location within the system and not because of any perceived inherent qualities, such as their shape, COLOUR, dimension, pattern, or relationship with other types of visual representation. Despite the insignificance of the shapes of marks in defining writing, it remains a subset of mark making, conforming to many aspects of theories of DRAWING. Considered as a DRAWING activity, the writing that contributes to the COMICS REGISTER has been discussed as autographic, that is, inferring meaning from the INDEXING or TRACING a drafter's bodily actions (Gardner 2011: 64).

Simon Grennan

## *References*

Gardner, J. (2011) "Storylines," *SubStance* 40(1), pp. 53–69.
Grennan, S. (2017) *A Theory of Narrative Drawing*. London: Palgrave Macmillan.
Harris, R. (2002) *Rethinking Writing*. New York: Continuum.
Halliday, M. (1985) *Spoken and Written Language*. Geelong: Deakin University Press.

## Zine

A zine is a SELF-PUBLISHED publication made by an individual or a small group of people that instantiates a philosophy of not-for-profit, non-institutional cultural PRODUCTION and AESTHETICS (Duncombe 1997). The zine is strongly associated with the photocopier and "how it impacted knowledge and cultural production … opening new possibilities for the dissemination of art and writing while simultaneously laying the groundwork for new communities of practice and resistance" (Eichhorn 2016: 7) such as FEMINISM (Piepmeier 2009). Zines are also produced on analogue PRINT TECHNOLOGIES such as the risograph, letterpress printing, and mimeograph. A zine can be a specific text produced in a small print run for a local community or event, or a long-running SERIAL publication that circulates through established modes of distribution such as online distributors and annual fairs or CONVENTIONS. Zines are also sold in independent bookstores and ARTIST-run spaces in many cities. A growing number of NATIONAL, academic, and community libraries collect zines in recognition of their importance as a site of independent artistic production. There is often overlap between zine culture, print artists, graphic DESIGNERS, and independent comics PUBLISHERS in a context that can be approached as "post-digital aesthetics" (Cramer 2013).

Anna Poletti

## *References*

Cramer, F. (2013) "Post-digital Aesthetics." *Jeu de Pame Le Magazine*, 1 May 2013. Available at: http://lemagazine.jeudepaume.org/2013/05/florian-cramer-post-digital-aesthetics/ [Accessed 29 July 2020].

Duncombe, S. (1997) *Notes from Underground: Zines and the Politics of Alternative Culture*. New York: Verso.

Eichhorn, K. (2016) *Adjusted Margin: Xerography, Art and Activism in the Late Twentieth Century*. Cambridge: The Massachusetts Institute of Technology Press.

Piepmeier, A. (2009) *Girl Zines: Making Media, Doing Feminism*. New York: New York University Press.

# Correction to: Introduction: Key Terms in Comics Studies

*Erin La Cour, Simon Grennan, and Rik Spanjers*

**Correction to:**

**Chapter 1 in: E. La Cour et al. (eds.), *Key Terms in Comics Studies*, Palgrave Studies in Comics and Graphic Novels, https://doi.org/10.1007/978-3-030-74974-3_1**

The original version of the chapter 1 has been revised and an updated bibliography has been incorporated in this chapter.

The updated online version of this chapter can be found at https://doi.org/10.1007/978-3-030-74974-3_1



E. La Cour et al. (eds.), *Key Terms in Comics Studies*, Palgrave Studies in Comics and Graphic Novels, https://doi.org/10.1007/978-3-030-74974-3_2

# Index




E. La Cour et al. (eds.), *Key Terms in Comics Studies*, Palgrave Studies in Comics and Graphic Novels,
https://doi.org/10.1007/978-3-030-74974-3

**D**

CPSIA information can be obtained
at www.ICGtesting.com
Printed in the USA
LVHW081358291122
734248LV00015B/764

9 783030 749736